THE CONFESSION

THE CONFESSION

MAUREEN MYANT

HOBECK

This edition produced in Great Britain in 2022

by Hobeck Books Limited, Unit 14, Sugnall Business Centre, Sugnall, Stafford, Staffordshire, ST21 6NF

www.hobeck.net

A CIP catalogue for this book is available from the British Library.

ISBN 978-1-913-793-89-0 (pbk)

ISBN 978-1-913-793-88-3 (ebook)

Cover design by Jayne Mapp Design

Printed and bound in Great Britain

Created with Vellum

Praise for The Confession

'Well what can I say? This is one of the most cleverly written books I've ever read!' Carole Gourlay

'Really enjoyable read ... the sort of book many will read in one or two sittings.' Pete Fleming

'A very clever crime thriller, with more twists and turns than a helter-skelter!' Angela Paull

Are you a thriller seeker?

Hobeck Books is an independent publisher of crime, mystery, thriller and suspense and we have one aim – to bring you the books you want to read.

For more details about our books, our authors and our plans, the chance to enter competitions, plus to download *Crime Bites*, a free compilation of novellas and short stories by our authors sign up for our newsletter at **www.hobeck.net**.

You can also find us on Twitter **@hobeckbooks** or on Facebook **www.facebook.com/hobeckbooks10**.

To Martin, the light of my life

Prologue

JUNE 29TH 2019

One bluebottle can lay 600 eggs in a day

DS Mark Nicholson donned the protective body suit before following the police constable into the house. He blinked as his eyes adjusted to the darkness. He was breathing through his mouth but it didn't help. The stench was overwhelming. 'So, what's the story?' he asked.

'Best see for yourself.' The PC showed Mark into a room at the back of the house. Mark scanned the scene. The floor was covered with bluebottles, dead and dying, but a fair number of live ones still buzzed around. Mark swatted one away, cursing. The corpse was a woman. It was hard to judge her age, but her hair had no grey in it and her clothes were fashionable. She was sitting at a desk, an almost empty bottle of fifteen-year-old Bowmore and a scattering of pills beside her left hand. A MacBook Air was open in front of her. Maggots heaved under what was left of her skin. Mark turned away.

'What's the problem? Looks like suicide to me.'

There were beads of sweat on the PC's forehead. 'I thought you should see this.' He tapped the touchpad and the screen came to life. 'See what I mean?,' he said as Mark started to read.

PART I
Confiteor

'He's half absolv'd who has confessed.'

It's as simple as this: I'll be dead before sunrise.

A number of years ago, I went to a dinner party where we talked about what we'd listen to or read if we had only a few hours left to live. Mahler or Strauss, Shakespeare or Dickens, what would it be? Shakespeare yielded to Beckett and Mahler to Nono as the choices became ever more obscure. The discussion went on for hours; you should have heard us, trying to outdo each other until it came to what we'd eat. I shut everyone up with my choice of shiokara. Look it up. Lovely. And yet now my time is up, I quite fancy scrambled eggs – *baveuse* naturally – but there's no time if I am to tell my story. Listening to music will have to do. It will help me relax. Various people at that dinner party went for the obvious choices: *Vier Letzte Lieder*, the finale of *Tristan und Isolde*, but these are too sombre for me. Excruciatingly so.

In these, my dying hours, I will listen to the music I love, music that has inspired me. I won't tell you what I'm listening to, though. You can work it out for yourself.

I want you to know about my life as a serial killer, about how I do not fit the pattern. After reading my story, you will never again look at your next-door neighbour without thinking – *are they capable of murder*? Psychologists think they're so smart with their profiles, their reports. But these reports are little more than guesswork. Look at this drivel from a basic psychology textbook. I can see them now, those spotty eighteen-year-old students, straight from their safe, middle class homes, revelling in the details, wondering how they can use this fascinating information to pull that boy or girl they fancy. *The typical serial killer is a white male of 20–30 years, above average intelligence, with a sociopathic type personality and a job that leads to travel.*

Oh dear. Right, wrong, wrong, right, wrong, wrong. Two out of six – worse than chance. I am white. I am a woman. I am forty-five years old. With an IQ of 132, it's safe to say that I am of above average intelligence. According to various personality tests, I am a stable introvert. I am a teacher of music. I wouldn't fit their profile even if they had one. And they don't, because they're not looking for a serial killer, for one single person. Anyone serious about being a serial killer these days has to be ahead of the game. There's no easy link between *my* victims. My killings were all different; so different they haven't picked up the pattern, because there isn't one, no modus operandi and no convenient little clues to latch on to.

Where to start? The beginning is the obvious choice, but it hurts to think of my first killing, the one that went so badly wrong. Let's go to the last one then. That's so much easier to write about. But wait. I need music and nothing springs to mind. I'll listen to something jolly while I think what would be appropriate for the old woman. Here's a clue, just like a crossword. I like crosswords but I'll never do another one now. Let's see... 'This Spanish hairdresser sounds Italian to me (2,8,2,8)'. Easy. Too easy, really. An insult to your intelligence.

It's taken me some time to get a handle on the music for this particular murder, but I've got it now. It's what was playing on the radio as I drove her home. It's how some people, those psychologists perhaps, would describe me, though it's a little non-PC for them. More suitable for a tabloid really. Maybe it inspired me, but it's also how I felt as I drove her home: I hate people who aren't polite. Don't you? And she was as rude as you get. She deserved all that was coming to her.

It was late November last year. A wild, wet, windy night of the type that encourages people to stay at home, cosy in their soft, lamplit living rooms, smugly snug by their fires. But I had to go out, to get milk.

I was in a foul temper. My last pupil had been so slow; his little fingers unable to cope with the Beethoven Allegro his parents had demanded he should try. He stumbled and tripped his way through the first few bars until my nerves were screaming *stop, stop, STOP*. Did I say it aloud? I don't think so, but I almost pushed him off the stool in my impatience to play the piece as it should be performed. It soothed me, as I knew it would, and we parted on friendly terms. I stood at the front door chatting to his mother, one of those thin, brittle women who are so common these days. They could be clones with their caramel-coloured hair, their perfectly groomed eyebrows and clothes straight from a Boden catalogue. Her clipped middle class tones grated on me as the wind gathered around us, making me colder and colder.

'Harry, why don't you go and sit in the Range Rover, darling, while I speak to your teacher.' Typical of gas guzzler owners to specify the make. Anyone else would refer to 'the car'. Harry scuttled off, his mother watching him, greedily maternal. 'I really think he's making excellent progress, don't you? Ross thinks he should sit the grade 6 exam, but I think the grade 5 will do. After all, we don't want to pressurise him, do we? Now, I've been meaning to say to you for some time... I think it's time we moved on from that little Beethoven piece. He's been playing it for months. I've brought along this Mozart – what do you think? Try it for next week?'

I took the sheets of music from her and glanced at them before handing them back. Harry would murder the Mozart, but to my horror I found myself agreeing not only to that, but also to him sitting the grade 5 exam even though I had only intended to enter him for grade 3. He'd never pass and I'd get the blame. She prattled on for several minutes, boasting about her family, the warmth of her self-satisfaction protecting her from the cold. My smile grew increasingly strained and I wondered if I'd ever get my face back to normal. After I'd glanced at my watch for the fifth time, she took the hint and left. I hurried inside to the kitchen to make myself hot chocolate; my nerves needed quietening and my hands could do with warming.

I switched on the light. The bulb flickered for a second then gave up. I had none spare and the gloomy light from the streetlamp in the back lane barely lit up the dark kitchen. I opened the fridge to see only the remains of food that had once been edible. The crusty cheese, the cured ham, now curling, the milk with the tell-tale weight of true sourness. My tentative calm slipped away as I realised I had to go out to the shops. Cursing aloud – why not, there was no one to hear me? – I shrugged on a jacket and grabbed my car keys from the shelf by the front door.

Outside, the wind flung the rain around in horizontal sheets. I bolted to the car, only a few metres away, but I wasn't quick enough to avoid a soaking. Once inside, I turned on the interior light and studied myself in the mirror. I was a sight. The rain had smudged my make-up; two black streaks of mascara trailed down my face, giving me the look of someone bereft. I thought about tidying myself up, but there are times when one just can't be bothered and this was one of them. On the way to the supermarket, I checked in the mirror once or twice to see how I looked. Deranged would be the best description.

The shop was deserted, save for two other shoppers: an old woman leaning on a trolley for support and a teenager loitering by the alcohol section. I wandered round, barely aware of the background music, filling my basket with basic provisions as well as some pacifiers for my bad mood: a magazine, some chocolate, a bottle of wine. I paid the acne-scarred boy at the checkout. He smiled a greeting without looking at me; no doubt he dreaded seeing the pity in people's eyes as they registered the pustular pits and bumps of his complexion. Well, that suited me fine; I was having a bit of a bad face day myself. I stood at the door of the supermarket for a few seconds before dashing across the unlit car park, two plastic carrier bags battering against my calves. As I got into my car, I saw the old woman struggle against the wind and on impulse offered her a lift.

She was a whinger; straight from the 'it's all right for you' school. She moaned all the way to her house, which was in the opposite direction from where I lived. Her children didn't come to see her; her neighbours were scroungers; she didn't get any of the benefits she was entitled to. I listened in silence. Not once did she thank me for stopping to pick her up; not once did she ask if I was going her way. She took me for granted, a total stranger offering her a kindness. 'I'm not surprised your children don't come and see you, you ungrateful old witch,' I muttered, but either she was deaf or, more likely, she wasn't listening, too intent on her list of grievances to hear my words.

'Here, here, stop here,' she demanded as we approached her house. She waited in the car for me to open the door. 'Do you need any help with your bags?' I murmured, but she just handed them to me before she turned to march up the path, her tiny bent figure rigid against the wind. Furious, I followed her into the house.

I won't give you the details of what I did to her. They're all there in the newspaper reports. Wait a minute, though – I must just quote you an excerpt from the local rag. No need for me to look. I know it off by heart. *Yesterday, police found the badly battered body of eighty-three-year-old Margaret Aintree in her house in Mitchison Crescent. It had lain undiscovered for several days. Mrs Mitchison was a well-loved and respected figure in the area.*

Aye, right. So well loved nobody noticed she was missing for several days. So well thought of, the journalist confused her name with her address. That amused me. So well respected that only nine people attended her funeral. How do I know this? Simple. I gate-crashed another funeral at the crematorium that day. Crept in at the back of another (well-attended) ceremony, gave my respects to the grieving family, sighing, 'I used to work with Maggie, a long time ago. A lovely person, so sorry for your loss,' all the time glancing sideways at my victim's party. No one shed a tear. I reckon her family were glad to be shot of her.

You're probably wondering whether I'm sorry for what I did. You're not going to like this, I'm afraid. The answer is no. No twinges of guilt, no sleepless nights. Frightening, isn't it? No remorse, therefore no redemption. Except for the child; I do regret that, of course I do. But it's not time to tell that story yet. I need to tell you a little about me first.

I can see you as you read this. You're horrified by my words but just a tiny bit fascinated. You need to believe that killers have a motive for their deed and that somewhere in the past lies the reason for their wickedness. Evil has gone out of fashion, or so it is claimed, with not even Catholics prepared to admit its existence. Maybe I'm evil. What do you think? Murdering an old woman is hardly a good act. Or perhaps there is some horrible trauma in my past that helps account for my behaviour. We'll see. I'll tell you one thing for sure, though. I am very respectable and my delightful neighbours will be rather dismayed when all this comes out. It won't be all that good for house prices, I imagine, or maybe it will. Who knows? One thing for sure; they won't be terribly surprised. Or they shouldn't be.

I had a long discussion with them once, about murder, amongst other things. One of these silly conversations that goes on long after bedtime, where you reveal rather more than you'd hoped you would. You know the sort of thing. Everyone's pissed, someone pipes up with, 'What was your most exciting sexual experience?' and many, many hours later you know more than you want to about other people's sex lives. I may be old fashioned, but I think it's best not to know that your boss likes to wear a nappy and drink milk from a baby's bottle. And what about that mousy colleague who turns out to be a masochist and nothing turns him on like nailing his testicles to the floor? Worst of all is the sneaking suspicion that it's a set up and you're the only one to have told the truth about a quick fumble in a train carriage.

I am digressing. Time to get back to the neighbours.

It was a summer evening and my neighbours had come round for a drink. We sat in the garden and listened to the city sounds: the siren of an ambulance hurtling towards the nearby hospital, shouts from the crowds leaving the pubs on the main road, the occasional football song, the background hum of a large city. The garden looked mysterious in the twilight with the garden torches casting shadows on the ground. The old apple tree in the corner was gnarled and misshapen, and if you narrowed your eyes the trunk became an old hag's face; it could have been an illustration for a fairy tale. I'd planted night-scented stock that year and the sweet perfume filled the air. For once the summer had been very dry and there were none of the infuriating midges we all dreaded. Wine had flowed all evening; a chilled white Rioja if I remember rightly, from the Sunday Times Wine Club, and when that ran out, a Pinot Grigio, which we drank like lemonade. We were pleasantly tipsy, a little tired and beginning to talk nonsense.

'I was at a party last week,' said Jan, my next door neighbour, 'and we played this really interesting game.'

'What, strip poker?' smirked her soon to be ex-husband.

'No, shut up you.' She tried to hit him but missed. Her chair wobbled and I steadied it for her. She was unaware she had almost fallen over. She continued, 'It's a game to show how well you know a person. You have to tell lies or something. It's really funny. Right, OK, so everyone needs to take a partner.'

We all groaned. Party games. But we were drunk enough to oblige and we sorted ourselves out without too much protest

Marianne leaned back in her chair and yawned, showing a mouthful of perfect teeth. 'Now what? Sex?'

A glare. 'Just shut up and listen, won't you? You write down three statements about yourself.'

'No paper, can't do.'

Jan rolled her eyes. 'Give me patience. Just say them to each other, then. Three statements. One hash to be a lie and your partner hash, *has* to guess which is the lie.'

I looked at my partner, Joe who lived at the bottom of the street, and smiled. 'Me first, OK? Here we go. Statement number one... I once ate raw snails. Number two, my worst fear is of flying, and last but certainly not least, I am a serial killer. Over to you, Joe. Which one's the lie?'

'No, no, no. Too easy,' said Jan. 'The point is, it should be something absurd but not too absurd. Listen, listen – last week I was told that someone had a pet monkey when they were a child. I thought that was a lie, but it wasn't, it was true. It was so funny.' She laughed at the memory. We looked at her, bewildered.

'You probably had to have been there,' I whispered to Joe before turning back to Jan. 'And why's it absurd that I'm a serial killer?'

'Don't be stupid. It just is.'

'Such reasoned argument impresses me,' I said (a bit pompously, to be honest), 'but you haven't answered my question. Why is it absurd that I'm a serial killer?'

'Well, for one thing you're a woman. Everyone knows serial killers are always men. And for another you're the wrong age and... Oh, this is ridilicous... ridiculous. You couldn't hurt a fly.'

I stared into her eyes. They were unfocused and the whites were that very pale yellow that comes from years of drinking too much. 'I think we all have it in us to kill someone,' I said.

Jan grimaced. 'Given the right circumstances, I suppose so,' she said, sounding surprisingly sober, 'but you've not had the right circumstances, so you haven't killed, just like everyone else here.'

The little seed of irritation had germinated in me. 'But that's the point of this game, isn't it? That we don't know even our closest friends all that well. And we certainly don't know every situation that they've got themselves into. So, you have to see that I could well be a serial killer.'

Jan laughed. 'I've never met anyone less likely than you to be a murderer... You've led a charmed life. You're intelligent, attractive and musical. You have lovers. All this and you want to be a psychopath too? Give us a break.'

Poor thing, she had no idea. For one thing, she'd only known me for a few years, so her statement about a 'charmed life' was a bit of a nerve. I thought about carrying on with the argument, but it was getting late. I was pretty drunk and I fancied my chances with Joe, whose wife was in hospital.

Ignoring Jan and the others, I leaned a little closer so he could smell my perfume and stroked the fine hairs on his arm.

'What about you, Joe? Do you believe I'm a killer?'

He looked straight into my eyes. 'Oh yes, you're a killer all right. A real man eater.' And then under his breath so that only I could hear, 'and I'm a real man.' Dear God, more corn than a seafood chowder; I almost changed my mind. But for once I was in a forgiving mood.

That was several years ago now. I'd only killed twice, so it was a bit of an exaggeration to claim I was a serial killer. Wikipedia, today's source of all knowledge, defines a serial killer as someone who has killed three or more people. Still, that night I added to my tally. Trying to live up to my claim, I suppose. By the way, my second statement, my worst fear is of flying, was the lie... My worst fear is of dying and I'll be confronting it in less than eight hours' time.

Why are we so afraid of dying, do you think? If it was like sleep as some writers have suggested, then no problem. But we know better, you and I – sleep is something you wake from; death isn't. If only we could follow Somerset Maugham's advice and have nothing to do with it.

I'm hungry now. I didn't expect to eat tonight and there's nothing in the house. I don't want there to be too much of a mess when they find me. Lately, I've been careless in my housekeeping, too often coming home to the smell of dead food. Yesterday I cleaned the house, sorted things out. It reminded me of times long past, when I cleaned and scrubbed and prepared for happier events than this. Days when I had prospects, when I had hope, when I had a future. Enough. I'm becoming melancholic and tired and I've put off writing this for too long. It is such an effort to get it all down.

After the garden party, it was hard to get rid of Joe. He hung around after we'd had sex, when all I wanted was to be left alone. He was in an inquisitive mood.

'Why do you live on your own, a lovely woman like you?'

'None of your business.'

'No, really, I want to know. I've often wondered why you're not married. You must have had offers. Have you never been tempted?'

I said nothing, hoping he'd take the hint and go.

'Well, aren't you going to answer me? Come on.' He leaned over me, smiling. I noticed the soggy bread caught in his teeth and wondered again at human sexuality. Love is blind and lust is short sighted. It's amazing how satiation improves the eyes.

'Jennifer getting home from hospital tomorrow? I hope she won't take too long to get over her hysterectomy.' That did the trick nicely, just as I'd hoped. He left.

Alone in the semi dark, the room lit by the orange glow of streetlamps, I thought over my confession and how my friends had reacted. Their reaction pleased me on the whole, confirmed my belief that you never really know another person. It made me feel safe from detection, justified in my assumption that we all have preconceptions about the act of murder. I smiled to myself and turned over to sleep. But it evaded me. The bed smelled of sex and I was restless; the feeling of wellbeing from the alcohol had worn off and I had to either change the bed linen or get up. After a second or two of thought, I decided to go for a walk. No. I may as well tell the truth. *Shame the devil*, as my dear, departed mother used to say without the least hint of irony. A stranger to the truth, that woman. But I don't have time to go into that now. I know that even as I was speaking in the garden I had decided to kill again.

This third killing was my only truly premeditated killing. As I got dressed, I started to plan it in my mind. I would follow an opera plot. Final act. Kill the first person I saw. It's playing now, as I write.

You can't perhaps imagine just how absurd that is. I am five foot three and weigh less than eight stone. How could I possibly murder the first person I came across? He or she could be six feet tall, with the build of a rugby player. The secret, of course, is to be well prepared. In the pocket of my cheap plastic mac, I carried a kitchen knife, Sabatier, sharpened before I left the house.

Have you ever walked city streets just before dawn? There is an uncanny stillness about them. Only the occasional car reassures you that other people have lives to live. Even so, I was surprised to see how few cars there were on the road. I walked along Newlands Road, past the detached sandstone houses that I had long admired, seeing the odd squirrel run fleet foot up a tree. A fox trotted alongside me for a few seconds; we looked each other up and down, two predators out on the prowl. The fox left me when I reached Pollokshaws. I fear it didn't like my company. I passed the flat that had featured in the first Trainspotting film. The derelict flat where the baby died while her parents lay in a heroin-induced torpor. A terrible scene. For years a pair of hideous purple patterned curtains had hung crookedly in the window, clinging to the condensation. No longer. The flats had been modernised, the condensation gone now they had double glazing, and smart blinds replaced the grubby curtains. I carried on walking, in my stride now. I was wearing trainers and my footfalls were silent. I felt as though I was walking above the ground – the effect of too much wine, no doubt. Within ten minutes, I was on Barrhead Road, Pollok Country Park to my right and the golf club to my left. The half-light of dawn was behind me and the sky ahead was brighter than when I'd left the house, though thin streaks of dark cloud still trailed their fingers over it. Out of the corner of my eye I caught movement; a man on the other side of the road. He was small and slightly built. That was good. He wouldn't be too difficult to manage. I started to cross over, aware this could be a busy road at times and therefore not the best place to kill someone. I looked both ways. No sign of any cars.

'Excuse me,' I called out as I drew near, 'Can you help me? My dog's fallen down a hole.' (Yes, yes, I know it's weak, but it was the best I could do at the time. I had drunk more than a bottle of wine, you know.)

He came bounding across the road. I read later that he was well thought of by everyone. Well known for his helpfulness and courtesy. There were still no cars, but there was no point in taking any chances.

'You're out early?'

'I couldn't sleep and Mandy loves her exercise...'

'Mandy?'

'My dog,' I explained. 'A westy. She's not barking.' I put a tremor in my voice. 'I hope she's all right. I couldn't bear it if anything has happened to her.'

'We'll soon have her out. Where is she?'

'Oh, thank you.' I was all charm. 'She's in here'. I walked into the woods and he followed.

Not far from the road, I stopped and pointed vaguely at a bush. I allowed him to get slightly in front of me. 'I think the hole's around here somewhere.'

'Aren't you scared walking alone? It's very quiet here.' He smiled at me. Or it might have been a leer. For the first time, I felt a little uneasy. What if I had picked up a rapist or a serial killer? I shook myself. What were the chances of two serial killers being out and about at the same time and in the same place? Yet, stranger things had happened. Better get my knife in first.

He kneeled down to peer at the earth. I pulled out the knife and as hard as I could I thrust it into the side of his neck. Blood gushed out in a huge arc, pumping with the dying beats of his heart. He fell to the ground, clutching his throat, and thrashed around for a few seconds before giving up. I think, although I wouldn't want to swear to it, that he said *why?* in that dying moment. But it might just have been a sigh. My heart was beating fast, the light was getting stronger and I could hear more traffic on the road. And there was blood – *yet who would have thought the man to have so much blood in him?* – I was covered in it. I thought I had planned for it by wearing a revolting plastic mackintosh, which I had intended to bury, but the blood was everywhere, on my face, in my hair, over my hands. I almost lost it then. Panicked. Started to dream up stories of how I had interrupted the murder and had frightened the murderer off, falling into the path of the dying man. Knew at once it wouldn't wash; any competent forensic scientist would know exactly what had caused the precise pattern of the bloodstains. I even thought of rolling in the earth to try to cleanse myself. Yes, that's how desperate and muddle-headed I was. Then I remembered the river.

I checked he was dead, though with losing so much blood he could be nothing more than an empty vessel. I made sure I had left no clues. Even though it was becoming lighter bit by bit, it was difficult to see. I used a fallen branch to sweep over my tracks and left, hoping it was enough. I walked in what I prayed was the direction of the River Cart, and within a few minutes I was there. There was no option. I waded into the river fully clothed and started to wash myself. Over and over again I dived beneath the murky waters to rinse out my hair. I took off all my clothes and scrubbed at them. After a time, the whole scene became dreamlike and I relaxed. I was the Lady of the Lake. Once I visited an art gallery in Edinburgh that had several paintings by the Scottish artist John Duncan on show. In one, Morgan le Fay held Excalibur aloft in triumph. Did I do something similar in the river that morning? I'm afraid I did. That Sabatier knife became my Excalibur. I have to confess: I have a tendency to over-dramatise at times.

With difficulty, I dragged myself back to reality. The plastic mac cleaned easily; my other clothes were thin and light, and while they would not have passed the close scrutiny of a forensic scientist or anyone who wasn't registered blind for that mattter, they looked fine to me. After a while I got dressed, shivering in spite of the warmth of the early morning sun. I had no idea what I would say if anyone did see me; perhaps that I had fallen into the river, drunk. The walk home was not a long one. I stayed close to walls and hedges and felt myself to be invisible to the few cars that passed me. I must have been. No one reported seeing a woman out walking that morning. I showered when I got home and went back to bed. I slept well.

His body was found later that morning. Apparently he'd been on his way to work at the local supermarket, Morrisons, walking in order to save money because his wife was pregnant. She appeared on television, a frantic sight, all snot and tears, appealing for witnesses. I almost felt sorry for her until I learned that the baby she was expecting was their sixth. Six children! Hadn't they learned how to tie a knot in it?

Do you know the opera? I'm listening to it now. It doesn't work out quite as well as my foray does. Characters in opera are so stupid and short-sighted.

There are times, though, when I wish I'd killed Joe instead. Not because he was a more unpleasant person, more deserving of a bad end than my poor young man, on his way to work. No, because it would have been fitting to kill as the Black Widow spider does, after mating. I did, after all, use him sexually. It would have been so satisfying to end the evening in that way. And he was an opportunistic adulterer. Yes, reluctant as I am to admit it, I suspect I made a mistake that morning.

It's no use. I'm ravenous. I really did not expect to have an appetite tonight. I'll have to leave you for a few minutes and visit the late night garage.

Forty-three minutes later. Unfuckingbelievable. I was stopped by the police! For speeding. Tonight of all nights they have to do their job properly. They got out of the patrol car and strolled towards me. They walked all round the car checking tyres and lights. It must have been a quiet night for them.

'Good evening, madam. In a bit of a hurry, are you?'

What could I say? *Well yes, I am, as a matter of fact. You see I've only got a few hours left to live and I'm in the middle of writing my confession to five murders.* It was tempting, but I needed to be on my way so I apologised and accepted the speeding ticket.

So here I am. A sizeable chunk of my remaining life taken by PC Plod. A speeding ticket, which surprise, surprise I'm not going to pay, and the indignity of having to blow into one of those little glass tube things. I was close to the limit, they said. Bloody Scottish government and their attempts to stop people drinking. They gave me a verbal warning and sent me on my way. I didn't get my snack after all.

On reflection though, maybe it's better not to eat. Less mess. And hunger will concentrate my thoughts on what needs to be done.

When I was a child I used to enjoy fasting. I was very impressionable. I thought if I copied the lives of the saints I would become one myself. One of my favourite pastimes was to wander round the local park feeling hungry and holy and waiting for the Virgin Mary to appear. After all, I reasoned, if she could appear to three peasant children in Portugal who hadn't even been looking for her, then how much more likely was it that she would appear to a pious girl like me? And so, one summer, I spent many hours looking for her among the branches of trees. I longed for a glimpse of a blue robe, a dazzle of a smile or a hint of a halo. One day my parents took me to a well-known beauty spot, the Whangie, an impressive geological formation north of Glasgow. As soon as I saw it I knew this had to be the place. I made them take me there every Sunday for weeks after that, and looked inside every crack. It seemed such an ideal place for my apparition. Then my father told me about the legend of the split in the rocks. A coven of witches was waiting to meet with the Devil on Auchinden Hill. As he arrived he whipped his tail across the top of the hill, resulting in the chasm which is known as the Whangie. That ruined it for me. The Blessed Virgin would never appear there, in a place tainted by Satan. Undaunted, I returned to the trees I knew and continued to practise my response to her. How I would smile shyly, look down and never ever look her in the eye for fear of being blinded. I would speak clearly but softly and I would go immediately to the parish priest with any secrets she might want to pass on through me. I truly thought she would appear. But she didn't hear my prayers and her non-appearance was the beginning of my disillusion with religion.

I'm sleepy now and I've only told you about two of the killings. They never got anyone for those two but they did get someone for my second murder. Derek White took the rap for that one. They police reckoned he'd done it, murdered his wife.

But before I tell you about it I need some appropriate music. Another opera of course. Though the woman in the opera is wanton and young, whereas my victim was wanton and middle aged. They weren't really married, of course. She was his common-law wife, a poor soul, who it turned out was regularly beaten up by him.

I was on my way home from the King's Theatre. I'd been to see a famous musical. It's based on a series of poems. If you've any knowledge of literature at all you'll know what it is. If you don't, you really need to read more.

A woman approached my car when it was stopped at traffic lights. I hadn't put on the central locking, and before I could stop her, she was in the back, cowering on the floor, begging me not to let on she was there. I looked all around. The streets were empty and we were totally alone. I was a little put out but intrigued too. She was clearly terrified of something or someone. The lights changed and I drove off with one last look round to see if there were any witnesses. Not a single one.

I drove for ten minutes without saying a word. It wasn't up to me to make polite conversation. I felt no fear, though you might have expected me to be more than a little apprehensive. I just wanted to see what would happen. Perhaps it was a scam and she was going to mug me. Maybe she was completely out of it and I would be left with piss on the back seat. I had no way of knowing, and in a way the uncertainty was liberating. Finally, she spoke. Her voice was guttural, thick with the tar of many cigarettes.

'Thanks, hen. My ex was after me. He was about to do me.'

'Where was he? I didn't see anyone.'

'Up Pitt Street, cursing and swearing. One of my pals seen

him, snorting and foaming at the mouth like the old bull he is. He was livid. Heard I had another man. Well, what if I do? Derek's boring. I was fed up with him; he thought he owned me. Listen, hen, can you drop me off at the bus station?'

'Not at all. I'll take you home. It's no trouble. Where do you live?'

She didn't suspect a thing. 'You're a doll. That's real good of you. Dennistoun, near where the tobacco factory was. I used to work there, afore it closed down.'

I turned the car round. 'Aren't you too young to have worked there? I thought they stopped production years ago.'

She lit up a cigarette. 'Aye, it shut in 1982. I was seventeen – I only got a year's work out of it.'

'Sorry, I have asthma,' I said. 'Could you put your cigarette out?'

She rolled her eyes. 'Och, it won't do you any harm.'

My lungs were already tightening. I pressed the button for the electric window. 'I mean it.' I said.

'Fuck's sake.' She took a long drag before throwing the cigarette out.

'Thank you,' I said. We drove on for another five minutes in silence.

'Here, where are we?'

It had taken her long enough to realise we weren't on the road to Dennistoun. 'I took a wrong turn back there,' I lied. 'Don't worry, you'll be home soon. We were passing through a large patch of waste ground, near Glasgow Green. It was deserted.

'Shit. The oil warning light's on.' I stopped the car. I had decided to kill her. She shouldn't have crossed me. But first I had to get her out of the car. 'Look', I said, 'I'm going to have to ask you to help me here. Do you know anything about cars?' She didn't. No surprise there. It took a little persuading to get her out of the car. I think she was frightened I'd drive off and leave her in the middle of the wasteland. If only. It took one blow. I'm sure that first blow killed her. The cracking of her skull seemed to echo through the dark night, but just to make sure, I hit her three, maybe four times with the heavy spanner I keep in the car. The viciousness of the attack apparently convinced the police that her ex-husband was behind it. That and the many witnesses who came forward to say they'd heard him swear he was going to 'do that fucking whore good and proper'.

The character in the opera was stabbed, but I don't always have a knife in my pocket. What do you think I am, some kind of psycho? No, sometimes I just had to use what was at hand.

Well, well, well. Nearly three a.m. Not long to go. I wonder when my body will be found. Marianne next door is going away for a few months to do charity work. Some ghastly place like Malawi. So she won't be around, and Jan on the other side is away for a week so it could be a while. Ugh, but it won't be my problem.

Sometimes when I think about my victims they seem to me to be a true random sample; a child, the middle-aged downtrodden woman, the respectable family man, the OAP and the young woman. I wonder if there's any significance in that. Maybe the psychologists will be able to tell.

Time to put on the music that defines this killing. No opera this time – the music is simple: a string quartet, written by the composer when he was ill; hence its gloominess. Though I prefer to think of it as lyrical and haunting. I'm sure you'll enjoy it. And if you really don't know what it is, there's a play of the same name. That's your lot, no more clues.

Looking back, it seems to me that I took a real chance killing her – the young woman, that is. She wasn't really random and she could easily be tracked back to me. For months after the murder I half expected to be taken in for questioning, especially after the *Crimewatch* feature. But I wasn't and it confirmed yet again my belief that middle-aged women are the invisible seams of our society. They hold everything together: caring for children and elderly parents, working all hours, but nobody sees them. Everyone notices young women, even unattractive ones. Men, no matter what age they are, draw attention to themselves all the time. The way they dress, the way they walk, even the way they sit, legs apart, balls exposed. It's the posture of the dominant with nothing to fear. If you were afraid, would you open up your tender bits to attack? No. They sit there, manspreading, ballsharing, call it what you will; safe in their certainty that no one is going to bother. Middle-aged women, on the other hand, sit with their legs entwined, arms across their expanding bellies in the hopeless belief that this hides their girth.

I used to see her every Wednesday evening at the gym. I called her Goldeneyes, although in reality everything about her was golden. Her highlighted hair, the perfectly toned limbs, the discretely expensive jewellery, the little flecks of gold studded around the perimeter of her irises. She didn't do anything as gaudy as shine. She shimmered. In the gym, all eyes turned to her. She was graceful on the treadmill; her movements on the machines were perfect. While others sweated through their exercise, she glistened slightly with a few diamond drops of perspiration. I was drawn to her. Once, in the crowded Jacuzzi, I sat thigh to thigh with her and felt a slight pressure, a hoped-for invitation. I've had many lovers, men and women. I decided early on in my adult life not to limit myself to one sex. I preferred to double my chances. Lazy with lust, I lay half asleep. I imagined turning to her with a smile, how we would arrange secret meetings, how I would draw energy from her vitality, how we would make love every day. The pressure grew and I felt a hand on my thigh. I hardly dared breathe. It seemed so bold to openly seduce a stranger in this way. I half opened one eye and glanced down. The bubbles frothed beneath my chin and I could just make out the outline of a large hairy hand. Without a sound I allowed my hand to travel up the thigh of the repulsive male who had somehow secreted himself beside me, while Goldeneyes was nowhere to be seen. I found his testicles, cupped them in my hand and squeezed. Hard. I was pretty sure he wouldn't have his wares on display for a while.

It pleased me to think of him hobbling around, but the amusement wasn't enough to make up for the disappointment of losing that glorious body. For several weeks after that, I watched her, desperate for any sign that the pressure in the Jacuzzi had been deliberate, but she seemed unaware of my existence. I carried on hoping though. Then one Saturday, late in October, I bumped into her in town. Without thinking, I greeted her like an old friend, approaching her with open arms. She stepped back, frowning.

'Hi. Um, do I know you?'

'Yes, well not really. We go to the same gym.'

'Really? I'm afraid I don't...'

'The Carlton gym.' I named another well-known gym, in an attempt to salvage something from this appalling gaffe.

'But I don't go to the Carlton. I'm a member of Newfields.'

'I'm so sorry. I've confused you with someone else.'

This horrible exchange seemed to last for ever, although in

reality we only said a few more mutually charming words to each other before I sloped off, the redness creeping up my neck. I was livid.

I didn't go back to the gym for over six weeks, until, fed up one evening, I decided that the social embarrassment did not warrant me spending sixty-five pounds each month for nothing. I returned but avoided Wednesday evenings. Of course anyone who spends that much for membership of an exclusive gym is not going to spend just one evening a week there, and it wasn't long before I saw her again. She was with a group of friends when she saw me, and she smiled a cruel smile before whispering something. They all laughed and stared at me. Did they know my secret desire or were they laughing at something else? That night I followed her home. She lived on a main road two or three miles from the gym. I parked near her house and watched her go up the garden path, house keys jangling. The house was dark.

I followed this pattern for a few weeks. She was becoming an obsession. I swear I didn't set out to kill her that Thursday evening. She was beautiful; I wanted to worship that beautiful body, not destroy it. But when she got out of her car in King's Park Avenue that evening, she started walking towards my car instead of going into her house. There was a grim set to her face and somehow I knew she was about to confront me. Although I had parked several doors away from her house, I panicked. I started to reverse the car to try to get away but she kept coming at me. Almost before I knew what I was doing, I had put the car into first gear and was driving hard at her. I don't remember much of what happened next. Something must have alerted the neighbours, for lights were coming on in the dark houses all around me. Somehow I managed to drive off.

The papers said she died immediately. Although I had not hit her that hard – I couldn't have done, there was only a small dent on the bumper – she had landed badly, striking her head on the edge of the kerb.

The next evening a neighbour was interviewed on the local news. I watched, terrified that something might have given me away. The usual questions were asked. You know the kind of thing: 'Mrs Morton, have you any idea who might have carried out this appalling act?'

And the appalled neighbour, anxious to help: 'No, I can't imagine anyone doing this, but I saw the car as it drove off. It was a white BMW. I didn't get its number, though. Laura had complained for weeks that someone was following her. She thought she was being stalked. I reckon it was one of those dirty old men that hang around the gym. She always complained that she was watched. Mind you, she was a lovely girl.'

I didn't know what to think. My car was a blue Golf. Where had the white BMW come from? Was it a bluff to lull me into a sense of security? I was very worried. It wouldn't take much to link the victim to me, and yet if they followed this false trail, I might just get away with it. I had washed the car thoroughly when I got home. There was a bump on the front, which concerned me. For two days I fretted about what to do. The police would surely have tipped off garages. I decided to brazen it out, not get it fixed. I had a story ready for when I was asked about it, as surely I would be. I continued to go to the gym, reasoning that it would be more suspicious to do anything out of the ordinary. Nevertheless, it was a shock when I turned into the car park at the gym and saw the police cars there. The car park had been cordoned off and police were everywhere, interviewing the clientele. I could scarcely breathe. This was it then. My life of crime was about to come to an end. I thought over the weak story I had prepared about the bump on my car and saw too late that it was full of holes. I even wondered whether it would be worthwhile getting a lawyer before I answered any questions or whether this would just antagonise the police.

'Good evening, madam.' The voice broke into my thoughts. 'Could I trouble you for a few minutes of your time?'

'Of course.' I smiled at him; there was no point in being uncooperative.

'You'll have heard that one of the members, Laura Henderson, was the victim of a hit and run accident three days ago. We have reason to believe that she knew her killer and that the incident was in no way an accident.'

I looked suitably shocked. Not too much though. Mustn't overreact.

'It's been suggested that Laura was being stalked, perhaps by one of the men here.'

My heart lifted. I wanted to kiss him, to dance around the car park. I kept my face expressionless, however.

'I see. How can I help?'

'Did you know Laura at all?'

I made a rueful face. 'Not really. I recognised her photograph when it was shown on TV the other night. But we were only on nodding terms.'

'So you don't know who her friends were or if she had been complaining of being stalked recently?'

I shook my head. 'Sorry, I've heard nothing at all.'

'Right you are then, madam. Can I just ask you a few more questions?'

We then went through the usual routine. Name, address, whereabouts on the night of the incident, had I seen anything. Not once did he examine my car. Just asked if it was mine and whether I had any other car and if I had been driving it on the relevant night. I answered smoothly, my voice belying the inner turmoil. Finally, he confirmed what I was scarcely daring to believe.

'Do you know if any of the members here drive a white BMW?'

'Any particular model?'

'We have a witness who saw a white BMW being driven away at speed from the incident the other night. Unfortunately, she isn't clear about the exact model. She thinks it was fairly big, though.'

No wonder they weren't giving my small blue Golf a second glance. This was too good to be true.

'I'm really sorry,' I said, 'but I don't mix socially with the other members and I don't take much notice of cars.'

'Thank you, madam. We may contact you in the next few days if anything else comes up. You will let us know if you hear anything, won't you?'

Quite frankly I would have laid myself down in a puddle for him to walk all over me, but I just quietly promised that I would, of course, let him know if I thought of anything else and we started to move apart. Then it came, so much worse because I had allowed myself to relax.

'That dent on your bumper, madam. Can you just tell me where and when it happened?'

While I had been preening myself, simpering at this man who I thought gullible and naive, he had been noticing everything. Not such a dull old plodder after all.

I blushed, feeling the heat rush to my face. 'It's awful, isn't it? Someone bumped into me in Sainsbury's car park yesterday when I was doing my shopping. I came out and there it was. Not a note, nothing.'

'I see. Can anyone confirm this?'

Shit, shit and shit again. I was beginning to feel unreal, as if I wasn't really there. I was sure he must see how guilty I looked.

I was probably puce coloured now. The sweat was gathering at the base of my spine. 'Gosh, sorry, no. No, I can't think of anyone who would confirm it. There was a woman I spoke to in the car park. You know, we exchanged a few remarks about how dishonest people are these days, but I've no idea who she was.'

'I see. Well, that's all for now, madam. We have your number if we need to ask you any further questions.'

The days that followed were among the worst of my life. I read every local paper, watched every news bulletin and listened on the hour to Radio Clyde. The police were getting nowhere. And then came *Crimewatch*. The white BMW featured largely in this programme but there was one dissenting voice. A young boy who lived in the same street said that he had noticed a car that evening, parked several doors away from Laura's house. It had been there before, many times. It was not white. It was blue, a blue Golf. I almost passed out. Then I realised I wasn't breathing. I took a deep breath, waiting for the bombshell that he collected car numbers. He looked just the type; small, pasty faced, glasses hanging off the edge of his nose. No, no car number. But definitely a Golf and most certainly blue. I almost phoned the police there and then and gave myself up. I was sure that they would be round to interview me again and I thought with regret of the silly story to explain the bump. Although at least I'd had it repaired by now, so there shouldn't be any forensic evidence on the car.

They never came. I still don't know why. A few days after the programme, a man was arrested. At his trial the verdict was 'not proven', that peculiarly Scottish, highly unsatisfactory outcome. It was enough to satisfy the police though. After the trial, they said that in the lack of any new evidence coming forward they were closing the file and were not actively seeking any other party. They clearly thought, though they could not say, that they had the right man all along. Well, they'll know better soon.

We could have had fun, Laura and I. If only she hadn't been such a tight-arsed little bitch. If only she had come to me that night with a smile instead of that look of what? Intense fury? Sadly, it was not even that. When I close my eyes and relive those last few moments of her life, I can see that look on her face clearly as she strides towards the car. It is a look of boredom. Boredom. How *dare* she?

4.51 a.m.

4.53 a.m.

4.54 a.m. I cannot do this. I cannot tell you about the boy. My son.

DEEP breath. Breathe slowly. It has to be done.

I was thirty-seven and in love. Like Jean Brodie, I was in my prime and married at last to the man who had been my lover for five years. I had been his mistress while he pondered and fretted about how to leave his wife. Five years is a long time to listen to someone's doubts. I grew sick of his procrastination, and so one evening after a particularly fraught and angst-ridden session, I phoned her. Told her just what had been going on.

Well, she was furious of course. Packed his bags, ripped his clothes, the usual clichéd stuff. But she must have had regrets soon after, for she started to fight back. I don't have time to go into all that. But she did have style, I'll grant her that. One morning, about three months after he had moved in with me, he got a CD through the letterbox. Paul Simon – 'Fifty Ways to Leave Your Lover'. We laughed long and hard about that. I admired her feistiness. I could afford to be gracious.

We married as soon as his divorce came through. I was pregnant. Gloriously, radiantly pregnant. I was so happy. So very, very happy. He was too. I'm sure of that. We laughed a lot, ate good food, sensuous finger food. We even drank a lot. I was not going to let doctors turn me into one of those pregnant women who feel guilty if they have even one glass of wine in an evening. I had never felt so good about myself and we abandoned ourselves to sensuality for the first six months of the pregnancy.

Happy days. Happy daze.

I wasn't aware of things going off. Too wrapped up in myself, I suppose. I started to become obsessed by the baby. The nesting instinct hit me hard and I spent hours cleaning and fussing over household tasks. I was still happy. He was less so. By the seventh month I had decided that sex was too risky and I insisted on celibacy. My mistake. He was very keen on sex and I should have realised that his ex-wife would be only too happy to supply what I would not.

God, was she smug. She came round to see me one day when he was at work. I didn't recognise her at first. It had been over a year since I'd watched her coming and going. She had lost weigh since then. Her hair was cut very short and showed off her fine bone structure. Her clothes were cheap but she was ten years younger than me. She would have looked good in a dress made out of newspaper. She looked great. I looked great too, as in huge.

'Can I come in? I think we have quite a lot to talk about.' She squeezed past the small space I had allowed between the door and me.

'Sit down, why don't you?' I said as she settled herself into the sofa.

'I'm not going to waste time. My husband...'

'Excuse me? *Your* husband? Mine, surely.'

She carried on as though I hadn't spoken. '...is desperate to leave you, but he feels tied by this... baby. He's frightened you'll be really upset. But you and I know that you'll survive.

You had years on your own, after all. Don't kid yourself that he stopped loving me just because you were available for a quick fuck.' She paused to revel in my shock. 'Here's the deal.' She threw me an envelope, which I didn't even glance at, just felt its weight on my lap. 'I think you'll find that the brat is provided for adequately. He won't be back, so I'll take his things now, or at least what I can carry. I'll come for the rest tomorrow.'

My heart stopped. I swear it stopped. I could feel panic rise inside me. She went through to the bedroom, *our* bedroom. The baby was moving inside me, sensing my agitation, and I tried hard to calm myself.

If the same thing happened today, I'd kill her. I've had enough practice now. A garrotte, I think, round that long slender throat. No, that's far too quick for the bitch. I'd torture her. Or better still, lock her in a small room, a cellar, maybe, and leave her there, dying of thirst and hunger. A small glass of water now and then to give her hope, to prolong her suffering. How can I make you understand that nothing, *nothing* would be too bad for her? She's to blame for everything.

In those days though, I was quiet and submissive on the whole, reluctant to take control of my own destiny. The phone call I'd made to that woman when she had been his wife was out of character. It had taken a lot out of me, and I suppose when she came to claim him back I felt I could do nothing; that he was, after all, rightfully hers. I sat and watched while she carried out two suitcases (mine) full of my husband's clothes. I cried. I even begged her not to do this to me. What a wimp I was.

After she'd gone, the contractions began. I'm not going to relive the horror of that birth, the pain that tore me apart. Perhaps if there had been someone there to support me, I would have survived the experience better. I might have avoided the terrible depression that came over me after the birth. A deep, dark and all-consuming melancholy, where there is no point to life, when you wake up in the morning and there isn't even a fleeting glimpse of how things could be better. Dreams turn into nightmares and a terrifying lethargy comes upon you. Washing yourself is a major exertion, so why bother? No point in eating, when all food is dust.

He was a beautiful baby. Even in despair, I recognised that. But he was difficult. I sat for hours while he gnawed at my raw, cracked nipples. Milk mixed with blood, and all the while, tears would run unchecked down my face and onto his. We tortured each other. I couldn't give him the food he needed and he couldn't give me the love I was desperate for. He cried almost as much as I did, but he was noisier. Sleep became a distant memory. We struggled on for five or six weeks. My husband tried to get custody of the child, but I had a good solicitor who argued that my depression had started as a result of him leaving. I had no family to help me and I had lost contact with most of my friends during my obsessive period with my lover/husband.

I have little memory of that time. I cracked, of course. Tried to suffocate my child as he slept. That's what they told me. I blocked it out. For years I didn't remember what happened in the immediate aftermath. I suppose I signed papers to have him adopted. What does happen in these cases? I don't know. They told me later (much later) that I had begged them to take him away from me. Maybe I did. I don't remember.

The pain... the pain of it all still attacks me at times. Creeps up on me and silences me with its viciousness. The treatment for depression went on for three long years. I saw psychiatrists, counsellors, psychologists. None of them helped, but I learned to say the right things, and eventually, one bright summer's day, I was released from the hospital that had been my home for so long. I never went back to my own house when I left the hospital. My solicitor took care of the sale and I lived in a rented flat for a while before I bought this house. I cut all the ties. Nobody knows me from my past life; from before. They all think I'm childless: pupils, their parents, neighbours. 'A charming woman,' I heard one parent say to her friend on the way out from a lesson one evening. 'Such a shame she never married. She'd have made a wonderful mother, don't you think?'

It took me two weeks to find out where they'd gone, my bastard husband and his bitch of a wife. They were ex-directory, of course. Didn't want their past catching up with them, no doubt. I watched them one evening as they sat in their sitting room; the curtains open, inviting the world to look in on their happiness. They had a baby by now, and as I watched they sat and talked to each other late in the evening, the baby nuzzling at her breast, a glass of wine by his side. She, however was the model of a perfect mother. No wine for her.

I knew what I had to do. They all had to die. I was dead inside and it was because of them. I had tried to kill my own child and had lost him to another couple because of them. I set a fire.

What a fool I was. It should have been obvious to me what had happened to my child. They had adopted him, of course. I had signed over my child to my worst enemies. When I heard the news of the fire on the radio, I thought there had been some mistake. I listened to the announcer, my heart thumping. 'A four-year-old boy died in a house fire in Bearsden early this morning. His parents and baby sister survived the fire, which is thought to have been the result of an electrical fault.'

Ironic, isn't it? I killed my own child in an attempt to get even. It sounds like the plot of a soap opera. It is – almost. It was the first opera I ever saw, and from the opening bars I was hooked. I wept as the gypsy woman unknowingly threw her own child into the flames. I should have heeded its lesson. Those who seek revenge will not go unpunished. *Il figlio mio, Mio figlio avea bruciato!*

Every death since then has been insignificant. I wanted others to suffer. I hope they did. I have no remorse. Dead people can't feel sorry, and since that morning, I've been dead.

It's nearly time to leave you. I have a large number of sleeping pills and some malt whisky, a good one – Bowmore. I should be asleep in a few minutes, dead in half an hour.

Have you learned anything from me? An ordinary, insignificant woman. My final choice of music is playing now. After all, I find I need something appropriate to sugar the pills. What better than the final notes written by Mozart just before his death...

Lacrimosa dies illa
Qua resurget ex favilla
Judicandus homo reus
Huic ergo parce, Deus
Pie Jesu Domine
Dona Eis requiem

PART II
Absolution

Ego te absolvo

Chapter One

Mark

DI ALEX SCRIMGEOUR picked up the tabloid lying on Mark's desk and read aloud from the front page. 'Blah, blah, blah... Although it hasn't yet been confirmed, it is rumoured that the woman left a note confessing to five murders.' He threw the paper down and glared at the roomful of police officers. His face, normally florid, was redder than ever and beads of sweat stood out on his forehead. Mark moved back a little. He'd experienced Scrimgeour's temper in the past and his rants usually involved a lot of spittle. But he was too late, Scrimgeour had already started.

'Where the fuck did they get that from? I made it very clear last night that this was to be kept quiet. If I find out there's been a leak from this team...'

Robbie McPhee stiffened and looked down at his desk. It was well known that his brother worked for that particular rag. Mark spoke before Scrimgeour's gaze settled on McPhee. He'd make mincemeat out of the boy. 'What do you make of this confession, sir?'

Scrimgeour looked at him, a little glint in his eye. 'Are you changing the subject, Mark? Was it you who leaked it?'

Mark took a deep breath before answering, 'No, it wasn't me.'

'Right.' Scrimgeour glared at the team. 'Who's read this so-called confession? I know you have, Mark. And I have, obviously. Anyone else?'

Two people slowly raised their hands.

'I think that the officer who was first at the scene read at least some of it,' said Mark.

'Find out,' snapped Scrimgeour. 'And tell whoever it was to keep his or her mouth shut. I don't want this passed around and I want to keep tabs on those in the know. No one else reads it without my permission. There's been too many tip-offs to the press recently. Right, Mark, I want you to check out the details. Look at all the databases, HOLMES, CHS, the lot. Check out any names that come up. I don't think for a minute that there's anything in it but we have to be sure. Especially if there's some arsehole ready to blab anything to the press. And talking about the papers, once you've done that, you can call a press conference. Tomorrow morning at the latest.'

'Is that really necessary, sir? I can't believe this confession's serious. I mean if you look at it objectively, a woman like that – a murderer? One or two of the descriptions were really violent. It's not really a woman's...'

'Careful, son. I'll need to send you on an equal opportunities refresher course if you don't watch out.' Scrimgeour snorted at his own joke and several people joined in, Robbie McPhee laughing loudest of all. Moron, it was the last time Mark would do anything to protect him.

McPhee was still laughing. Big mistake. Scrimgeour's eyes narrowed as he focused on him. 'It wasn't that funny, son.'

Robbie flushed. 'Sorry, sir.'

'Your brother, isn't he a journalist?'

'I... um...' It was no use; he couldn't let Robbie go through a Scrimgeour interrogation. The kid was barely out of his teens. Mark tried again. 'Could it have been one of the neighbours, maybe? After all, according to the confession we found she did tell them she was a serial killer.'

Scrimgeour shook his head. 'Doubt it. The ones next door are tenants, just moved in. Apparently the owner is off doing good works abroad.' He snorted. 'Do-gooders. I can't stand them. There's plenty to do round here. You don't need to go to Malaysia or wherever the fuck she is to help. But it sounds better than volunteering at your local soup kitchen.'

'Malawi, sir.'

'What?'

'The neighbour's gone to Malawi, not Malaysia.'

'Who the fuck cares? They're all the same to me.' Scrimgeour looked down at his notes and carried on. 'Anyway, the tenants are clueless. They noticed the smell right away but thought it was the drains. They were interviewed yesterday. They moved in on the 20th June. They knocked at Ms Campbell's door the next day to introduce themselves but got no answer so we can probably assume she was dead by then. But the neighbour on the other side is yet to be interviewed. A – he consulted his notes – Mrs Jan Stevenson. How the fuck she missed seeing those bluebottles, I don't know. They were fucking everywhere.'

Mark shrugged. 'She did notice them. Thought they were the result of the hot weather.'

Scrimgeour ignored Mark's comment. 'I want you to go and interview her, Mark. It might help us pin down when she died.

Pathologist is being a bit vague about it. Take McPhee with you.'

Mark tugged at his tie. 'Actually, I promised Karen I'd be home early tonight. It's my turn to bath the weans.' Karen was always on his back these days. He should have held his peace; Scrimgeour, a middle-aged man with no kids, had no understanding of family life.

'You're a policeman, what does she expect?'

Scrimgeour was right. Everyone knew police had to work long hours. Mark shrugged and nodded at Robbie to follow him.

Once in the car, he turned to McPhee. 'Robbie, don't ever do that again.'

The kid tried to bluff his way out. 'What? I don't know—'

Mark interrupted him. 'Look, I know your brother works for the Daily Shitstirrer. Everyone knows... even the boss. You've no idea how close you were to the bollocking of your life.'

Robbie swallowed, his Adam's apple gross in his skinny neck. He flushed then paled. 'I'm sorry, it's just that he's under so much pressure to get stories.'

'I don't care, Robbie. This is an ongoing investigation. It could turn out to be a murder investigation. We can't go giving out information like sweeties. What exactly did you tell him?'

Robbie licked his lips, his voice cracking as he spoke. 'Only that there was a confession to five killings. That's all.'

'Sure?'

'That's all I knew. The station was buzzing about it this morning, but nobody gave any more info than that. Honest.'

'Cross your heart and hope to die?' Mark grinned as Robbie's index finger crept towards his chest. Where the fuck did they find them these days? 'No, there's no need to do that.

But I'm warning you. No more sneaky wee leaks to your brother.'

Mrs Stevenson, wasn't at home. If she'd any sense she'd gone to stay with a friend, away from all the papers and publicity. The scene of crime team was still working, and Mark and Robbie called in to see how things were going. They chatted for a while, Robbie gawping at the young female forensic scientist. 'Put your tongue back in,' Mark managed to whisper to him before she noticed. Any hint of sexism or inappropriate behaviour and she would quite rightly complain. McPhee had a lot to learn. Mark spoke to the officer in charge.

'OK if we go and have a look at the room where the body was found?'

'On you go. Just make sure you have protective clothing on.'

The smell had dissipated somewhat and the floor was clear; Mark shuddered as he remembered the sight that had met them the evening before. As he walked across the polished wooden floor, he imagined the crunch of the dying insects beneath his feet.

Without the distractions the room was even more elegant than he remembered. The heavy, cream curtains that had been drawn when the body was found were now held back by black iron curtain holders. He fingered them; the material felt cool to his fingers – some sort of silk? He wasn't sure.

There was no sign of the laptop that had been on when they walked in on the scene; it had been taken as evidence. The smell had indeed been horrific but not as bad as the sight of a decomposing body sitting at a desk. Now the curtains were open and light was streaming in, he saw that the desk was antique. A captain's desk, with two sections of drawers. He opened the largest one. It was empty save for a pencil and a sharpener. The others were stuffed full of theatre and opera programmes. Mark took one of them out. A French production of Shakespeare, *La Tempête.* He searched his memory for Shakespeare plays. It must be *The Tempest*, he thought. That sounded right. He put the programme back in its place. Not quite how he'd choose to spend an evening. A lack of even basic French would ensure that he'd be asleep within five minutes of its beginning. He thumbed through the other programmes looking for something he'd recognise. He'd been to the theatre a few times and loved it, but Karen hadn't really enjoyed it – romcoms were more her sort of thing. Defeated, he put them all back; there was nothing there that he'd seen.

He carried on looking around the room. It wasn't large, perhaps sixteen square metres. Probably it had been the dining room originally, but a modern extension with a dining kitchen had made this redundant. One wall was covered in built-in bookshelves filled with a collection of books. He had a quick look at them. It was an eclectic choice, carefully ordered so that fiction and non-fiction were separate. There were many art books, mainly about Renaissance art but a few on more modern artists. One caught his eye, Joan Eardley. He'd been to an exhibition of her work in Edinburgh last year, though he hadn't been able to spend as much time there as he would have liked. Karen and the kids combined were a formidable force and he'd given in quickly. He plucked the book from the shelf and leafed through it. Her work had really appealed to him. She captured perfectly the expressions of the young children she'd painted and their chaotic lifestyle. He wondered what would happen to the deceased's possessions, and whether she had any relatives. Stifling a sigh, he stuffed the book back in its place and moved away. An expensive-looking rug, with an intricate pattern, lay in front of the carved wooden fireplace. Mark had seen similar rugs in the Burrell collection and knew it was eastern, Turkish possibly or maybe from Pakistan. He'd read once that you could tell if a rug was genuine by looking for an error in the pattern. The weavers of these carpets would deliberately put in an imperfection, as only Allah could make something perfect. Mark stood in the centre of the rug and scanned it systematically until he found the flaw. The rug had a border of rectangles, each with a cross inside. Four red rectangles alternated with a cream one, but in the top left-hand corner there were only three red rectangles with two cream ones. He continued checking to make sure that it wasn't part of the design, but the pattern of four to one was repeated all the way round. It was genuine then. He bent down to stroke it, marvelling at its richness. The rest of the room was simple. There were few ornaments: a reproduction of an ancient Greek horse, a terracotta disc with hieroglyphics spiralling round it, a plain glass vase, empty now though he remembered it as having been full of dead flowers.

Mark picked up the disc. It looked familiar. It was about six inches in diameter and had different figures engraved on it. In the centre was a flower. Some of the other shapes were recognisable – a walking man, a man's head – but many were more symbolic; some were shaped like letters, others were more abstract. Mark looked at it for a while, trying to make sense of it, before it came to him that he'd seen it on a television programme about ancient Greece. He searched in his memory for its name. Not the Rosetta stone; he'd seen that on a trip to London and knew it was Egyptian. The Phaestos disc, that was it. Some thought that the engravings told of the adventures of Hercules, others that they represented the evolution of humankind, but the overwhelming view was that it was indecipherable. He put it back on the mantelpiece. He had nothing to add to its story.

Before leaving the room, Mark took one last look round; it was all very tasteful and understated. The sofa was upholstered in dark grey wool with two scatter cushions that picked up on the red tones in the rug. There was little else in the room save for a couple of side tables made of dark oak that also looked antique. No Ikea furniture for this woman. He grimaced as he thought of his own house, untidy and overcrowded. He'd love to live in a house like this where there was plenty of room for his books – books that Karen saw as useless clutter – and where the shelves were adorned with tasteful ornaments rather than plastic toys.

Mark looked up from his reverie to find that Robbie had disappeared. He went through to the light, modern extension with its painted kitchen units. They looked expensive. Robbie was there, way too close to the forensic scientist, who was making some tea. Mark refused her offer of a cuppa for them both and they made their way back to the car. Robbie had a sullen look on his face.

'I was just about to ask her out,' he said as he pulled the seat belt over his shoulder and fastened it.

Mark sighed. 'What age are you, son?'

'I'll be twenty next week. Why?'

'Sarah is thirty-two. She's married with twin daughters aged eighteen months. She's off limits. You were that much off – he held his thumb and forefinger a centimetre apart – a sexual harassment complaint in there.' She was also gay. But that was none of the wee shite's business. He glared at Robbie, noting the tic at the corner of his right eye. Good, he needed to get the message. 'This isn't a dating agency, son, nor is it somewhere where you can pick up stories for your big brother.

That's two stains on your copybook in one day. Get a fucking grip, will you?'

It was nearly ten o'clock before he got home. Mark hadn't had a chance to phone and say he was going to be late. Truth to tell, he'd chickened out. Why have two confrontations if you can get away with one? But there was no avoiding it now.

The key didn't turn in the lock. Mark took it out and shook it, then laughed when he realised what he'd done. 'That won't do any good. Pencil lead, that's what it needs, or WD40 to grease the lock.' He rang the door bell. No reply. He rang again.

'Karen? Are you in there? Karen?' He stooped down and shouted through the letterbox. No reply.

He tried the key again. This time, after careful manoeuvring, it turned and he pushed the door open. Immediately he knew there was no one there. The air was thick with that dead atmosphere that empty houses often have and his heart sank. No doubt there would be a note on the mantelpiece again. 'I've taken the kids to Debbie's. We need to sort things out. Blah bloody blah.' He spoke aloud, listening to his words mock him. His face felt hot and his voice rose out of control.

'Fuck you, Karen,' he shouted into the empty room. 'I've had enough of these fucking games. Night after night of sulks and silence, running round to that bitch Debbie when things get too much, blaming me for everything. You can stay at your bloody friend's house forever. I just don't care any more.' Mark was sweating now. The feelings of sickness that had threatened him since yesterday returned forcefully. An image of the maggot-ridden body rose up before him. With some effort, he forced the dreadful picture out of his mind and considered that his emotional state might be the cause of the nausea. Then again, he hadn't eaten for hours. It must be hunger. Mark went straight to the kitchen in search of something to feed the gnawing in his stomach. The tiny room was untidy, dirty dishes littering the worktop and sink. What on earth did she do all day?

He cleared the sink and filled the bowl with hot water. The mundane task soothed him and he thawed a little. After the tensions of the past two days, he was in an almost dream-like state and his thoughts flowed easily: maybe her life was harder than he thought. It wasn't all that usual to have three children these days and there was probably a good reason for that. Maybe he was using his work as an excuse to get away from their demands. Sophie always wanted a story, Oscar to play football and Emma... Christ alone knew what she wanted. He had never known a child to cry so much. She needed time and patience but he just couldn't give it to her. She was the unwanted third child. There. He had admitted it to himself. He would have been happy with two but Karen as usual had got her own way. Maybe Emma sensed she wasn't wanted. Who knows? But she had the most difficult temperament he had ever come across in a child. He felt guilty about how he felt and compensated by giving in to her every demand, with the result that she whinged even more. Christ, she was a fucking dictator and she wasn't even two years old. Karen tried to tell him he was ruining Emma but he never listened. Maybe they did need professional help like Karen claimed, he thought. They should talk more. He needed to give her a treat. He shouldn't work so hard. Next time, he would stand up to Scrimgeour. Tell him to stuff the job. They should have a holiday, get away by themselves, have that honeymoon they never had. By the time Mark had finished washing the dishes, he was completely calm and regretted his harsh words when he had entered the house. He'd phone Karen after he'd eaten. He could charm her into forgiving him if he really tried. After all, he'd had plenty of practice.

Once he'd put away the dishes, Mark looked in the fridge. He winced as he saw the dish half full of tuna mayonnaise, covered by a blue mould. The little bit of cheese that lay there was caked with a rind like the sole of an old man's foot. He took out three eggs and looked at the date stamped on them. Only two days past their best. He made himself an omelette. Not a perfect omelette. That would need fresh eggs. Nearly perfect though, runny on the inside just as he liked it. As he ate it, he recalled the times that he and Karen had fought over this. Her omelettes were overcooked, rubbery, a sop to salmonella. Fruitlessly he had tried to explain to her that salmonella was little risk to strong, healthy adults like them. He never managed to work out her logic. She was happy to keep horrible bits of left-overs breeding bacteria in the fridge, yet was frightened of a perfectly made omelette.

Mark made himself coffee, pulverising the Colombian beans in the expensive grinder he'd treated himself to, knowing as he did so that he'd regret the intake of caffeine so late at night. Small cup in hand, he moved through to the living room. No note on the mantelpiece; that was a surprise. Mark put down his coffee and picked up the phone. The icon on its screen was flashing to show there was a message. He picked up the receiver and went through the menu to the answering machine. *You have three messages: Message one received at two forty-seven a.m. on Wednesday the fourteenth of January.* He really had to do something about the timer on the phone. They'd never set it up properly and it was months out.

The first message was from Karen's mother reminding her of her father's birthday next week. Poor Jeannie, she lived in hope that there would be a reconciliation between Karen and her father. The old man, a freemason and Orangeman, had been furious that she'd moved in with a Catholic, even though Mark hadn't been to church since he was a small child. He hadn't spoken to Karen since and had stopped his wife from seeing her. She'd stood up to him briefly as she wanted to see her grandchildren, but he made her life a misery when she did. She was frightened of him, so the visits became less and less frequent. She did everything she could to keep in touch and to try to breach the distance between Karen and her father. Mark lived in fear of her succeeding. Bitterness like his father-in-law's was hard to swallow.

The next message was almost finished before he'd registered it; he was so full of resentful thoughts about the old man. It was from Karen; she'd sounded upset. Something about hospital. His heart started to beat faster. Damn this machine; there was no way of replaying messages easily. You had to go through the whole lot again. The third message rang into his ears: Karen's voice, upset, angry. *Where the hell are you, Mark? Sophie's been knocked down. We're at the Royal Hospital for Children. Just get here as quickly as you can and bring...*

He was out of the door before the message finished.

Chapter Two

Mark

THE PRESS CONFERENCE WAS A DISASTER. Mark was ill prepared for it after his shock of the night before. He had reached the hospital at midnight to find his wife pacing up and down the corridor, two children at her side. One of them had a dirty nappy. Mark caught the warm farmyard smell as he ran towards them. 'Where's Sophie? Is she all right?'

'In the operating room.' The words came at him bleakly and he felt himself start to sway. Karen noticed his pallor and took pity. 'She's going to be fine. Her arm's badly broken and the operation takes some time. Where the hell have you been? Did you bring nappies? I left a message on the answering machine.' Her face was tight and Mark noticed fine lines creasing across her forehead and round her mouth. Dammit, she looked like her father. Mark made himself smile.

'Thank God she's OK. No, I didn't bring nappies. I'll go and get them.'

Karen thrust the children towards him. 'No, you wait here. I'll get them. Give me your car keys.'

'Drive carefully,' he called after her, but she was already gone.

The night had been a long one. It was well after three in the morning when he finally got home. The operation had finished soon after his arrival. When Karen returned she had insisted on staying. He hadn't wanted to leave either her or Sophie, but Emma's fractious cries made it impossible for him to stay. When he left, Karen was asleep on a camp bed beside Sophie, a deep frown line etched on her forehead. He took the other children home. Oscar was excited to be out in the middle of the night and kept asking questions. 'Where's Mummy?' 'Will Sophie only have one arm?' 'Why did the bad car hit her?' As Mark listened, he realised he didn't even know what had happened. Why had Sophie been allowed out alone? 'I don't know, son. I just don't know.' He said this over and over again until Oscar, bored, drifted off to sleep beside the twitchy body of his younger sister.

Stupid with fatigue, he drove the wrong way home. Coming out of the new hospital campus, which housed both the Royal Hospital for Children and the Queen Elizabeth University Hospital, he took a wrong turn so that he went into the Clyde Tunnel by mistake. Swearing under his breath, he took the first exit and found himself in Whiteinch. North of the river when he should have stayed south. Making matters worse he went into automatic pilot mode and followed the route he used to take when he was younger and had lived in the West End and worked in Castlemilk. He was in Shawlands before he realised his mistake. Cursing, he drove through the dark streets. When he reached Barrhead Road, the dead woman came to mind and he looked across at Pollok Country Park. Too many bodies had been found there over the years, but none corresponded to what had been described in her confession. Mark sighed; the city was a paradox. It was a great place; he loved it, loved the people, their patter and friendliness. But there was an underlying darkness here as there was in any large city – of deprivation and desperation, with drugs and alcohol ruining lives.

A fox ran out in front of the car, jolting him out of his reverie. He swerved to miss it. He loved seeing wildlife in the city, even though he knew many people regarded the foxes as vermin. Looking in his rear view mirror he caught a glimpse of its tail as it ran into the park. There were deer in the park too, but he'd never seen one, never been around at a quiet enough time. He drove on past Peat Road roundabout along Brockburn Road, which had gone up greatly in the world. He should know – he'd been brought up here and he remembered the demise of the council flats. Doors and windows boarded up with large sheets of metal, odd bits of unwanted furniture littering the street. He'd almost crashed his car once when he'd swerved to avoid a mattress someone was flinging out of a window. The flats were long gone, replaced by neat semi-detached houses with cars on their tiny driveways. As he continued to drive he wondered again at the diversity of the city. There were still slums in the city – fewer than before, but they were there. And often within walking distance of houses worth hundreds of thousands of pounds. He turned on to Crookston Road, relieved to be nearly home at last. A few minutes later he turned into the little estate, driving slowly over the speed bumps and up to his house. He'd get a couple of hours' sleep at most if he was lucky. Moving slowly so as not to wake them, he lifted the two sleeping children out of the car, into the house and up to bed. They didn't stir.

Getting them up again in the morning had been a nightmare. They were exhausted, Emma especially, and he groaned as she picked up her plate of cornflakes and threw them onto the floor. His jaw was clenched as Emma continued to scream while he cleared up the mess. Her screaming didn't stop all through the phone calls that he made trying to arrange child minding for the day. No wonder no one wanted to help. There was nothing else for it. He'd have to try Karen's friend, Debbie. She hated him and the feeling was mutual. She made a show of checking her diary and muttering about being very busy before she at last agreed.

'Thanks, Debbie, I owe you one.' He put the phone down before she could change her mind.

Now, only five hours after he had left the hospital in the middle of the night, he was in front of a group of reporters, poorly briefed, with no Alex Scrimgeour to help him. 'Where's the boss?' he asked every policeman he saw. The shrugs were indifferent. Scrimgeour was not an easy man to work for and no one saw any need to help his sergeant. Pale and sweating, Mark sat down in front of the pack. His eyes, stinging from lack of sleep, blurred the features of the men and women before him, so that he imagined he saw a pack of wolves, slavering, ready to pounce. Well, he was right about the pounce. The questions came at him, so many stinging arrows, and he could hear his voice cracked with nerves, trying to answer.

'This woman, Julie Campbell, right?' The journalist

glanced at her notes. 'Is it true she killed five people, including a young child?'

Mark picked up the intake of breath as the others digested what she'd said. He could see them mentally sharpening their pencils, thinking of the bylines and the money to be made out of a serial killer, one who had murdered a child.

'We don't know for sure.' Shit. He shouldn't have said that. The pack gathered round him, sensing a kill.

'You don't know for sure.' His words mocked him. 'So there's a possibility she *was* a murderer after all?'

Mark backed off. 'We only know that the body of a woman was found, in an advanced state of decomposition. She left a lengthy suicide note.'

'This suicide note – was it also perhaps a confession?' The Kelvinside drawl of the *Herald*'s crime reporter needled its way into Mark's head.

'No comment.'

'So it was a confession.' The voice of the *Herald* reporter held only the faintest quiver to betray his excitement.

'No comment.' Mark rose to leave the press conference, his face scarlet with annoyance and embarrassment, knowing his performance had been poor. He stumbled as he strode to the door. Behind him, he heard a colleague laugh, and in his touchy state, imagined that she was getting at him. He turned and glowered at her.

'What's so fucking funny?'

Her brown eyes widened in surprise. 'Er... I was just telling the others a joke.'

'Aye, right.' He saw her surprise turn to anger.

'Would you like to hear it, Mark? Looks like you could do with lightening up a bit.'

Several of his colleagues were looking on in interest. Best not give them anything to gossip about. Mark held his hands up and smiled in apology. 'I'm sorry, Clare. It's been a bad night. My daughter's in hospital. She had an accident yesterday.'

'Sorry to hear that, Mark. But please don't swear at me again. There's no need for that.' Her eyes were cold. She wouldn't forget his outburst in a hurry. He gazed after her as she hurried out of the room, her back tense.

'The old charm never fails, does it, son?' Scrimgeour had sidled up without him seeing.

Mark clenched his fists. Scrimgeour always seemed to know just how to get to him. 'Calm, calm, calm,' Mark thought to himself and tried to force a smile. It stopped a mile short of his eyes. 'Ah well, you win some you lose some.'

'You've lost her, all right. Her father's a minister. She hates swearing. With any luck she won't complain about you. Anyway, enough of that. You made a right cock up of that press conference, didn't you? Christ only knows what the papers are going to say. What's wrong with you, anyway? You look knackered. Up shagging the wife half the night?'

Mark winced. He looked silently at the man and considered telling him about Sophie. No, someone else could do that. He changed the subject. 'I didn't manage to see Mrs Stevenson, sir. You know, the neighbour. Should I try again today?'

'Good idea. Tell you what, I'll come too. Get a sense of the scene.' Scrimgeour threw a set of car keys at Mark. 'You can drive.'

Mark raised his right hand and caught them without looking. He was used to his boss trying to catch him out.

Jan Stevenson opened a door that was decorated with original stained glass and beckoned them into the hallway. An enticing smell of coffee greeted them.

'I've been expecting you,' she said in a voice that betrayed a love of cigarettes. 'Come in.'

Scrimgeour pushed past Mark and followed her into the front room, which was full of what would be described as 'charming original features' by the estate agents. The cornicing was pristine and the fireplace had been stripped back to its original pine. The doors too had been stripped and waxed, but the oak floor appeared to be new. She must have seen Mark looking.

'I know,' she said. 'It's a crime not to have the original floorboards. We had them for one winter and then had to cover them up with new ones. There were just too many draughts.'

Mark felt wrong-footed. 'No, no. They're lovely.'

Scrimgeour glared at him before turning to Mrs Stevenson. 'We need to talk to you about some things.'

'Of course, but first things first. Would you like some coffee? It's freshly made.'

'Yes please... Not for me.' The two policemen spoke together.

She raised an eyebrow. 'One at a time, please.'

'Coffee for me please,' said Mark, 'with milk. I smell real coffee. Am I right?'

'But of course. Freshly ground. I wouldn't give instant house room. And as for those stupid machines...' She turned to Scrimgeour. 'And what about you? Some tea?'

'Nothing for me. I'm working.'

Mrs Stevenson looked inquisitively at Mark as she left the room. He thought the look was saying, 'How can you put up with that?' His reflection was interrupted by Scrimgeour's sneering tone.

'*I smell real coffee. Am I right?* Who're you kidding, son? You couldn't tell real coffee from instant. Where are you getting these notions from anyway? Not from Karen, that's for sure. She wouldn't put up with that nonsense.'

'I just happen to like coffee, that's all. And I think it should be made properly. Everywhere else in the world can make decent coffee. Why can't we?'

'You're so right, inspector. Well-prepared food and drink are one of the joys of life.' Neither man had heard Mrs Stevenson return to the room. She placed a tray on the coffee table in front of them.

Scrimgeour's face reddened in irritation. Mark hurried to correct her. 'I'm Detective Sergeant Nicholson, Mrs Stevenson. This is Detective Inspector Scrimgeour.'

A smile skimmed across her lips, so faint that Mark wondered if he had imagined it. She knew what she'd been doing all right.

'Whatever. Now how exactly can I help you, gentlemen?'

'We're just trying to get a sense of what happened. When did you last see your neighbour? When did you notice something was wrong? Take your time.'

'Mmm. Let me see. I saw her before I went on holiday. That was two weeks ago.'

'So, you saw her on what? The 15th June?'

'No, it would have been before that. The 13th most likely. It was a nice day and we were both out in our gardens. We chatted over the fence for a bit.'

'Did you notice anything unusual about her? Did she seem stressed or upset at all?' Scrimgeour was leaning forward in his seat, intent on every word.

Mrs Stevenson thought for a moment. 'No,' she said. 'She was just as she always is. Chatty, normal. Nothing out of the ordinary.'

'What did you talk about? Do you remember?'

'We talked about Marianne going away and how brave it

was of her to volunteer like that. And then we chatted a bit about the book we were reading for the street book club. Neither of us liked it much.'

'Anything else?' asked Mark.

'No, she said she was going away for a few days so not to worry if I didn't see her when I got back.' Mrs Stevenson blinked and wiped away a tear. It was the first time she'd shown she was upset. 'I didn't realise I'd never see her again.'

It wasn't much to go on. Mark felt it was a waste of time but he carried on with his questions. 'What made you think something was wrong?'

'It was the tenants in Marianne's house. I bumped into them two days ago and we had a chat about how they were settling in. Nice young couple – have you spoken to them?' She sipped her coffee. 'They asked about the smell, whether there had ever been any problems with the drains.'

'Was this the first time you noticed the smell?' asked Mark.

She shook her head. 'No. I noticed it as soon as I got home from my holiday. At first I thought it was a mouse, dead in the cellar. So down I went through the little trap door under the stairs. I hate going exploring. My husband always took care of that sort of thing but we separated last year.' She laid the coffee cup down on a Rennie Mackintosh. 'It can be a little tricky, you know. You could have a nasty fall. Careful, I thought, no point in doing yourself an injury. You could lie there for weeks, making a nasty smell. Humph. Anyway, down I went, taking my time, and of course the light bulb was out, wasn't it? I certainly wasn't going to go down there in the dark. So I left it. It's a mouse, I told myself. Small. It'll be gone in no time, taking its nasty smell with it. Well of course it didn't go. And then I thought it was a rat, or perhaps a dead cat. There's always cats going missing round here. I didn't know what to do. I was going to call environmental health, but between you and me they're absolutely no use at all. That time I had bees nesting, or whatever it is they do, in my cellar. They wouldn't touch them. "Oh no, Mrs Stevenson, they're harmless." And then I had wasps in the attic. They wouldn't climb up a ladder to spray them. No, they stood in the garden with a spray on the top of a long wobbly stick and puffed uselessly at where they thought the wasps' nest might be. Might be. I ask you.' Her voice rose in indignation. 'Anyway, I wasn't going to bother with them. So I called you. Not 999, of course. That would have been a waste of resources.' She stopped to take a breath and smiled at Mark. 'I'm not telling this very well, am I? Maybe it would be better if you asked me questions.'

Mark demurred just as Scrimgeour was starting to speak.

'Aye, it would be better. There are quite a number of things that we need to get straight, Mrs Stevenson. I just don't get it why you didn't call someone in before? I mean, the smell was overpowering.'

'I don't know really. I did smell it, of course. But as I said, I thought it was a dead rat or something. To be honest I thought it would just go away.'

Scrimgeour's voice rose. 'You thought it would go away?'

Mark interrupted before Scrimgeour could go off on one. 'I imagine you've not had much experience with dead rats and such.'

"Not exactly. As I said, my husband always dealt with that sort of thing.'

Scrimgeour stood up. 'I'll leave my DS to finish this interview. I need to get back to work. Mark, can I have a word, please?'

Mark followed him to the door. Once outside he took out a cigarette and lit it. He drew on it deeply. 'I can't be bothered with this. She's a bit of a flake isn't she. See what else you can get out of her and I'll get back to the station and start the paper work. No, you keep the car,' as Mark went into his pocket, 'I'll call for a squad car or maybe I'll walk. The exercise might do me some good.' He patted his gut and walked down the path.

Mrs Stevenson raised an eyebrow as Mark walked back into the room. 'Bit abrupt isn't he?' she asked. 'No, don't answer. It's not fair to ask you that. I used to hate it when people asked me to comment about my boss. I mean, what can you say? Yes, he's a mean bastard and I hate his guts.' She laughed softly as she saw him try to control his face. 'Oh dear, looks like I struck a chord somewhere.'

'Yes, well.' Mark was embarrassed. He had thought he had better control over his features than that. Two minutes in her company and she was reading him like a book. 'Mrs Stevenson,' he began.

'Please, call me Jan.'

It was best to keep things formal. 'Mrs Stevenson, I realise that this must be distressing for you, but I must ask you some questions.'

She looked a little put out by his refusal to use her first name. 'Go ahead.'

'How well did you know your neighbour?'

'How well did I know Julie? Well enough to know that she wouldn't kill anyone. Did you see those articles in the papers? Simply absurd. She was gentle, cultured, well read. She couldn't have killed anyone.'

'What about herself? Does it surprise you that she took her own life?'

Mrs Stevenson looked down at her nails, lost in thought. 'I suppose, if I'm honest, it doesn't surprise me. She suffered from depression. Not often, but she did tell me once that there were periods of her life that she would rather forget. We had quite an argument once, about the Piaf song... *Je ne regrette rien...* She said it was laughable, that anyone who had no regrets either had no conscience or had led an impeccable life. Me, I was struck by the defiance of the song. I found it admirable that someone could have such self-confidence, could look ahead all the time rather than back.'

'Have you any idea what caused the depression?'

'I'm not sure. She let slip once that she had a child. A boy. But when I asked about him, she clammed up and her eyes filled with tears. I never mentioned children again.'

'So, you weren't really close, were you?'

'I suppose not. She was a very private person.'

'Was she acting strange in any way? Anything out of the ordinary that you can think of?'

Mrs Stevenson sighed. 'No, I really can't think of anything.'

'Mrs Stevenson, do you recall Julie holding a garden party once? I'm not sure how long ago, but it was in the summer.'

She thought for a second. 'Yes, she did have a small party once, just for the neighbours. Rather a dull affair. I got rather tipsy, I'm afraid. I tried to liven it up with a party game but she wouldn't take it seriously.' Her eyes opened wide. 'No, she couldn't have been serious. She couldn't have been.' She rose from her seat, twisting her hands, and turned away from Mark. She walked over to a perfectly arranged vase of flowers and fiddled with them. She spoke as she worked, never once looking at him. 'Sergeant Nicholson, at this party we played a game, just one of those silly games you play at parties. You get into pairs, tell each other three things about yourself, and one has to be a lie. I was really irritated by her because she kept claiming she was a serial killer.' She snapped the head off a chrysanthemum and threw it in a wastepaper bin before turning to look at Mark. Her face was pale. 'She was kidding, surely.'

'That's the most likely explanation. There's nothing more

at present, but you've been very helpful. I may need to speak to you again though. Do you have a mobile number I could use?'

Mrs Stevenson nodded and wrote down a number on a piece of paper. She looked worried, Mark thought. He smiled at her. 'I'd be grateful if you kept what you just told me to yourself for now.' He held out his hand. 'Thank you for all your help. I'll be in touch.'

Chapter Three

Mark

MARK LOOKED ROUND as he closed the garden gate. Mrs Stevenson was standing at the window. She turned away without acknowledging him. He got into the car, pulled his seatbelt across and leaned back. His mind was made up. Twenty minutes and he could be at the hospital. He had to see his daughter, to see for himself that she was all right after the operation. How on earth had she come to be knocked down? He hadn't had a chance to ask Karen last night. Surely she hadn't allowed Sophie out to play unsupervised? Karen knew his views on this. He was dead against it, even though they lived in a quiet cul-de-sac. Only last week they'd argued about it and she had accused him of wanting to wrap the children up in cotton wool. He didn't. He just wanted them to be safe. He also felt that they should both spend more time with the kids. Do more interesting things with them. He had a nagging feeling that sticking them in front of a DVD was less beneficial than just spending time doing ordinary things. Karen was a mug for anything with an educational tag, but it was more to do with giving herself a break than helping the children's development. Before long he found himself thinking about what an easy life she had. And yet she was never happy. Fuck, he was becoming a right old grump. She was probably just as fed up with him.

He reached the hospital and started the difficult job of finding somewhere to park. This was a new hospital built only a few years ago, but already it was obvious there weren't enough spaces in the car parks. Doctors, nurses, porters, patients, visitors all having to fight over the few places available. He crawled round the multi-storey carpark, wondering if he'd find somewhere. His luck was in; a car indicated its intention of moving out in front of him. He slowed down and waved the woman out. She half turned in her seat and held up a hand to thank him. Once she was out he started his manoeuvres. He parked the car less than expertly, aware of cars waiting behind. The space was smaller than he would have liked. Backwards and forwards he went until it was done to his satisfaction.

The hospital was busy, and rather than wait for the lift, he bounded up the three flights of stairs, thankful for the chance to work off some of his energy and frustration. He found Karen beside Sophie's empty bed, her head on the cover, sound asleep. He shook her gently. 'Karen, wake up. Where's Sophie?'

'What?'

Mark drew back from her. Her breath smelled; she hadn't cleaned her teeth. Sleep had gathered in the corners of her eyes, and in the harsh fluorescent light she looked haggard and ill-kempt. Despite this he felt a rush of tenderness. She was exhausted. He spoke again. 'Sophie. Where is she? Is she OK?'

Karen shielded her eyes from the light. She yawned. 'She's in the playroom. She's fine, Mark. Woke up at eleven and immediately demanded something to eat. I thought you were supposed to be groggy after an anaesthetic.' She laid her head down again. 'I'm shattered. I need a break from this.'

'Go on home then. Debbie's got the other two. I'll take over here.'

She shook her head. 'You don't understand, do you? I need a break from everything.' Her voice rose and Mark was aware of curious glances from other parents in the ward. He remained calm.

'OK. Why don't you go away for a couple of days? You could visit...' He stopped, unable to think of anyone. Her parents were out of the question and she didn't have many friends. In fact, the only one he really knew was Debbie; others were fleeting... women she'd met at mother and toddler groups or at WeightWatchers. They were never around for long. She'd told him once she found women difficult. 'They always want to know everything about you, all your problems. And it's just so they can gossip to one another. Debbie's the only person I trust.' She kept herself to herself; she hadn't even told him much about her past when they'd met, dismissing it with, 'It's gone, no point in going there.'

'You could arrange to go on one of those weekend breaks with Debbie. There's always something on Groupon.'

She grimaced. 'Oh, forget it. I'm just tired, that's all. Have you finished work for the day?'

Mark braced himself. 'Well, if you're sure I'm not needed here, I ought to get back to the station. We're in the middle of a really bizarre case. Some woman killed herself and left a note claiming credit for five murders.' He waited for an explosive outburst against his work, but there was no predicting Karen's reaction.

'You'll be working overtime then. Good. We could do with the money if I'm going away for a weekend.' She smiled at him, a genuine warm smile that reminded him of how crazy he had been about her once. 'Oh God, I'm so relieved that Sophie's going to be all right.'

'What happened?'

She shook her head. 'I don't know really. It was all so quick. We were in Shawlands. One minute she was beside me, the next she was running across Pollokshaws Road. She'd seen one of her friends from school. I had her by the hand but she broke free. The driver didn't have a chance. She was lucky only to break an arm.' Karen's eyes filled. 'Oh, Mark, I thought she was dead. She was so white, lying in the street. She just lay there for what seemed like hours and then she started screaming. It was such a relief to hear her, but then I was terrified that some terrible damage was done. It seemed like an age before the ambulance came, though someone said it was only five minutes. And then the traffic... You know what it's like at rush hour. It seemed to take an age to get here. I needed you but I tried your mobile and couldn't get through, and of course you're never at home.' The tears spilled over and ran down her face. Mark offered her his hanky and she blew her nose noisily.

'Ssh. It's over now. She's fine. You said so yourself. No point in going over it again. You know what children are like. They mend in no time at all.'

Karen nodded. 'Yes, I know. I'm being silly. It's just... I'm so tired and I'm sick to death of always snapping at you. I was fun once, wasn't I?' Her voice wavered.

It was true. Karen had always been good for a laugh. She had a wry sense of humour, which hadn't been apparent for some time now. But this wasn't the time or place for a long discussion about their relationship or their faults, and Mark, now he knew Sophie would be fine, was impatient to get back to work. All he wanted to do was to see for himself that she was all right and give her a cuddle.

'You go back to sleep. I'll go and see Sophie before I go.' He smiled to himself. Karen was already asleep, worn out by the powerful emotions of the past day.

Chapter Four

Mark

Scrimgeour put the phone down. The look on his face was enough to curdle milk. Mark decided against asking what was wrong and went back to the massive cardboard box that contained files on murder cases that they had thought were closed. He waved a bulky brown package in the air. 'Got it, sir, the White case. Shall we go through it now?'

Scrimgeour shook his head. 'No, the pathologist wants to see us. We'd better get down there.'

Mark thought he wasn't quite hearing right. What on earth had the pathologist said to Scrimgeour to get him to behave so meekly? He thought about saying something, teasing the man, and then thought better of it. Scrimgeour was dour and didn't take well to banter. He was good at dishing it out right enough but he couldn't take it. Mark smiled as he thought of the fortieth birthday card some of the younger police officers had sent a few years back. A harmless enough message for most people; most would have laughed it off. 'Happy birthday, you pompous old fart!' Not him. Scrimgeour had sulked for days, and his acerbic tongue had hit out at most of his colleagues for several weeks after. Well, the truth must hurt after all. It was rich really, considering what Scrimgeour could dish out. One police officer had run from a briefing in tears after being told that he'd seen dead sheep with more active brain cells than her.

'What about this file? Will I take it with us? I could go through it in the car.

'Fine. Whatever you want.'

On the way to the pathologist's office, Scrimgeour was unusually quiet. Mark glanced once or twice to see if he seemed to want to discuss the case, but Scrimgeour was lying back in his seat, eyes closed. He looked exhausted. There were rumours that he looked after his elderly mother, who had dementia, but no one wanted to risk his wrath by mentioning it or asking after her; he was notoriously private about his personal life. It was only because one of the civvies lived near him that they knew anything about him at all. He opened his eyes and caught Mark looking at him. 'What?'

'I was just wondering about this case. I've looked through it and we remembered right. White did confess to his wife's murder and there were several witnesses who saw him threaten his wife earlier on the night of her murder. The forensic evidence wasn't particularly great though.'

'The woman was murdered with a spanner that matched with one found in White's possession. She had been hit from behind by a right-handed person. He had previous convictions for beating her up. He's right-handed and he had always used a weapon for hitting his wife. What more evidence do you need?'

'All I was saying was that the main evidence really came from his confession. It was that that convicted him. Everything else was circumstantial. I mean, why was there no blood on the spanner? Everyone knows how difficult it is to get rid of all traces.' Mark was rattled. He had been in interview rooms with Scrimgeour and his presence could be very threatening. Scrimgeour had interviewed White.

'Listen, son, he was a wee shite. He did it all right. I know he did it. In any case, even if there was no blood, there were traces of bleach. He'd cleaned that spanner thoroughly. Why? When every other tool in his possession was filthy?'

'OK, OK, keep your hat on. Well, if that's the case, then this woman's confession is rubbish. Although I suppose there might be something in the other cases. I mean just because you don't remember them...'

'Listen, son, I remember everything.' He looked at Mark meaningfully. 'Everything. Of course it's rubbish.'

Mark looked away. He didn't like Scrimgeour's tone. Was he going to bring up the past again? He'd hoped it was forgotten. He forced himself to speak, willing his voice not to shake. 'Makes you wonder though, doesn't it? I mean why would a middle-aged woman leave a confession that she had murdered someone like White's wife?'

'I've no idea. Timewaster? Nutter? Attention seeker? We need to find out if she did have a psychiatrist like she says in the confession. If she did we'll have to speak to them, and then it'll all come out, you'll see.'

They drove on in silence. Mark continued to read the file but it didn't help.

Dr Siddiqui was waiting for them near the reception. 'I'll take you to see the body. You might like to wear masks. The smell is a little overpowering.'

'I know, I was there,' he reminded her.

'Bet you wish you'd been wearing a mask then.' She grinned at him.

Mark beamed back; her smile was so infectious. Scrimgeour saw the smile and opened his mouth. Mark got there first, not wanting to hear Scrimgeour's riposte.

'You're right. I'll take a mask. We both will.' He changed the subject. 'I saw you on TV last week on *Question Time*. How did you get to go on that?

The ploy worked and he was spared Scrimgeour's venom. The pathologist talked all the way down the long corridors to the morgue and Scrimgeour couldn't get a word in without being even more of a bore than he actually was. They reached the room and accepted the gowns and masks without demur.

Once in the room, an assistant pulled out a drawer where the remains were kept. Dr Siddiqui asked for them to be moved to the table in the centre of the room. 'The light is better there,' she said.

Both men flinched when the cover was taken off the body. Even though it had been cleaned up, it was worse than they remembered. 'If you look in here, you'll understand.' She pointed to inside the woman's mouth. 'Look closely and you'll see that the left side of her mouth is less well cared for than the right. Although her teeth are perfect with no fillings or extractions, you can see that those on the left have more plaque than those on the right-hand side.'

'So?'

'So, chief inspector. She was left-handed. It's common to see this discrepancy in oral care. Right-handed people have better teeth on the left of their mouth and vice versa. They spend more time brushing that side. Also if you look at her left hand, the middle finger has a callous on it that usually comes from writing.'

Mark thought he understood. 'What you're saying then is that she couldn't have murdered Derek White's wife. Mrs White was killed by a right-handed person. So the confession is a fake after all.'

Dr Siddiqui frowned. 'What on earth are you talking about? No, don't bother going into it. Whatever it is, it probably isn't important. But yes, I do think that the confession is most likely a fake. Think about it. Think back to the scene when you walked into the room. What did you see?'

Mark started to speak but was immediately interrupted by her.

'Was there a mouse?'

'Yes, there was. One of those fancy cordless Apple ones that cost a fortune.'

'Where was it?'

'Where they usually are. On the right of the laptop.'

'It's well seen you're not caurie-fistit. No. In this case, you wouldn't expect it to be there. If Julie Campbell had typed that confession, the mouse should have been on the left-hand side. It was on the right; chances are she didn't type the confession. So you'll have to ask yourselves – who did?'

Mark tried to put his thoughts into some order on the way back to the station. This case, which had seemed quite straightforward when they had discovered the body, was becoming more complicated by the minute. If Julie Campbell had been murdered, and it was a big 'if', who had murdered her and why? She seemed to have been a quiet woman with few friends and no known enemies. What was the confession about? Was it genuine, referring to real murders? They knew for sure that at least one of them was a real murder, although it was a closed case with someone locked up for it. They were still checking on the others but had drawn a blank so far. There were no missing persons fitting the profiles of Julie's so-called victims. No, the confession was most likely a fantasy. Why would someone murder Julie though and leave a confession purporting to be from her? Were they trying to set her up as a murderer? With no bodies? It was all too confusing. He turned to Scrimgeour.

'What do you make of this latest, sir?'

For once Scrimgeour was subdued. 'I have to admit it, Mark – I'm stumped. I haven't a clue what's going on. Look, we'll have to find out more about Ms Campbell's past, see if she did see a shrink, get the low down on her recent mental state. As soon as we get back I want you to get on to that. Phone her GP or something. But if there was a psychiatrist, I want an interview set up as soon as possible.'

'What are we looking for?'

'I want to know about her mental state. Why she was in hospital, did she have a baby as she claimed in the confession or is that fantasy too? We also need to talk to her ex-husband.'

Mark looked perplexed. 'That might not be that easy, sir. We don't have a name or anything. None of the neighbours even knew she'd been married and he hasn't come forward.'

There was no reply for a moment. Scrimgeour was looking out of the window, miles away. He often lapsed into dreaminess, something he wouldn't tolerate in others. He rubbed his nose and sighed. 'Try the NRS.'

'NRS?'

'The National Records of Scotland. They're responsible for registering births, marriages and deaths. We have her name; shouldn't be hard to find. I'm surprised you didn't think of that, Mark.'

Wrong footed again. Shit. It was best not to underestimate Scrimgeour. Mark nodded. 'Yes, of course. Do we have her date of birth?'

'It'll be in her passport. Or other documents. The house will be full of them.'

Damn, he really wasn't on form today. This was elementary stuff. But it was hard to keep his mind on the job when he was worried about Sophie. Karen had phoned earlier and left a message that they were keeping Sophie in for further observation, something about a high temperature. He'd tried Karen's mobile but it was switched off. He needed to find out how she was. If only he could get to the hospital... but he knew Scrimgeour wouldn't approve of him going off like that during the day even though it was almost the end of his shift. A little cunning was needed.

'If you like, sir, I could get off at the Queen Elizabeth and make inquiries about how to find out who has what psychiatrist and so on.' He didn't think for a minute that the ploy would succeed, but Scrimgeour nodded in agreement.

'Good idea. I'll let you off just after we get through the tunnel.'

Mark waited until the car was out of sight then bolted across Langlands Road, towards the hospital. It had started to rain as soon as he got out of the car. He would phone about the psychiatrist later, from home if necessary or first thing tomorrow morning. He had no intention of spending precious visiting time on police business. As he ran up the stairs to the ward, he tried to tidy his hair and shake some of the raindrops away. It clearly didn't work, because a nurse stopped him as he went to go into the ward. Too late, he remembered that his shave had been cursory that morning. He had a heavy growth at the best of times; no doubt he was presenting an unruly, perhaps even threatening figure. He tried to smile reassuringly. There was no answering smile.

'Can I help you?

'Um, yes. I'm here to see my daughter, Sophie. Sophie Nicholson. She was brought in here with a broken arm last night. My wife phoned me to say she was being kept in for further observation.'

Still no smile. 'Yes, of course. She's through here.' The nurse pointed to a small side room. 'She's quite tired now though, so don't stay too long.'

'Is she all right?'

'She's fine. We were a little worried because her temperature went up, but Calpol sorted that out. We'll keep her in for one more night, just to check. But you'll see, she'll be as good as new in no time.'

'Is my wife still here?'

'I think she went home about half an hour ago. Once she knew Sophie was going to be fine she said something about needing to see to the other kids.'

Mark nodded. Probably Debbie had had enough and had got on to Karen to pick them up. He felt drained suddenly as he thought of the evening to come. Karen was so exhausted he wouldn't blame her if she had a go at him about work, childcare, everything. She'd been very subdued last night when she'd phoned from the hospital. He had no idea how to make things better. Flowers had never worked, neither had chocolates. Perhaps if he booked a weekend away... but there was no one to look after the children. He wished his mother was still alive. She would have loved the children. Fuck, he shouldn't be thinking about this now. He was here to see Sophie and she needed his full attention.

Sophie looked up as he went in to the room, a lively smile dancing at the corners of her mouth. She was fair like her mother, a beautiful child with large hazel eyes. Her eyebrows and lashes were dark and this made her appear very striking. He bent down to kiss her. Although she was not his, he loved her as much as his own children.

'Are you going to sign my plaster, Daddy?'

'Of course. Would you like me to draw something?

'Peppa Pig.'

He looked inside his jacket pocket. By chance there was a red biro there. He took it out and set to work on the pure white plaster, his troubles forgotten for the time being.

Chapter Five

Suzanne

It was the street name that struck me. I looked up at the television and wished I'd been listening properly, but I'd been preoccupied with some sales invoices while watching the news, multi-tasking as usual. The newsreader's voice tailed off. '...not yet formally identified but it is thought to be that of a woman who lived there alone. Police are asking for anyone with information to come forward.' She shuffled her papers and moved on. 'Today in the Scottish Parliament, the First Minister outlined proposals for...' I picked up the remote control and switched it off, my heart pounding as it always did when I heard or read the name Braeside Road.

I brushed the invoices aside and picked up my laptop. I took a deep breath and typed in the words *Braeside Road, Glasgow*. The results came up on Google immediately. Mostly houses for sale. But four lines down, there it was on the *Herald*'s website, a link to an article. My mouth was dry as I clicked the mouse and started to read.

A woman's body was discovered last night in a house in Braeside Road in Glasgow's Southside. First reports suggest the body had been there for some weeks. The woman has not yet been named. A neighbour, who wishes to remain anonymous, says the woman was well known and liked in the area. However, it is not known whether the woman had any living relatives. Anyone with any information is asked to contact Police Scotland on the non-emergency number, 101.

There was nothing else, nothing to suggest it was the house in which I had grown up, but the feeling of dread had settled on me like a heavy blanket, weighing me down. I sat on the sofa plucking at a cushion, wondering what to do.

Less than an hour later, I was standing in the street at a safe distance from my childhood home. A police car was parked in front of it. I had barely set foot in the Southside for well over twenty years, and when I did go, I made sure to stay away from Newlands. God knows why I'd come now. All it did was bring back bad memories. I jumped as someone tapped me on the shoulder.

'Are you all right, dear?' It was an elderly woman, her features creased into a kind smile.

'I... yes, I'm fine thanks. I think I must have the wrong address. This isn't Braemar Street, is it?'

'Oh no, dear. That's in Battlefield, but it's not far from here. I can give you directions if you like.'

I listened as she gave very good and clear directions to a place I had no intention of visiting. When she had finished I couldn't resist nodding towards the police car and asking whether they'd been plagued with break-ins.

Her smile faded. 'If only it was that. But I'm afraid the owner's body was found there yesterday. Suicide. They think she'd been lying there for about two weeks. Terrible.' She shook her head. 'We're all so upset as you can imagine. Julie was a lovely person. Quiet, you know, but friendly. None of us can believe it.'

'Julie?' I asked.

'Yes, Julie Campbell. She was all alone in the world so who knows what will happen to the house now. I expect some distant relative will get it, or the government.' She broke off and peered into my face, 'Are you sure you're all right, dear? You're terribly pale. It must be this heat. Why don't you come in and I'll get you a glass of water?'

Julie was dead. My gut feeling had been right. Last time I heard anything about her, she lived in Shawlands. What had possessed her to come back here? Somehow I managed to stave off the woman's concerns and convince her I was fine. I desperately needed something to drink – my mouth had dried up – but I wanted to be alone to digest what she'd told me, and anyway, I had a bottle of water in the car. I thanked her and escaped.

I've no memory of the drive across the city to the West End. For once I found a parking space with no difficulty. I sat in the car for a while, then shook myself out of my lethargy and went inside. At the entrance to the close, I fumbled in my bag for my keys, pushed open the door and stumbled upstairs to my flat on the first floor. Once inside, I pulled down the blinds, locked the door and fell onto my bed, stunned.

It was dark when I awoke three hours later. I looked at the clock on my bedside table: 11.28. I wanted to turn over and go back to the oblivion that sleep promised but my mind was jumping with questions. Tomorrow I had to go to the police and I needed to be prepared, to know what I was going to say.

I shook my head as I typed my sister's name into the search engine. How many times had I thought of doing this and stopped myself, frightened of what might come about if we met again? Well, she couldn't harm me now.

I looked in disbelief at the screen: around 49,400,000 results. I'd forgotten to put quotation marks round the name. It made a difference – I was down to 340,000 possibilities now. Still too many. I added Glasgow, at 7,800 still too many, and a quick look through the first few pages drew a blank. Adding the address helped – 564 results. I would never have thought of that if I hadn't known, because I would never have believed she would go back to live there after what had happened.

The results didn't tell me much. There were a couple of adverts from local papers; she was a piano teacher – that made sense. She'd always been very musical. Nothing about the body being hers. The police obviously hadn't released her name yet. I shut the lid of the laptop. I would go and see them after her name had been released, because otherwise there would be too much explaining to do. When you're lying you need to keep it simple. Otherwise you lay traps for yourself.

Chapter Six

Mark

Mark arrived home at six o'clock. With some difficulty he had found out who the psychiatrist was, a Dr Elaine Cumming, and had set up a time to interview her the next day. He and Karen would have to visit the hospital to see Sophie again, but he planned to take Karen out for a meal afterwards. He had booked a table for them at Karen's favourite restaurant, and had called in to their next door neighbours, who had a sixteen-year-old daughter, Caitlin, who was always desperate to look after the children. They kept telling him how fond she was of the kids, but it was the money she liked, that and the snacks and free access to booze that babysitting allowed. He also suspected that she brought in her boyfriend and was fairly sure that the stains he had spotted on the sheets after their last night out had nothing to do with him or Karen. In any case he'd changed the bed linen immediately; he wasn't going to sleep in someone else's mess. He wondered what her father, Jimmy, would think of it if he knew, and resolved that his daughters were never going to get such freedom. Poor old Jimmy thought that Caitlin was studying for her Highers, but he could well be in for a shock when the results came out in the next couple of weeks. Still, it was none of Mark's business. He opened the door and called out to Karen.

She came out of the kitchen wiping her hands on a dish cloth. As she walked towards him he couldn't help noticing that she had made no attempt to tidy herself up.

He dredged up a smile. 'I thought we'd eat out tonight. I've booked a table at La Trattoria and I've asked Caitlin to babysit. It's all arranged.'

Almost immediately she started to protest. He put his hands on her shoulders and looked into her eyes. 'Karen, we need a break. The past couple of days haven't been easy, especially for you. Now, go and get ready and I'll bath the kids and put them to bed. Caitlin's coming in at quarter to seven and we can go and see Sophie on our way to the restaurant.' Her head lifted slightly; there was a hint of a smile on her lips.

'Mark, I'm too tired. Can't we just get a takeaway after we've been to the hospital?'

He shook his head. 'No, we're going out. It'll be good for both of us.'

She raised her eyebrows. 'OK, you're the boss.' Halfway up the stairs she called down to him. 'Smart but casual or posh?'

'Posh.' Mark went into the living room to see what damage the two younger children were doing to each other. Emma had scribbled on a book of Oscar's and it took some time to calm him down. The promise of a special story did the trick and Mark took Oscar on to his knee to tell him tales about when he was a baby. It worked like a charm; Oscar loved hearing about how high he'd been able to wee when he was a baby and about how he'd been sick all over his mummy's head once. Emma played quietly in the corner as he and Oscar talked on. It was an unexpectedly peaceful scene. After a while he took them upstairs and bathed them both. The bath with its lavender scented bath oil worked its usual trick, and before long Mark tucked them up in bed. They were quick to fall asleep, tired after the long and no doubt boring day at Debbie's.

Caitlin was prompt for once. There was an air of suppressed excitement about her and Mark suspected there was a new boyfriend on the scene. He stood to one side as Karen went through the usual instructions with her. At last they were ready to go. Karen was wearing a short black dress, which clung to her figure. Her short hair with its blonde highlights was carefully teased into the just out of bed look that he liked so much. She looked good. Mark eyed her with appreciation. 'You look very pretty,' he said as they left the house.

Karen looked at him with a slight frown. 'Pretty? Isn't that a bit girly for a woman of my age?'

He shrugged. 'It's how I see you. Like it or lump it.' Even as he spoke the words he could hear how ungracious they were. He must make more of an effort. Forcing a smile, he turned and kissed her. 'Ignore that last remark. You look just gorgeous.'

She smiled back. 'That's more like it. Come on, let's get a move on. It's nearly visiting time.'

Just over two and a half hours later they were back at the house. Sophie had fallen asleep shortly after they'd got to the hospital.

They sat on by her bed for a few minutes, but she was so deeply asleep they didn't want to wake her up and instead decided to leave. They left instructions for one of the nurses to call them on Karen's mobile if she woke up, but Sophie was a sound sleeper and they knew they had the rest of the night to themselves. When they arrived at the restaurant it had been quiet, with only an elderly couple sitting in an even greater stillness than theirs. So there was nothing to distract them, no one to whisper and point at. After they had discussed Sophie and the hospital they fell into a deep silence and looked at their food rather than each other. Karen pushed her food around the plate. She never finished a meal these days. From time to time, Mark tried to revive the conversation but Karen's replies had been monosyllabic. Eventually he gave up. Why bother striking a dead match? He toyed with the idea of saying out loud the words that had been going round his head all evening. 'Karen, this isn't working. We're not happy as we are and I want a new life before it's too late.' If only he wasn't such a coward. Saying something like that would lead to such a scene. He smiled as he thought about the other couple in the restaurant; at least it would have given them something to talk about. But as usual, he had copped out; he couldn't bear the thought of losing the children. At ten past nine they paid the bill and fifteen minutes later they were home. They had driven home in silence.

Karen marched up the path ahead of him. The gravel crunched under her feet. She threw the door open and Mark nipped in behind her before she had time to let it close in his face. No point in giving Caitlin something to gossip to her parents about. As he set foot in the hall, he could hear the sounds of unmistakeable enthusiastic lovemaking coming from upstairs. Clearly Caitlin had more on her mind than whether

her neighbours were talking to each other or not. He looked at Karen and simultaneously they started to laugh, sinking down together onto the bottom stair. 'Perhaps we should go for a drink,' whispered Mark. And they crept back out of their house, the evening not quite ruined after all.

Chapter Seven

Mark

Dr Cumming was putting away some files as Mark and Scrimgeour entered the room. She was a good looking woman in her late thirties. Mark clocked Scrimgeour tucking in his shirt and trying to pull in his beer belly. The psychiatrist stopped what she was doing and looked at him with a slight frown when she noticed his hand down the front of his trousers. Scrimgeour turned puce.

'Just tucking my shirt in,' he stammered.

She gave a curt nod. 'Of course.'

Scrimgeour held out his hand, which she ignored.

'Sit down.' She indicated two low chairs in front of her desk.

'No consulting couch, Dr Cumming?'

Mark winced. Scrimgeour's social skills weren't always up to the mark. The psychiatrist ignored him.

'Well, I'll just sit here and you can answer my questions. No need for me to speak when you can read minds.'

Her face revealed nothing. 'What is it you want to know?'

Mark fumbled for his notebook. 'We're investigating the death of a woman called Julie Campbell and we know she was a patient of yours some years ago. It would be helpful if you could give us some background information. I realise there are confidentiality issues' He gave her a professional smile. 'It would be most helpful.'

Doctor Cumming nodded. 'I have a report here that sums up the involvement of psychiatric services. Will that do, or do you need to speak to me further? I'm sorry but I am extremely busy.' She had thawed a little but Scrimgeour's attitude had clearly rankled.

Scrimgeour interrupted before Mark could reply. 'That's fine. The file will do. I'll need to take it away with me though.'

Dr Cumming bristled. She turned to her filing cabinet and pulled out a thick file. She flicked through it and handed a report to Scrimgeour. 'You can have a copy of the report, but if you want to look through the file, you must go through the proper channels. The secretary will photocopy the report for you. Now, I have a patient waiting, so if that's all?'

Mark gritted his teeth. He was sure he could have charmed the file from her, confidentiality issues or not, but Scrimgeour had completely fucked up. The two men stood up and got ready to go.

At the door Mark turned to look back. Dr Cumming was sitting at her desk tapping a pen on the wooden surface. 'Sorry,' he mouthed. She shrugged and started to write.

Back in the police station, he made another copy of the report and gave one to Scrimgeour to read. The two men read in silence; Mark quickly, Scrimgeour more slowly.

STRICTLY CONFIDENTIAL
Psychiatric Report – 24th September 2014
Re Julie Campbell (3/6/74)
53 Woodlands Avenue
Glasgow G41 4TX

This report summarises the involvement of Psychiatric Services in the case of the above named woman. It is confidential and has been co-written by Dr Elaine Cumming, MRCP (Psychiatrist), Antonia Whelan, B.A. DClinPsychol (Clinical Psychologist) and Roger Blackwood, BSc (Psychiatric Nurse). No part of this report should be disclosed without prior permission of the authors.

Julie Campbell was admitted to hospital on 13th September 2011. She was suicidal and had taken an overdose of sleeping pills. She had also tried to suffocate her child, a baby boy aged 4 months; fibres from a pillow were found in his nasal passage. A neighbour of Ms Campbell had called the police because she was alarmed by the prolonged crying of the baby coming from the house. The police had broken into the house and immediately called an ambulance. Julie was brought here after her stomach was pumped, as the duty psychiatrist had been alarmed by her state of mind when he had interviewed her. He suspected severe postnatal depression and this was confirmed by Dr Cumming who assessed her on admission. She was treated immediately with anti-depressants and thereafter offered counselling.

Family background

At the time of admission to hospital, Julie was living at the above address with her baby son. The boy was born at 38 weeks after a prolonged labour. He was 7lbs 6ozs and healthy. Julie chose to breast feed initially but had difficulty with milk supply. After several unsuccessful days of trying to breast feed she was advised to discontinue by her health visitor as the baby was failing to thrive.

However, it appears that she persevered up until the time she was admitted.

Initially Julie refused to speak about the baby's father. It transpired that they had been married briefly but that he had returned to his first wife just before the baby was born. Although he never visited Julie, he applied immediately for access to his son. After the usual checks this was granted.

Julie had no other obvious family supports. Her husband, John Allen, when interviewed, mentioned she had a sister from whom she was estranged. He had never met her. Julie's depression was most probably reactive, arising from a difficult birth followed by feeding problems with the additional emotional problems arising from her recent separation. It was hypothesised that she had difficulties in bonding with the child after the difficult labour and feeding problems and that she at least in part blamed the child for the break-up of her marriage.

Julie

Julie, as already mentioned, was suffering from postnatal depression on admission to hospital. Assessment showed a high degree of suicidal ideation and she was thought to be at risk of suicide or self-harm. Following the prescription of anti-depressants, she was offered counselling. After an initial reluctance she accepted this treatment. Counselling was supervised by clinical psychology and carried out by the psychiatric nurse.

Ten sessions were offered initially as part of in-patient treatment. Julie said little during the first four sessions and indeed it was thought that she was unlikely to respond to a counselling approach as she appeared unable to accept what she had done to her child. However, during the fifth session she started to talk, and following this successful session, a further ten sessions were offered.

It appeared that our initial hypothesis was accurate. Julie did indeed blame the child for her marriage break-up. She was possessive towards her husband, and personality testing revealed a borderline obsessive personality. Julie reasoned that her husband left her because of the child, an idea not borne out by her husband's actions after the birth. She was insistent that he had left because he did not want to be burdened with a child. We put it to her that it was she who did not want a child, that her husband was very keen to have children and that he had left her only because he realised he was still in love with his first wife. Julie categorically denied this and maintained throughout her treatment that she did want the child. Julie was unable to rationalise the attempted suffocation of the child and consistently denied that she had done it. She was also unable to give any account of her suicide attempt. During treatment, her GP contacted the hospital with information that changed our approach. It transpired that Julie had had another baby when she was a teenager and that she had suffocated that child. Her father had abused her for a number of years and had impregnated her. He was imprisoned but died of a heart attack soon after. Julie spent some time in a private psychiatric hospital in Perthshire, but no details were available as a fire at this hospital had destroyed many files including Julie's. We immediately contacted the hospital and spoke to the only remaining member of staff who had known her. He could tell us very little. As far as he could remember, Julie had been admitted when she was fifteen. She had killed her child soon after it was born. He didn't remember any other details. We asked Julie about this period but she refused to discuss it. Counselling was discontinued at this time, as she was so uncooperative. She continued to receive medication, however. It was with reluctance that we agreed that the child was in danger and should not be allowed to remain with Julie. Social Services were involved throughout and Julie eventually signed over the baby for adoption. Following this, Julie was on suicide watch and remained in hospital.

In early 2012, Julie had a severe psychotic episode. She alleged that John Allen was stalking her and that he was going to kill her. At times she was violent towards staff. She was prescribed anti-psychotics and responded well to these. However she remained at risk of suicide. Despite several trial periods of living at home she was unable to sustain this and each time returned to hospital voluntarily after a few days. When she was well enough she agreed to cognitive behaviour therapy and was eventually released from hospital in 2014.

Julie had experienced two highly traumatic events, one in her teens and one in her thirties. Both led to hospitalisation. Although she was not always well enough to cooperate she did respond to medication and eventually to cognitive behaviour therapy. On release she was offered community psychiatric services but declined. She can, of course, be re-referred if necessary.

Mark put the report down, blowing out his cheeks as he did so. Christ, that poor woman. She'd been through so much. But the fact remained that she had killed one child and tried to kill another. Was it possible that she could have killed any of the people she mentioned in the confession? He waited as Scrimgeour read on.

'Well?' he said when Scrimgeour finally put the report down.

'Well?'

'What do you think?' Mark was impatient. He could see that the older man was in one of his difficult moods.

'Not sure. What do you think?'

Mark managed not to raise his eyes to heaven with a great effort of willpower. 'I think she could have killed more than just her baby. She was clearly a very disturbed personality.'

'Aye. But there's no bodies.'

'The White case, sir.'

'Oh, for fuck's sake, change the record, will you? Derek White killed his wife and that's all there is to it.'

Mark nodded with some reluctance. He had been through the file twice since yesterday and he had to agree that Scrimgeour was most probably right. The evidence that White had killed his wife was overwhelming. 'And we've come up with nothing for the others?'

'Nothing. Well, that's not strictly true. There's been shed loads of batterings and stabbings. This is Glasgow after all. But none of them fit any of the details in the confession. No unsolved hit and runs and no wee boys dying in arson attacks. I think we have to accept that she's a fantasist.'

'What if she was murdered?'

'She wasn't murdered, Mark. Everything points to suicide. Fingerprints on the glass, heavy overdose of narcotics, depressed state. And the report. She was considered a risk to herself for years.'

'But what about the pathologist's evidence that she was left-handed?'

Scrimgeour shook his head. 'Ach, that's nothing to write home about. Apparently lots of people swap the mouse around to avoid RIS, especially if it's wireless like the one she had. It being on the right side means nothing. In any case the glass was on her left-hand side. It was likely that she drank as she wrote. There was a lot of alcohol in her system.'

'RIS? Oh, you mean RSI. Repetitive strain injury. Yes, I see. But what about the callus on the middle finger of her left hand? That's evidence for her using her left hand to write.'

'Ach, it was barely visible. I bet if we'd looked hard we'd have seen one on her right hand too.'

Mark wasn't convinced but he decided to leave it. 'We're getting nowhere with this.'

'Well, I'm sure she wasn't murdered. I got IT to check the computer. Just in case it was all a set up and she was killed and someone put the confession on her computer using one of those memory sticks.'

'And?'

'Well, it was definitely written on that night, the fifteenth of June. The file was opened at nine p.m. It was worked on during the night and there was a blank period coinciding with the time that she said she went out. A search of speeding tickets showed that she was issued with one that night in Barrhead Road. Unpaid, as she predicted. The last words of the confession were written just before half past four in the morning. We're as sure as we can be that she wrote it.

Mark sighed. He put his hands behind his head and leaned back in his seat. 'But why? We still don't know why.'

Scrimgeour threw the report down on the desk. 'No, we don't know why and it's likely we never will. I'm going to recommend that we close the case. I don't want to waste any more time on this woman's fantasies. Once we've got a positive identification of the body, that'll be it.'

'Well, at least we know the name of her ex-husband now. He should be easy enough to trace. We'll have to find her sister as well.'

'She'll come forward once she's read about Julie's death. We could do a check on all Campbells in the area, but I think it's a bit of a waste of time. We don't know her first name, and even if we did she could have changed it, or moved away from Glasgow.'

'What about if I say something to the press, get them to put out an appeal?'

Scrimgeour thought for a second. 'Good idea. On balance, even if this Campbell woman hasn't been murdered, I'd like both the sister and the ex to be interviewed. There might be something we're missing here.'

Mark picked up the phone. 'I'll get on to it right away.'

Chapter Eight

Suzanne

I TOSSED and turned all night, unable to sleep. All of my instincts were screaming at me, telling me to run and hide. No good could come of her being back in my life, even if she was dead. But it would only be a matter of time before they found me. I had to decide what I was going to tell them. Not the truth, that was for sure. Or at least not the whole truth. I wondered how much they already knew. They would find out about her period in hospital when we were teenagers. That was a given. It would be in her medical notes somewhere. So, I had to tell them about that. The trouble was I didn't know what had transpired there. And they would want to know when I last saw her. Over twenty years of not seeing your only sister when you lived in the same city was going to take some explaining.

I was desperate to get it over with and wondered whether I shouldn't just go and see them, but as it happened, I didn't have long to wait. When I finally struggled out of the heavy sleep that had descended on me at five a.m., I switched on the radio in time to hear that the police had released her name. I immediately decided I would go to the police station later that day. They suggested phoning if you had information. But I wanted to meet face to face. I had to know who I was dealing with. First though I would paint. I had a commission to finish and I needed the money.

It was after four when I arrived at the police station. I had done what I could on the painting and driven over, parking in a nearby street as I wasn't sure if the public were allowed to park in the station car park.

There was a child on the reception desk. He was in uniform but he looked no more than fourteen years old, little pimples poking through what he no doubt called stubble, but which was little more than a light dusting of fuzz.

His eyes lit up when he saw me; more proof of his age. He must have been rampant with hormones.

'How can I help you?' he asked when I approached the desk.

I swallowed, trying to calm myself before I spoke. 'I'd like to speak to someone about the body of the woman found in Braeside Road.'

'I see. And you are?'

My mouth had dried up. 'I... I think the body may be that of my sister.' I tried to think how I should be reacting but all I felt was fear. Perhaps it showed in my face, because the young policeman reacted with sympathy.

'I see,' he said. 'I'll just take a few details from you and then someone will see you.'

'Is there somewhere private we can do this?' I asked. I was

aware of two young girls sitting nearby who were whispering and nudging each other. They had the alert look of people avid for some good gossip. My eyes slid sideways towards them and he immediately knew what I meant.

'Of course. I'll see if the interview room is free.'

He was back within the minute. 'Please, follow me.'

The interview room wasn't as stark as I thought it might be. Someone had made an attempt to make it comfortable, though the welcome it gave was rather institutional. There were four low chairs covered in a blue woollen fabric. They were placed round a small coffee table, which was beech laminate. On one wall there was a matching bookcase, which was stuffed full of information leaflets on subjects such as Victim Support and Neighbourhood Watch. He indicated that I should sit down before taking a seat opposite me.

'Can you tell me your full name, please?'

'Suzanne Yates, née Campbell.'

'No middle name?'

I shook my head.

'Date of birth?'

'The nineteenth of November 1977.'

'And your address.'

I told him.

'West End, eh? I'd love to live there.' With a slight smile he got up and told me to wait while he fetched someone who was on the case. I settled back in my seat to wait, fighting the urge to run.

Mark

Mark stared at Robbie. 'What the fuck does it matter what she looks like? Five star looks? What's that supposed to mean?'

The young constable looked down at his boots, his face

bright red. Mark almost took pity on him, but there was too much sexism in the police as it was. In his experience if you gave them an inch... He continued, 'This woman is a grieving relative. Her "five star looks" are totally irrelevant. You have to stop treating women like objects, Constable McPhee, is that understood?'

'Yes, sir.'

At least he looked ashamed; the last officer Mark had warned about sexism had all but laughed in his face. 'OK, enough said. Where is she?'

'Interview room one.'

Mark nodded. 'Get back to the front desk and relieve the officer there, please.' He set off to find the woman. This should be interesting.

Robbie had been right. The woman in the waiting room was a stunner, no doubt about it. Mark paused for a second to take her in, thinking as he did so that he was a total hypocrite. He'd better not let McPhee see him ogling her. No, not ogling – that was disrespectful. He was appreciating her. She was older than he usually went for, wasn't really his type, but he could see how elegant, beautiful even, she was. She was in her late thirties, he guessed, but she was nothing like most of the women he knew who were that age. She had fine skin and good bone structure that would ensure she looked good even in her later years. Her hair was skilfully highlighted in warm tones of honey and caramel and framed her face in soft waves. It was a pleasant change from the over-straightened hair that most women went in for. He looked down at the sheet of paper Robbie had given him.

'Ms Yates?'

She nodded and stood up, 'Suzanne Yates, yes.'

'Please, sit down, Ms Yates.' He sat down opposite her. 'I've been told that you are Ms Campbell's sister. Please accept my condolences for your loss and for the fact that we didn't contact you, but we only found out yesterday that she had a sister. However, we had no information other than that and no way of finding out, so thank you for coming forward. Did you read the appeal in the press?'

'Yes, I know it said to phone in but I wanted to speak face to face.'

'Of course.'

'As I'm her only relative, I presume you'll want me to identify her.'

Mark thought quickly. The body was not in a state that made good viewing. 'I'm afraid...' he began and then stopped, uncertain how to go on.

She caught on at once. 'It's all right, I wasn't thinking. She was lying there for weeks, wasn't she?'

'She was last seen two weeks before her body was found.'

She looked down then, shielded her eyes with her right hand. 'I see. Yes of course.' She took a deep breath. 'We were never close, you know. In fact, we hadn't seen each other for more than twenty years. But I never expected... I never knew...' She shuddered. 'I read in one of the reports that she left a confession. To some murders. Is it true?'

Mark hesitated before answering. 'It's being investigated. There are many anomalies though, and I have to say we think that it's most likely a bit of a fantasy. I'm sorry that you had to hear about it this way. We didn't know...'

'That she had a sister. You said already. Why do you think it's a fantasy?'

'There are no bodies. She names names, you see, and... well, they're made up, all except one. That's real all right. But there's no possibility she could have done that one. There's a guilty man in jail for that.' He hesitated, wondering how much to tell her. All of it, damn it; she was her sister after all. Better hear it from him than the tabloids. How they got hold of so much, he didn't know. He looked at her with sympathy; this was going to be hard, even if they had been estranged. 'There is something else though that you should know. We did briefly suspect that she might have been murdered herself.'

Suzanne bowed her head, sunlight catching the different highlights in her hair. A faint perfume rose from her, not one that Mark knew. Her voice intruded on his thoughts.

'I don't understand. She confessed to murders that aren't real but she's been murdered herself? It's just not possible. What on earth is going on?'

Mark shook his head; he shouldn't have said anything about that. 'We honestly don't know. There was something that suggested it might not be suicide; the mouse was on the wrong side of the computer for someone who is left handed. But everything else points to suicide. The techies looked at her computer in case someone had planted the confession but it was clear it had been typed at the relevant time. She also mentioned being caught for speeding that night and when we checked, a speeding ticket had been issued to her. Look, can I get you a cup of tea or something? This must be such a shock.'

He looked at the woman in front of him. Everything about her was perfect. Expensive clothes, everything toned in together, matching bag and shoes, carefully chosen to complement her trouser suit, which should have looked masculine but just emphasised her femininity. He thought about Karen and her liking for cheap leggings and short lycra skirts – comfort clothes, she called them. As often as not, they were stained and creased. Inevitable, he supposed, with young children. 'Do you have children?' he asked.

'Excuse me?' The voice was less soft.

'I'm sorry, none of my business.' What on earth had he been thinking?

'No, it isn't. I'll have a coffee, thank you. Black.'

Mark felt himself dismissed. He crossed to the door, opened it and spoke to Constable McPhee. 'Two coffees, please, Robbie. Now. One black, one white.' He spoke more sharply than he had intended, still embarrassed by his faux pas. He turned back into the room. 'There were a number of items of jewellery on the body. A garnet ring for one. Perhaps you might be able to identify those?'

'I'll do my best. Did the garnet ring have five stones in a row? If so, it was our grandmother's engagement ring. She could also have been wearing a gold watch and little gold earrings, hoops with a Celtic design engraved on them. They were our mother's. Her mother's.' She stood up and walked round the little space that there was in the room. Mark thought she was agitated. The reason for her tension dawned on him and he spoke without thinking.

'You didn't really like her, did you?'

She stopped at that and looked directly at him, her green eyes glinting. 'No. I didn't. I shouldn't admit that to you, should I? Especially if you're considering the possibility that she was murdered. But,' she waved his protests aside, 'you've ruled that out, I know. I didn't like her though and she hated me. She was jealous of me from day one.' She sat down again, smoothing her trousers beneath her. 'Mum used to tell a tale of how she found her in my pram, just after they brought me home. Mum thought it showed how fond she was of me. I believed it for years and years. Then Julie told me the truth, during one of our many fights. "I hated you," she said. "I wanted to kill you when you were a baby. All those presents, everyone making a fuss. I climbed into your pram. I was going to smother you with one of your teddies. Mother thought I was trying to give it to you. What a fool."'

Suzanne paused for a second, closed her eyes before saying, 'I was devastated.'

'That must have been hard for you,' murmured Mark.

'Yes, well... I never got over it really. You don't. I thought the world of her, and to find out during a stupid petty fight that she had tried to *murder* me. Well...'

'It's difficult though. I mean, can you be sure that she meant it? She was only a child after all.'

Suzanne

Only a child. The words resonated in my ears. I felt rage build up inside me and tried to quash it. The door opened and the boy came in with the coffee, giving me time to calm myself.

'And children never kill? Surely you as a policeman know better than that.' I gave him a tight smile. 'Oh, it was deliberate, all right. She meant to kill me then and she meant to kill me twenty years later.' I sipped my coffee and watched as he struggled with this information.

'What happened?'

'She tried to knock me down, with that damn Golf she was so proud of.'

I don't know what it was that I said but his demeanour changed. He became more alert, more aware. If I didn't know better, I'd say he was excited. His eyes never left mine as he said, 'A Golf? Are you sure?'

I'd hit on something, but I didn't know what it was. 'Am I sure about what make it was, or sure that she tried to knock me down? I suppose it might have been another type of car. What does it matter?'

'Go on. Tell me about the incident.'

I didn't really want to talk about it and I was aware that I'd told him far more than I'd intended. I lifted my coffee cup, but the bitter smell made me feel nauseous and I put it down again before I was tempted to have another taste. I'd have to tell him now I'd started. I closed my eyes, and for a moment I was back in that cold, dark street with her car racing towards me.

'Ms Yates, are you all right?'

I shook myself out of my reverie and stared at him. 'What happened? Well, I was coming home late one night, alone. I was at art school at the time and lived over in the West End, in Kelvinbridge. A crowd of us had been out drinking and I was slightly drunk, I suppose. Anyway, I insisted on walking home alone. God knows why; parts of Kelvinbridge are really dark and it was a particularly nasty night. Rain lashing down, wind howling, that sort of thing. I was a bit nervous, I can tell you, so I was glad when I turned the corner into my street. Something, I don't know what, sixth sense maybe, made me turn round. I certainly didn't hear it; because of the wind you know. It was racing towards me, no lights on. I'll never know how I got out of the way.'

He leaned towards me. 'But what makes you so sure it was her?' Again there was that undernote of excitement.

I studied my nails. The varnish on my right index finger was chipped. I'd have to do something about that. I looked up. 'She wrote to me.'

'What?'

'She wrote to me and confessed. I hadn't heard from her in years. I still have the letter.'

'She confessed?' The policeman didn't bother to hide his surprise. 'Why didn't you go to the police?'

'My mother begged me not to. Before she died she made me promise I'd never tell anyone. Well, I've broken that promise, haven't I? But Julie's dead now, so...' My voice trailed off.

The policeman fiddled with a paper clip, opening it out

then shaping it into a question mark. 'Your sister saw a psychiatrist.'

'More than one, I believe.'

'The first one when she was fifteen. After the abuse by your father and the subsequent trauma of the death of her baby. We don't have much more information than that. Her medical records were destroyed in a fire apparently.'

The words were out before I could stop them. 'Probably started by her.'

He jabbed the paper clip into the desk. 'Are you serious?'

I backpedalled. 'I don't know... maybe.'

'Did she ever speak to you about the abuse or the baby that she killed?'

I wasn't prepared for this. I stalled, rummaged in my bag for a tissue, and wiped my nose before answering. I hoped it wasn't too obvious I was giving myself time to think.

'No, I found out about that from my mother just before she died. Julie became pregnant when she was only fourteen. She never told anyone she was pregnant and she killed the baby as soon as it was born.'

'Doesn't it bother you? That she killed her child?'

I looked away to hide the twitch that was starting up beneath my right eye.

Mark

Mark thought he saw a look of annoyance in her eyes but it was gone almost instantly. Her eyes when they looked at him were wet. He must have imagined the irritation.

'It's not something I like to think about. No doubt a psychiatrist would say I'm in denial. Can we change the subject please?'

Mark thought for a second; it probably wasn't all that relevant to the current enquiry. He returned to the alleged attempt to kill her. 'This note that she sent you. I don't suppose you have it with you, do you?'

'Hardly. No. It's at home.' She looked directly at him and smiled. Her whole demeanour had changed. There was an invitation in the curve of her mouth, the lowering of her eyes, he was certain. 'Perhaps you'll need to call round to see it.'

'Perhaps.' His reply was curt. Never mix business with pleasure; he'd always stuck to that. 'We've strayed off the subject a bit, haven't we? I'll call the morgue to see if they've got your sister's personal effects ready for viewing.'

It was less than a fifteen-minute drive to the city morgue, a squat building on the other side of the river. Mark followed her. She'd insisted on taking her own car. They parked in King Street car park and walked to the morgue in silence. Outside, she hesitated.

'You OK?'

She didn't answer but pushed open the door. Inside it was cold; it always was. Mark was never sure whether it was the white tiled walls that made it seem so cold, or the frosty stares of the attendants, or whether it was all in his imagination. Suzanne shivered.

'Freezing, isn't it?'

'Yeah. They have to keep it cool for the bodies.'

She flinched. 'I did love her once you know; when I was a child. And she is... was, all I had left of my family. This is very hard for me.'

Mark said nothing. He couldn't get the measure of this woman. Earlier she'd seemed unconcerned about the death of her sister. They walked on in silence towards the main office.

Her heels clicked on the hard surface, echoing down the corridors. Mark was very aware of his shoes squeaking as he walked along. The toe of his right shoe stuck on the surface momentarily and he stumbled, but if Suzanne noticed she didn't show it and just kept on walking. He hurried to catch up with her. At the door of the viewing room, he paused. 'Are you ready for this?'

'As much as I ever will be.'

He opened the door for her and they went in.

The room was small with only a table in its centre and three chairs lined up around the wall. It was painted an institutional pale green colour that gave it a cold and unwelcoming air. Various items were laid out on the table, evenly spaced: two rings, a watch, earrings, some bits of clothing. Suzanne picked up one of the rings. Five garnets in a row, the middle one larger than the others, set in ornate gold. She held it up to the light and pointed to an inscription on the inside. It was very worn and hard to read.

'Look,' she said, 'CC to MT, May 1923. CC is Charles Campbell, my grandfather. MT is Moira Thomson, my grandmother.' She put it on her finger. It was a tight fit, even though her fingers were long and slim. 'Too tight for me. They were tiny, those Edwardian women. I think my grandmother was less than five foot tall.' She tugged it off and picked up an earring. 'Yes, this was my mother's. These definitely belonged to my sister. Putting down the earring she stroked a silk scarf. 'I wouldn't recognise any of her clothes. As I said, we hadn't seen each other for years. From what I remember though, this is the sort of thing she'd wear.'

'That's very helpful,' Mark said. 'Would you be willing to give a sample for DNA testing?'

Suzanne looked down at the ground. 'I'm sorry, but that won't be possible.'

'I can assure you it's completely painless. They'd use it to match it with a sample from the body.'

'I'm sorry, I should have made it clearer. I was adopted. We are not blood relatives. Our parents thought that as they couldn't have another baby they would adopt one to keep Julie company.'

'I see,' said Mark slowly. 'Well, these details should be enough. And we might be able to get DNA from her toothbrush or hairbrush. And there's always dental records.'

'She had perfect teeth. Not a single filling or extraction. At least she did when we were children. We both did. Our parents were pretty strict about sweets.'

She smiled at him, showing a row of white even teeth. Her eyes flicked towards his lips. There was definitely an invitation there. He shook his head; he needed to get a grip on himself.

Mark walked with her to the morgue entrance. At the door, he shook her hand, 'I'll need to see you again, take a statement, that sort of thing.'

She nodded, turned away and was gone, leaving only a hint of perfume behind.

Chapter Nine

Mark

Mark was late again. He opened his front door to an unusual quiet, the silence thrumming with tension. When he went into the living room, the children were lined up on the sofa watching television. They were subdued, their faces pale and solemn. Sophie gave him a weak smile, as far from her usual exuberant greeting as you could imagine. 'What's going on here?' he asked.

'We've been bad,' said Oscar.

'Really? How bad?'

'Don't you fucking dare.' Karen came into the room.

Mark frowned at her to warn her not to swear in front of the children. She narrowed her eyes.

'I mean it, Mark. I'm totally pissed off with this. You leave me alone every day with three young kids. Then when I discipline them you come in with your nice daddy act, all *ooh, you've been naughty. Well never mind, Daddy's home now*. I'm sick of it. You're never around to help. I do everything around here...'

Mark rounded up the children as she ranted on. He spoke soothingly to them, determined not to let her ravings get to him or to them. They went to bed with none of their customary playfulness; just how grumpy had she been with them? After he'd tucked them up and read them a story, he went back downstairs where Karen was now sitting staring at a police drama on the television. He sat down and allowed his thoughts to drift as the TV droned from its position of power in the corner. The house in Newlands with its peaceful study came into his mind, and he imagined himself sitting there, waiting for a compatible companion to join him in a bottle of red wine. He imagined an elegant woman sitting at the piano, long fingers drifting over the keyboard, strains of Beethoven lilting through the house. He pulled his thoughts together; he was getting mixed up with thoughts of Julie Campbell. He closed his eyes and slipped into a doze.

Some time later he woke with a start. He looked at his watch – nearly nine o'clock. He'd been asleep for over an hour; he'd never get to sleep tonight. And he hadn't eaten yet. He squinted at Karen. She was looking at him as if she expected him to do something. A rhythmic thumping was drumming its way into his consciousness and he realised that Caitlin next door was alone again and entertaining some of her yobbish friends. He gritted his teeth. 'Do you want me to do something about that racket?'

Karen smiled a little. He wondered if she was regretting her earlier outburst. 'No. Just go and see how the kids are. Check it hasn't woken them. I'll make us something to eat.'

Mark picked his way through the toys that were scattered across the floor. He thought of how much money they had spent on expensive pieces of plastic that, frankly, were rarely played with. The children got more enjoyment out of playing with the boxes they came in. He shook his head; he was a right old fogey at times.

After checking on Oscar, he looked in on Emma. She was lying on her back, her cheeks flushed. She had thrown off her duvet; rarely a night passed without her doing that, she was such a restless sleeper. She was fast asleep, looking angelic, and he wondered how any adult could harm a child. Who was he kidding? After all, how often had he found his hands clenched when confronted by his difficult youngest child? Who was he to judge a depressed woman who tried to kill both herself and her child? He doubted if he'd be any better in the same situation. No one had the right to judge people who'd been through hell. Bending over to kiss Emma goodnight, the smell of baby shampoo made him sneeze and he tensed, waiting for her to wake up. She stirred and he shushed her. For once it worked and she turned over without opening her eyes.

Mark went back downstairs where Karen was preparing their evening meal. He watched her from the kitchen door. She was chopping onions, unaware of him watching. A tear rolled out of the corner of her eye and down to her mouth. Mark didn't know if she was crying or if the onion was irritating her. She was a mystery to him. They'd met four years ago; Sophie had been little more than a baby at the time. It hadn't been Mark's intention to get involved with a single parent but they'd got on so well, it was hard to resist her. And Sophie was an adorable toddler. The first time she'd called him 'Daddy' he'd resolved to be a proper father to her. Her own father was out of the picture. Karen never talked about him. All she'd said was that that part of her life was over. He'd tried to discuss it once or twice when they were relaxed after a bottle of wine, but he was always met with resistance. Tears were rolling down her face now and he turned away. Best leave her to it.

He tidied up the living room, putting away the piles of Lego into their toy boxes, lining up soft toys on top, careful not to tread Playdoh into the expensive rug they'd bought at Ikea only two months ago. Already it was showing signs of wear. He called through into the kitchen, 'Shall I set the table?'

It was a second or two before she answered, 'Yes, please.' Her voice was thick.

He went into the kitchen to get what he needed and pretended not to notice her tears. By the time Karen served their meal there was no sign of them. She was smiling as she waved a bottle of wine in front of him. 'Want some?'

'What's the celebration?'

'Do we need an excuse?'

Mark didn't like drinking when he was working the next day. He found it hard to stop once he'd started and too often the bottle of wine turned into two. But he sensed trouble if he refused. 'Go on then.' He held out his glass for her to fill.

'Tell me about this case,' said Karen as she spooned spaghetti onto his plate. 'Is it true what they're saying in the papers? That she killed five people?'

Mark's mouth was full. He chewed until he was able to speak without food spilling from his mouth, glad that he had the chance to think. 'I'm not supposed to talk about it.'

Karen smiled. 'I know,' she said. 'It's just that it's so interesting and unusual, you know, a woman being a serial killer.'

Mark relented. 'You mustn't talk about this to anyone, I mean it.'

'Cross my heart and hope to die.'

Mark laughed. 'OK then. She confessed to five killings but we don't think they actually happened. In fact, we know that four of them didn't. And the one that did is the Derek White case. Cast iron case. You remember it?'

'Battered his wife to death with a spanner for going off with another man?'

'That's the one.'

'So what were the other murders?'

'Let's see. Battered an old woman, hit and run involving a young girl, arson that killed a wee boy and stabbing a man in Pollok Park when he was on his way to work.'

She made a face. 'Lovely. But she didn't do any of them?'

Mark hesitated; he'd said too much already. 'It doesn't look like it. She had... an unfortunate past. It seems she was very disturbed. But no, I don't think she killed five people.'

Karen's grip tightened round her glass. 'What sort of unfortunate past?' She said the final two words in a sardonic way, as if she was putting them in inverted commas.

Mark put his hand on top of her free one. 'I'm sorry, Karen. I've said more than I should.' He got up from the table. 'I'll load the dishwasher and you pour us both some more wine.'

'OK,' she said, smiling up at him. He wasn't sure but he thought there was the shine of unshed tears in her eyes. He hoped he wasn't in for a rough time.

Chapter Ten

Suzanne

AFTER THE VISIT to the mortuary I drove home, but my mind wasn't on the route. At the traffic lights at Charing Cross – gridlocked as they always were at rush hour – I almost drove into the back of a white van. It brought me round. I had no wish to be involved in a road rage incident. The rest of the way I drove with care, and twenty-five minutes later I parked as near to my flat as I could. The journey of less than three miles had taken the best part of an hour, but that's the West End for you.

Once inside, I prepared a salad and reflected on my afternoon, but mainly I thought about the policeman. It took me some time to remember his name. Mark something, Williamson, or Davidson. No, that wasn't it, but I was sure it ended in son. Not that it helped; there must be hundreds of names in that category. He was very attractive, ages with me I thought, though he might be younger. He looked a little like a young Hugh Grant but rougher, less of a mummy's boy. He wasn't wearing a wedding ring but he'd have someone; nobody that fit was alone for long. I hoped he'd follow up on that promised visit to get further information. It would be good to see him again.

The next day, I took longer than usual with my make-up. I wanted to be prepared if the handsome policeman called. The more I thought about him, the more I was sure he was interested. His eyes had swept over me when we'd met – not that barcode sweep that some women do, appraising your hair, your make-up, your outfit, mentally cataloguing it all and pricing it down to the nearest penny. No, this was sexual. His eyes had lingered on my eyes, my lips, my breasts and on my legs. I had been wearing a pale grey linen suit from Hobbs, with cropped trousers that showed off my ankles.

Make-up and hair done, I turned to my outfit. A dress, I thought. I had a new one from Jigsaw that I'd never worn, saving it for a special occasion. Was this enough of a special occasion? I decided it was.

I was pleased with what I saw in the mirror. The teal of the dress brought out the green in my eyes and the dress itself was sexy and demure at the same time. With a round neck and elbow length sleeves it didn't reveal too much skin, but the flared skirt ending just above the knees flattered my legs. A pair of cream ballet pumps completed the outfit and I twirled like a schoolgirl to admire my reflection. I settled down to wait.

What was it they said about counting chickens and crossing bridges? Two hours later, the doorbell rang. I opened the door with what I hoped was a suitably welcoming expression only to find two policewomen standing there. I hope they didn't notice my face fall. But they're trained to observe, so they most likely did.

They didn't stay long. I showed them the letter from my sister, which they copied into one of their little black books before one of them asked if they could take it away with them. I agreed. To be truthful, I didn't know why I'd kept it. It had been a hurtful, no, a devastating thing to receive and I didn't want to be reminded of that time any longer. Time to move on, I thought. Put her behind me for ever now she was dead.

I showed them out after about ten minutes. As they went down the stairs, I heard one of them remark to the other that I was a dressed-up tart. I sighed. What is it about some women that they have to be so jealous?

My encounter with the policewomen depressed me, and that afternoon I found I couldn't work. I had changed into my usual work clothes. I tended to make a mess when I was painting and so I used decorators' overalls. I found the key and opened the door to the room I used as a studio. I always kept it locked. I didn't want anyone wandering into it while they were 'just looking for the bathroom'. I hated anyone watching me paint and I loathed anyone examining my work in progress. I walked over to the easel and studied the canvas. This was the last of a set of paintings commissioned by a GP practice, a young trendy one not far from where I lived. They'd wanted a series of paintings based on a variation of those old anatomy posters you sometimes saw in antique shops. Bodies with the skin peeled back to show the muscles or skeleton or central nervous system beneath. Although they had expressed delight at the sketches I'd shown them, one of them came back to me the next day to ask if the paintings could be 'rawer, a bit more visceral'. My heart sank. This was one of the problems with doing commissioned work: you never knew exactly what the client wanted. And in this case there were five of them. But the money was good, so I redid the sketches and this time no one came back with any further demands.

I was almost done, apart from this last one, which was a study of the female reproductive system. The others stood upright in a row against the wall in my make-do studio and they were so bloody they looked like something from a pathologist's table, and that, of course, reminded me of my sister. I left the room to make myself some coffee.

Could she have written anything to implicate me, or was my secret safe? I shook myself. They hadn't known about me until reading the psychiatrist's report, so it figured that I hadn't been mentioned. After all, only Julie and I knew for sure what happened all those years ago. And she was dead.

Chapter Eleven

Mark

MARK CURSED as he drove to work. He was late again, the third time that week. Emma had a fever and she had spent most of the night wedged in between him and Karen, whimpering each time one of them touched her. At five thirty he'd given in and gone downstairs to try to grab some sleep on the couch. When he woke, three hours later, it was to the knowledge that he should have started work half an hour ago. He also could barely move his head, not because of a hangover for once, but because of the crick in his neck from his unnatural sleeping position.

For once luck was on his side. Scrimgeour wasn't in his office and Mark managed to get to his desk without the inspector noticing he was late. He pulled a case file from the middle of the mound on his desk and thumbed through it. Another unsolved murder. He read through it but it was entirely unrelated to anything in Julie Campbell's confession; a young Asian shopkeeper stabbed late at night for a few quid in his till. He started as Scrimgeour's voice boomed in his ear.

'Have you reached a conclusion yet? About that damned confession. I think it's a load of shite myself.'

Mark nodded; he couldn't think of anything to say that he hadn't said already.

'Fucking nutcase and timewaster.'

It was as good an explanation as any. They were wasting their time looking into all these old cases. The body had been formally identified as Julie Campbell. They had taken hair from a hairbrush in her bedroom and compared it with that of the corpse. The DNA results were positive. He'd wanted to interview Suzanne Yates again, to discuss her sister further, but Scrimgeour had sent out two women police officers to speak to her. They came back with very little of value from the interview. They confirmed what Suzanne had already told Mark; that her sister had tried to kill her, and they gave him the note. Interesting as this was, it was not particularly helpful and didn't provide a way forward, so Mark had continued to work through the files. There was only a handful to go but a picture was emerging, confirming what he'd thought all along. Julie Campbell could not have done what she claimed to have done in her confession. He sighed and picked up one of the remaining files.

It was the case of a woman beaten to death in her house. Her body had been discovered by her daughter, who had been worried when she didn't answer the phone. There had been no obvious suspects. She lived alone, was popular with her neighbours, had many friends and no enemies that anyone knew of. It was put down to a burglary that had gone wrong. There were signs that someone else had been in the house but there were no fingerprints or other forensic evidence left. An over-eager officer had followed the line that it was probably the daughter, but that proved a non-starter and led only to a near lawsuit when the daughter found out. She was a lawyer in a top defence firm known for its dislike of the police and her letter of complaint to the chief constable was a masterpiece. As he read through the file, Mark's heart began to beat a little faster. There was a bag of unopened shopping on the kitchen table. One hypothesis was that someone had followed her home from the local shops. He looked at the address: Kelvinside. It didn't tie in with the one Julie Campbell had left in her confession but maybe there was something here. He took the file to Scrimgeour.

'Sir, have a look at this.'

Scrimgeour looked up from the report he was writing on his laptop. 'What is it?'

'It's probably nothing, but this file is the unsolved murder of Mrs—' He broke off to remind himself of the victim's name. 'Mrs Roberta McMillan.'

Scrimgeour stopped typing. 'Go on.'

'She was found dead in her house by her daughter. There were no clues; none of the neighbours saw or heard anything, but she was battered to death and there was an unopened bag of shopping on the kitchen table.'

'Interesting. When was this?'

Mark looked at the date of death. Fuck, they should have been more careful in what they were looking at. 'Sorry, sir. My mistake, she was murdered when the Campbell woman was in hospital.'

Scrimgeour waved him away. He was lucky to get off so easily, though the truth was it was actually Scrimgeour's fault. He was the officer in charge, and once they'd found out that Julie had been in hospital, in a locked ward, murders carried out during that time should have been eliminated. Mark went back to his desk, pink with embarrassment. It wasn't like him to make elementary errors.

He spent the rest of the morning looking through the rest, checking first to see if dates matched up. They all drew a blank. He looked at the piles surrounding his desk. All unsolved, all dead ends. Nobody had been killed on their way to work. Children had died in fires, too many of them by far, but the fires hadn't been caused by arson, and although there were two hit and runs that remained unsolved, neither involved a young woman. Now they had to determine that no one had murdered her. It seemed unlikely, but Scrimgeour wanted to be sure.

'I want you to go out and see Julie Campbell's ex-husband today. See whether he's got anything that might shed some light on this pile of crap. And then we close the case. It's taken up far too much time already.'

Mark nodded. The address and phone number were in front of him. He picked up the phone and dialled.

It didn't take long to find the house. John Allen was living north of Milngavie in a farm conversion. Mark had a young policewoman, Kerry, with him.

'Bloody hell,' she said. 'This must have cost a packet.'

'Best part of a million.' Mark loved to look through property sites on the internet and dream of better places to live. This place looked like something out of *Grand Designs*. What had been a farm and outbuildings had been converted into four separate dwellings with a central courtyard. Allen lived in what must have been a barn. It was the largest of the buildings and stood apart from the rest of the development. A side wall had been removed and replaced with plate glass. Most of the front of the building was also glass. It was different, Mark thought, but he wasn't sure he liked it. A woman came to the door as Mark drew the car to a halt in the courtyard. Mrs Allen, he presumed. She waited as they got out of the car.

'Do come in, please. My husband is in his study. I'll go and get him.' Her smile went nowhere near her eyes.

They followed her into the house. He'd expected it to be open plan and wasn't disappointed. It was a vast space, fifty feet by twenty-five feet, he guessed. The original building must have been extended. At one end was the kitchen – white gloss finish, stainless steel fittings. It looked coolly intimidating. Mark thought of his beech Ikea kitchen with the doors that didn't hang properly. These doors would never dare fall out of line. Next to the kitchen area was a large solid oak table, simple but expensive. Eight dining chairs, upholstered in dark red leather, were spaced evenly round it. The only other furniture in the room was a coffee table, made from oak and glass, and two huge sofas. They were suede. Mark's children would have destroyed them in five minutes.

No television – that was interesting. Then he spotted the plasma screen on the far wall. Of course. And on the opposite wall a massive oil painting of a half-naked man, all bulging muscles. Mark went to look at it more closely. The style looked familiar.

'Peter Howson.' The voice came from behind him. 'Do you know his work?'

Mark turned round. 'One of the Glasgow boys. Yes, I've heard of him. This is an early one, I'm sure.' Allen nodded. He looked disappointed. He was probably a snob and believed police were all thick and lacking in culture.

'Please, take a seat.' Allen's wife flapped a hand in the direction of the sofas.

As soon as they'd sat down, Mark realised their mistake. Allen and his wife sat at the table, making them dominant. He cursed his stupidity. Worse, the sofa was so soft he had sunk right into it and struggled to get his notebook out of his inside pocket. Kerry was oblivious; she settled into the sofa, looking as if she was at a party.

'You know what this is about so we'll just get started.' Mark's voice was curt. 'You're a psychologist, right?'

Allen nodded. 'Consultant, private practice.'

'Tell me about your relationship with Julie Campbell.'

Allen made a steeple with his fingers. 'What do you want to know?'

'Let's start with where and when you met.'

Allen smiled up at his wife. 'Don't you have dinner to make, darling?'

Mrs Allen got up and left the room, quick little steps betraying her rage. Mark wondered at Allen's lack of tact. 'I imagine your wife doesn't like hearing about that time.'

'Lynn? Why should it bother her?'

Mark reddened. 'Well, you left her for Julie Campbell...'

'Oh, I see. No, you've got it all wrong. Lynn is my third wife. We're not long married actually. Kaye, my first wife, left me a few months after our daughter was born.'

Kerry interrupted. 'This all sounds very complicated. Can you explain?'

'If you could just answer my question first, please.' Mark frowned at Kerry. She was meant to follow his lead, not interrupt with her own thoughts. 'Where and when did you meet Miss Campbell?'

'Um... it was 2005, I think. I was out with the lads and she chatted me up. I ended up going home with her; she had a nice little flat in Shawlands.'

'And what happened then?'

'What do you think? We shagged like rabbits. Went on for

a few years, then Kaye found out and that was that. I married Julie when the divorce came through.'

"OK, so just let me get this straight. You were married to Kaye... When was that exactly?'

'Fuck, I don't know,' he laughed. 'Do you know your wedding anniversary? Does any man? And I've had three to remember.'

Mark kept his face impassive. What an obnoxious shit this man was. No doubt those popular psychology books that Karen loved so much would call him an alpha male. Wanker, more like. 'I don't need the exact date; the year will do.'

Allen puffed out his cheeks, which made him look like a hamster. 'It was 2004. I was thirty, Kaye was nineteen.'

'Quite young to get married these days, I mean for Kaye. Not many women get married so early.'

'She was cunning, that one. Wouldn't deliver until she had a ring on her finger, know what I mean? The solitaire got me halfway there but she insisted on waiting until we were married for the full show. Christ, my balls were aching, I can tell you.' Allen grinned, showing white, even teeth.

'So, within a year you were unfaithful?' Kerry's voice held a hint of censure.

'Oh, sooner than that. I had some fuck buddies from university days – they helped me out, both before and after I married Kaye.' He lowered his voice and glanced towards the door, 'Still do, to tell you the truth.'

It was hard not to raise an eyebrow at that but somehow Mark kept his face straight. 'Whatever. It's your relationship with Miss Campbell that concerns us. After you married her, what happened then?'

'She got pregnant, and look, I'm not proud of what happened next but I have needs and she wasn't delivering.

Kaye got in touch – she'd lost weight, learned some new tricks, and before I knew where I was, I was back with her.'

This fitted perfectly with what was in the confession. Careful not to show any emotion, Mark leaned forward. 'So, when exactly did you leave your second wife?'

Allen got up and went to the door. 'Lynn, any chance of a drink?' There was no reply. He returned to his seat. 'Well, it was a bit unfortunate but there was a bit of a scene between Kaye and Julie, and after Kaye left, Julie went into labour.'

'Miss Campbell must have been under a great deal of stress. Didn't you realise she had a history of mental illness?'

John Allen looked offended at this slur on his professional judgement. 'I didn't know her past history. She certainly showed no signs of mental illness when she was with me.' He made it sound as though this was down to him. 'We were together for seven years in all, and she was charming, fascinating.' His voice softened. 'There was never a hint of anything untoward.'

'When did the current Mrs Allen arrive on the scene?'

Mark wished Kerry would butt out. He wanted to get on to the subject of Julie's son and whether there had been any arson attacks or even threats on the family but he let Allen answer.

'We got married last year. Orlando needed a mummy.'

Orlando, Christ! How would that go down at the local comprehensive? What was he thinking? Orlando was most likely at an expensive private school. Mark had put up with a bit of ribbing over Oscar's name. Now, only three years later it was in the top thirty of boys' names in Scotland. He had no doubt Orlando would be much further down that list. 'Orlando being Julie's son?'

'As far as he's concerned, he is our child. Mine and Lynn's. He knows nothing about his real mother. And he's forgotten Kaye.'

'Doesn't she see him?'

For a moment, the glistening veneer dulled. 'No,' he said in a voice that was meant to put an end to that line of questioning. Mark sensed a story here. He'd decide whether it was relevant when he heard it. 'Why is that?'

In response, Allen stood up. 'I'll make us some coffee. I think I need some.' He walked over to the door without asking Mark and Kerry what they took.

'What do you think?' said Mark in a low voice.

'He's hiding something about Kaye; there's definitely something he doesn't want us to know.'

'Mmm. He's been pretty upfront so far but I agree. There's more to this than we thought. We'll need to find out if he had a child with Kaye, as suggested in Julie's confession.

Allen came back after a few minutes, carrying a tray with a cafetière and some cups. He put it down on the glass table in front of them. 'We'll let it brew for a moment or two. Now where were we? Ah yes, Orlando. Lynn treats him as her own.'

'Actually no,' said Mark. 'You were about to tell us about what happened to your first wife, Kaye.'

A flicker of annoyance passed over John Allen's face. He gave them a thin smile. 'She left me. Got up one day, packed some clothes and made off with half of our joint bank account and the baby.' He looked more upset at the loss of his money than the baby.

'When was this?'

'Well, the baby would be five now, so just under five years ago.'

It sounded strangely impersonal, that phrase: the baby. 'That must have been very difficult for you.'

Allen nodded to acknowledge what Mark had said, but he was lost in his own thoughts. 'There's never a day goes by when I don't wonder about them.'

'Did you go to the police?'

He laughed. 'Fat lot of good that did me. She'd left a note, she'd taken money, she was an adult. They weren't interested and I understand why not. I'm not unreasonable. I know the police have better things to do than search for someone who disappeared of their own accord.'

'What about a private detective?' asked Kerry. 'They can get good results.'

'Tried that. Trail ran cold. She went through the Eurostar terminal, took the train to Brussels. She could be anywhere in Europe. Cost me several thousand and many sleepless nights to find that out. After a year or so I decided to move on.'

'You must have some idea why she left though,' said Mark.

Allen closed his eyes and leaned back in the sofa. 'Look I just don't see what this has to do with Julie's death. Can we get to the point please, because I have clients later this afternoon and I need to prepare for them?'

He was right; this was a side line, though Mark felt that there was more going on than he was being told. He decided to turn to Julie. 'Tell me what happened when Julie had her baby.'

'Julie was unbelievably vindictive, got herself the most vituperative lawyer it has ever been my misfortune to meet. She even managed to stop me seeing my son when he was born. Oh yes, Julie was a woman possessed all right. It was the best thing that ever happened to me when she had that breakdown. Otherwise I don't think I'd have managed to see him, let alone get custody and eventually adopt him.'

'To get back to your first wife, Kaye. Is it possible she was frightened of Julie?'

Allen poured out coffee and indicated they should help themselves to milk and sugar. He sipped his, eyeballing Mark. Mark waited. Experience told him it was best to say nothing.

Eventually Allen put the cup down. 'Perhaps. Why do you ask?'

'When we found Julie's body it was by a laptop. There was a confession on it and extensive enquiries tell us it was written by Julie. You may have read about it in the press. At the moment, I'm not at liberty to tell you anything other than the part that directly affects you. Obviously we know that what she said wasn't true, but I'd like your take on it.'

Allen sat up straighter, alert as Mark told him about Julie's confession. Mark's voice was emotionless as he told him how Julie claimed to have killed their son accidentally in a fire. When he'd finished, John Allen gave a snort of laughter. 'That's Julie for you, what a woman. A real game player. God, I miss her at times. She could be difficult, but God, what a woman.'

Mark made notes as Allen continued to chuckle.

'My God, your face. I wish I had a camera. No, it's just too funny. She was taking the mickey. That's the plot from one of her favourite operas. We saw it together actually. *Il Trovatore*. Verdi. In the amphitheatre in Verona.' He lowered his voice. 'Don't let on to the wife. She's always banging on about going and I can't face it again – those stone seats don't half give you piles.' He shook his head. 'No, it's Julie's idea of a joke all right. Azucena, the gypsy woman, throws her own child on to a bonfire in an attempt at revenge. Of course she doesn't know it's her child, it's a horrible accident. You know these operas, they're full of nonsense.'

Mark and Kerry drove back to the station in silence. Kerry tried to ask Mark about his thoughts but Mark said nothing. His mind was busy trying to process what he'd heard. Taking it at face value, Allen's statement should be enough to close the case. It would be argued that Julie Campbell was at worst a fantasist, at best a woman with a weird sense of humour. However, the fact that Allen's first wife was missing niggled at Mark. He thought back to the confession written by Julie, the poisonous words about her husband's first wife. Could Kaye and the baby have come to harm at Julie's hands? It was possible. Mark made a mental note to check up on the report about her being missing. Christ, this was some tangled web. Traffic duty would be preferable. He parked the car and went into the station.

Mark settled down to do some work. He'd have to report back to Scrimgeour later so he wanted to clear his thoughts. Missing wife and baby first. John Allen had been holding something back there, he'd swear to it. He thought back to the interview and how Allen had kept steering the conversation back to Julie. He was uncomfortable discussing his first wife. But why? Did he suspect something had happened to her? And why was he so unconcerned about the baby being missing? He'd been more upset about the money she'd taken. He picked up his phone.

An hour later and he had some answers but just as many questions. Mark slammed down his phone. 'Kerry? You free? We need to go and see Allen again.'

She popped her head round the door. 'Any particular reason?'

'He's been lying his arse off, Kerry. And I want to know why.'

Chapter Twelve

Mark

ALLEN OPENED the door and scowled through the gap. 'What is it now?'

'Can we come in, please? We have some more questions to ask you.'

'I'm in the middle of a session. I told you I was working this afternoon.'

Mark smiled. 'Then I suggest you rearrange your session. Or we could arrest you for obstructing the course of justice?'

The door opened fully. 'Give me five minutes, I'm almost finished. You can wait in the living room.'

Kerry and Mark settled themselves at the dining table. Mark wasn't going to make the same mistake again of falling into that sofa. This was very much a business meeting. Allen kept his word and appeared five minutes later, his wife at his side.

'What's this about?'

No preamble, no offers of coffee, no smirks. Mark noted his

nervousness. 'Earlier on today you told us your first wife Kaye left you, taking your baby with her. You reported this to the police and then hired a private detective. Is that right?'

Mark watched Allen grow pale. Four seconds passed. 'Well? Do you have anything to say?'

Allen sat down opposite him. He rubbed his forehead with both hands. 'Shit. I should have known you'd check.'

'Of course we checked. There was no report of a missing woman and child at that time.'

'Kaye's disappearance isn't relevant, I assure you.'

'So why lie about it?'

Beads of sweat were appearing on his upper lip. 'It's personal.'

'Go on.'

'Oh fuck.' He looked at his wife.

'John didn't want to let you know that he had been taken in by Kaye,' she said.

'Taken in?'

'Yes. She lied about the baby being his child. When he found out, she left.'

'I just didn't see that it was any of your business.' The bluster and arrogance had disappeared. 'It was between me and Kaye. It almost destroyed me.'

'Tell us what happened.'

Allen took a deep breath. 'I suppose I was suspicious from the start. The dates didn't tie up. I had been working in Singapore for a few weeks, some consultancy stuff. Two months later she tells me she's pregnant. I was thrilled at first. I was desperate for a brother or sister for Orlando, but then I started to worry.'

'What concerned you?'

'She wouldn't let me go to appointments with her. Then the date for her first scan came in. I really wanted to go with her but there was some sort of misunderstanding about the time and I turned up too late. A couple of weeks later I was talking to a neighbour who was also pregnant, and she was complaining about the fact that Greater Glasgow Health Board were behind with their scanning programme. She'd gone private because she wasn't prepared to wait until sixteen weeks, which is when the twelve week scans were being done.'

'I see. What did Kaye say about that?'

'Oh, she spun me a story about how she'd put pressure on them, threatened to go to her MSP, and they'd caved in and made an exception. I chose to believe her. I wanted to.'

Mark made a few more notes. 'So, when did you stop believing her?'

'The baby was born allegedly two weeks early. She was over four kilograms, a big bruiser of a girl. I caught sight of her notes and they said "born at forty-two weeks gestation". I knew then but I didn't say anything. I kept telling myself there was a mistake. We went home and played happy families for a week or so. But then the baby developed jaundice and needed a blood transfusion. I remember the doctor coming in cheerily and asking which one of us was blood group A and did we want to donate?'

'I assume neither of you were.'

A half smile and a nod. 'That's about it. We never discussed it. I left the hospital there and then. Kaye disappeared soon after and I was back on my own again.'

Mark reckoned he probably hadn't been alone for long. 'So, you divorced her?'

'Divorced? No. We had never remarried. I divorced Julie when she was in hospital but Kaye didn't want to get married again.'

'And do you know where she is now?'

'She's got another bloke and at least one other child. Lives over on the Southside. I'll get the address for you.' He got up from the table.

Mark, Kerry and Lynn sat in an awkward silence while they waited, broken only by Kerry's inane attempt at small talk. 'Quite cold for July isn't it?' Lynn spotted Mark rolling his eyes and smiled. 'It is, yes,' she said. Allen came into the room and handed Mark a piece of paper. He glanced at it and his eyes widened.

'Everything all right?' said Allen.

'What? Yes, yes of course. You're sure this is her address?'

'Yes, she's been there for about four years now.'

'Are you in touch with her?'

'No, I haven't spoken to her since that day in the hospital. She sent a friend round to pick up her belongings.'

Mark nodded. 'So, how do you come to have her address?'

Allen looked shifty. 'I saw her one day in town, followed her home.'

Beside him, his wife stiffened. He'd have hell to pay for that slip up later.

Mark got up out of his chair. 'OK, well that will be all for now. If you could just read through this and sign for me...'

Kerry chatted all the way back to the station, nattering on about nothing. Mark wished she'd shut up. He was trying to think what to do now. He ought to get those items back to Julie's sister but there was something else much more pressing to do. 'I'll drop you off at the station,' he said when Kerry paused for breath. 'There's another witness I need to see. You can process John Allen's statement.'

'Oh, all right. Where are you going?'

Mark gritted his teeth and didn't reply. He was her senior officer and he didn't like the tone of her voice.

'I'd like to come with you if that's OK.'

His hands gripped the steering wheel tightly. 'And I'd rather you typed up John Allen's statement.'

Kerry opened her mouth to speak, but before she could he said, 'That's my final word, Kerry.'

Ten minutes later he was on his way, seething at Kerry's attitude. She had had the nerve to suggest he was skiving off early and he'd snapped at her in a way he'd never had to do with anyone junior before. She had then sulked for the remainder of the journey. Where the fuck they got them these days he didn't know.

It was after four p.m. when he drew up at the small terraced house. He parked the car and got out. 'Here goes,' he muttered as he opened the door.

'You're early,' said Karen. 'Good, you can go and get the kids from Debbie's. She's been looking after them while I got some painting done. I managed to get Oscar's room finished.'

'Sit down, Karen. We need to talk.'

She paled, looked at him aghast. 'We need to talk? You never want to talk. So, this is it, you're leaving me?'

Mark sat on the sofa. 'No, I want you to tell me about John Allen,' he said.

Chapter Thirteen

Mark

KAREN TURNED to leave the room, her face white and tense, but before she could, Mark grabbed her arm. 'Let me go,' she said.

'Karen, this is serious. You have to tell me.'

'There's nothing to say. We were married once, he cheated on me, we divorced. End of.'

Mark shook his head. 'Karen, I know all about it. I know you went back to him after the divorce. I know Sophie isn't his child.'

'Have you been spying on me?' Her voice rose. 'I told you, I told you when we met that I didn't want to talk about my past. It's over. But, no. You couldn't let it be, could you? You've poked your nose in where it isn't needed.'

Mark felt his temper rise, took a deep breath. 'Karen, again. This is serious. Please, sit down. I haven't been spying on you.'

'Then how the fuck did you find out?'

Mark took a deep breath and told her about his interviews

with John Allen and why he had had to speak to him. When he finished he waited for her to say something.

Karen was shaking her head in disbelief. 'I don't believe it. That fucking bitch. She ruined my life once; now she's at it again.'

'Karen, she's dead. She can't harm you.' Thank goodness he hadn't told her any details of the confession, just that there was one. She'd never cope with the knowledge that Julie Campbell had fantasised about garrotting her. Or that she had wanted to kill her and Sophie in a fire.

Karen stared at him, 'You have no idea, do you? This woman ruined my life. She stole my husband.'

Mark felt something twist deep inside. Did Karen still have feelings for Allen then? What about him, his children? 'It sounds as if you want to be with him still.'

'Oh for heaven's sake. That's all over. It was over when he left me. I only took him back in order to show that I could. I wanted her to see that I was in control. And I was. She went to pieces after I went to see her.'

The hate in her voice repelled Mark. He understood that she had been badly hurt by the actions of Julie Campbell, but Julie had paid for this by losing custody of her child and ultimately she had taken her own life. 'You do know that what you did caused her to go into premature labour, don't you? And that as a result she became depressed.'

Karen shrugged. 'As far as I'm concerned, she brought it on herself. She chose to have an affair with a married man; she had to take the consequences.'

'But she was married to him. You did to her what she had done to you. You're just as bad!' Mark didn't like the Karen that was appearing in front of him. Her bitterness was sickening, as was her self-righteousness.

'You don't get it, do you? John was mine. Yes, she might have married him but he was MY husband.'

'I can't take this in, Karen. I don't feel that I know you any more. You've been lying to me from the moment we met. I don't even know your name! He paused, studying her face as if somehow, it would reveal her true nature. 'Who are you? Karen or Kaye?'

Her look was full of scorn. 'Karen, of course. John just used my initial.'

'You say "of course" as if it's my fault I don't know. But don't you see what this means? How can I trust you now? I...' He tailed off, not knowing what to say.

Karen shrugged. 'Trust? You can't trust anyone, believe me.'

Mark got up. 'I'll go and get the kids but we have more talking to do. I want you to think about this, Karen, about where you want our relationship to go. Because if we're to stay together you need to be honest, and you can start by telling me about Sophie's father. Who is he and is he likely to come marching into our life any time soon?' He was pleased to note that she paled when Sophie's father was mentioned. Good. At least something made her uncomfortable.

Outside in the car he leaned his head against the headrest. He ought to tell Scrimgeour about this latest development, but he didn't want anyone knowing about the mess his life had become. He didn't know what to do.

Chapter Fourteen

Mark

THREE DAYS on and Mark was no further forward either in the investigation or in his home life. Karen wasn't speaking to him. Ironic when for once she was the one in the wrong. But whenever he tried to raise any questions about her past she blocked him and refused to answer. He took to staying on at work late. The money would come in useful, but as it happened, they were busier than they'd been for some time with a spate of gang attacks. In the end he had decided not to mention his connection to the case. Mark couldn't see the relevance and the case was all but closed. Only a few loose ends remained.

'Sir.' It was Robbie, phone in hand. Mark tried to wave it away but the young constable persisted. 'It's the morgue, sir. They've still got Julie Campbell's jewellery and clothes and they want to know where to send it.'

Mark opened his mouth to tell him Suzanne Yates' address then thought again. He could take it round. It would get him out of here for the rest of the afternoon. 'Give it to me,' he snapped and waited until Robbie was out of earshot before speaking into the phone. 'I have to go over to see Ms Campbell's sister this afternoon. Some more questions to ask her,' he lied. 'I'll pop in and pick up the things later.'

He put the phone back and prayed no one had heard him.

Suzanne's tenement flat was in the West End, near Hyndland. There was a secure entry system and he pressed the buzzer beside her name. A first floor flat – preferred, as the estate agents said.

'Yes.' Her voice was abrupt.

'It's um, it's Sergeant Nicholson. I have your sister's jewellery and er, some other things.'

Silence. 'Hallo? Ms Yates? Are you there?'

There was no reply, but two seconds later a click indicated that the door was now open. He went inside. This was what was known locally as a 'wally close'. It smelled of disinfectant as though it had just been washed and there wasn't a speck of dirt on the stone staircase. The centre of each step was a little worn from over a century of feet treading on them. He walked slowly up the stairs, admiring the art nouveau tiles on the wall. He was sure he had seen them before, or something very like them, on a popular postcard sold at Kelvinbridge Art Gallery. The colours of the stylised flowers were vibrant and the tiles looked as fresh as the day they had been fired.

He carried on up to the landing and looked to see which of the two doors was hers. The first door had two names on a brass plaque, neither of them hers, so he went across to the other flat. He stood in front of an impressive wooden door and gazed at the leaded glass inset. A womanly figure holding a bunch of spring flowers was outlined in the stained glass. It was probably a representation of one of the four seasons, a common theme for Victorian times. It was stunning; he'd love to have a front door like that instead of the white plastic one at his house. If only... but there was no point dreaming. It would be years before he could afford a place like this and even then, Karen would never agree to it, obsessed as she was with having a garden.

The door opened, taking him by surprise. Suzanne was wearing a boiler suit and was covered in paint. If anything she looked more beautiful than she had when he'd seen her earlier in the week. Her hair glowed with life and her eyes were laughing as she invited him in.

'You've caught me at a bad time, sergeant.'

'I'm sorry. Are you decorating?'

She laughed. 'Heavens, no, I'm an artist.'

He felt at a disadvantage. 'Oh,' was all he could think of saying. He stepped inside. The hall was large and square with several doors leading off it. They were panelled and had been stripped and varnished to show the original oak. Most wooden fitments from houses and flats of the Victorian period were pine, but the more expensive flats had oak floors, skirting and doors. He followed her across the hall and into the sitting room. The door had a brass plate on it, beneath the doorknob. Once again it was engraved in an art nouveau style. Everything seemed to be architecturally correct. Like her sister, she had good taste.

She stopped him before he could enter. 'I'm sorry, do you mind removing your shoes?'

He put down the package he'd picked up at the mortuary and bent down to untie his shoe laces, worried about the state of his socks. He'd grabbed the first pair that came to hand in his rush to get out that morning. At least they were clean. A quick glance showed him they were respectable, no holes as he'd feared, and he went into the room.

Suzanne's style was quite different from her sister's. A thick camel-coloured carpet covered the floor giving an air of rich comfort to the room. The walls were painted a pale yellow, and with the sun streaming in through the large bay window, the effect was one of light and space. On the wall were three modern paintings, bright splashes of colour. They looked like originals. Abstract paintings, yellows fading into more shades of yellow; just looking at them made him feel happy. The furniture was more modern than her sister's, although there were one or two older pieces mixed in with what looked like Habitat style but was probably more expensive than that. Conran or BoConcept, he guessed. She indicated he should sit on the sofa, and to his surprise she sat down beside him. She looked directly into his eyes. 'You have my sister's jewellery?'

'And some other things – the clothes she was wearing and so on.'

'What about the suicide note? Do I get that too?'

For a moment Mark was silent. Usually there was no problem with giving relatives suicide notes, but this one had been slightly different. 'To be honest, I don't know. It's not really a note—'

She interrupted him. 'It may well be strange, but as her next of kin, surely it reverts to me?' There was a hard edge to her tone and Mark wondered why it meant so much to her.

'It's a confession to five murders... Although it appears to be false, it had to be investigated, so a great deal of police time was wasted. I have to confess I don't know what happens in these cases because I've never come across one quite like it before...' He tailed off.

'But perhaps you could get me a copy?'

'I'm sorry, I honestly don't know. Once we're sure that it's not evidence it will be released to you. That's all I can say at the moment.'

For a brief moment he thought she looked angry, but it was gone before he could be certain. She smiled. 'Can I get you a coffee? Or something stronger?'

Suzanne

The buzzer had broken my concentration and I swore aloud in disbelief. I was midway through a delicate part of the painting and the last thing I wanted was an interruption. I considered ignoring it and then remembered I was expecting a delivery. I strode to the intercom and picked up the receiver. 'Yes?'

It was the policeman. With my sister's things. He hadn't come earlier in the week when I was ready for him – no, he had waited until I was in a boiler suit covered in paint. I considered telling him to go away, but when he asked if I was there something in his voice, a neediness perhaps, made me press the buzzer. I took a quick look in the mirror. I would pass, I decided, and I opened the door.

He looked better than I remembered. There was an air of weariness about him that was attractive. We went through into the living room and sat down. I think he was a little disconcerted when I sat down on the sofa beside him, but that was good. I wanted him off guard. I wasn't interested in the jewellery or in Julie's clothes. I might keep her grandmother's engagement ring but everything else could go. What I really wanted was to see that suicide note but he was remarkably unforthcoming. Eventually, after some to-ing and fro-ing, he agreed it ought to come to me but not immediately. It wasn't enough; I had to try something else. I offered him coffee. To my surprise he agreed to have 'something stronger' after making it clear he was off duty and was just passing on his way home.

When I asked him where he lived, he mumbled something about it being not far and I knew then he had volunteered to do this in order to see me again. I got him a Highland Park and moved a little closer.

Mark

Suzanne leaned forward. He could smell her perfume, light and flowery. It was the one she'd worn that day at the police station. It reminded him of summer evenings, walking in the local park with his mother and sister, free for an hour or so from the fear of his drunken father. His mother would point out the flowers, naming them: marigolds, nasturtiums, alyssum, lobelia. Without thinking he moved closer to her. Her hand brushed against his thigh.

'You want to fuck me, don't you?' She laughed aloud as his mouth dropped open. 'Don't deny it. It's what we both want.'

Mark looked down at her hand resting on his leg. It was a small hand, smudged with paint. Her nails were immaculately manicured, coloured a bright red that looked like drops of blood. It was strangely erotic. His breathing quickened as he thought of her fingers stroking him, of her mouth closing round his penis. He raised his eyes to hers – he had to put an end to this now. It was completely inappropriate. 'I don't know what you mean.'

'I think you do,' she smiled.

Mark had seen sexual scenes in films that he had never believed. Hands everywhere, tearing off clothes. Bodies ramming each other against doors. Pure lust. And now it was happening to him. He was totally unprepared for the passion that erupted between him and Suzanne. He came within fifteen seconds of entering her.

They rolled apart. 'I'm so sorry.'

'Don't be.' She traced round his mouth with the tip of her finger. 'You were excited, very excited. I'm flattered. And I'm sure there will be other times.' She smiled into his eyes.

They lay together quietly for a time. He felt more at peace than he had for many months. 'Suzanne,' he started to say.

She shushed him. 'Don't speak.' Her mouth started to explore his body; little fluttering kisses. It was too soon; he'd never manage...

Suzanne

After he'd gone, I lay on in bed. I hadn't really intended that to happen and I had been astonished at how good it was – well, the second time anyway. Poor boy, he only lasted a few seconds first time round. But the second time... I turned over and stretched out, feeling the cool cotton on my body. I told myself I was just doing this to get hold of the suicide note but deep down I knew it was the beginning of something else.

Chapter Fifteen

Mark

THE JULY DAYS SPED PAST. Sometimes it rained, sometimes it was sunny. Mark noticed none of it. He was consumed by Suzanne. He thought of nothing else. Karen was there in the background, increasingly remote. Had anyone asked, he would have been hard pressed to remember any meaningful conversation with her. If she was puzzled by his sudden withdrawal, she didn't say. She could put it down to her deceit. Mark didn't care. He had other things to think about. His sex life for one.

There was a constant smile on his face. At work, the other police officers made lewd remarks, which he ignored. No one knew that he was fucking – no, it was more than that – making love to the most desirable woman he'd ever known. Just thinking about her made him hard.

It wasn't all about sex though. Everything about her drew him in: her knowledge of art, literature and music. Her intelligence, her wit. She made him laugh. He loved listening to her talk about what her paintings meant to her. She played her favourite music to him. His knowledge of classical music and jazz was growing fast. Three weeks ago, he might have been able to recognise a few popular pieces like Tchaikovsky's piano concerto; now he had chamber music, opera and symphonies by composers he'd barely heard of before on his smart phone, along with Etta James and Nina Simone. Suzanne was well read, had a huge library of books. When Mark first met Karen he had tried to share his love of literature with her but she'd laughed at him: *real men don't read books, they're too busy living*. In vain he'd tried to explain what it meant to him, but she never listened. *It takes me all day to read a magazine, and it would take me a year to read a book. Books are for school*. Now, at last, he had found a soul mate. They liked the same books, felt strongly about the same things.

By the end of July, he and Karen were barely speaking. She appeared not to care about where he was late at night, she accepted every lame excuse without question. The only thing she ever mentioned was the amount of time he worked. That was still a sore spot and she'd bring it up whenever he was around for more than five minutes.

'You need to get a better job,' she'd say. 'One that lets you work normal hours. You never see the kids these days. They'll grow up not knowing you.'

And there it was: the only bit of mould on the jam. Used to working long hours, Mark spent every spare second with the kids, especially Oscar. Boys needed their fathers. He didn't doubt it. But there were other pressures on his time now. He had turned down overtime to spend time with Suzanne, knowing there would be hell to pay at home when his salary reached the bank. He didn't care.

Late one night, as he was getting dressed and ready to leave, he said to Suzanne, 'I'd do anything for you, you know, anything.'

'I don't believe you,' she said.

'Try me.'

'Anything?'

'Anything.'

She smiled at him. 'That's lovely, but there's no need. I'm happy as I am.' He smiled back, happy that she was happy. Then she spoiled it all.

Suzanne

I had what I wanted. Soon after the affair started he'd brought Julie's confession home for me to read and I managed to scan it onto my computer when he was having a shower. That was tense, I can tell you. He wanted me in the shower with him and called through to me several times. 'Just a minute,' I'd shouted back, all the while willing the scanner to work faster. I was terrified he'd catch me. He'd told his boss I wanted to see the confession and the answer was a firm 'No'. I was never sure why. Mark was putting his job on the line by letting me see it. I had read it over and over to see whether there were any little clues there for me, or anything that might implicate me, but as far as I could see there was nothing. I considered ending the affair then, especially as I had found out he had a live-in partner and three children. But he was too much fun to give up easily and so I held on to him, wishing he was mine. Then one night as he was leaving he said he would do anything for me. I told him I was happy as I was, but inside I was shouting *leave her, leave her and come to live with me.* But the thought of his face falling, his dismay as he thought of his children and how it would affect them was enough to stop me. I didn't want to go to war with his children. I swear I didn't mean the words to come out, but they did.

'Come live with me, and be my love, and we will such new pleasures prove.'

'John Donne,' said Mark. This was one of the games we played. We loved to test each other.

He said nothing else, carried on dressing, not looking at me. I studied his face, trying to read his expression. 'You haven't replied.' My voice was flat. He looked at me then and I could see the hurt in his eyes.

'Leave her, Mark. She's not good enough for you. You know she isn't.'

He tensed. 'Suzanne, listen to me. I will not leave my children. Nor will I discuss Karen with you. My family life is not up for discussion.'

God knows what devil was inside me. 'I'll say what I like and you won't stop me.' I got up out of bed and stood naked in front of him, 'You've spent weeks with me and ignored your little family. Seems to me you've more or less left them already. So what's the difference? Make it official. Shall I tell them or shall you?'

I winced as he smashed his fist into the wall behind the bed.

'Temper, temper,' I taunted. He took a deep breath and turned away from me.

'I think it's best if I go.' He stooped to pick up his jacket. Only a twitch beneath his right eye betrayed him.

I stepped towards him. 'I'm sorry. I should have said nothing, but...' The remaining words came out in a rush. 'I love you, Mark. I didn't mean to fall in love but I did and I'm jealous. I want to be with you all the time.'

The tension left his body and he sank down on the bed. He

looked up at me, shaking his head. 'No, I'm sorry.' He held out his arms to me. 'Truly sorry.'

I lay down on the bed beside him. 'You... you seem to have quite a problem with anger.' He tried to say something. 'No, let me continue. What's behind it? You have to tell me.'

'I don't know that I can.'

'No, that's not good enough, Mark. If we are to have a proper relationship, we have to talk about this. You punched the wall. I thought you were going to hit me. And I'm warning you, I will not tolerate anything like that.'

Mark shook his head. He was devastated by what he'd done. 'Of course not. I'm sorry.'

'So?'

'You won't like it.'

I said nothing for a moment, then I stood up. 'In that case...'

He closed his eyes. 'I had a very violent upbringing. My dad...' Mark stopped, unable to continue.

I took his hand. 'Go on.'

'He beat me and my sister.' He turned away so that I couldn't see his face. I continued to hold his hand and waited.

'My sister was five years younger than me. Mum always told me I should protect her and I tried, I really did.'

'What happened?'

'He lost it one night when she wet the bed. She was four at the time and he went crazy. She was crying and it woke him up. I can still hear him shouting as he stormed upstairs. He was calling her a bitch. Can you imagine? A father calling his daughter a bitch?'

I shook my head, though in truth I knew better than he thought.

'I ran after him. Mum was out and I knew he was going to hit my sister.' Mark's voice trailed away. 'It was... I'm not sure I can talk about it.'

'Yes, you can. You must.'

'They sent me to anger management classes, you know.'

'What?'

'The police, after the incident with Johnson.'

I frowned. 'You've lost me now. Please, Mark, just tell me what your father did.'

'He dragged her out of bed by the hair. I was running after him, begging him to leave her alone. He brushed me aside as if I was a wasp buzzing around him. Mandy was screaming; she must have been terrified. He lifted her up and tossed her down the stairs as if she was a bundle of dirty washing. And she just lay there in a heap, not screaming any more, not moving.'

I couldn't speak for a moment. I was horrified. 'Was she dead?' I managed when the silence grew too oppressive.

'She had massive brain damage. She was in a coma for weeks, and when she awoke, her life spirit had gone. I remember going to see her in hospital. It wasn't her, just an empty breathing shell. She looked at me and didn't smile. Mandy always smiled when she saw me, but she didn't smile that day. That's when I understood what Mum had been trying to tell me. I had been so happy when she told me Mandy wasn't dead and I couldn't understand why Mum spent every day in tears. And then it hit me. Mandy was as good as dead.'

'Is she still alive?'

He blinked. 'She died a few years ago. An infection. Otherwise she could have gone on for years, lying there, eyes open, seeing nothing. I used to visit every month even though there was no point.' He went on. 'It killed my mother, you know. She was never the same after that night. She blamed herself. I thought it was my fault. My father of course didn't feel the slightest guilt. Everyone was to blame but him.' He spat out the last word.

I stroked his arm and he caught hold of my hand and held it fast. 'I've never forgiven him and I never will.'

'What happened to him? Did he get caught?'

'Oh yes. I shopped him. I had to; he would have gone on to kill me one day, or Mum. I told the police everything.' He paused for a second, remembering. 'The police constable was so kind, so understanding. She listened to everything I said. I had been so afraid that no one would believe me. No one at school talked about their dads hitting them. Maybe the odd cuff round the head, but nobody admitted to the sort of violence that I had experienced. So it was hard for me to talk about it. That's when I decided to join the police. I wanted to give other children that feeling of safety that she gave me.' He laughed. 'Well, I was only nine and completely idealistic.'

After a pause he added, 'They sent me to anger management, you know.'

I looked at him, puzzled. 'Yes, you said. But why?'

'Because I kept losing my temper.' He said it slowly as if to a child. 'The counsellor said it was because I was angry with my father. Angry? I could have fucking killed him. Angry doesn't even begin to describe my feelings towards him. But it wasn't just because of that.'

'What then?'

'I did keep losing my temper. I do keep losing my temper. With the kids, with Karen, people at work and now you. Christ, I'm sorry.'

'It doesn't matter.'

'Oh but it does. Because you see, there was one time when I totally lost it. I nearly killed a man. And in my eyes that makes me as bad as my dad.'

Mark

Mark woke up the next morning feeling as if he had never been asleep. They had talked for hours about his childhood and his feelings for his father. They'd never got round to talking about his anger problems or the man he'd attacked so viciously. When they finished talking, they made love. Afterwards, Mark had fallen into a deep sleep and jumped up startled when Suzanne woke him just after three thirty. She wanted to make love again but he knew he had to get home. He kissed her with a fierce intensity.

'We'll sort this out. I know we will.'

'I hope so,' was her brief reply.

He dressed quickly and went out to his car. The starter screamed every time he turned the key, the noise piercing the silence of the street. He tried maybe fifteen, maybe twenty times before getting out and hailing a black cab. It cost him over fifteen quid to get back to the Southside. He should have called a mini cab. God, they were heading for real money problems at this rate. It was nearly five when he opened his front door. He crept up the stairs but couldn't bring himself to get into bed beside Karen. After the closeness of the last few hours, he felt it would be a betrayal of Suzanne. He stood outside the bedroom door, his heart thumping so hard he felt it must wake her. 'Tell her. Tell her.' The beat pounded on. He breathed deeply and thought – I'll do it. His hand was on the doorknob, sweat making it hard to get a proper grip, when he heard his son stir in his bed. Defeated, Mark turned away from his bedroom and resigned himself to having to stay. He slipped back downstairs and curled up on the sofa where he slept for what was left of the night.

He woke two hours later. He could hear movement in the house as the children did their usual morning rituals of shouting and jumping and crying. Karen was in the kitchen, standing at the sink washing last night's dirty dishes. Her back was rigid.

'Where were you last night?'

'Work.'

'Don't you dare lie to me. You were not at work until five in the morning.' The words were clipped and precise. Mark had never heard her so angry. He opened a cupboard door. 'Cereal?'

'What?' She turned to face him. Her face was blotchy with tears. 'We need to talk, Mark.'

We need to talk. This was his chance. Mark felt an instant sense of relief quickly followed by a grip of terror in his abdomen. He couldn't do this to his children. He just couldn't. He put on his most convincing face and forced himself to smile. 'We need to talk? That sounds serious. Do you really want to know what I was doing last night?'

'It's another woman, isn't it?'

Mark made himself look straight into her eyes. 'I should be so lucky. No. It's the car. It broke down again. I called the breakdown company and waited for over three hours for them to come and then they couldn't fix it. They spent an hour on it, you know. Useless bunch of wasters. I know they're cheaper than the AA but honestly! I'd have been much better just leaving the car and getting a taxi right away. I'm knackered, you know. God knows how I'll cope at work today.' Well, at least part of what he'd said was true.

Karen stared back at him. He could see the yellow flecks that made her eyes look hazel at times. Her voice was quiet as she started to speak.

'I don't really care. Our relationship sucks. You're never here. The kids are beginning to forget who you are. Whenever you do speak to me it's just to whine on about how I deceived you. OK, so I was wrong not to tell you but you're doing a damn good job of punishing me.' She rubbed her forehead. 'I don't know why you just don't go.'

Because of our children, he thought. Aloud he said, 'Because there is no other woman, and you're right, I haven't been the greatest father recently but I'll make it up to you all, I promise.' To his relief she appeared to relax.

'You'd bloody better.' She turned back to what she was doing. 'It's Sophie's birthday soon. I thought we could have a party for her.'

A kids' party. The last thing they needed. More expense. 'Good idea,' he said. 'But let's do everything ourselves. Have a good old-fashioned party with party games. No entertainers, no brought in food.'

'Someone I know does Elsa from *Frozen*. She only costs £250 for an hour and a half and she arranges everything: food, party bags, games.'

Only £250. He could do it if he went into his savings, but then there was Christmas to think about...

'Come to think of it, you're right. We can do it ourselves, but you have to promise me you'll be there.'

Trying hard not to show his relief at saving what was after all not that great a sum, Mark agreed. He looked at his watch. 'Shit! Is that the time? I'll have to dash.'

Karen gave him a tentative smile. 'I'm sorry,' she said. 'I'm sorry I didn't tell you about my past. It was just so hard to talk about it.' She went over to him and put her arms around him. 'Am I forgiven?'

He said nothing for a few seconds; the carousel of his thoughts wouldn't stop long enough to allow him to think of a suitable response. Fortunately, she took his silence for assent. She squeezed his arm. 'You'd better go. We don't want you getting the sack.'

Chapter Sixteen

Mark

MARK RAN to the bus stop. For once a bus came quickly and he got on. No change. He had to put a fiver in for a fare of just over two pounds. Fuck. What a start to the day. He sat on the bus with a heavy heart. He dreaded the day ahead and his worries all flooded in on him. The car would need to be fixed; he'd have to get over to the West End to meet the breakdown company. He'd have to see Suzanne; well, that wasn't strictly true but he needed to see her. He should do some overtime. If the car needed fixing it was going to cost him. What a mess. He got off the bus in the city centre, bought a newspaper so as to get change for the next bus and walked to the stop in time to see his bus pulling away. It was ten minutes before the next one came. Once on the bus, he opened the paper and started to read, his eyelids drooping. He shook himself awake and looked out of the window, realising with a start that he had gone past the station. He leapt out of his seat and shouted to the driver to stop. The bastard drove on.

The lights in the office were bright; Mark screwed up his eyes. He went to his desk and looked at the day's work. A hit and run accident had been reported in the early hours of the morning and a young woman had been killed. Mark read through the initial report with half his mind at home and half with Suzanne. He blinked and started again, forcing himself to concentrate. 'I must try harder,' he whispered to himself. 'Concentrate.' Mark read through the report with a rising sense of disbelief. He had to check it out. He rummaged through the bottom drawer of his desk where he had kept a copy of Julie's confession. He swept through the pages muttering to himself, 'I'm right, I know I am', and with a small cry of triumph he found the passage he was looking for.

'I swear I didn't set out to kill her that Thursday evening. She was beautiful; I wanted to worship that beautiful body, not destroy it. But when she got out of her car in King's Park Avenue that evening, she started walking towards my car instead of going into her house. There was a grim set to her face and somehow I knew she was about to confront me. Although I had parked several doors away from her house, I panicked. I started to reverse the car to try to get away but she kept coming at me. Almost before I knew what I was doing, I had put the car into first gear and was driving hard at her. I don't remember much of what happened next. Something must have alerted the neighbours, for lights were coming on in the dark houses all around me. Somehow I managed to drive off.'

'King's Park Avenue, same as our little accident last night. I knew I recognised that address. I knew it.' Mark slapped the papers down on his desk. Several colleagues in the room turned to look at him. 'Breakthrough on the hit and run,' he muttered as he made his way to Scrimgeour's office.

Two minutes later he left the office, Scrimgeour's sarcastic comments drumming in his ears. His boss had not spared his feelings.

'A breakthrough? You call this a fucking breakthrough? What the fuck do you think you're playing at? It's a coincidence, son, a fucking coincidence, that's all. Have you any idea how long King's Park Avenue is? Over a mile. And in any case, as it so happened, our hit and run last night was in King's Park Road.'

'It says Avenue in the report,' muttered Mark.

'I don't fucking care! It's a typing error, nothing more, and even if it wasn't... What are you thinking, man? That Julie Campbell has risen from her grave to finish off her imaginary crimes? You've lost your fucking marbles, son. The woman's dead. She made it all up. Get that into your head.'

Mark opened his mouth to interrupt but was thwarted by the look in Scrimgeour's eyes.

'Get back to your work, son. Proper work and stop trying to pretend you're Sherlock fucking Holmes.'

Sitting at his desk, Mark wondered why he had been so presumptuous. Lack of sleep, he decided, and started reading the report thoroughly as he should have done in the first place. Of course it was a ludicrous conclusion to jump to. Yet something niggled still. What was it? Yes, there it was in the statement given by the young woman's father: *she had been at the gym in the local school.* He knew the gym. It was part of the city council leisure facilities, not the private one mentioned in Julie's confession, but still... Mark rubbed his eyes. They stung from lack of sleep and too much booze. Two coincidences. But they were just that. Nothing else.

Mark went through the motions for the rest of the day. He

caught up on paperwork, filed reports and generally carried out mindless routine tasks. The coincidences wouldn't give him peace though, and just before he was due to sign off he made a decision.

As he stood in King's Park Road, Mark wondered whether he was doing the right thing. He'd told the rest of the team that he wanted to see the scene of the crime, but really he was hoping to talk to Daisy Palmer's parents. He looked around. On one side of the road there were tenement flats, on the other a row of red sandstone terrace houses.

Daisy Palmer had lived with her parents in one of the terraced houses. A large rowan tree dominated the tiny front garden. Its branches were heavy with red berries; they were early this year. Tradition held that a good crop of rowan berries heralded a cold winter. Well, they were in for an Arctic one this year if there was any truth in the folklore. Many of the berries had fallen to the ground and lay spattered like tiny drops of blood. They were a strange contrast to the bouquets of flowers that had been laid at the front door. They ranged from simple hand-bound garden flowers to elaborate bunches of lilies and orchids. Daisy had been popular by the look of things. Mark stooped to read the tributes. Some were personal notes from friends; others must have been put down by locals shocked by the tragedy so close to home.

'Daisy, we love you and will miss you always. Sarah, Paula and Katy xxxxxx'
'To a dear friend, all my love, Anna'
'With deepest sympathy, the McManus family'

As he looked at the flowers, Mark remembered the days after his sister had been so terribly injured. There had been no bouquets for her, no sympathy for his mother. Only whispered comments from passers-by. *The mother was out at the Bingo, you know. She left the kids with him.* Pursed lips emitting little drops of poison. *She knew what he was like, the bastard – she's as much to blame.* Even now he didn't know why they had judged his mother so harshly. It had been her one night out in months. She had been a good mother. She cared for him; she cared for his sister, visiting her every day until she had been so riddled with cancer that she couldn't make the hour-long journey to the hospital. Eventually she died in hospital, eaten up by cancer and guilt, believing she could have saved her daughter if only she had been at home.

Mark forced his thoughts back to the present. There was no point in picking at these old sores, and whatever the rights and wrongs of his tragedy, one thing was certain: this poor young woman was entitled to flowers and sympathy and so were her family. He was so lost in thought he didn't see the middle-aged man until he was standing in front of him.

'Can I help you?' The man's face drooped with sorrow and Mark realised immediately that this must be Daisy's father.

'Mr Palmer?'

'Yes.'

'I'm sorry to disturb you. I'm Detective Sergeant...'

'Come in, please.' Mr Palmer interrupted him and ushered him through the door.

In the immaculate living room, Mark tried again to apologise, but his inept mumblings were swept aside. He could see Mrs Palmer out of the corner of his eye – a dignified figure dressed in a neat, navy suit. Mr Palmer indicated to Mark that he should sit down.

'We've been expecting you.'

'I'm sorry?' Mark was puzzled.

'My wife spoke to the policewoman earlier today. She called to see if there was anything we could think of that was unusual in Daisy's life recently.'

'A policewoman? Did you get her name?'

'Ah now, let me see. Aitken, I think.'

'I don't know an officer of that name. Did she say what division she was from?'

Mrs Palmer rose from her seat and stood in front of Mark. She plucked at her skirt, brushing away imaginary crumbs. 'Does it matter where she was from? Our daughter's dead, killed by a stalker, and no one is listening to us.'

'I was told it was a hit and run.' Mark's voice was cautious.

'Yes, a hit and run carried out by a stalker. Daisy has...' She paused for a second. Mark thought she was going to cry but she drew herself together and continued, her voice strained. '...had been saying for some time that she thought someone was following her. I told the policewoman about it and she said a detective would be out to see us. Are you interested in hearing us, or do you just want to quibble about names?'

'I... Yes of course, I'm truly sorry. Please go on.' Mark knew he was blushing; his hands felt clammy with embarrassment. He was sweating – it was hot and stuffy in the room and he imagined he could smell his own body odour.

'It started about a year ago. Daisy was always out and about, coming in late, spending a fortune on taxis. We were always nagging her about the cost.' Mrs Palmer stopped, her eyes full of tears. 'You tell him, John. I can't talk.' She rushed from the room, her body shuddering with sobs.

Her husband looked after her, tears streaming down his face. 'We can't take it in. It just seems so unreal.'

'I'm so sorry.'

The two men sat in silence. Mark could see his watch out

of the corner of his eye and he studied the second hand as it crept round. Ten seconds, twenty seconds passed, every one seeming like a minute. Mr Palmer composed himself.

'Would you like a drink?'

'Uh, no thanks.'

Mr Palmer poured himself a large brandy. 'We bought her a car for her twenty-first birthday. A Volkswagen Polo – five years old but she loved it. We joked that it was cheaper than paying for taxis all the time. Anyway, shortly after she started driving it she began complaining that she thought someone was following her. She'd be driving along, late at night, and nine times out of ten there was always this little black car behind her. It was never near enough to get a number but she was sure it was the same one.'

'Black? You're sure it was black and not blue?'

The cut-glass goblet stopped halfway to Palmer's lips. 'Definitely black. No doubt about it. I think the colour spooked her.'

'What make of car was it?'

'God knows. Daisy's hopeless about that sort of thing. She can't tell one make of car from...' He put his head in his hands and groaned as if he was being tortured. 'Oh, God. Oh, dear God. How will we cope without her? She was our only child. We waited years for her, had given up hope, and then when we were in our forties, my wife conceived. She was our little miracle. Our own little miracle and now she's gone.'

He put the glass down and started to sob. Mark sat in his seat, wanting to offer words of comfort, knowing there were none. But there was something he had to ask. 'Did Daisy ever mention a woman being over friendly towards her, an older woman?'

They looked at each other. 'Why do you ask?' said Mrs Palmer.

For a crazy second, Mark considered telling them the truth, then he thought of Scrimgeour and what might happen if the press got hold of this through the Palmers.

'Oh, I just wondered if she had a sense of it being a man or a woman who was following her?'

'We just assumed it was a man. And so did Daisy.'

'She didn't get a look at whoever it was?'

They both shook their heads. The doorbell rang and Mark leapt up, glad to have an excuse to leave.

'Don't get up, Mr Palmer. I'll get that on my way out. Let us know if there's anything else you remember.' He almost ran out of the room. Mrs Palmer was already at the door, hugging two young women who must have been friends of Daisy's. He squeezed past them, avoiding eye contact. This sounded like more than coincidence to him, but what could he do?

Chapter Seventeen

Mark

MARK PUT the visit to the back of his mind over the next few days. The Palmers did not contact the police to give any more information about the stalker. Mark filed a report on what they had said and carried on with the investigation as normal. A bus driver reported a near miss with a red Mercedes at the traffic lights at the nearby junction at the time of the accident, and as this was the only real clue the police had to go on, they concentrated on following it up. There had been a lot of traffic in the area but no one else came forward.

While he was sitting at his desk, his mobile phone rang. It was Suzanne. She sounded young and happy. She must be in the flat, for he could hear music playing in the background.

'Is that Schubert?'

'You're a quick learner, well done. How are you?'

'All the better for hearing you.'

'I've booked dinner for us at the Chip.'

'What?' The Ubiquitous Chip was a busy, popular restaurant in the West End. He couldn't possibly risk going there with her.

'The Chip, my treat.'

'I'm sorry, Suzanne, but it's Sophie's birthday and we're having a party. I told you some time ago.' He tried to make light of it. 'Fifteen five-year-olds – aren't you jealous? The highlight will be pass the parcel.'

There was no reply. Mark looked at the screen to see if they were still connected. They were. 'Suzanne?'

Her voice had an edge to it. 'You know where to find me when you've stopped playing happy families.'

Mark grimaced as he put down his phone. This was becoming tedious. Whenever he mentioned his children she became distant and cold. Was it worth it? Perhaps he should put a stop to it but oh, fuck... the sex. It was so fucking amazing. Fuck, he couldn't think of that now. Not here. Think about Sophie's party... A roomful of five-year-olds wasn't his idea of fun. He tidied his desk in an attempt to put off the dreadful hour, but ten minutes later with a huge sigh he left his desk and started on the journey home. He needed to give himself plenty of time to visit a toyshop.

The house and garden were decorated with red and yellow balloons so guests would know where the party was. He parked the car and took the parcel out of the boot. As he walked up the path to the door he resisted the temptation to burst the balloons and struggled past with the huge package in his arms. He put it down on the doorstep and threw open the door. Sophie ran and hugged him for a second before jumping on the package.

'Is this my present, Daddy? Is it? Can I open it?'

'Yes, yes and yes.' He laughed and bent down to help her.

She squealed with delight when she saw the doll's house inside.

'It's beautiful. It's gorgeous. It's mine, mine, *mine.*' The last word was screamed as Emma tottered towards them, putting a sticky hand out to touch the brightly painted surface.

'Come and see what Daddy's got for you,' said Mark, grabbing the sticky little fingers and averting two major temper tantrums.

'Well done,' whispered Karen as he rushed Emma along the hall.

'Superdad to the rescue.' He lifted Emma up and made her fly through the air. She giggled; the danger point had passed. 'When do the hordes arrive?' he asked Karen.

'Any minute now.' The doorbell rang and they both laughed. Mark looked in appreciation at Karen. She had done her hair differently and her face was shining. She looked young and wholesome, and Mark felt a surge of warmth and affection towards her.

'Superdad and psychicmum – the super heroes of the Southside. Well, here goes.' Karen opened the door. The party had started.

Two and a half hours later, having amused and fed fifteen small children and delivered them safely back into the hands of their loving parents, Karen and Mark slumped exhausted on the sofa. Their own children were, at last, asleep in bed. Mark fretted about Suzanne, about their last phone call. He ought to put a stop to it now before he became any more involved, but his relationship with Karen was terrible. He closed his eyes, willing sleep to come.

Karen's voice broke into his reverie. 'Mark, I'm sorry.'

He opened his eyes slowly and looked at her, waiting to see what she'd say.

'I should have told you I'd been married.'

'Why didn't you?'

Karen got up from her chair. 'If we're going to talk about this, I need a drink. Do you want one?'

'I'll have a beer, thanks.'

Karen came back two minutes later with their drinks, a bottle of Staropramen for him and red wine for her. She picked up her wine and gulped down half of it. 'Why didn't I tell you?' She shook her head. 'I think I was ashamed. No, don't interrupt. John was a very controlling person. He was older than me, more than ten years, and it's a lot when you're only nineteen. Looking back, I suppose I saw him as an escape route. I wasn't happy at home. You know, because of my father.'

Mark nodded. 'Let's not talk about him. Tell me about your ex.'

'He was cheating on me right from the start. Not just with Julie, but with other women too. Fuck buddies, he called them.' She wrinkled her nose. 'But I'm getting ahead of myself. I didn't find that out until later. Anyway, to begin with I thought it was only Julie. She phoned me. God, it was horrible. It destroyed my life.' She took a deep breath. 'I left John, divorced him. Not long after, they got married. I was making a new life for myself, then I bumped into him in a night club. I was drunk and invited him back to my flat and that was it. Sucked back in again like the fool I was.'

Mark swirled his beer in his glass. 'But how did you get together with him in the first place? I mean he's quite a lot older than you.'

She wouldn't look at him. 'I thought it was chance but I found his diaries. Oh God, what a fool I was.'

This was useless. She was going back and forwards in time,

making it impossible to keep up with her. 'Karen, I'm finding this hard to follow. Start at the beginning. Don't jump about from one year to another; start with how you met and go from there.'

It took her two hours to tell her story. A depressing tale of a harsh father, low self-esteem and a manipulative older man.

'When I interviewed him, he said he had to have you, that you held out for a ring.'

Karen nibbled at her nails. 'I was a virgin. I had been brought up in a really strict way. I wasn't after marriage, but he was so persuasive and yes, I suppose he could be romantic. He completely took me in. He was my tutor at college. He taught psychology on a part-time basis. He'd just started the consultancy and he needed a back-up in case it didn't take off. Turned out he was screwing half the tutorial group.' She shook her head.

'How do you know?'

'By the time we got back together, the consultancy was successful. He was always off on trips abroad. He was away in Singapore and I found his diaries. They catalogued every woman he'd slept with, gave them a mark out of ten.' She gulped her wine. 'I thought I was in love, I thought he loved me, but his "affairs", if you can call them that, had gone on all the time we were together. I was devastated when I found out what he'd been up to. Christ, I can't believe I was so naïve. I phoned up Debbie and we went out. I'm so ashamed of what I did. I picked up a complete stranger and slept with him. I didn't know his name. That's why I didn't tell you any of this. It's so damn sordid.'

'And that is Sophie's father?'

She nodded; a tear rolled down her cheek. 'John came back from Singapore. I felt nauseous all the time. At first I thought it was psychological then I realised. I was terrified he'd find out. And of course he did. I left immediately, and not long after that I met you.' She smiled. 'I couldn't believe my luck. But I didn't dare tell you in case you left me too.'

'Oh, Karen. Do you think I'm that lacking in compassion?'

She gave him a watery smile. 'I know better now, but at the time... and now I've probably lost you. Can you forgive me?'

It wasn't the time to hesitate so Mark answered immediately, 'Yes.' He had to forgive her, for the sake of his children.

Mark went through to the kitchen to get more drink. This was it; he had to choose – his children or Suzanne. There was no competition. Suzanne would have to go. He returned with the drinks and sat down on the sofa beside Karen. They were at either end of the settee, mirroring each other. He was at the right-hand side, with his legs curled up to the left, while Karen sat at the other end, her legs curled up to the right. 'We're like a pair of china dogs,' he commented when he noticed how they were seated.

'Are we? Are we really still a pair?' asked Karen, her face serious.

'Well of course we are.' To his surprise, Mark meant it. He sipped at his beer and then raised his glass. 'We could be a great team, you and me, if we tried.'

Karen raised her glass back, her eyebrows elevated in slight puzzlement. 'Do you think so? How hard will you try?'

'As hard as I need to.' Mark looked down at his hands. 'Look, Karen, I know I've been awful recently – late nights, too much work...'

'Not enough play.' Karen finished his sentence for him. 'Yes, that's certainly true. But can you change?'

Mark reached over and took her hand. 'Look, I'm going to try. I appreciate you telling me about Allen, though I'm hurt that you couldn't have trusted me earlier. We shouldn't have secrets.'

'I know. I'm sorry.'

Mark poured himself some more beer. What a hypocrite he was, no secrets. He'd end it tomorrow. Karen had shown her commitment by coming clean about her past. It was the least he could do. 'We'll need some ground rules, you know.'

'Absolutely.' Karen leaned over to kiss him. She stopped as Mark stiffened. 'What's wrong?'

'Nothing. I thought I saw someone pass the window and look in, that's all. It gave me a fright. We should shut the curtains at night, you know.'

The doorbell rang. 'Looks as though you didn't imagine it.' Karen got up. 'I'll get it.'

Mark couldn't move – his legs were like dead weights, his heart pounding. The face at the window had been Suzanne's and now she was at his door. He wanted to call out to Karen to leave the door, not answer it, pretend they weren't at home, but the words wouldn't form. Instead they lingered at the back of his throat as a low groan.

Chapter Eighteen

Suzanne

I WAS SEETHING as I drove away from Mark's house. I had thought he felt the same way about me. How often had he told me he was bored with Karen, that they had nothing in common? I sat outside their house for hours watching. Their curtains were open and the lights on, giving a clear view of the living room through the window that was almost to the floor. It was a shock to see them sitting close together on their cheap sofa, drinks in hand, deep in conversation. At first I thought it was *the* conversation, that he was telling her he was leaving. She was in tears at one point, I'd swear. But then I saw them holding hands. At that point I got out of the car.

I crept closer to the house wanting to try to hear what they were saying. It was impossible of course – they had double glazing and I couldn't make out a thing. I could see everything though with my grandstand view. Karen leaning in to kiss him. Mark smiling at her. Then he saw me. His face! It turned purple, then white. Karen saw something was wrong. She frowned and I moved away. I didn't want her to see me... and yet I did. The door was only a few steps away.

My plan was that Mark would answer; we would have a whispered conversation, Karen would interrupt, he'd turn to her and apologise: *I'm so sorry, Karen. This is Suzanne. We love each other.* But it was Karen who opened the door, a welcoming smile on her pretty face.

She was lovely. She looked a little tired but the bloom of youth was still there. Once you're past forty like me, you can do all sorts of things to enhance your appearance but all the facial peels in the world don't bring back that glow. And her figure was perfect. I stared at her without saying anything.

'Hello,' she said. 'How can I help you?'

I gathered my thoughts. 'I'm so sorry to disturb you,' I said, 'but my car won't start and I've stupidly left my mobile at home. Would it be possible to use your phone?'

'Come in, come in.' I followed her into the cramped hallway; I've seen bigger cardboard boxes. She talked nonstop. 'My husband's good with his hands – he'll have a look and see what he can do. Mark, this lady's car has broken down. Do you think you could have a look at it for her?'

We were now in the living room, where Mark seemed to be stuck to the sofa. He scowled but said nothing. Karen frowned at him. 'Mark? Have a look at her car, won't you?'

He nodded and I gave him the keys. Once he was outside, Karen started to apologise. 'Sorry about my husband. He can be a bit shy at times.'

I laughed, trying to make it sound natural. 'Please, don't apologise. I'm disturbing you.' I nodded towards the helium balloons that were gathered on the ceiling. 'Someone's birthday?'

'Our eldest. Can I get you something to drink?'

At least he'd been telling the truth when he refused to

come out earlier. 'No, not for me thanks.' She chatted on, telling me about the party they'd had for Sophie's birthday. I nodded and smiled, not really paying attention. Mark was taking an awfully long time to fix a car that wasn't broken. What the hell was he doing?

He returned several minutes later, by which time I'd refused three more offers of something to drink and heard several anecdotes about their children. I felt sick. This was not the unhappy family I'd been told about and Karen was anything but boring.

'It's fixed.' He gave me the keys, fixing me with a hard stare, which fortunately Karen didn't notice.

'Thank you so much. I'll get on my way.' Thankfully, Karen, who by now had drunk another glass of wine, didn't press me to stay. She showed me to the door. 'Well, thanks again, Karen. You have a lovely family. Enjoy the rest of your evening.'

A faint look of confusion passed over her face as she closed the door behind me. I cursed myself. She hadn't told me her name. But it would be fine. I was going to be out of her life from now on. Tomorrow I would end this relationship.

The car was across the road where I left it. I pressed the remote control and it beeped to tell me it was open. I got into the driving seat, moved it back into position and got ready to drive away.

Mark

Karen came back into the room.

'What on earth's wrong with you? You were appallingly rude.' She poured some more wine. 'Well?'

Mark forced a smile. 'Nothing. I'm a bit tired, that's all.

And I didn't want her hanging around. I was enjoying having you all to myself.'

'Mmn.' Karen smiled back. He sank into the sofa, his heartbeat returning to normal, and told himself it was an omen. Suzanne had had her chance to tell Karen and had lost it. He would finish with her tomorrow. He would make it work with Karen.

Later, after making love, as he was about to drop off to sleep, Karen said, 'It was funny, when that woman left. She used my name and I'm sure I didn't tell her.'

'You're pissed, Karen. You most likely did and you've forgotten.'

Karen's voice was sleepy. 'I don't think so, oh well...' Her voice tailed off; she was asleep. Mark stared into the darkness. Sleep was a million miles away.

Chapter Nineteen

Mark

MARK LAY in his bed not wanting to move his head from the pillow. He opened one eye and shut it again when the light struck it. Suzanne coming to the house had shaken him and he'd had far more to drink than he intended.

Did he have the strength to finish with Suzanne? He had to find it from somewhere. It would be hard, but her appearance at his house last night had been a warning. Better end it now before Karen found out. He started humming Paul Simon's 'Fifty Ways To Leave Your Lover'. That made him think of Julie Campbell's 'confession' and in turn of the bereaved parents he had seen yesterday. The throbbing in his head intensified. He couldn't think straight. Something was evading him, but whenever he seemed to be getting there, the pain screamed at him to give up. He turned over and tried to get back to sleep. He was falling down a lift shaft when Karen shook him awake.

'Tea, sweetheart?'

He groaned. 'What time is it? Do I have to get up?' Even as he spoke he knew he'd have to go to work, alcohol poisoning or not. He held a hand out in front of him and watched the slight tremble. Not too bad. He tried to sit up and immediately beads of sweat stood out on his forehead. His head reeled and he lay back. 'Aspirin and water, and Irn Bru if you haven't already finished it.'

'It's here already. Come on, get it down you.'

Karen stroked his forehead as she handed him the drink. Her fingers were cool against his hot face. He was in for a day of suffering; the malt whisky that had been so seductive in the evening was intent on making him pay. He threw the bright orange drink with its sweet metallic edge down his throat and belched as the bubbles reached his stomach. He took the second glass with the water and aspirin and almost immediately felt better but not up to facing Suzanne. How had he got into this mess? Lack of willpower – that was it. He'd have to do something; there was too much at stake. But first he had to deal with the hangover.

'Any chance of a roll and bacon?'

'Get yourself into the shower and I'll see what I can do.'

'Hmm. I must have done something right last night.' He tried to grab her as she padded round the bedroom, picking up clothes, tidying the chaos that they lived in. She put down the towel that she had just picked up from the floor and looked down at him.

'It isn't earth shattering, you know. You were there. You listened to me when I told you about John, you didn't judge. I should have told you years ago, trusted you.'

Mark could see the tears in her eyes and pulled her towards him. 'I'm glad you told me.'

'And you said you'd be home for the birthday party and you were. You said you'd get the birthday present and you did.

It doesn't take much to keep me happy, Mark. All you need to do is keep your promises.'

'I know. We can make this work, I'm sure we can.'

She leaned into him. 'I hope so, Mark. I really do.'

Mark stopped dead when he got outside and saw the car. There was a huge scratch along one side. He was sure it hadn't been there yesterday. Damn her – this must have been Suzanne. It was too much of a coincidence for it not to be. Well, that settled it. It wouldn't be too hard to end it after all. He looked closely at it. It was more than a surface scratch; it went deep. Fuck, it would cost hundreds of pounds to fix it properly. This wasn't something that could be sorted with a DIY scratch kit. Damn her! He got into the car and drove to work, desperate to get there so he could phone Suzanne and tell her what he thought about her.

'Phone call for you, sir. Can you take it?' called out one of the younger officers as Mark strode through the building. Mark nodded and made his way to his room foregoing the coffee he desperately needed. The ringing of the phone seemed shriller than usual. He picked up the handset. 'Mark Nicholson.'

'Mark, I'm so sorry about last night.'

He looked round to check no one was in earshot. 'What the hell were you thinking about?'

'I know, I'm sorry. I shouldn't have come to your door. It was unforgiveable.'

'And the damage to my car. That's really crap.'

There was a pause. When she spoke, her voice was quiet. 'What damage?'

'Come off it. You took your keys and scratched all along the right side. Don't bother denying it.' She started to speak and his temper flared. 'I'm not interested, Suzanne. It's over.' His voice must have risen for two of his colleagues looked very busy all of a sudden in a way that said they'd been listening to every word. Shit. He put the phone down and looked at his desk. There was a shed load of paperwork to do. He'd find a quiet place where he wouldn't be disturbed and he'd stay there until it was done.

Suzanne

I put the phone down and sat stunned on my sofa. That hadn't gone the way I'd planned. He'd sounded so angry, and although I knew it had to end, it shouldn't be like this. I thought over the events of last night. Surely I hadn't scratched his car? And yet there was a little niggle in my mind.

It was years since I'd done something like this. My psychiatrist had called it dissociation, said it was common among children who'd been abused or who had been traumatised. Apparently it is a defence device. The brain switches off, there is memory loss. Could I have been angrier than I thought when faced with the evidence that Mark had a happy family after all? I thought back over my return home last night.

I had driven home carefully. I was devastated but I managed to keep the tears in check until I got into the flat. I opened a bottle of Australian merlot and poured myself a large glass. I swallowed it quickly, wincing at its slightly sour taste. It hadn't had time to breathe. The second glass was better, and I made myself sip it slowly. I went over the scene with Mark again and again in my head. I had been so stupid, believing him when he said his relationship with Karen was dead.

The wine went to my head. I'd eaten nothing all day as I'd been savouring the prospect of a good meal at the Chip. It was to have been a celebration. The doctors who had commissioned the anatomy paintings were thrilled with them and had promised to recommend me to friends. And, sure enough, that afternoon I had two enquiries that were extremely promising. I preferred doing my own work – what artist doesn't? – but commissions such as this paid the bills. So, I'd booked a table then been turned down. Perhaps if I'd eaten...

I was going off-piste; I should be concentrating on remembering. I sat on the sofa trying to picture the previous evening. There had been a third glass of wine, of course there had. I went through to the kitchen. A bottle of merlot with only half an inch left in it stood on the worktop. It was as I feared. I had drunk a bottle of wine on an empty stomach.

Did I leave the flat, get into the car and drive over to Mark's and vandalise his car? I didn't remember doing that. But I did remember where I had parked the car last night. I put on my shoes and went out to check. It was two streets away in Dowanside Road.

It wasn't there. An image came to me of headlights flashing at me, a glimpse of an angry face. I was imagining things, I told myself, but if I was, where was my car?

I wandered round for thirty minutes before I found it, badly parked partly in front of someone's driveway. There was a note under my windscreen wipers. I took it out and put it in my pocket without reading it and got into the car. Before anyone could come out and start shouting at me, I drove away, hoping it hadn't been reported to the police. People round here get very heated about parking.

Back in the flat I made myself some strong coffee. I didn't have a hangover; I didn't feel as though I'd drunk a whole bottle of wine on an empty stomach last night, but the evidence was there in the kitchen and in the fact that the car wasn't where I had left it. I was in the danger zone of dissociation and it scared me.

Chapter Twenty

Mark

IT FELT good to have finished with Suzanne. The affair had been madness, an infection of his brain. He had not been himself and now it was time to get back to normal. Mark hadn't worked in such a focused way for ages, not since he'd become entangled with Suzanne. He went through to the back office, which he sometimes used if he had a lot of work to get through, and was delighted to see it was empty. He settled down to work and flew through reports, case notes and other administrative duties until satisfied, he sat back with a smile. He leaned back in his chair with his hands clasped behind his head and looked up at the clock on the wall, astonished to see it was nearly half past ten. He hadn't been disturbed all day. Mark went out into the corridor to see if any of his mates were around. A group were standing huddled chatting near one of the shared offices. One of the men greeted him.

'Mark! Thought you weren't in today. Where have you been?'

'In the back office, working. Got a load of paperwork done.'

'Oh. We thought you must be on the early shift.'

'No, just been holed up working. Anyone going for a drink? We could go to O'Neil's – it doesn't shut until midnight.' The words were barely out of his mouth when the phone in his room rang. Mark dashed back into the room and picked up the phone, silently mouthing fuck offs at the mouthpiece. One of the women saw him and giggled. Mark made a face at her and spoke into the receiver.

'Nicholson here. Tell me it isn't important.'

It was the desk sergeant; Phil Evans, a man not easily amused. His voice was abrupt.

'Right, so you are in. I wasn't sure. We need someone to call round at 39 Barlogan Drive.'

'Any details?' asked Mark.

'Not really. The report's just come in of an old woman being beaten up. It's not clear exactly what happened but she's dead. The ambulance is there already and a patrol car, but they need a DS as well. It'll have to be you, Mark.'

'Come on. I should've finished at eight. I'm bloody knackered.'

'Too bad, Mark. Just think of the overtime. Word on the street is you need it.'

Mark put the phone down. 'Sorry, lads, it'll have to be a rain cheque.' He ducked under the table as a pen followed by a curse flew across the room. Pulling a hanky out of his pocket, he waved it. 'Truce. Truce. I swear I'll buy the next round.'

'Aye, that's what you always say.'

Mark laughed and made his way to the door. He rang Karen from his mobile. 'I'm sorry, love, but I've been called out on a case. Some old biddy's been mugged and it's pretty serious by the sounds of it.'

To his surprise, Karen was understanding. She told him to

take care; he could hear the warmth in her voice. They chatted easily for a minute or two, light inconsequential chat that had been missing from their relationship for some time. Things were definitely looking up. Humming tunelessly, he went out into the yard and got into his car.

There was a police cordon already around the street when he got there. Mark was ushered into the street by a policewoman he vaguely recognised. He acknowledged her with a brief smile and walked on up to the house, an ex-council house built in the thirties, semi-detached. The garden was untidy, overgrown with grass and weeds. A wheelie bin was overturned on the path and a lawnmower lay rusting in the long grass. Flower beds busy with weeds gave testament to a past when someone had cared about appearances. Some houses in the street looked prosperous with tidy gardens and white PVC doors, but this house had the air of a middle-aged man who'd had a midlife crisis and then given up trying. A number of people stood outside the front door with its chipped paint and cracked glass. Among them was Dr Siddiqui, the pathologist. Her face was serious as she approached him.

'Mark, hi. We get the best cases don't we? It's a bit grim in there.'

'Do we know what happened?' He took a protective suit from the PC at the door and put it on.

'I don't have a clear idea yet. Maybe you should speak to your own officers. What I can tell you though, is that she died about an hour ago, most likely from a blow to the head, but we'll need to wait for the post-mortem to know for sure. There's some evidence of a struggle, but she was a frail old woman – she wouldn't have been able to defend herself.'

Mark nodded his thanks and went to find someone who could brief him. Inside, the house was spotlessly clean, though the furnishings were poor and it looked as though it hadn't been decorated for many years. The wallpaper was woodchip and had a shiny look as though it had been painted with gloss paint. Easier to clean, of course. The kitchen had what seemed to be original fifties units and a gas cooker, which although it hadn't a mark on it should surely have been condemned as unfit for use. What could be seen of the floor showed worn linoleum of a type he hadn't seen since his childhood. It was a grim scene right enough, just as the pathologist had said. Blood everywhere. Mark looked round; the neat surroundings didn't really fit with the mess outside. He supposed the garden had become too much for her. A young police officer approached him and started to tell him what was going on.

'It looks as though she'd just come in from doing some shopping. There are some Asda bags with their contents everywhere. Also she's wet as if she had just come in from the rain. The floor has been wiped though. We reckon the murderer wiped it with the floor mop over there. He's probably left footprints.' The police constable pointed to an old-fashioned squeegee mop that stood like a sentinel at the back door. 'But as you can see it didn't make much difference. She must have carried on bleeding after he'd left. We've tested the mop for fingerprints but it's been wiped too.'

'Any hints as to the perpetrator?'

'Actually, sir, we've made an arrest.' The young policeman couldn't keep the hint of pride out of his voice.

'Already?' Mark was impressed.

'Local druggie, boy of about sixteen. We reckon he followed her in to try and grab her purse. There's obviously been a struggle. See the food all over the floor? She was probably carrying the bags when he attacked and they've just spilled out.'

'Is her purse missing?'

'We found it on him. Neighbour next door saw him rush out of the house and put us on to it right away.'

'Good work. Better get back to the station and get the paper work done. What's the suspect's name?'

'Laird, sir. Dylan Laird. He's in the car over there.' He indicated with his head.

Mark looked over but it was too dark to see clearly. Only a slight shape in the back let him know that there was anyone there. He turned back to the constable. 'Anything else I should know?'

'Only one thing. I was first on the scene. When I got here, that song was playing.'

'What song? I'm not a mind reader.'

'I think it's called 'Psycho Killer', something like that. Don't know who sings it, though.' He hummed a few bars.

'Talking Heads,' said Mark. 'But so what? It's just a coincidence. Not a pleasant one, admittedly, but I doubt there's anything in it.'

The constable pointed to an evidence bag on the table. 'No, I think it was deliberate. There's nothing but that song on that tape; it just plays it over and over.'

Mark stared at the young police officer. 'Yes,' he said slowly. 'That is odd. Make sure you've noted it. I'll see you back at the station. Let me have your report as soon as possible. Everything's under control here so I'll get back and do the first interview.'

Back at the station, Mark sat in the interviewing room and stared at the vision of pathetic humanity that sat across from him. The boy had been blubbing for at least twenty minutes now.

'It wisnae me.'

How often had he heard that refrain? Thousands of times over the years, it must be now. Nobody had ever done anything. It was always someone else's fault. And yet there was something believable in the boy's terror-struck eyes.

'OK, son. You've already said that. Now can we just go over again what happened?'

The boy sniffed hard but it was not enough to stop watery snotters falling from his nose. He was in a wretched state, desperate for a fix, shivering from fear and cold. The temperature in the interview room was low and the boy was wearing only a thin T-shirt and trackie bottoms.

'I never hit her.' There was no defiance in his voice as was usual with guilty suspects, only a quiet despair. 'I never hit her. I did take the purse. My dealer was on at me for money.' He started to cry again.

Mark found himself feeling sorry for him. He never judged drug addicts, seeing them as how he might have been if he hadn't had his dream of becoming a police officer to sustain him during the difficult teenage years. Mark knew several people who had been at school with him who had turned to drugs to help them escape the dreary reality of their lives. He tried smiling at the boy. 'I know, son, but I need to hear from you what actually happened.'

'I was just passing the house and I saw the door open. So I thought I'd take a chance and nip inside and see if there was anything worth stealing.'

'What time was this?'

'About eight o'clock.'

'Where had you been before then?'

'At home, in my bed. I never got up until two o'clock.'

'That leaves several hours unaccounted for. We need to know exactly where you were before that.'

'I was watching *Countdown*.'

Mark raised an eyebrow. '*Countdown*?'

The boy looked defiant for the first time. 'Aye, *Countdown*. I watch it every day. I learned to read afore I went to school because of *Countdown* and I like the wee sums.'

Christ, what a waste. He must have been a bright spark to teach himself to read like that. Life wasn't fair. A better family and the boy would be studying for his Highers, getting ready to go to university. Mark held up his hands. 'And after that?'

'More telly. I like quiz shows: *Pointless*, that's my favourite. I got two pointless answers today. And then, I was needing a fix and I had no money so I went out on the rob.' He looked straight at Mark, a strange sort of pride in his eyes. 'I'm no denying that and I'm no proud of it. But I never killed the old woman. She was deid already.' The eyes went down then and he started to cry again. Mark pushed the box of tissues towards him and waited until he had calmed down. After a few moments the boy went on. 'I wandered about looking for a likely house and it seemed like a miracle when I saw the door open.'

'What happened then?' Mark prompted.

'I went in. There was something playing on the radio but the house felt empty as if there was nobody there. I called out just in case and got ready to run. There was no answer so I peeked inside the living room. There was nobody there but the door to the kitchen was open so in I went. Christ what a sight.' He stopped.

'Go on.'

'Well, you saw her, didn't you?'

Mark nodded. He examined his nails, waiting for the boy to continue.

'I thought to myself, I'd better get out of here, and I was just going when I saw the purse on the floor, so I picked it up without thinking and stuffed it in my pocket. Well, I was fucking desperate. There was a mop so I cleaned away my foot-prints.' He said this as though he was proud of what he'd done.

'What was playing on the radio?'

'Dunno. I'd no heard it before.'

Mark fumbled in his pocket for his phone and scrolled through his playlist before pressing play. 'Is this it?'

Dylan listened, a bemused look on his face. 'Aye, I think so. I'm no very good with music. Tone deaf.'

Poor sod, thought Mark, but aloud he said 'OK, son, that'll do for now.' He ignored the look of disbelief coming from the other police officer in the room, a young woman not long in the force, and switched off the tape recorder after saying 'DS Nicholson ending the interview of Dylan Laird concerning the murder of Mrs Mary McLeod.' He left the policewoman to take Laird back to the cells after warning her to keep him on suicide watch.

'Sir, can I have a word?' The policewoman caught up with him outside the interview room.

'What is it?'

She hesitated. 'Sir, I feel that I have to express my discomfort at that interview.'

'Really?' Mark's tone was dry. He knew what was coming.

'Yes sir. I felt that you gave him much too easy a time of it. After all he's just killed a defenceless old woman.'

Mark shook his head. 'Excuse me? It may be unfashionable, constable, but I still believe it's our job to gather evidence. We can leave the rest to the procurator fiscal and then the jury, surely?' He waved her aside as she started to speak again. 'Not interested. Go tell it to the mountains if you have to.'

He left her standing, mouth still open. 'Watch out for flies,' he called as he strode away.

In Scrimgeour's office an hour later, he was beginning to regret his treatment of the new recruit. Too late he remembered that Scrimgeour had a personal interest in her; she was a niece or something.

Scrimgeour let him stand. A tic flickered under his right eye, a sure sign that he was angry. His voice was controlled though. 'I've had a complaint about how you handled our prime suspect. It's our job to see that justice is done, and by all accounts, it sounds as though you've decided that that piece of human shit is innocent when we all but caught him with the knife in his hand.'

'She wasn't stabbed, sir, she was beaten. The blood came from a head wound.'

'Don't play funny games with me, Nicholson. You know perfectly well what I mean. The boy was in the house; he had her purse on him when he was picked up. It has to have been him.'

Mark took a deep breath. His hands were in his jacket pockets and he fiddled with his car keys. He let the index finger of his right hand trace the outline of the key ring. It was Peppa Pig, Daddy Pig to be precise, complete with briefcase, given to him as a Christmas present by Sophie. 'Doesn't it strike you as funny, sir, that this is the second murder in a matter of days that fits almost exactly with those in Julie Campbell's confession?'

Scrimgeour leaned over Mark so close that Mark could

almost taste the coffee on Scrimgeour's breath. He tried not to breathe in. Scrimgeour exploded, words spitting out of his mouth. 'I'm fucking sick of you rabbiting on about that fucking loony. She's dead, you eejit. You're totally obsessed with her and her posh sister. Oh yes, we all know you're screwing her. You might as well have had it tattooed over your forehead. You wander about in a daydream, not doing any proper work, and every time we put you on a case the only solution you come up with is "This is very like the Julie Campbell case".' He did a passable imitation of Mark's voice.

Mark gritted his teeth and clasped the key ring. He made himself think about something positive, Sophie's face when she gave it to him. She'd picked it herself and been so proud of it... He was not going to say anything. He had to stay cool. 'Calm, calm, calm.' He repeated the words over and over again to himself, picturing Sophie's sweet face while Scrimgeour ranted on. It worked, so that when he finally spoke, his voice was quiet but firm.

'Several things you should know, sir. There was a tape playing at the scene. The same song had been recorded over and over: 'Psycho Killer'. He mentioned hearing it but didn't seem to know the track. When I played it to him there was no reaction. Nothing. He couldn't be acting; he's desperate for a fix.' Mark paused.

Scrimgeour frowned. 'Go on. I'm listening.'

'Dylan Laird has a history of theft but there's nothing in his past to suggest violence. Nothing whatsoever. There was no blood on him when he was picked up. I saw the kitchen floor; I was there at the scene. Whoever killed that woman would have had some blood on them, maybe not a lot but some at least. We've still to have his clothes fully tested but there's nothing visible to the naked eye.'

Scrimgeour was silent for a second. He looked uncomfortable. 'No blood, eh? Well, maybe he changed his clothes.'

'There was no time, sir. He was picked up barely half an hour after Mrs McLeod died. He hadn't had time to go home, change and be back out on the street. I'm just not convinced that he did it.'

Scrimgeour made a noise that sounded suspiciously like humph and waved Mark out of the room. Mark left the room feeling a slight triumph that he had managed to state his case calmly. Maybe there was something in this anger management stuff after all. He made his way to his car, happy to be going home, to Karen, to his children.

Chapter Twenty-One

Mark

LIFE WITH KAREN returned to normal. Mark stopped taking every shift he could get; he was determined to spend more time with his family and it was paying off. Oscar was growing in confidence the more time he spent with his father and even Emma was becoming less of a tyrant. Mark grew calmer and a little content with his lot. Once or twice a little voice in his head would say, 'Call this being alive, man? You're suffocating,' and Mark had to bring all his will power to the front of his mind to help push this thought back to the hidden depths. It had to be suppressed. He did his best not to think of Suzanne, but at odd times of day he'd wonder what she was doing. Several times he picked up the phone; one time he dialled her number but put the handset down before it started ringing. He felt virtuous when he did that, strong willed and in control. Afterwards though, his mood was dark.

Mark plodded through his work. He didn't voice his suspicions again about the hit and run accident. No one was arrested for it. There were two further eyewitness statements, but they were in conflict with each other. One said Daisy had stepped out in front of the car and the driver had had no chance of missing her. 'He was panic stricken, just a lad, drove off.' The other, from an elderly widow, said that she had seen the car in the street several times before. She was adamant that a woman was driving. 'I know it was a woman because if it was a man I would have taken more notice – I would have thought he was casing one of the houses – I might even have taken down the number.' She shook her head at her failings. She even agreed to be hypnotised in an effort to remember the car's number plate, but all that came out of that was a previous life as an Egyptian slave. Mark had had to put up with a lot of ribbing about that, as the hypnotist had been his idea. Too bad she turned out to be a charlatan. No way would he voice his suspicions about the similarities between the confession and this case again.

But the murder of Mrs McLeod continued to worry him. Robbie Laird, the drug addict, was the main suspect even though tests had shown no traces of blood anywhere on his clothes. Unfortunately, however, there was some on the soles of his trainers. The boy's lawyer was adamant that this could have got there when he entered the house, and Laird had admitted to mopping the floor to get rid of his footprints. Other than that it was only circumstantial evidence. Scrimgeour passed on the reports to the Procurator Fiscal and it would be up to him to decide whether there was enough evidence. Mark didn't know what to think but he continued to be baffled by the similarity between the cases and those outlined in Julie Campbell's confession.

Against his better judgement Mark photocopied the confession to take home. He snuck out of the station with it in his inside pocket feeling like a shoplifter. It was against policy, and if he was found out he could expect to get his balls nailed to the floor. He wanted to read it through in peace to see if he could get any more sense out of it. It just seemed like such a strange thing to do – to confess to imaginary murders – but when he raised it with anyone they blew him off. He needed time to put it all together. There was something there, of that he was certain. Once the children were in bed he brought it out and sat on the couch with a highlighter in hand ready to underline anything significant. He started to read through it and within minutes was completely engrossed.

'What are you doing?' said Karen, who had come into the living room without him noticing.

'It's work.'

'What work?'

He considered lying to her but decided against it. 'It's Julie Campbell's confession.'

Karen stared at him. 'Really, can I read it?'

'I can't let you see it, Karen. You know that.'

'But I might be able to help.'

'No. I shouldn't even have it here. I'd be up to my neck in it if anyone found out that you were connected in any way.'

'But...'

'No, Karen.'

He'd been so firm with her it had never occurred to him that she would look at it. But two evenings later he arrived home to find her trying to stuff it down the side of the sofa.

'What the hell are you doing?'

Her smile was nervous. 'It's quite intriguing, isn't it?'

'Karen! I told you not to read it.'

She jumped up, ran to him, grabbed his hands. 'I know, but I had to see what was in it for myself. Don't you see that? She ruined my life.'

'Well, we could argue about that. Is being with me so bad?'

'Of course not! But the hurt from what she did...'

'How far have you got?' he asked, thinking of the part where Julie talked about killing Karen.

'I've read it all.'

He sat down. 'Oh, Karen. Apart from everything else, I wanted to protect you from that poison.'

'Mark, I'm an adult. I knew Julie hated me. It's no surprise.'

He looked at her, a question in his eyes. She seemed invigorated by the confession, rather than disturbed as he'd thought.

Shrugging in response she said, 'You know, in spite of everything, in spite of how she hurt me, I *can* see why John was attracted to her. She's quite something, isn't she? And those musical clues – have you worked them out?'

'We do know one of them. The story about burning her child comes from an opera. What was it called?' He thought for a moment, remembering times when Suzanne had played opera music to him. Karen was looking at him, the line between her eyes deepening. 'I didn't know you knew anything about opera?'

'I don't. Allen told us about it. It was something about an old gypsy throwing her child into a fire. No, I can't remember. As for the others, I don't really know enough about music to get them and no one at work thought they were important.'

'Why not?' The frown had disappeared.

'Oh well, I suppose once we found out that it was all a lie then there seemed little point in looking any further at it. The case is closed, the body buried.'

'Would you mind if I tried to work them out?'

'What? You? You've never shown...' Mark stopped. He was falling back into his old habit of denigrating any interest that Karen showed. Her face began to close up, her lips tightened and little lines appeared at the corners of her mouth. He started again.

'Well, OK, I don't see why not. But for God's sake, keep it to yourself. You mustn't speak to anyone about it. I'm serious, Karen. I'd get into real bother if they found out I'd taken a copy home. You know what they're like about evidence.'

'It's not a real confession though.'

'I know that, but even so...'

Karen nodded. 'My lips are sealed.'

'Fine then. Let me know if you find anything. Keep me informed, won't you?'

'Yes sir!' said Karen, jumping to mock attention. 'Anything else, sir?'

'Yes, come here.' He grabbed her and kissed her, determined to eradicate the last of those little lines he had seen lingering around her mouth. As they kissed he thought, we'll make it, we have to make it for the sake of the children if nothing else. And yet still there was a little niggle at the back of his mind that would not go away, and as he started to make love to his wife, Suzanne's face and body drifted into his mind. No matter how he tried they were there, mocking him, and they weren't going to budge. He gave a mental sigh and gave into them, letting the images take over as he literally and metaphorically screwed the mother of his children.

Chapter Twenty-Two

Suzanne

Every day was the same, so when I thought back over what I'd done in one week it was impossible to say: Sunday I went for a walk or Monday I met friends. They merged into one big blur. I was working hard on the paintings that had been commissioned, but now and again I'd take out my sketch book and draw; horrible images of things I wanted to forget emerged and I'd sit on the floor staring at them, wondering if they would ever go away. I had to accept that I probably had scratched Mark's car and I was deeply ashamed of myself. I was careful not to drink too much, limiting myself to two small glasses of wine in the evening three times a week. A few days after we broke up I sent Mark a short note apologising for what I'd done and offering to pay for the damage, but he didn't write back.

It was hard without him but work kept me sane. And there were other things to deal with too. The police released Julie's body and there was no more talk of her being murdered. The evidence pointed to suicide and I accepted that. She was much more likely to have murdered someone than be a victim herself, but that too had been dismissed. A rather grumpy DCI met with me to explain that they'd wasted a great deal of time trying to find out if any of the murders in her confession coincided with unsolved ones. They hadn't and there was nothing to suggest she had been murdered. The only 'evidence' for that was that something about a mouse being on the wrong side of the laptop for someone left-handed. I knew that already of course because Mark had told me but I didn't say anything. To tell the truth I wasn't sure she was left-handed; I'd been a child when I'd last seen her but I thought she was, so that was that – case closed. I left the police station reluctantly. I'd hoped I might bump into Mark but he was nowhere to be seen.

It was a strange experience arranging a funeral for someone I barely knew. I thought about contacting one of the neighbours to ask about friends, but in the end I contented myself with a brief notice in the *Herald*, giving the date, time and place of the cremation and nothing else. The funeral directors had given me the name of a woman who performed eulogies in lieu of a service, so I met with her to discuss what I wanted said. She asked a multitude of questions in one of those low, serious voices that are so often used for solemn occasions.

'Tell me about your sister,' she said.

I stared at her stupefied, no words coming to me. She must have thought I was grief stricken, because she patted my arm.

'Take your time,' she said. 'I know how difficult it is. The loss of a sister is a terrible thing.'

'I... She wasn't my sister,' I stammered.

A frown crossed her forehead. 'I was told her sister was

arranging the funeral.' She looked at me as though I had cheated her of her pension.

I'm adopted,' I said in a rush.

The frown disappeared. 'But no less sisters for that,' she said. 'I'm sure you have just as many fond memories of her as a real sister would.'

I never fail to be astonished at the naivety of people. Every day we read headlines about horrific abuse of children and women and occasionally men. Families everywhere hold horrendous secrets to their bosoms. And yet, and yet... when someone dies we are expected to be overwhelmingly positive about them with perhaps only the odd aside: *Michelle wasn't perfect, of course. She could be difficult at times.* I knew sisters who hadn't spoken to each other for years, brothers who beat up their younger siblings, women who couldn't be in the same room as their mother without a screaming match developing within seconds. Fond memories indeed.

A requiem mass would have been easier; few priests bothered with saying much other than prayers, but I didn't want to have anything to do with church so I told her the music I wanted played and continued to ignore her pointed requests for 'more personal information'.

The funeral was in Linn Crematorium on a bright September morning. I had chosen the first slot of the day; it was cheaper and as I had no relatives to placate I could please myself. There weren't many people there: two of her neighbours, the parents of a couple of her pupils and a man who slipped away before I had a chance to speak to him. Her ex-husband, perhaps? There was a representative from the police, the boy who'd signed me in that first day, but no Mark. I accepted all of their condolences with a smile, saying as little as I could. They hung around for several minutes afterwards, looking a bit lost, and too late I realised I should have organised some sort of a buffet. For a moment I considered inviting them back to my flat, but then I remembered my empty fridge – with not even as much as a carton of milk in it – and decided against it. Who cared what they thought? I would never see any of them again.

When I got home there was a letter waiting for me from a firm of lawyers saying they were the executors of her will. They wanted me to meet with them two days later.

Their office was in Renfield Street, in a Victorian building that still had its original lift. I ignored it and walked up the stairs. A rather dashing young lawyer took me into his office and told me everything had been left to me. I was both dismayed and astonished but managed to keep my face blank.

'What if I don't want the money?'

His poker face was nowhere as good as mine. His mouth dropped open. 'I... Well it's yours so you can do what you want with it, I suppose. But surely...'

I didn't want to get into a long discussion with him so I stood up. 'I'll think some more about it and get back to you. Meanwhile, I'd be grateful if you could arrange for the house to be cleared and then put on the market.'

'But surely there are personal effects, mementoes that you would like. Your sister told me it was your childhood home.'

By this time my hand was on the door knob. 'It was and I can assure you I have no wish to set foot in that place ever again.'

He sprang up from his seat. 'Nonetheless I strongly recommend that you at least visit the property. I have the keys here.' He pressed them into my hand.

I looked down at the expensive key ring with its silver charm, tempted to shove it right back at him. Instead I shrugged and took them. He'd never know whether I visited or not.

That afternoon I settled back down to work. The past few weeks had been disruptive and I was behind with the commissions I'd taken on. I was keen to finish them as I had an idea for a landscape, and as always, I wanted to do my own work but not before finishing my orders. The painting I was working on was a portrait of a young woman. Her parents had asked me to do it for her twenty-first birthday. I was using photographs as they wanted it to be a surprise and I was finding it difficult. I loved doing portraits but I preferred having a real live person in front of me. That way I could chat to the sitter, get to know them, and that helped with my interpretation. Although I'd explained all this to the parents they were not budging, but they had agreed to send some video footage of their daughter, which I decided to watch before going any further with my painting.

I was glad I had insisted. The photos they'd sent me showed a beautiful but rather bland young woman, carefully made up with straightened hair and a perfect smile. On the other hand, the videos gave me a better picture. She was funny, sardonic and warm; qualities that hadn't come through from the photos. I went into the room I used as a studio eager to translate these on to the canvas.

I knew something was wrong as soon as I entered the room. Nothing was immediately visible; it was more a sense of the air being disturbed. The room was in its usual state of disarray. I looked around but it was several seconds before I spotted it. The portrait was on the floor, destroyed. An open bottle of white spirit was beside it. It had fallen over and the liquid had spilled on to the canvas, making a smudged mess of my work. I cried out in dismay and rushed over to it. How had this happened? I had left the canvas on the floor, as I sometimes prefer to work this way, and I had had the white spirit open, but surely I had put the bottle away again? I tried to remember. Yes, I definitely had put it away, and in any case how could it have spilled? My jaw tensed; this was Mark's revenge for his car. I picked up the phone and dialled.

Mark

Mark was late for work again. He hadn't been sleeping well and every morning was a struggle to get out of bed. It was worse during the night. He missed Suzanne. He was trying hard with Karen but the spark wasn't there. She sensed it and they were growing apart again. Usually he fell asleep with no trouble; a double whisky, sometimes a treble before bedtime saw to that, but he often woke at three a.m. with his heart thumping, mouth dry. Once, after he'd had too much to drink, he woke to find himself in his living room, fully dressed with no idea of how he'd come to be there. That had been an especially bad night. His pulse had galloped as he paced the room trying to remember.

This morning the alarm had gone off as usual at six thirty. He'd switched it off and promptly fallen asleep. Two hours later, he was woken by a slobbery kiss from Emma. He greeted her with a smile, which disappeared when he saw the time.

After a quick shower, Mark ran downstairs and picked up the mail. Mostly bills, a postcard from one of Karen's friends and a letter for Karen. It wasn't often that Karen got letters addressed solely to her. Maybe it was an application form; last week she'd mentioned going back to work. It would be great if she did; they really needed the money, though no doubt child-care would eat up most of what she earned. He put the type-written buff envelope on the mantelpiece in the dining room and flicked through the rest of the mail. His pay slip was there.

Feeling slightly sick, he opened it. Shit. His pay was way down this month as he'd done so little overtime. He shoved the paper into his pocket, praying Karen wouldn't ask about it. It wasn't likely; he dealt with most of their finances. Next month would be different though; Oscar's birthday was coming up and she'd start on about a party and presents and then there would be Christmas and she'd want to know how much they could afford to spend on the kids. No point worrying about it now though, he thought as he left the house and started the drive to work. He felt less than happy, however, as he sat down at his desk, switched on his laptop and opened the file he'd been working on.

He yawned as he read through the boring, uninspiring prose he'd written. At first he'd been pleased that he'd been asked to write the Equality Impact Assessment. But this was dull. He closed his eyes and opened them almost immediately. He was falling asleep. Coffee was called for and he allowed himself to leave his task and make his way through to the staff canteen.

The front of the station was busy. People were coming in to report house break-ins and bicycle thefts for insurance purposes; the days were long gone that they'd solved any of these petty day-to-day crimes that were part of city life. One man drew a second glance from Mark. He was tall and striking looking, a bit like Rupert Everett but older, and very well dressed: dark woollen coat over a grey suit, shoes highly polished and expensive. Mark wondered if he was some high up police officer come to check them over. No, more likely he'd had his Jaguar done over and was coming in to complain. Mark carried on to the canteen.

The strong coffee did its job, waking Mark up. He felt much better as he walked back through to his office. The front of the station had calmed down and he noticed that the distinguished man had gone. He stopped to talk to Robbie. 'What did that bloke want?'

'What one?'

'You know, the tall one with the greying hair.'

Robbie shrugged. 'Claims his ex-wife has gone missing. He's through making a statement now.'

'Ah.'

'Yeah, she's supposed to be abroad working with a charity. She rented out her house, there's been a problem with the boiler, and when the letting agency tried to contact her through the charity they said she hadn't turned up.'

'Ah right. Well, it'll be the usual thing – another man.' Mark moved towards his office.

'Suppose so. Interesting though, that they live next door to that Campbell woman.'

'What?' Mark turned round. 'What did you say?'

'They live next d...'

'I heard you. Where is he?'

'What're you asking for, if you already heard? Interview room five, I think.'

Mark almost ran down the corridor. He peered in through the window of room five. Empty. Trust Robbie to get it wrong. He tried the next room along. Bingo. He opened the door and went in.

'Thank you, constable, I'll take over from here.' He waved the young policeman aside. The man being interviewed looked up in surprise.

Mark held out his hand to the older man. 'I'm DS Nicholson. I was one of the officers working on the case next... I assume you have heard about the unfortunate events next door to you?'

The man stood up and shook Mark's hand. He looked like a firm handshake man but his hand was like a dead fish in Mark's. 'David Fitzwilliam. Yes, I have, but I don't see what that's got to do with my ex-wife.'

'I understand that your wife, sorry, your ex-wife, had gone off to work abroad for a while?'

He rolled his eyes. 'It was a stupid idea. Mid-life crisis if you ask me. Like the affair she had but anyway, yes. She's let—'

Mark interrupted him. 'Her house out... Yes I've been told about that. I know you're divorced, but when did you last see Mrs Fitzwilliam?'

Fitzwilliam took out his diary, a small black Moleskine, and leafed through it. 'She was due to leave for Malawi on the fourteenth of June. We went out for a drink a few days before. Ah yes, here it is. The tenth of June.'

Mark did a quick calculation in his head. It was within the time frame. 'Do you know if anyone saw or heard from her after that? Did anyone go to see her off at the airport, for example?'

Fitzwilliam shook his head. 'I was meant to be going to see her off, but the next day I got a text asking me not to come. She said it would only upset her.'

'Do you still have this text?'

'I think so. Let me see.' He brought out his phone and scrolled through several messages before handing it over to Mark. There it was, a brief message thanking him for the drinks the night before and asking him not to go to the airport.

'What airline was she flying with?'

'KLM. There were two stops, Amsterdam and... I'm sorry, I can't remember the other one.'

Mark stood up. 'That's all right. Do you mind waiting here,

sir? I'm just going to get someone to check that she was on that flight. What is her first name?'

'It's Marianne.'

'And she used your surname?'

'It was on her passport, yes. She talked about going back to her own name but she renewed her passport only two years ago and decided to leave it as it was.'

'Thanks. I'll be back shortly.' Mark left the room and went downstairs to the main office.

There were two messages there for him, one from Karen and one from Suzanne. He screwed up both pieces of paper and threw them in the bin. He beckoned McPhee over. 'Robbie, I want you to call KLM and find out if Marianne Fitzwilliam was on a flight to Malawi, going through Amsterdam, on the fourteenth of June.'

Robbie nodded. 'Will do. Er, Mark?'

'What is it?'

'Your wife called. She sounded pretty angry.'

'OK, thanks.' Shit, he'd taken his pay slip out of his pocket and left it on the table. What had he been thinking? She must have found it. The phone rang; he was tempted to leave it in case it was Karen but thought better of it. He picked up the receiver, 'Mark Nicholson.'

'Is this some sort of retaliation?'

'What do you want, Suzanne?' He lowered his voice. 'I've told you it's over. Please don't call me again.'

'You destroyed my painting.'

'What are you talking about? What painting?'

She was crying now. 'I told you before, Mark. I don't remember scratching your car. I've said I was sorry. You've destroyed weeks of work.'

Mark shook his head. He didn't have time for this. 'Look, Suzanne. I have no idea what you're talking about. Please leave me alone.' He replaced the receiver and tried to put her out of his mind.

'Mark?' The interjection startled him.

'Yes, what have you got for me?'

'She wasn't on that flight, nor any other before or since. I got them to check.'

'Taking the initiative? Well done.' Mark got up from his desk then hesitated, wondering if he should check with Scrimgeour. It was probably best.

He should have known better. Mark blushed as Scrimgeour laughed in his face. 'What? You think that the body we found wasn't that of Julie Campbell but someone else completely? For fuck's sake, Nicholson. You're losing it. We have DNA evidence that it was her. No room for error there.' He held up his right hand to stop Mark saying anything else.

'No, Mark. I'm not entertaining it. It's a completely ludicrous idea. Tell the man to phone round all of his ex-wife's friends. She'll be off for a jolly somewhere.'

'For three months?' Mark didn't bother to hide his contempt.

Scrimgeour sighed. 'I don't know what's got into you lately. Your head's all over the place. What the fuck's going on?'

Mark avoided eye contact.

'You're not still seeing that woman's sister? I thought you were better than that.'

'It's over, sir. Over before it began, really.'

'It had fucking better be. I'm telling you, Mark. I'm this close to putting you on a warning.' He held his thumb and forefinger a centimetre apart.

Mark waited. 'Go,' said Scrimgeour. 'Get rid of the man, give him the usual platitudes and then get on with some detecting. All this supposition is just that. You have no evidence. Make sure someone checks out her bank accounts and the like.

But don't come to me again with any fairy stories. And don't mention your thinking to that man. We don't need him going to the press with your daft theories.'

Mark left Scrimgeour's office, subdued. He told Robbie to finish the interview, knowing even as he did so that Fitzwilliam would most likely complain at having been passed from one police officer to another. It would just be his luck if he turned out to be a lawyer. He gave Robbie instructions not to rile him any further and to find out what bank and credit cards his ex-wife had. Back at his desk he set about finishing his report. He'd just started when the receptionist phoned through.

'Your wife phoned again. She says you've to phone her immediately.'

'Right, OK. When did she call?'

'About five or ten minutes ago. Listen, Mark, I'd better warn you. She sounded really angry.' Mark put the phone down and swore. It'd be all over the station in an hour. He took out his mobile and switched it on: five missed calls. Fuck. He dialled Karen's mobile. She answered immediately.

'Karen? Are you all right?' He sounded irritated, he realised, and at first he thought that her furious response was because of this. He paused as an angry stream of words erupted from the telephone. Gradually he made some sense of them. 'Hang on. What letter? What are you talking about?'

Karen's voice was taut. 'You could at least have told me face to face. But to write me a letter, Mark. You are such a cowardly piece of shit.'

'Told you what? What are you talking about?' Even as he spoke, Mark's suspicions were growing. He guessed what was in the letter but waited anyway for Karen's reply. His stomach twisted; he felt sick. This couldn't be happening.

'About your fucking precious Suzanne. About how you can't live without her.' Karen started to cry.

'I'm on my way home.' He got up and started the walk towards the front door. The whole office, it seemed, turned to look at him. 'Family crisis,' he announced. 'I've got to go home. Tell Scrimgeour for me, won't you?' This last was directed at the desk sergeant as Mark left the building, shrugging on his jacket.

On reaching the house, Mark took a deep breath. How was he to get out of this? He opened the door as quietly as he could. There was no sound from any of the rooms. Surely Karen hadn't gone out? He made his way to the kitchen. It looked as though a battle had taken place. The table was overturned; the breakfast plates lay broken on the floor. There was a coffee stain on the wall. It hadn't been there long; the coffee was still seeping down the wall. Mark blew out his cheeks in a gesture of disbelief. This was so unlike Karen. There was still no sound from the house. It was beginning to feel eerie. He went into the dining room. Nothing. It was as neat as he'd seen it for some time. He looked around. On the mantelpiece was a large sheet of paper with the word 'Bastard' inscribed on it in large untidy letters. He lifted it up; behind it was the letter that had come for Karen that morning, a single sheet of A4 paper. Mark picked it up and started to read.

Dear Karen,

First of all, I want you to know how sorry I am about this. I have been trying to pluck up the courage to tell you for weeks now, but the time never seemed right. You see, I've fallen in love with someone else. Her name is Suzanne and we've been seeing each other for some time now.

Mark was bemused. It sounded as if the letter was written by... No, it wasn't possible. He glanced at the bottom of the page and there it was, half way down; his distinctive signature. Just that, no sign off, no other handwritten words. Mark felt the familiar rage boil up inside. This was the work of Karen's friend, Debbie. It had to be. He had thought he had seen her once when he was out with Suzanne and he'd worried about it for a few days, but when nothing was said, he had persuaded himself it was just someone who looked a bit like her. So it had been her after all and now the payoff had come. He wondered why now, why wait so many weeks? He turned back to the page to see what else was written.

I won't bore you with details of how we met. You have probably realised that I have not been happy for some time. I'm happy now. I've never felt this way about anyone before, Karen. It's as if Suzanne is my soul mate. We like the same things; we think the same way. I would die rather than lose her.

I know this will come as a shock to you but I feel that it's better if we make a clean break. It will be very hard for me but I think it's best if I don't see you or the children again. In time you will meet someone else and he can be the children's father. They're young; anything else would confuse them and they will soon forget me.

My solicitor will contact you soon to arrange the sale of the house.

Once again, Karen, I am sorry about this. I wish you and the children no harm.

Mark

Dizziness swept over him. He grasped the side of a chair

and lowered himself into it. The words seemed to mock him over and over. 'I'm sorry,' he whispered. 'Oh, Karen.' He groaned as he thought of the children. Damned by his own words. What would solicitors, judges, courts, make of such words? He imagined himself ostracised by his friends and colleagues. The deserting husband who couldn't even tell his wife that he was leaving but had to send her a letter, a cowardly letter. Debbie would answer for this. Bitch, she'd always had it in for him. And then it struck him. She'd only seen him, if indeed it had been her – he wasn't sure. But even if it was her, how could she know details like Suzanne's name? He felt cold. Only one person knew for sure. He ran to his car and set off. He would kill Suzanne for this.

Chapter Twenty-Three

Suzanne

I RESTED my head on the back of the sofa, the receiver still in my hand. He sounded so sure of himself when he said he didn't know what I was talking about. Perhaps I was wrong to blame him, perhaps I had forgotten to put the top back on the white spirit and it had somehow fallen over. I was lightheaded in a way I'd almost forgotten, confused, uncertain of what was real and what wasn't. I closed my eyes and wished for sleep.

I awoke with a start. Someone was banging on the door. I pressed my fingers against my forehead and swore. I wasn't in the mood for visitors. I ignored it but whoever it was wanted an answer. I hauled myself off the sofa and went to the door.

It was Mark. I opened the door. 'Not using your key this time?' I said.

His face was twisted with rage. 'I could kill you.' His voice was venomous.

I was already regretting letting him in. 'I've already apologised about your stupid car. I offered to pay for the damage, which by the way, I don't think I even did. It's me who should kill you. Weeks of work ruined.'

'I'm not talking about the car. The letter you sent,' he said, 'to my wife. How dare you send such lies to her?' He moved towards me, his fist clenched.

'I have no idea what you're talking about. But go on, hit me,' I goaded. 'It's what you want to do. It's in your blood after all. You're just like your father. You know you are.' I was furious at him for turning up here like this.

Mark raised his fist slowly. He towered above me, looking into my eyes. His fist moved and I flinched then sighed with relief as he punched the wall just above my head. I moved away from him. 'You should go.'

'Why did you do it?'

'I don't know what you mean.'

He was calming down. 'You didn't send the letter?'

This was getting boring. Against my better judgement I said, 'I need a drink. What about you?'

My heart was beating hard as we went into the living room. It was partly fear, but mostly I was excited to see him again.

Mark

Mark followed her, flattened by the jibe about his father. That had hurt. His teenage years had been rough. Depression had him in its grip and he had tried to kill himself; a half-hearted attempt with aspirins, which he had hurriedly thrown up, ten minutes after he had swallowed them. Deeply ashamed, he'd never told anyone. His stomach twisted and churned at the thought of it and his fear he might once again fall into despair.

He walked over to the window. It was raining outside, a slow light drizzle. Soft weather, the Irish called it. He watched the people below; they looked happy for the most part. No one hurried to get out of the drizzle. There were one or two umbrellas, but for the most part people strolled by. One couple huddled up together, but Mark suspected that was from desire rather than from the need for comfort. He dragged his eyes away and looked across the wide street to the tenements on the other side. In a flat directly across the road, a woman stood at the window, mirroring his stance. A man came and stood beside her and together they looked down, pointing at a dog that was chasing its tail. Mark turned away.

'Well?' said Suzanne.

'Karen received a letter this morning. It was typewritten, allegedly signed by me and told her about... about our affair. She's devastated.'

Suzanne put a hand on his arm. 'I swear to you, Mark. It wasn't me. I would never do something like that.' His arm burned where she had touched him. 'But now I have to ask you something.' She paused. 'Someone poured white spirit over one of my paintings. It's a commission; I'd been working on it for weeks. Was it you?'

He looked into her eyes. 'No.'

Suzanne

As soon as he looked at me I knew he wasn't lying. And there was this little niggle of doubt that I might have been responsible, though I was almost sure I wasn't. 'All right,' I said. 'I believe you. Now, show me this letter.'

I read through it in disbelief. 'Why would you think it was me who wrote this?'

He shrugged. 'No one else knew about us.'

'What about that person you thought you saw once, Karen's friend?'

'The letter mentions you by name. Even if Debbie did see you she couldn't know your name.'

A thought struck me. 'Is it possible Karen wrote it? Perhaps she suspected something and wanted it brought out into the open.'

'Again, how would she have known your name?'

He was right. It was very unlikely that either of them would know who I was. Although I was reasonably well known in artistic circles, I didn't flatter myself that I would be recognised by anyone else. I nodded, defeated. 'What are you going to do?'

'She'll probably be at Debbie's. I suppose I'll have to go round and try to patch things up.'

'You could always...' I stopped.

'I'm not leaving her,' he said. 'I won't leave my children.'

I didn't reply. He might think that but there was every possibility he would have no choice in the matter. After a few seconds in which we stared at each other I said, 'You need to go now. I hope it works out for you, Mark, but if it doesn't you can always stay here. No strings...'

He half smiled and nodded and then he was gone. I watched from the window as he ran to his car and prayed she wouldn't take him back.

Mark

Karen refused to see him. Debbie came to the door and stood there impassively. Her double chin quivered with rage as she spat the words at him. 'No, she's not going to speak to you. No, you can't see the children. You're a right bastard, Mark.' She leaned in towards him. 'Frankly, I'd cut off your fucking balls. Now, fuck off.'

He'd gone back to their house and drunk half a bottle of

whisky. Not a malt, not even a decent blend. Half a bottle of supermarket crap, which burned his throat as he tossed it down. He kept trying Karen's mobile but she'd turned it off. At one o'clock he gave up and crawled upstairs to his bed. He sprawled across it, not bothering to undress, and sobbed into the pillow before falling asleep half an hour later.

When he awoke it was already light and he realised he'd overslept. He felt grubby and unwashed and his hangover was beginning to kick in. He took out his phone and called the station, telling the duty officer not to expect him in. 'I think it's flu,' he said. 'I'll let you know.'

He crawled back under the covers and fell asleep again.

It was three o'clock before he woke up. The stubble on his chin was itching and he felt filthy. He went for a piss, noting the dark yellow colour. Serious dehydration. He drank straight from the tap, then turned on the shower, emerging refreshed ten minutes later. Downstairs he made himself coffee and toast, and having devoured that, he rummaged through the fridge to see what else he could find. He could have wept when he found some bacon. The ideal thing to make him feel better. He had just finished his second bacon sandwich when Karen walked in.

'I want you to leave,' she said.

He waited for her to go on but she said nothing more. Behind her he could see Debbie, hovering around the front door. Safety in numbers, he thought. 'Aren't we going to talk about this, Karen?'

'No.'

'It's over, you know, between me and Suzanne. I didn't write that letter. I don't know who did but it wasn't me.'

She waved this aside. Her eyes were dull. She looked tired and five years older. 'I don't care who wrote the letter. That's not the important thing, Mark. You slept with another woman. You spent money on her, money we don't have. Do you remember what I said when we moved in together?'

Mark looked at the floor. He remembered it well.

'You don't, do you?'

He rubbed his eyes. 'You said that the one thing you insisted on was stability, that you didn't want me coming into yours and Sophie's lives if I was just going to walk out a couple of years later. But I didn't! Don't you see? I chose you and the children.'

Her eyes narrowed. 'And I'm meant to be grateful for that, am I? The point, Mark, is that you should never have had a choice to make. You supposedly made that choice years ago, when we moved in together. There should never have been another woman in your life.' The tears were streaming down her face now and she could barely get the words out. 'It's over, Mark. You need to find somewhere else to live. I've already contacted a lawyer about money and access visits to the children. You can see them once during the week and have them every second weekend.'

'No! You can't do this, please, Karen. I'm sorry, I'm so, so sorry.' He was crying now too. The thought of not seeing his children every day tore him apart.

'You have until tomorrow to leave,' said Karen. She turned and walked away without looking back.

Mark sat on in the kitchen until it was dark. The house felt dead without the cries and laughter of his children ringing through it. This was a terrible mess he'd got into. Financially as well as emotionally. His savings had almost gone; they were barely managing on his salary as it was. And now he had to find money to rent a flat for himself. God knows what even the smallest flat would cost. He had no relatives to speak of and the few friends he had were all married. Their wives would never countenance having an unfaithful partner around their men. He shook his head as he took out his phone and dialled. This was a terrible idea but he didn't know what else to do. The ring tone stopped. 'Suzanne?' he said, 'I have a favour to ask.'

PART III
Penance

The safest and most suitable form of penance seems to be that which causes pain in the flesh...

Ignatius of Loyola

Chapter Twenty-Four

Mark

By late October Mark had reached the conclusion that it had been a mistake to move in with Suzanne. What was it his mother used to say? You didn't really know someone until you lived with them. How true that was. Suzanne was immersed in her work in a way he didn't understand. She'd spend hours in the bright south-facing room she called her studio, emerging from it late in the evening dazed and distant, her mind still on her work. Sometimes, when he tried to speak to her, she looked at him as if she didn't know who he was. If he mentioned his work she'd yawn. At least Karen had tried to look interested.

Karen hadn't been the best cook in the world but she put meals on the table and ate with him. He didn't expect Suzanne to cook for him; he was more than happy to do his share, but when she was working on a painting she'd go for hours without eating. If Mark made her something to eat she'd snarl: *Go away, I don't have time for this.*

And although the flat was twice the size of his house it felt too small for the two of them. Suzanne hated clutter and sighed loudly as she tidied away his socks or a cup he'd dared leave lying about. Huh, she should try living with three small children if she thought he was messy.

As for her insistence on watching every highbrow programme that there was... It was no joke, there were hundreds of them: documentaries, foreign films, operas. Every day of the week. It was exhausting.

He thought back to the first weeks and how he'd thought of her as his soul mate. Now he pined for Karen's less intellectually demanding chatter and a chance to talk about the latest episode of *Masterchef* or dissect the antics of candidates on *The Apprentice* rather than try to keep up with Suzanne's analysis of opera. He loved opera – well, those that had tunes – but the finer nuances were beyond him, and sometimes when they were discussing the merits of *recitatif* versus *opera seria*, he felt unreal, as though he was outside himself looking on. He didn't like what he saw. But, as his mother used to say, he had made his bed, and uncomfortable as it was, he had to lie on it.

He missed his children; their chatter, the funny things they said, the smell of them, the feel of their small, sturdy bodies as he carried them to bed. Their absence made him ache.

Today though, it was Oscar's birthday party, giving him a chance to see them all. An extra longed-for visit. The access visits were killing him, reminding him of how much he was missing. He smiled in anticipation.

'What are you looking so happy about?' Suzanne came into the room. He didn't answer. He hadn't told her about the party. But she didn't seem to be expecting a response anyway because she went on.

'There's an exhibition on at GOMA I thought we could go to see,' she said, passing the cafetière to him.

He shook his head. 'Sorry, I can't go, but you go and we'll meet for dinner.'

She frowned. 'I didn't know you were working today.'

'I'm not.' He cleared his throat and swallowed, dismayed at how nervous he felt. 'Actually it's Oscar's birthday party and I promised I'd be there.'

Her mouth tightened, emphasising the faint lines round her lips. 'At least take me with you,' she said.

'I don't think so, Suzanne.'

'Why not? It's time I met your children. Can't put off meeting the ankle biters forever.' She sipped her coffee.

He grimaced at her choice of words and stood up. 'Don't call them that. It's disrespectful.'

'You what?' Her face was ugly with anger.

He held up a hand. 'Leave it, Suzanne. You're not invited. End of. I'll see you later.'

Her response was terse. 'Fine.'

God knows how she knew where they were having the party. She must have followed him. When she spotted Suzanne, Karen turned to him, her voice brittle.

'Get her out of here, now!'

Mark muttered an apology and went towards the door, where Suzanne was standing with an amused smile on her face. He sidestepped her as she went to kiss him.

'What the fuck do you think you're doing?'

'Excuse me?' she said, arching her right eyebrow.

Christ, she behaved in such a fucking *entitled* way sometimes. He grabbed her elbow and pushed her towards the door, waiting until they were out of earshot of the other parents before saying anything else.

'What part of *no, you can't come* did you not understand?'

She stared at him, her eyes blank, before turning and leaving without a word. He stood at the door of the soft play area and watched as she went towards her car. There would be hell to pay later, but for now he had to get back inside and try to explain to Karen what had happened.

'Trouble in paradise?' she asked as he got near. There was a hint of *Schadenfreude* in her half smile.

'I'm so sorry, Karen. I didn't tell her where the party was and I told her specifically she couldn't come.'

'She *asked* to come? She actually thought she might be *welcome* here?'

'I...' He couldn't think of anything to say that would make things better but it didn't matter. She held up a hand up to silence him.

'I could kill her, you know.'

'You don't mean that, Karen.' He put out a placating hand, which she pushed away.

'Don't I? First her sister and that bastard John Allen. It was a bad day I met him, I can tell you. Between the two of them they ruined my life, and then when I thought I was back on track, Lady Muck comes along. At least Julie had the sense to kill herself. I wish they were all dead! Tell your fancy woman from me, that if I see her anywhere near me or my children again, I'll not be responsible for what I do.'

Out of the corner of his eye, Mark noticed the other parents looking at them with interest. 'I'll keep her away from you, don't worry. Come on, we'd better get back to Oscar's guests.'

It was late when he got back to Suzanne's flat. And it was *Suzanne's* flat, entirely her space. After the party he'd gone drinking with some friends from work and he felt better than he had for weeks. Relaxed, more himself. He let himself in quietly, hoping he wouldn't disturb Suzanne, but when he went into the living room the light was on.

'I thought you'd be in bed,' he said, sitting down to take off his shoes.

'Not likely,' she said.

Taken aback by the sharpness of her voice, he glanced at her. 'What the...?' he said. Her arm was in a sling.

'What happened? I honestly don't know. One minute I was walking along the pavement, the next a car was coming straight for me. I jumped out of the way and sprained my wrist in the process.'

She looked so frail sitting there that he forgot how angry he'd been. 'Are you all right? What can I do? Can I get you anything? Did you get the number of the car?'

'Woah, so many questions. I'm fine. It's a slight sprain, that's all. Fortunately, it's my left hand so I'll be able to work.' She smiled. 'I'm sorry. I shouldn't have come today, but I was just so angry.'

'Ssh, forget about it. Tell me about the car. Did you get a number? Have you told the police?'

She shook her head. 'It was a family car, like the one you had. Well, it was the same colour anyway. Silver. Don't know what make, sorry. I'm hopeless with cars. I think, but I'm not sure, that there was an X in the registration and it was quite old, registered in 2015.'

'And what did the police say?'

'Nothing. I haven't told them.'

Mark frowned. 'Why not?'

She shrugged. 'It was dark, there were no other witnesses. I don't know the make of the car. It was an accident. What can the police do with that? I don't want to waste their time.'

She was right. Without a registration number and with no witnesses, there was little they could do. He was furious though. Most likely the driver was pissed.

'Come to bed,' she said. 'It's after midnight. Time to sleep.'

Sleep was far from her mind though. Afterwards, Mark lay in bed, smiling. Perhaps things weren't so bad after all. Beside him, Suzanne muttered something.

'What was that?'

'The number of the car – I've remembered part of it: MX65.'

'Oh, OK,' he murmured in return. 'I'll write it down in the morning.' He turned over and went to sleep, the alcohol and the satisfying sex promising a good night's rest.

The next day Mark was back on shift. The police station was buzzing when he arrived. 'Scrimgeour's called a meeting,' said Robbie as he passed his desk.

'What's up?'

'There's been a murder, sir,' said one of the new recruits to the force, a boy of about twelve. Mark had never believed the hype about 'policemen getting younger' until he met this year's lot. Fourteen-year-olds – the lot of them.

Mark raised his eyebrows at one of the not so young police officers, Jane. 'Taggart lives on,' he said and they burst out laughing. The boy looked at them, baffled. Scrimgeour walked into the room and glowered at them all.

'Murder is no laughing matter,' he started to say and stopped, furious at the sight of Jane and Mark trying to hold themselves together.

'Sorry, sir,' gulped Mark. 'I...' He stopped, unable to think of any reasonable excuse.

'Save it. Let's get started.'

Mark studied the carpet tiles at his feet, reluctant to look up in case he caught Jane's eye and it started him off again. He barely listened as Scrimgeour outlined the case for them. With an effort he concentrated, exclaiming when he finally focused in on what his boss was saying.

'Sorry, sir, could you just repeat that last sentence?' Scrimgeour glared at him. Shit, he'd pay for his inattention later.

'Forgotten to bring your brain with you this morning, have you? The body of a man has been found on Glasgow Green, battered to death. There's nothing on him, no car keys or wallet, so he was most likely mugged. Our priority is to identify him.'

'Most likely a junkie,' muttered someone at the back. 'Waste of time, if you ask me.'

Scrimgeour looked up from his notes. 'Who was that?'

Silence. Mark noticed that one of the new recruits was blushing but it didn't necessarily mean it was him.

'Let me make this clear,' said Scrimgeour. 'We work for everyone, from the poorest people to the richest. We do not discriminate; we work as hard to help a homeless person if they're the victim of a crime as we do for anyone else. Is that understood?'

Mark managed not to roll his eyes. It was a laudable sentiment and one in which he strongly believed, but everyone knew that in practice, those who shouted loudest got the best service. And somewhere along the line, the poor and the dispossessed had lost their voices. He mumbled, 'Yes, sir,' along with everyone else.

'However,' Scrimgeour continued, 'the victim is unlikely to be a junkie or a homeless person. He's in his mid to late forties, well dressed, expensive suit – Armani – no less, polished shoes.'

'Dealer?' asked Robbie.

'Well, we can't rule that out, certainly. But for now we'll concentrate on missing persons. See if any match his description. Mark, I'd like you to go through the latest list. Robbie, Megan, phone round all the taxi firms and find out if anyone dropped a man in his forties off at Glasgow Green last night. He has to have got there somehow. Get the addresses of where he was picked up from.'

'If he came by car, it'll likely have a ticket by now,' said Mark. 'Perhaps someone should check up on any parking tickets issued in the area.'

'Good point.' Scrimgeour allocated the task to two of the newbies. 'Right, we'll meet back here at four thirty for an update. Get cracking.'

Back at his desk, Mark opened up his computer ready to search the database of missing people. It always depressed him. So many lost souls, so many families left in limbo, wondering what had happened to their dad, their brother, their daughter. Some were high profile, their families unable to let go. They filled Facebook with appeals to come home and posted messages on the timeline of their lost one. Others were sucked into a vacuum of hopelessness, accepting that the person was gone for good, waiting for the knock on the door to tell them a body had been found, matching their description.

He shuddered; best get on with it. He'd start with those reported missing in the past twenty-four hours. Around a hundred people vanished every day in Scotland, a handful of them in Glasgow. Across the United Kingdom as a whole, two people disappeared every minute. It was a horrifying statistic, although of course most of them turned up safe and well.

Mark skimmed the first three reports: a fifteen-year-old girl who had left her foster home the day before to go to school but hadn't turned up; an elderly woman who went out shopping and didn't return; another teenager. Nothing there. He scrolled down to the next one and read it without really taking it in. Robbie was talking loudly in the background, showing off to the new recruits, beefing about Scrimgeour. Mark shook his head; he'd have his bollocks for lunch later.

'OK, let's see. Where was I?' he muttered. He read through the last report for a second time. '*Mrs Allen phoned in to report her husband missing. He went out on Friday evening and didn't return home. Says it's not in character but when pressed, admitted he'd gone out on the tiles several times before. Mr Allen is medium build, six feet, late forties. Advised wife to phone again Monday if he did not return during the weekend. No further action at present.*' It was impossible. Surely it couldn't be John Allen, Karen's ex? He looked at the address given. Fuck. There it was: The Old Barn, Millhouse Farm, Milngavie.

Mark leaned back in his chair, his heart racing. John Allen. It must be a coincidence. Yes, that's what it was. There was no firm evidence as yet to link him with the poor soul found dead on Glasgow Green. He closed his eyes. Who was he kidding? The links were all there. A man was dead on Glasgow Green, battered like that woman in Julie Campbell's confession. A coincidence? He didn't think so. But what did it mean? Julie Campbell was dead and her ashes left at Linn Crematorium. She couldn't have murdered him, so who had? He swallowed hard as he thought about Karen. Was she involved? Two days ago he would have laughed at the suggestion, but he thought back to her face when Suzanne had turned up at Oscar's party. It was murderous. And the venom in her voice when she spoke about Julie and 'that bastard I married' and how she wished they were all dead, including Suzanne. No, it wasn't possible that she had anything to do with this. Something was niggling him, but try as he might he couldn't bring it to the front of his mind. A ping alerted him to an update on the missing persons' database. Please let it be another middle-aged man. He looked at the screen. No such luck. An update on John Allen. His wife had phoned again to say he was still missing. He put his head in his hands.

'You OK there, Mark?'

He forced a smile. 'Think I had some dodgy prawns in my sandwich at lunch time. I'll be fine.'

Jane laughed. 'They were well dodgy. They looked like ham to me.'

Mark got up. 'I'll need to go and check something. If Scrimgeour asks, tell him...'

Jane's laughter changed to concern. 'You look awful. Go home. I'll cover for you.'

'Thanks, Jane. I'll see you tomorrow.' He ran to the door, pushing his arms into his jacket sleeves as he went. The thing that had been niggling had forced its way into his mind. He wished it hadn't.

He'd have to tell Scrimgeour about Karen's relationship with John Allen if he was the dead man. It was bound to come out that they'd been married. Fuck, fuck, fuck. He should have disclosed that information when he'd had the chance. What a mess. But before he spoke to Scrimgeour he had to see Karen and find out what was going on.

Chapter Twenty-Five

Mark

THE HOUSE WAS quiet when Mark approached it. No screams from the children, no sounds of chatter, no balls bouncing along the scuffed laminate floors. The life had been sucked out of it. Mark rang the doorbell. It rang out in the hall; funny how you could always tell when a house was empty. He wondered where they were. It was almost five o'clock; they should be in, having their tea. He prayed Karen hadn't made it up with her father now she'd kicked Mark out. He couldn't bear to think of the old man spouting his hatred at them.

If she was in, she wasn't answering the door. He tried his key but the lock had been changed. His neighbour from across the road, an elderly man called George, stood at the edge of the driveway.

'You all right there, son?'

Mark nodded and bent down to pick up a piece of litter. He had no idea whether or not anyone knew about him leaving but they most likely did.

'She's not in. Probably round at that pal of hers. You know the one. Her with the mouth on her like a sewer. And her with wee weans an all. I told her that – she didn't like it one wee bit.'

Mark interrupted him before he could get on to his favourite subject of how women weren't feminine any more. He'd had to listen once too often to tirades on the subject. 'Oh yes,' he lied. 'I'd forgotten she said that's where she'd be.' He got into his car, hoping George wouldn't start interrogating him. For once he was lucky. A passing dog walker was allowing her Labrador to shit in the gutter and George moved away to tackle them. As Mark drove off he heard George's plaintive voice telling the woman just what he thought of her. In vain she showed him the little green plastic trowel and bag she'd been going to use. He was in full flow and not to be interrupted. One day he'd pick on someone who'd take a punch at him.

Debbie's house was in Mosspark. She had a chip on her shoulder about living in what she called a 'scheme', although in reality the council houses that had been built in the nineteen thirties were solid and would outlast their own recently built house in Crookston. Even in the rain that made most parts of Glasgow look grim, the area looked welcoming. Most gardens were well kept. Some were tasteful and restrained; others, like Debbie's, were a riot of colour. Mark looked closer at the flowers climbing up a green plastic trellis in Debbie's front garden. He touched one; it was some sort of firm unyielding fabric. He shook his head as he walked on up the red gravel path. The rain started to come down in torrents and he ran up the last few steps to the porch. He shook his rain-soaked fringe away from his eyes; time to get a haircut. He pressed the doorbell; had it rung? He wasn't sure so he tried again.

'Coming, coming.' It was Karen's voice. She opened the door and laughed at the sight of him before she remembered she hated him.

'What do you want?'

'To talk.'

'Bit late for that now, isn't it?'

'Is Debbie in?' He had no intention of talking to Karen in front of her.

'What's it to you?'

He stared at her and she gave in. 'No, but she'll be back soon. She's taken all the kids out to the soft play area.'

Mark moved further in, away from the rain. She recoiled, held the door in front of her as if it was a shield. She must really hate him. 'It's important, Karen.'

She opened the door and let him in.

'Debbie's been decorating again, then?' Mark looked round the small living room, which was dominated by a 'statement wall' covered in a wallpaper patterned with large black and pink flowers.

She wasn't going to be tempted to slag off Debbie's decorating skills. 'What do you want, Mark?'

'A man's been found dead on Glasgow Green.' He watched for her reaction. Nothing.

She shrugged. 'And?'

'We're trying to find out who it is. There was nothing on him to identify him.'

'Why are you telling me this?' Either she was a very good actress or she knew nothing about it.

He sat down on the over-stuffed leather sofa. 'John Allen has gone missing. His wife phoned it in on Saturday and again today.'

Her face paled then reddened. Tears came to her eyes and she bent her head quickly in an attempt to hide it. He'd swear she knew nothing. He waited for her to compose herself. After ten seconds or so she lifted her head and spoke.

'Are they sure it's him?'

'No, I wanted to see you first before setting things in motion.'

She frowned, 'What things?'

This was the difficult part. Mark reached out to take her hand and winced as she snatched it away.

She glared at him. 'What things? Tell me, Mark.'

'Well, I have to report back to Scrimgeour about whether any of the missing men I've been looking at could be the dead man on the Green.'

'You mean you haven't already told them? Why not?'

Exasperated, Mark puffed out his cheeks. 'Karen, think for a minute. We have two dead bodies here, Julie Campbell and John Allen. Both with links to you.'

'So?'

She was going to make him spell it out. 'I'm sorry, Karen, but I have to tell them you were married to Allen. They're not daft. They'll see immediately that you have a motive.'

'Motive?'

'You said yourself that they had ruined your life, that you were glad Julie was dead. The other day you also said you wished John Allen and Suzanne were both dead.' He took a deep breath. 'Suzanne came in later that evening and said that someone had almost run her over in a car.'

'Shame about the "almost",' muttered Karen.

Mark continued as if she had said nothing. 'The car was a silver one, just like yours, and she has a partial registration, MX65.'

Karen stared at him, her eyes bright with fury. 'You're not

serious! You can't surely think... Get out. Now!' She got up from her seat and went to the living room door. She stood there, glaring at him. 'Fuck off, Mark.'

Mark rose from his seat. 'I'm sorry, Karen, but if the body is John Allen's, I'm going to have to tell the boss about your relationship with him.'

'Do what you want. You always do.'

Back at the station, Mark went through his list over and over again. There was only one missing person who fitted the profile of the dead man and the sooner he told Scrimgeour the better.

Mark was so nervous he forgot to knock before going into Scrimgeour's office. He was sitting at his desk, eyes shut. When he opened them, Mark saw the glint of tears.

'What do you want, Mark?'

'Is everything OK, sir?'

Scrimgeour shook his head. 'Your parents are both dead, right?'

'Um, yes. Years ago.'

'I never thought I'd say it but I wish my mother was dead.'

Mark waited.

'You know my mother has Alzheimer's, right?'

'I had heard, yes.'

Scrimgeour gave a wan smile. 'The office grapevine. More reliable than the *Herald*.'

Mark started to reassure him. 'It's not gossip, sir...' but stopped as Scrimgeour waved a hand at him.

'I know, I know. People are sympathetic; they know what it's like. But they don't, not really.' He massaged his forehead. 'She tried to strangle one of her carers today. That's it for home care. She'll be in a nursing home before the end of the week.'

Mark chose his words with care. 'It's not your mother who's done this. It's the disease.'

Scrimgeour raised an eyebrow, 'You always were a smooth talker, Mark. You'll go far.' He sat up straight in his chair as if sloughing off his cares. 'Now, what can I do for you? Have you found the identity of that man yet?'

Mark ran his tongue nervously round his lips before he started to explain.

'So, let me be sure I've got this straight. You think the body is John Allen's, the ex-husband of Julie Campbell. And at the same time you're telling me that Karen was also married to him?'

Mark nodded, not trusting himself to speak.

'I can't get my head round this. Tell me again why you didn't let me know of Karen's connection to Julie Campbell.'

'I only found out about it once the case was closed, sir.' Mark didn't want to lie but he wasn't going to let on that he'd known about it while he'd been working on it.

'When was that?'

'Um, a few weeks ago.'

'And how did you find out?'

Christ, this was what you got for lying. The more he said, the worse it was. There was nothing for it but to brazen it out. 'You know Karen and I are separated?'

'Yes, I heard, and I have to say, Mark, I know it's none of my business but you're making a real mistake there.'

Mark half smiled. Yesterday he'd have agreed, but after last night... 'Mm, well anyway, it all came out round about that time.' Well it was true, sort of.

'You should have told me as soon as you found out.'

'I'm sorry. You're right of course, but the case was closed by that time and I didn't see it as relevant. And I had other things on my mind.'

'You're a fucking eejit at times.'

Mark didn't reply.

'Ah well, no harm done, I suppose. Although...' The cogs were beginning to turn. 'It won't look good for Karen, if this bloke does turn out to be her ex. Two dead bodies in the space of less than four months and both with a connection to Karen. A strong, emotionally upsetting connection at that.'

Mark shifted in his seat. He ought to tell Scrimgeour about Suzanne's near miss with the car last night.

Scrimgeour frowned. 'There's something you're not telling me. Spit it out.'

Mark's mouth was dry. 'It's probably nothing...'

'But?'

Mark told him, finishing with, 'It's only a partial match to Karen's car. And also, Suzanne wasn't sure of the number. Not at all.'

Scrimgeour's fingers were drumming on his desk. 'OK. First things first. We'll have to get Mrs Allen in to see if she identifies the body as her husband's.'

Mark sent Megan and Robbie over to Mrs Allen and arranged to meet them all at the morgue. He hated viewing dead bodies with relatives and always tried to get out of it. He'd hoped that the boss would let him opt out, given the possible connection to Karen, but when he had suggested it, Scrimgeour passed it off with a wave of his hand. 'Time enough for worrying if it does turn out to be our man Allen. But for the time being, we'll assume it isn't.'

Lynn Allen looked small and tired. Her eyes were rimmed with red, though she wasn't crying. She squinted at Mark. 'I know you, don't I? Have we met before?'

'Yes, we have. In connection with the death of Mr Allen's ex-wife.'

'Oh, yes of course. I remember now.'

'I'm sure my colleagues have told you that the description of the body matches that of Mr Allen. We'd like you to look at the body. Is that all right?'

She nodded. 'Can we get it over with, please?'

'I'll just be a minute or two.' Mark wanted to ensure the body was in a fit state to be identified. The last thing he wanted was Mrs Allen looking at some ghastly wound. He checked with the mortician on duty and came back to her. 'Were can we go now.'

They walked down to the viewing room in silence, Lynn Allen's high heels clicking on the tiled floor. Mark paused before they reached the viewing room. 'Are you ready? You will see the body through a window. We don't actually go into the room where the body is.'

Mrs Allen nodded and they went in.

When the sheet was drawn back Mark wasn't sure it was him. There were similarities but he wouldn't have been able to swear it was John Allen. He looked smaller, a shrunken version of himself; the cockiness and confidence that had marked him out were gone. But Lynn Allen knew at once. 'Yes, that's him.'

Mark had been afraid of hysterics. Like many men, like many people, he found other people's grief hard to bear. But there were no tears here. They had, it seemed, all been shed elsewhere. 'I'm so sorry,' he said. 'Is there someone you can call?'

Lynn shook her head. 'I don't want anyone. Can I just go home?'

'Yes, of course.' He hesitated. 'But at some point we will have to interview you—'

'What! You think I did this?'

'No, no.' Mark hurried to reassure her. 'Of course not. No, it's routine... We need to know if he had enemies, where he was going when you last saw him, things like that.'

'Oh, I see. Right, let's do it now, get it over with.'

'We can't do it here. We can do it at the station, or at your home if you like.'

'No.' She shook her head. 'Not at home. My mother is there with Orlando. I don't want to risk him overhearing anything. I suppose it will have to be the station. 'Well, if you're sure.' Mark radioed the station to say the body had been positively identified and that he was coming back with Mrs Allen to interview her.

Scrimgeour met them as they came into the station. He gave his condolences to Mrs Allen. 'I understand you want to get the interview over as soon as possible. Are you sure there's no one you want to call? This must be very stressful for you.'

'I'll be fine.'

Mark and Scrimgeour exchanged glances.

'Well, if at any time it becomes too much, please say and we'll stop. DS Nicholson will take notes and write up your statement for you to sign. Do you understand?'

'Yes. Please, just get on with it.'

'We'll start with when you last saw your husband.'

'Friday evening. He got a text about seven thirty and said he had to go out.'

'Did he say who it was from?'

She shook her head. 'No, he never told me anything. But I know who it was from.'

"What? Who was it?' Mark heard the excitement in Scrimgeour's voice. What a breakthrough.

'His first wife, Kaye.'

Mark tensed, sensing Scrimgeour's bafflement. He'd heard people talk about blood rushing from their head, leaving them disoriented and dizzy. Scrimgeour's voice sounded as though it was coming from a long way away. 'How do you know this?'

'He left his mobile on his desk while he was showering. I knew immediately it was a woman. He always showered if he was meeting one of his "fuck buddies".' She paused, blinking to try to hold back tears. Her clenched fists betrayed her rage. A tear escaped from the corner of her eye. 'And he was singing in the shower too. A sure sign he was on to a good thing.'

'And you saw the text message?'

'Yes, it said "Call me", and it was signed Kaye.'

Scrimgeour stood up. 'I'm so sorry, Mrs Allen. Will you excuse us just for a second, please? Mark, a word.'

Mark followed him into the corridor.

'I thought Karen was this bloke's first wife? Who's this Kaye, then?'

Mark hesitated only for a second. There was no point in trying to bluff, 'It's... it's what Allen called Karen. Just her initial.'

'What the fuck! Karen's been meeting him?'

'I don't see how she could be, Sir. I...'

'Can you give her an alibi?'

Mark looked down at his feet. He shook his head.

'No, of course not. You're too fucking busy screwing elsewhere.' Scrimgeour leaned against the wall and sighed. 'I'm sorry, Mark. We're going to have to bring her in. You're off the case. No.' He held up his hand in front of him. 'I don't want to hear a word. Get one of the PCs in to the interview room so I can finish with this before seeing Karen.'

Mark opened his mouth to speak.

'No, I said, not another fucking word. Don't send that McPhee bloke though. We don't want him leaking everything to that hack of a brother of his.'

Mark asked if he could observe the interview and to his surprise Scrimgeour agreed. He went into the observation room before they brought Karen in. Mark's main thought was for his children and who was looking after them. Almost as if he could read his thoughts, Scrimgeour came to reassure him.

'Karen's here now. The children are being looked after by her friend. Debbie? Is that her name?'

'I should be with them.'

'I want you here. An extra pair of eyes. My gut feeling is Karen has nothing to do with this.'

Mark said nothing, thinking of the fury in Karen's eyes when she spoke about Julie Campbell.

Scrimgeour studied him, his face serious. 'Is there something you're not telling me?'

'What? Oh no, it's nothing. Just worried about the kids.'

'Hmm. OK, Bob will be leading this interview and Jane will be there too. Neither of them knows Karen, is that right?'

Mark nodded.

'Right, I'm going to observe too.' Scrimgeour settled into the only chair in the room.

They waited, the door half open. Bits of conversations hovered in the air: *battered to death... Nicholson couldn't be involved, could he... alibi... aye, they've got three weans but the eldest isn't Mark's... did you know he's left her, screwing the sister of the woman that was found in Newlands*. Mark stood there rigid, listening to the gossip and unable to meet Scrimgeour's eye. On and on it went until he wanted to scream at them to stop. He'd never live this down. Had he somehow brought this on himself by having an affair with Suzanne? He went to the door. 'I'm sorry, sir. I don't think I should be here. I'll be through in the office if you need me.'

Scrimgeour didn't try to stop him. He was lost in thought, making notes with a stub of a pencil that looked as though it came from Ikea. Mark knew he'd be noting down questions that had to be asked. No doubt he'd phone them through if he thought Bob and Jane weren't doing a good enough job.

Mark kept his head down, trying not to notice how everyone stopped talking when they saw him. It was all he could do to keep upright. He sat down knowing he should catch up with some paperwork, but all he could think about was Karen.

'DS Nicholson?' It was one of the new recruits, a young lad whose name he couldn't remember. 'DI Scrimgeour wants to see you.' When Mark didn't immediately get up, he coughed. 'He says you've to get there right away.'

Mark smiled. 'You mean he told you to tell me to get my arse into gear?'

The constable's rueful grin said it all.

Scrimgeour was standing at the window, with the light behind him. Mark wasn't able to make out the expression on his face – all he could see was his silhouette. 'Sit down, Mark.'

Mark took a seat but Scrimgeour remained standing. 'We've released Karen. She has an alibi for the time of John Allen's murder. We won't be taking things any further. I'm only sorry we had to question her at all, but it was inevitable because of the connection.'

Mark closed his eyes and thanked a God he didn't believe in. 'What about the text, though?'

'It was from an unregistered phone, nothing to connect it with Karen. And it was signed K – could have stood for anything, Kenny, Kieran, Katy.'

'And the alibi?'

Scrimgeour didn't look up. 'She was out with a friend.'

'Debbie? I'm not sure I'd trust her.' What was he saying? He should be pleased Karen was no longer under suspicion, but that look on her face...

'Not Debbie, no.' Scrimgeour paused. 'You didn't know?'

'Know what?'

'She's got a new man. A personal trainer. She met him at the gym. And that's where she was when her ex was being murdered. Well, there and then at the new man's house.'

Mark felt as though he'd been kicked in the balls. A personal trainer? He'd known one once; the man used to boast that he'd get women into shape and then he'd screw them. And now Karen was falling for the same shit.

'You OK?'

'Aye, fine.' He wasn't going to talk to Scrimgeour about his problems.

'It's just, you look a wee bit green about the gills there.'

Mark's smile was tight. 'I said I'm OK, didn't I? Karen's a free woman – she can see who she wants.'

'That she can, that she can.' Scrimgeour moved away from the window towards him. 'I think you should take a few days off, Mark. Let the heat die down. I did my best but you know what the station's like.'

'I'd rather work.'

'It's not a suggestion, Mark. I'm ordering you. You need to sort yourself out. Speak to Karen.'

'I've nothing to say to her.'

Scrimgeour raised an eyebrow. 'You have children to think of. And yourself. Don't try to kid me that it means nothing to you that she's seeing someone else.'

Mark opened his mouth to object but instead came out with, 'How long do you want me to take?'

'You have eight days leave left. Take the rest of the week off; you'll still have enough to take some time at Christmas. We'll manage without you.'

Suzanne wasn't in when he arrived at her flat. He didn't think of it as home. He knew he ought to go and see Karen, but she'd likely throw something at him after the day's events. Instead he poured himself a large Bowmore and settled down to see what was on TV. The usual daytime rubbish: self-righteous programmes about scammers and scroungers, thrown in with programmes about property, the great British obsession. It was like being force fed the *Daily Mail*. Eventually he found something to watch on Netflix, a thriller he'd missed when it had been on the BBC. He lay back on the sofa and tried not to think about work. But it was hopeless. His thoughts returned to Karen. How could he have doubted her? She'd be angrier than ever with him. He switched off the television, unable to concentrate on the complicated plot, and picked up the novel Suzanne had left on the sofa. He recognised it as being on the Man Booker short list but only because a sticker on the front announced it. He opened it and started to read. Fifteen minutes later he was asleep.

Suzanne

I was in a good mood when I let myself into the flat. A meeting with prospective clients had gone well and they had commissioned a painting of their favourite view. A somewhat clichéd one of Arran, but I knew I could do it justice and I was keen to start on it. But the sound of snoring coming from the living room stopped me. It was dark outside and there had been no light on. I opened the door and switched on the main light. The brightness woke up Mark. He looked at me with bleary eyes.

'I thought you were working late tonight.' My voice was unwelcoming, and not for the first time I thought that perhaps him living here was not such a great idea.

'Nice to see you too.'

I wasn't in the mood for banter. A quick look round the room showed me one hell of a mess. An open bottle of whisky (mine of course), an empty glass on the side table and a half-eaten sandwich on the arm of the sofa. And his feet with shoes on were on the sofa. I grabbed the sandwich and threw it into the wastepaper basket, swiping his feet as I passed.

'Hey!' he protested. 'Watch it.'

'Don't put your filthy shoes on my sofa,' I said. 'And use a fucking plate.' I turned on my heel and marched out of the room.

In the kitchen I leaned my head against the window and stared out. This was my safe place, my haven, but more and more the flat didn't belong to me. How had I got myself into this position, with this man, who after all, I barely knew, squatting in my flat? I had only ever lived with one other person after leaving home and that too had been a disaster. I was destined to be alone, or perhaps it was just that I had been on my own for so long that it had become my default position. I sighed and went over to the sink to fill the kettle. I'd have to make the best of it, at least for now.

'Tea or coffee?' I called.

There was no reply. No doubt he was sulking. I made a pot of tea and took it through to the sitting room with one cup. He could get his own if he wanted it. I pushed open the door to see him sitting on the sofa, head in hands.

'What's up?'

'Karen was questioned at the police station.'

'Why?'

'Her ex-husband was found dead on Glasgow Green.'

I said nothing for a moment. I hadn't known Karen had been married before. Mark never talked about her. 'What happened?'

'He was beaten to death.'

'Shit.'

'The thing is, Suzanne, there's something I need to tell you.' He paused. 'Karen was once married to John Allen.'

I frowned. 'Isn't that the name of the man married to Julie?'

Mark nodded and then told me about Karen.

Mark

Suzanne's reaction puzzled Mark. She had closed up completely when he'd told her about Karen being married to John Allen. He'd gone on to tell her how Karen had been questioned, and she'd listened, seemingly taking it all in, but had said nothing. Only when he admitted he'd been sent home from work, told to take the rest of the week off, did she react.

'You're going to be hanging about here all day?'

Mark clenched his fists. 'What else do you expect me to do?'

'I don't know. Can't you go away somewhere? I have work to do and I can't, I won't be disturbed while—'

'I'll be quiet.' He attempted a smile.

'No, Mark. It's not good enough. I've just agreed a commission worth forty k. I have to get on with it.'

Mark got up from the sofa. 'Fine. I'll make sure I'm out tomorrow.' He thought she might demur, but instead she said, 'You do that.' He left the room before saying something he might regret.

Chapter Twenty-Six

Mark

MARK HAD NEVER THOUGHT he'd miss work so much. He left Suzanne's flat before ten o'clock without saying goodbye. She'd probably not noticed he'd gone. He walked along to Kelvinbridge Art Gallery and Museum and spent a couple of hours there before going to the café for lunch. When he came out it was raining. Fuck. A woman passing with two small children, glared at him. Fuck, he must have said that aloud. He couldn't be bothered apologising, though he knew he should. Instead he swore again, but more quietly. 'Fuck, fuck, fuck, fuck, fuck.'

What was he going to do now? Suzanne had told him he could come home at seven. 'I just need you out of the house during the day.' Christ. Only six hours to go.

He was stuck. He couldn't go to a hotel as he had no money. Suzanne had offered to lend him some but he wouldn't take it though she could clearly afford it. Forty grand for a commission! Fuck's sake. It was almost as much as he earned in a year, before overtime obviously, but still! Forty fucking thousand.

Damn, he needed to pay attention. He'd walked straight into a puddle and now one of his shoes was sodden. A car drove past, splashing him with water.

'Nae luck, mate,' a passing bloke called out to him. Mark ignored him, looking round to see if there was a bus coming. He was in luck, a McGill's bus, 17. He'd go and see Karen, apologise.

For the second time that week, he found himself outside his own house. He had his hand up to knock on the door when it opened.

'Go to hell, Mark.'

'Karen, I'm sorry.'

Her arms were folded in front of her, her mouth tight. 'I was questioned in connection with a murder, Mark. How do you think that makes me feel?'

He bowed his head, 'I know, I know. But—'

'Daddy, Daddy!' Oscar was pulling at his hand, pulling him inside. Mark looked at Karen. She shook her head and stood aside.

'I'll pick Sophie up from school, if you like.' Mark didn't want to leave. Playing with Oscar and Emma for the past hour had been heaven. He wanted to be part of his family again.

'No, I'll do it. I need some fresh air, clear my head.'

Left alone with his two youngest children, who were now playing quietly together in a corner of the tiny living room,

Mark gazed at his surroundings. Yes, it was small. Yes, it was shabby, but he'd been happy here. His stomach hadn't been in knots all the time. *You were bored, matey*, a voice niggled in his head. *Suffocated by domesticity. It wasn't for you.*

'Shut up!' He only realised he had said it aloud when Emma started to cry. Shit. He rushed to pick her up and comfort her. He sat on the sofa, soothing her, barely noticing his own tears coursing down his cheeks.

Karen had been adamant. There was no chance; she was seeing someone else. It was over. She wanted him out of her life. He'd betrayed her, first with Suzanne, then by telling the police about her link to John Allen. He could fuck off and die as far as she was concerned. For an hour he pleaded with her, wept as his children watched, subdued, Sophie sucking her thumb as she used to when she was younger. He hated himself.

'It's over, Mark. I could never trust you again. I'll contact my solicitors about giving you more access to the children but frankly I'd be happiest if I never saw you again.' Karen stood up, her eyes glinting with what? Anger, tears? Mark couldn't decide. He followed her to the door. She wouldn't look at him.

'Goodbye, Mark.' The farewell sounded final.

Mark stumbled out of the door. 'I'm sorry, Karen, about everything.' He crunched his way down the path. As he reached the gate he turned to give her a final wave but she was already inside. He pulled up the collar of his jacket against the driving rain and held his face up to the sky to let the rain wash away his tears.

Chapter Twenty-Seven

Mark

THE FOLLOWING week he was back at work, thankful to be away from the oppressiveness of Suzanne's flat but worried about the reception he'd get. It wouldn't surprise him if he was met with stony faces and recriminations about what he'd done. But it was yesterday's news. No one frowned, no one sniggered. A few people nodded and said 'hi'. It was as if it had never happened. He sat down at his desk and turned on his computer. Two hundred and fifty-three emails. He sighed and set to work.

It was after eleven before he raised his head. He'd rushed out without breakfast and his head pounded from the lack of coffee and food. A visit to the canteen was in order. He stood up and stretched, wondering at how good it felt to be back at work. As he reached the door, his phone rang. He'd thought about leaving it – he was entitled to a break after all – but then he remembered how poor his performance had been at work in the past few weeks. He strode over to the desk and picked up the receiver. It was Scrimgeour. He listened, disbelieving. 'Sorry, sir, what?'

'I said there's been a stabbing in Pollok Country Park. A young man on his way to work. He was due to start at six a.m. in the Vicky. Worked there as a porter.'

Saliva rushed into Mark's mouth. This time, there could be no mistake. This murder could not be dismissed as coincidence. He barely registered Scrimgeour's request to come to his office.

Scrimgeour was sitting at his desk when Mark entered the room. He waved a hand to indicate that Mark should sit.

'What do you make of this murder then? Any theories?'

Mark was hesitant. 'Well, it does seem rather a coincidence, sir.'

'I'll say it does.' Scrimgeour sounded strange. There was a lightness to his voice that could almost be called enthusiasm. He carried on. 'Well, surely you've more to say than that. Go on.'

'That's four murders in the past few months that have been remarkably similar to the ones Julie Campbell wrote about.'

Scrimgeour nodded. 'Go over all the similarities for me. Let's look at the hit and run first of all.'

Mark thought quickly. He had been over it all in his mind so many times. Where to start though?

'Well, sir. Julie Campbell goes into some detail in her confession about her passion for a young woman she calls Goldeneyes who she later murdered. There are three definite similarities here. Firstly, the method of killing is the same in both cases. Hit and run. Then there's the place. In the confession, Julie says it happened in King's Park Avenue. In real life, that's exactly where it happened. Well, near enough. King's Park Road is a continuation of the avenue. Finally, Daisy

Palmer's parents made a claim that she was being stalked. Exactly the same as in the confession. I don't think this can be coincidence.'

Scrimgeour was non-committal. 'OK. What about the old woman?'

'There are coincidences here as well. She'd been out shopping like in the confession, but in Asda not Morrisons. The method of death was the same – battered to death. Place was the same – in her kitchen in both cases. Of course we already have a suspect here.' Mark couldn't resist this dig. He was certain that the kid who'd been charged was innocent of murder. Scrimgeour didn't react.

'Mm. The John Allen case doesn't quite fit though, does it? Yes, it happened in Glasgow Green, but in the confession it's a woman who was killed.'

'It never really fitted. After all, someone was already in jail for that one and it was the only real murder. Everything else was fiction.'

'Up until now. This latest case? Talk me through it.'

Mark was exasperated. How much more evidence did there need to be to link these killings to Julie Campbell's confession? He said as calmly as he could, 'Once again, method, age and sex of victim and place are all the same.' He hesitated before adding, 'It can't just be coincidence.'

Scrimgeour swung round in his chair. He tapped at his desk with a pencil. 'So, what does it mean? Could Julie Campbell still be alive? We need to find out, Mark, and fast. If it gets out that these killings are in her confession...'

Mark sighed. 'I don't see how she could be. There's DNA evidence. No arguing with that. They matched hairs that were found in the hairbrush with one taken from the corpse.' He hesitated.

'There's a "but", isn't there?'

Mark puffed out his cheeks. 'It may be nothing, but there's that woman who was reported missing. She fits the age and description of the body we found and she lived next door to Julie Campbell. That's some coincidence.'

'Yeah. Remind me again what happened when we looked at her bank statements?'

This was a sticking point and the reason Mark had dropped the theory he'd held. 'Her credit and bank cards have continued to be used, so we had to close the case. Her ex-husband wasn't happy but we got him to look at CCTV footage from one of the places where she took out money and he agreed it could be her. The pictures weren't as clear as they might have been though.'

Scrimgeour ran his fingers through his thinning hair. 'You're right, it just doesn't add up. One thing's for sure though; there are too many coincidences here for comfort. I've got another theory for you to think about.'

'What's that, then?'

'Copycat killings, Mark. I think someone who has read the confession is playing a little game with us.'

'Do you think so?' Mark was astonished. 'That leaves quite a few suspects then.'

Scrimgeour looked at Mark with narrowed eyes. 'You reckon?'

Mark shrugged, 'Yeah. Why?'

'Don't you remember? I put a ban on anyone else seeing it after someone leaked to the press. Only five people have read that confession in full, including you and me. That makes us prime suspects. I hope you've got watertight alibis. I've already got the Assistant Chief Constable breathing down my neck about it.' Scrimgeour threw his head back and laughed at that, showing a fur coated tongue and a mouth full of metal. Mark tried to join in, but his laughter was forced. He was desperately trying to think where he'd been when these murders had been committed. Most likely he'd been home in bed. He'd check later.

First though, he'd have to tell Suzanne about this latest development.

Chapter Twenty-Eight

Suzanne

I PUT the phone down and went back to work but I couldn't get what he'd said out of my head. Copycat killings; was it possible? He was right about it being worrying. I hadn't imagined so few people had seen the confession. Somehow I thought it would have been more public. He made no mention of the fact that he'd allowed me to see the confession. Perhaps he'd forgotten, in which case I was safe. But I didn't like it. I didn't want the police coming round and questioning me. I had too much to lose. I sat in the sitting room fretting for an hour or so until I shook myself out of it and returned to the canvas I was working on.

It was several minutes later when I was engrossed in a preliminary sketch that the doorbell rang. I ignored it at first, concentrating on the hatching I was doing, thinking as I did it that I ought to draw more, but the ringing became more insistent. I put down my pencil and went to the intercom. 'Yes,' I said, not bothering to hide my irritation. No answer. I slammed the receiver down and went back to my studio. A few seconds later I heard someone at the door. I got up and walked towards the hall. There was a scuffling noise outside the door and I knew at once it was someone trying to break in. That idiot old woman upstairs must have let him in. 'Mark,' I shouted. 'Phone the police.' Somewhere in my mind I thought if I called out a man's name the intruder would take fright and flee and they did. The scuffling stopped. I ran along the hall, almost falling in my haste, pulled open the door and went out onto the landing in time to see a figure disappear downstairs and out of the close. I couldn't chase them because I didn't have shoes on, so I ran back inside and to the window. They were easy to spot, running down the street, which was quiet; a slender figure in a hooded jacket. It looked like a woman and there was only one woman I knew who'd want to break in.

Mark

'Don't be ridiculous, said Mark when Suzanne had finished her story.

'It was her, I'm sure of it. Who else could it be?'

'An opportunist thief?'

'Mark, it was Karen. You'll have to speak to her.'

'No way. Things are bad enough between us. If I go to her and accuse her of trying to break in, she'll go straight to her lawyer and I could lose access to the children.'

'I doubt that.'

'Doubt all you like. I'm not doing it.'

'Well then, I will.'

'You will not.'

'Try me.'

Mark sat down, unwilling to get into another confrontation with Suzanne. 'Suzanne, please. Look at the evidence. Karen would never break in anywhere. She has too much to lose and also too much respect for other people's property. You didn't see the intruder's face so it could be anyone.'

'Who else could it be though?'

'It'll be some drug addict, desperate for a fix. They were probably casing out all the flats here until someone let them in. They'd be looking for cash, something easy to sell.' He paused for a moment, 'What were they wearing?'

'Um, trousers, black I think, and a hooded jacket, one of those puffa jackets, dark green.'

Mark laughed, 'Definitely not Karen then. She hates puffa jackets, says they make her look like the Michelin Man.'

Suzanne half smiled. 'Oh, OK then, you've convinced me.'

'Do you want me to phone it in?'

'Sorry, what?'

'To report it.'

She shook her head, visibly calmer. 'Is there any point? There's no damage and nothing was stolen. It would be a waste of time.'

Thank heavens he'd calmed her down. Mark couldn't imagine what Karen might do if Suzanne confronted her with an accusation of having tried to break into her flat. She'd take it out on him, that was for sure.

'Any news on the copycat theory?'

'No, they're checking out everyone's alibis first.'

'Do you think it's a copycat?'

Mark shook his head. 'I don't know what to think. It's baffling. I really thought for a time that perhaps it was Julie, still alive—'

Suzanne interrupted him, her face white. 'You don't think she could be alive, do you?'

'No, the DNA evidence is that the body was hers. She's definitely dead.' He paused. 'You look worried.'

Suzanne laughed. 'No, it was just a bit weird when you said that... the thought that she might not be dead after all. It was as if...'

'As if what?'

'Oh, nothing. I'm being silly. Look, I've got to get on with my work. I've wasted too much time today. I'll be ready to eat at eight if you want to cook.'

Suzanne

Back in the room I used as my studio, I leaned against the wall and sank to the floor. I was horrified at the prospect that she might still be alive. Could it be? No, Mark was sure about the DNA and I made myself dismiss the thought. I had to calm down; I'd become too agitated at the thought and had almost given myself away. The words 'as if she was coming after me' had been on the tip of my tongue a moment ago, and who knows what would have come about if I hadn't stopped myself in time. There would have been questions: why did I think that, what had I done to make her want to come after me? I took a deep breath. No need to worry; she was dead and that was all there was to it.

Chapter Twenty-Nine

Mark

SUZANNE WAS STANDING at the front door waiting for him; she must have seen him from the window. She held up a quieting hand as he started to speak.

'The police are here. A DI Scrimgeour and a PC Livingstone.'

'Why, what is it?' A sudden fear gripped his stomach. 'Nothing's happened to the children, has it?'

Scrimgeour appeared behind her. 'No, Mark. Nothing's happened to the children or to Karen.' His voice had a dark edge to it. 'Mark, there are some questions I need to ask you about the murders of Mary McLeod, Daisy Palmer, John Allen and Donald Paterson.'

Mark blinked. 'I don't understand,' was the only thing he could say as Scrimgeour indicated to him that he should sit.

The interview lasted nearly an hour. At first Mark had difficulty taking it seriously and he jested with Scrimgeour, but as the questions progressed he started to wonder whether he should phone a lawyer. Knew that he should when his light hearted 'Do I need a lawyer?' hadn't met with a 'Don't be soft, man,' but instead a serious gaze and 'I'll leave that decision to you.' Shit. He thought about picking up the phone but then remembered the weasel-faced duty solicitor; no way was that man getting to know his business. So Mark went against his usually sound common sense and allowed Scrimgeour to interrogate him unimpeded.

It started gently enough. 'Where were you on the night of the twenty-sixth of August?'

'I don't know. You've caught me by surprise. With Karen, I suppose.'

'Sorry, Mark. We've already checked.' He reached into his briefcase and pulled out a sheaf of paper. 'We asked Karen yesterday and she said, and I quote, "Mark came in very late that night. About five a.m. He told me he'd been at work. I didn't believe him." Scrimgeour put down the papers. 'I asked her how she could be so sure of the date and she said she'd been keeping a note of all the times you were late. She was right not to believe you. You weren't at work that night. We'd already checked. You'd left the station at a little before eight p.m.'

Suzanne was rubbing her hands on her trousers. She seemed agitated, Mark thought. When she spoke, her voice was a whisper.

'I've just remembered, inspector. Mark was here with me.'

'That's not what you said earlier on.' Scrimgeour was dismissive.

'But I was here,' insisted Mark. 'Karen's right, I did come home at five in the morning. I was here with Suzanne and I'd fallen asleep and then the car wouldn't start.'

'Ah yes, the car. Let's see what Karen said about the car.' He read aloud. 'He didn't have the car with him. Said it had broken down. It was two or three days before he got it back.'

Scrimgeour put the paper down and fixed Mark with his gaze. Mark had never before realised that the boss had such blue eyes. He jumped as Scrimgeour said in a firm voice, 'Where was the car, Mark?'

'In the garage, getting fixed.'

'I'll need the name of the garage.'

Mark jumped up and left the room. He came back with an invoice in his hand. 'Here, receipt for repairs made, £337.46. Details and everything. There was a problem with the starter motor and it took two days to fix because they couldn't get hold of a part. Phone them – they'll tell you.'

'We will. Don't you worry.'

Out of the corner of his eye, Mark saw Livingstone leave the room, taking out his mobile as he did so.

Scrimgeour carried on with the questions. 'Tell us about the evening of the fifth of September when Mary McLeod was murdered.'

Mark thought for a moment. 'Nothing to tell. I was at work all day until after ten. For God's sake, I went out to the scene of that crime.'

'No one remembers seeing you at work that day from about two in the afternoon until ten or thereabouts.'

'I was in the back room, catching up with paperwork. I was on a roll, getting through a huge backlog. I didn't want to be interrupted so I just kept on going.'

'And you didn't take a break?'

'I had lunch, which took about ten minutes. It's as I said. I wanted to get it all finished.' He raised his voice. 'This is ridiculous.'

Scrimgeour wasn't listening. He glared at Livingstone, who had come back into the room. 'Well?'

'The garage confirms there was a problem with the starter motor and that they had the car for a couple of days.' He bent towards Scrimgeour and lowered his voice so Mark had to strain to hear. 'There were no marks or bumps on any part of the car, sir. They always make a note in case there's any come-back from the customer.'

Those words confirmed what Mark had been thinking. They actually believed he might have had something to do with the murders of three people. He barely registered Scrimgeour's next words.

'What were you doing when Donald Paterson was killed?'

'Who's Donald Paterson?'

'Don't mess with me. The man who was stabbed on his way to work last week.'

'Oh, that Donald Paterson.'

'Watch it, son,' Scrimgeour warned.

Mark made a gesture with his hands. It was an open movement; an attempt to draw Scrimgeour back on to his side. 'Sorry, that came out wrong. I'd forgotten his name. He was killed in the middle of the night, wasn't he? I would have been here, asleep. And before you ask, I was here when John Allen was killed too.' He stared at his boss. This was fucking unreal. He was sitting here in his own living room – well, Suzanne's living room, being questioned for murders he had not committed. It was time to attack. His fists were clenched. The time for being open was over. 'With respect, sir, this is all a waste of time. You've nothing to link me to these murders. Nothing.'

'You saw the confessions, Mark. You know what was in them. You agreed the other day that they could be copycat killings. Only five people saw the full confession with all its details. Everyone else has alibis. Everyone except you.'

His temper was rising. Well, let it rip. Maybe it was time to remind Scrimgeour of how intimidating he could be. He stood up to his full height and raised his voice.

'And you really believe that one of your officers is a killer?'

'You wouldn't be the first, son. Nor the last.'

Mark shook his head, a slow movement of disbelief. 'How could you possibly think it was me?'

Scrimgeour looked at Mark. A long knowing look that Mark returned at first, then, furious with himself, found he couldn't continue. His face reddened and he looked at his hands. 'That's in the past. And it was totally different from this.' He was aware of both Livingstone and Suzanne looking at him with interest. Damn Scrimgeour – this would be all over the station. He'd never live it down.

'Can we speak alone, sir?' Mark indicated the two other people with a nod of his head.

'Livingstone, Ms Yates, please wait outside.'

Scrimgeour waited until they were out of the room.'You nearly killed a man, Mark.'

'That was different.'

'We both know you can be violent.'

Mark felt the surge of adrenalin. It was going to be too late to control it. He forced himself to visualise a calming shade of blue and breathed deeply as the psychologist had taught him. He remained still for some moments; it would do him no good at all to lose it now. He had to stay focused. Eyes shut, he concentrated all his energies on remaining calm. After a minute or so, he opened his eyes. Time for another technique to help him cope. The broken record.

'That was in the past, sir, and was quite different.'

'I shouldn't have covered up for you.'

'It was in the past and quite different.'

'You knew what was in the confession.'

'In the past, quite different.'

'You have no fucking alibi, Mark.' Scrimgeour spat out the words.

'Past, different.' It was definitely working. Scrimgeour wasn't getting to him. Mark could see the man was wavering.

Scrimgeour shook his head. 'I don't know about this.' He thought for a minute and then seemed to relent. He carried on. 'I don't believe it's you, Mark, not deep down. I've spoken to a forensic psychologist and she agrees. Anyway, you've no motive as far as I can see.'

Mark bridled. 'You've been talking to a profiler about me?'

'Not a profiler, no. A forensic psychologist. And you're in the clear as far as she's concerned. She says these murders have been thought out and planned. Whoever it is likes to toy with authority, sees himself or herself as very superior to others. And most likely they're very intelligent, so that lets you off the hook.' Scrimgeour laughed.

Mark didn't like the crack about not being bright enough. Bloody cheek, but he ignored it. 'I don't understand, sir. Why has the enquiry suddenly taken this line?'

Scrimgeour got up then and brushed some crumbs off his trousers on to the floor. He wouldn't look Mark in the eye. 'I'm off now, Mark, to follow up what you've told me. I think we've enough to be going on with to take the heat off you, but you know the ropes – stay around, don't go disappearing on us.'

Mark went with him to the door. 'I have to know, sir. What's going on?'

Scrimgeour bent towards him and hissed, 'Maybe you have a powerful enemy, Mark. Think about it. Who have you annoyed?'

'There's no one, sir.' Mark was puzzled. Scrimgeour was getting at something; he wasn't sure what.

'Oh well, if you don't know, I can't help you.' Scrimgeour would say nothing else.

Then the truth hit Mark. Of course. Karen's father, the Orangeman and freemason. He had friends high up in the police. He looked at Scrimgeour. There was sympathy in his eyes. He was on Mark's side. Mark decided to take a chance.

'How many people know I'm under suspicion? I mean, is this going to be the latest gossip back at the station?'

'Just me and Livingstone, Mark.'

'So everyone knows then?'

'He's sworn to secrecy.'

Mark snorted. 'He doesn't know the meaning of the word.'

'You've got my word, Mark.' He lowered his voice so that Livingstone couldn't hear. 'I've never told anyone about that night. God knows why not. If it ever got out that I lied for you, my career would be over. And I've warned Livingstone.' Scrimgeour grinned. 'You're not the only one with secrets, you know.'

'I'm very grateful, sir.'

'And so you fucking should be.'

After they left Mark went back into the living room. Suzanne had disappeared, perhaps giving him some space. Well, he had a lot to think about. A malt whisky was in order. Suzanne had an excellent selection. He opened the door of the cupboard where the drink was kept, Caol Ila, Bowmore, Laphroaig. He poured himself a good measure of Laphroaig and sat on the couch to think about what might happen next. But it was the past that came to mind, the night when he had so nearly killed a man.

He had been in his twenties. A new recruit to the force. He'd just finished his degree at Glasgow Caledonian University and had joined the police. A long-held ambition realised at last. He wondered why it had taken him so long to join when he'd always been sure about what he'd wanted to do. But his mother had always been keen for him to get an education, and so when he got the chance to go to university he went for it. A social sciences degree, covering subjects he suspected he didn't really understand and which would be of little use to him in his new career. He worked hard and it was worth it; it earned him a place on the graduates' fast track programme. That wasn't necessarily an advantage. The other young police officers made that clear to him. Still, he was thick skinned or could be when it was needed, and he shrugged off the insults and jibes at his so-called intellectual pretensions. They were wary of him; it was a common complaint among the graduates. But he'd got over that, and after his induction at the police training college at Tullieallan he'd learned enough to keep his head down, take the insults and just generally fit in. He'd gone along like that for several months, and then there had been the Johnson case. Even now he hated thinking about it. A little boy had been reported missing by his parents. There had been the usual searches in the neighbourhood. Days passed and there had been no trace of the boy. Mark was sent to interview the parents, and as soon as he saw the father he knew he'd done away with the boy. He put his suspicions to the officers in charge of the case but no one took any notice. Mr Johnson put on a very convincing face as the distraught father. But Mark recognised the signs, saw in him the anger that had marked out his own father. He had spoken to Scrimgeour about it. To his credit, Scrimgeour had listened and had agreed to them interviewing the man together. They'd still not found the body at that point. Sitting now, over ten years later, Mark could still see the lies in the man's face as he'd told them of when he'd last seen his son.

'It was Saturday, around teatime. He'd gone out to play in the garden.'

'Yes, I see. Yet it was four in the morning before you reported him missing? Why the delay?'

'We were sure he'd just wandered off.'

'He's six years old, Mr Johnson. Nearly twelve hours is a long time for a child of that age to wander off. What did your wife say?'

'Oh, I didn't tell her he was missing until nearly midnight.'

'What?' Scrimgeour's face was a picture. 'That's not what your wife said.'

The two policemen had exchanged glances then. Mark could see that his boss had misgivings. He could barely contain his excitement as Johnson was cautioned and told that questioning would continue in the police station. His disappointment when he was told to stay behind in the house was huge until Scrimgeour had told him he was applying for a search warrant for the house and garden. 'I think we'll find that the boy isn't that far from home, Mark,' he'd said.

Mark had been there when they found the body in the garden, hidden under a huge pile of rocks that the Johnsons had told them was for a rockery they were building. Mark had always wondered if they would have got away with it for so long if they'd lived in a council scheme rather than a large Victorian detached villa, if they'd lived in Castlemilk rather than Old Cathcart. He'd driven back to the police station, his anger simmering, fury at injustices of all sort bubbling up to make him a veritable ratatouille of rage. He strode into the station and demanded to know where Johnson was. Before anyone could stop him he was in his cell, with his hand covering Johnson's face.

'I'm going to suffocate you. There won't be a mark on you, save the one round your neck from the tie that you hid in your shoes, which unfortunately wasn't found and which you used to hang yourself. That'll be the story, you bastard.'

Johnson had been semi-conscious when Scrimgeour had hauled Mark off him. Mark knew that it was the end of his career and turned his anger on himself. He stood facing the cell wall and started banging his head off the rough surface. He was nearly unconscious himself when Scrimgeour turned him round and punched him full in the face.

'Say nothing. I'll do the talking.'

Mark would never have believed that Scrimgeour would protect him in the way he had. The investigation was thorough, but no matter how hard the pressure, how many disbelieving looks there were, his story remained the same. Scrimgeour had entered the cell and had found Johnson beating up a police officer – just look at his face – nobody had laid a finger on Johnson. The man was a maniac; hadn't he killed his son and threatened his wife, who was a terrified victim of the man's physical and mental bullying? No matter how many different ways they asked the questions, the answers remained constant. Mark was given a formal warning for abandoning procedure by entering a cell alone; Johnson was given life for the murder of his son; Mrs Johnson continued to insist that her son had been abducted, but three days after the verdict she took an overdose of sleeping tablets and left a note blaming herself for everything.

After it was all over, Scrimgeour had taken Mark aside and warned him very firmly.

'We all get angry, son. Especially when there's a wean involved, but the law's the law and we never, repeat never, take it into our own hands. I'm giving you one last chance. You've got a temper all right and it'll be the death of you if you don't get it sorted. I want you to get counselling for it. Go and see a shrink, whatever. But get it sorted. Comprenez?'

Mark didn't need to be told twice. He knew how fortunate he'd been, so he got himself a psychologist. He'd been very lucky; they'd hit it off right away and he quickly learned to trust her. She was trained to use EMDR, eye movement desensitisation and reprocessing, if he remembered correctly. When she'd told him about it, he had laughed out loud; it had seemed so ridiculous that moving his eyes back and forwards following her moving finger would help him. So she had agreed to carry out conventional counselling for his traumatic past, all the time telling him that they could try EMDR when they were ready. After many long months they'd tried it. She instructed him to think about the incident where his sister had been thrown downstairs, and while he was thinking, he followed her fingers as they moved rhythmically in front of his eyes. To his utter amazement, after only two exhausting sessions he felt better than he'd ever done and began to accept that the incident had not been his fault. Finally, she had started to go over various strategies to help with his rage. She taught him all about anger, how debilitating it could be, and at the same time took him through his childhood experiences, teaching him how to reprocess his thoughts. He was virtually cured of his terrible rages now, though shades of them still remained, and he shuddered when he thought of how close he'd come to killing someone.

Now, over ten years later, he wondered if he would ever be free of the past. He did still get angry; admittedly he could control it most of the time now, but the rage was still there. He threw the whisky down his throat without really tasting it. He rose to get another. Suzanne was at his shoulder and he jumped as he sensed her presence.

'You gave me a fright.'

'Sorry. I was just wondering; do you want to eat?'

The whisky was gnawing at his stomach. He could feel the acid burning; it was a mistake to drink on an empty stomach. And yet the thought of food made him ill. He shook his head and then changed his mind. 'Perhaps a cheese sandwich.'

'You sure? There's chicken and salmon in the freezer.'

'Sure, a sandwich will be fine.'

While Suzanne was in the kitchen he continued to think about the accusations. He pushed any worries about these to the back of his mind. He was in the clear. Or he hoped he was. Someone had it in for him; it could only be Karen's father. Christ, the old man had always hated him and he had some influential friends. He must be rubbing his hands with joy at all this.

Mark poured himself another whisky. Scrimgeour said five people had seen the confession and they all had alibis except him. Scrimgeour didn't know about Suzanne and Karen reading it and he wasn't going to tell him. He was up to his neck in shit as it was and anyway Karen had already been ruled out and Suzanne, well he knew where she had been for most of the murders, didn't he?

Chapter Thirty

Mark

Mark wasn't sure he was doing the right thing. His relationship with Karen was as stressed as it had ever been, and asking her this one question might destroy it forever. But he had to know. He raised his hand to knock at the door.

'What do you want?'

'Can we talk?'

'What about?'

'Please, Karen. I wouldn't ask if it wasn't important.'

He followed her into the house. 'Children here?'

'No, get to the point.'

'Karen, I was questioned about those murders today.'

'Well, now you know how it feels.' She started to laugh. 'Christ, first me now you. I never thought they were that desperate.'

Her reaction filled him with relief. If it was her father behind it, then she obviously didn't know anything about it.

'So, is that it? You want to compare notes?'

'No, I... This is a wee bit awkward. Have you seen your father recently?'

'What's that got to do with anything?'

'Well, you know how much he hates me.'

'It's not just you, you know. There's nothing personal in it.'

'Isn't there? After what I did to you?'

She turned away from him. 'I don't want to talk about that, so if that's all you wanted, Mark, please go.'

He had to say it. 'Karen, is there any way he might be trying to influence this investigation? I mean after you were questioned.'

She laughed. 'It would serve you right if he did.'

'I'm serious.'

'I don't think so. I hope not, for your sake.'

Suzanne was out when he returned to the flat – thank goodness. The visit to Karen had shaken him and he wished more than anything that whoever had sent that letter hadn't. It had destroyed his life. Yes, he was infatuated with Suzanne, but deep down he knew it wouldn't last.

His reflections continued as he made himself lunch. If it hadn't been for that damn letter. He found himself thinking back to that day, Suzanne's calmness when he had accused her. Had she been too calm? Did she perhaps already know about it? No, she wouldn't do something like that... and yet, she'd as good as admitted to that ugly scratch on his car, said she'd been very drunk, she wasn't sure, she might have. Fuck, what if... No, she wouldn't have. He finished his lunch and switched on the television but couldn't settle on anything to watch. His thoughts were driving him mad. He was deluded. Driven by sex, he had ignored what was right in front of him. Who else could have written the letter? Who would benefit from telling Karen? No one else even knew about them. Not for certain. His eyes were drawn to the laptop on her desk. Spying on someone, going through their things, opening up files on a computer – it was despicable but he had to know. He went over and sat at the desk, his fingers drumming on the lid of the laptop.

It was password protected – of course it was. But he knew she kept a list of passwords somewhere, because they'd chatted about how difficult it was to remember them. He looked at his watch. She was out until five p.m. and it was only two p.m. now. He opened the top drawer of her desk and began to search.

Ten minutes was all it took. Ten minutes to find them taped to the underside of one of the drawers. He memorised the line of letters and numbers and typed them in. He was in.

The desktop was neatly laid out with folders: work, letters, household bills, finances, music, miscellaneous. He started with the obvious one: letters. He opened up the folder to find around a hundred files. There would be no time to read them all, but if he remembered correctly you could do a search of what was actually in the Word documents. Now all he had to do was remember how it was done.

Taking a deep breath, Mark typed 'Karen' into the search facility. It offered him the choice of searching 'all my files' or 'in this mac'. He chose the latter. One document simply named doc 34 came up. It was in the folder marked Finance. He double clicked on it.

So, it was true. It was Suzanne who had written to Karen. He had the evidence there in front of him. The same letter the mother of his children had received. What was he going to do? Suzanne had been so dismissive when he'd accused her and he'd been too soft, too willing to believe her. Too fucking naïve.

What an idiot he was. Of course it had been her. Who else had the motive?

He must have sat there for an hour or more, thinking things through. He was managing to keep a lid on his temper – how, he didn't know – but he had to play this carefully. The first thing he had to do was print out the letter. He wanted proof to show her. He clicked on the print icon but nothing happened. Dammit, there was no paper in the printer. He opened the bottom drawer of the desk where it was kept and took out a handful to reload the printer. An envelope fell out of the packet and he picked it up. It was stuffed with paper, which he took out. His eyes widened when he read the first sentence.

Chapter Thirty-One

Suzanne

I WAS worried when I saw the police car just outside my flat. I hoped Mark wasn't being questioned again and I quickened my step so he would have me there to support him. 'Mark?' I called as I closed the front door behind me. 'Mark?'

'In here,' he said. He sounded angry and my heart sank. They must have come after him again. I went through to the living room. His boss was there again, Scrimgeour, and his side-kick whose name I'd forgotten. They were sitting on one sofa facing Mark, who was alone on the other. I crossed the room and sat down beside him, feeling for his hand as I did so. He withdrew it and I looked at him in surprise. His head was down and I was unable to see the expression on his face.

'What's going on?' I asked.

'We have a few questions to ask you. Do you mind?'

Did I have any choice? I nodded. It was always best to keep on the right side of the law. 'Of course, go ahead.'

Scrimgeour held up an envelope, which I recognised

straight away. My mouth dried up. Mark had made it clear that he would be in deep trouble if anyone found out he'd taken home evidence. I knew I shouldn't have copied it but I needed more than one quick glance at it. 'Oh, God. I'm sorry, Mark. I didn't mean to get you into trouble but I needed a copy, I know I shouldn't have but...'

'What the hell are you talking about?' His voice was hard.

'The suicide note left by my sister – isn't that it?'

'This is a copy of the suicide note, with comments on it,' said Scrimgeour.

'I stared at him. 'I'm sorry, I don't understand.'

'This is an exact copy of the confession that Mark found in your desk. It has comments on it with regard to the feasibility of carrying out the murders.' He flicked through the pages and started to read aloud. I recognised the words immediately. '*He kneeled down to peer at the earth. I pulled out the knife and as hard as I could I thrust it into the side of his neck. Blood gushed out in a huge arc, pumping with the dying beats of his heart.* And then here there's a comment.' He pushed the paper towards me, pointing towards a comment in the right margin. 'Would you read that, please?'

I squinted at it. It was hard to read without glasses; the comments section in Word is always smaller than the print used in the main document. '*Think about this,*' I read. '*There will be a lot of blood, better maybe to hit him with something?*' I looked round at them all. 'What is this?'

'Do you see who the comment is made by?'

I looked at it again. It was there, in black and white: Suzanne Yates, 11th June 2019. The words danced in front of my eyes. 'I... I didn't write this.' I stared at the policemen, who in turn were staring at me. 'You have to believe me...' They were unblinking. I turned to Mark. 'I didn't write this, Mark.'

'Just like you didn't write this letter to my wife?' He held out a piece of paper.

'Reality was slipping away from me, 'You know I didn't.'

'I found it on your computer.'

'No.'

Scrimgeour stood up. 'I've applied for a search warrant, Ms Yates. It will arrive any moment now. I need you to accompany me to the police station in order to answer further questions.'

I was barely able to stand. My whole body was shaking. I began, 'Mark, please, you have to believe me...' but he was already out of the room in front of me. I followed them out and got into the police car, shaking off the hand that always protects the suspect's head. 'I'm not a child,' I snapped. 'I can look after myself.'

I sat in the back of the car, trying to keep myself together, but it was hard. Still, once they looked at my computer it would be obvious that I hadn't written that document they showed me.

The interview room where they'd put me was cold and unwelcoming. No surprise there. What did surprise me though were the underlying smells. Someone had plugged in one of those awful air fresheners that puffed out scent at five minute intervals. I was sensitive to perfume, especially the types they put in air fresheners, and within a few minutes I had the beginning of an almighty headache. I sat down on the metal chair and put my head on the table. Breathing slowly, I tried to calm myself, but the atmosphere was not conducive to relaxation. After a few minutes I realised there was nothing to stop me pulling the offending Air Wick out of the socket and I did just that. Without the rose perfume the room smelled of booze and other people's sweat, but nonetheless I started to feel better. For three hours I sat there, cold, worried, terrified about what might happen. Around seven p.m. a woman brought me a cup of tea and a pack of sandwiches. I wasn't hungry but I hadn't eaten for hours and I thought I'd better get something inside me. I only managed one of the sandwiches, but once I'd eaten I felt better; my head was less fuzzy and I realised I should have asked for a lawyer. In fact, there was nothing to stop me walking out. They hadn't charged me; they hadn't arrested me. I was free to go. I took a deep breath and stood up. Defying authority in this way wasn't in my nature but I was damned if I'd sit here a moment longer. The door opened and Scrimgeour came in flanked by two uniformed officers.

'Sit down, please.'

'You've left me alone for hours. You have no right to hold me. I'm going now.'

He shook his head. 'No, Ms Yates. You're staying right here. I'm arresting you on suspicion of the murders of Julie Campbell, Donald Paterson, Daisy Palmer, John Allen and Mary McLeod. You do not have to say anything. But, it may harm your defence if you do not mention when questioned something which you later rely on in court. Anything you do say may be given in evidence.'

Mark

The next day was probably the most difficult Mark had ever faced. His position at work was precarious; word had leaked out that Suzanne had been arrested. No one was talking to him, except on work matters. Rooms fell silent when he walked into them. Everywhere there were huddles of people gossiping about him. His imagination told him what they were saying: *what a fucking idiot, thinks with his dick, wanker*. Somehow he carried on working, trying to pretend none of it mattered to him. He was in deep shit though. With Suzanne in prison he had nowhere to live; he'd booked into the cheapest bed and breakfast he could find, but knew he couldn't afford this for long. Money was running out fast.

He left work late. Outside, the sky was clear. Earlier rain had sped off to the east where it might even fall as snow. It was cold enough. Light pollution meant that even on a cloudless night like this, only the brightest stars were visible. Once and only once had Mark seen the night sky in an unpolluted atmosphere, far from artificial city lights. He'd been a teenager at the time, camping with half a dozen friends in northern France. The countryside was flat and boring there, or at least so he had thought until night fell and they had sat and watched the stars saturate the wide expanse of sky. One of his friends had pointed out Orion and then the Plough. They'd watched as these great constellations had been overwhelmed by the myriad suns that made up the galaxy. The flat countryside gave them an unimpeded view and they had sat up until late, drunk with warm farmhouse cider and the glimpse of eternity that they'd had. They'd fallen asleep one by one, leaving just Mark awake to wonder at its vastness. It had been one of the great moments of his life.

Out of habit he checked for the Plough and sketched its outline with his finger. It was all there. He started on his walk home. The city was quiet. There were some cars on the road, swishing through the still wet streets. The cold was beginning to pierce through his jacket and he jingled the coins in his pocket. He felt in his pocket for his mobile. Good, it was there – he could phone for a taxi; he had just about enough money. He took his Samsung and pressed the keys to unlock it. The backlight illuminated a tiny space around it briefly before fading. He knew as he started to press the digits that there wasn't enough battery power even for one call; it had been some time since he'd charged it. With a groan he put it away; it was going to be a long walk.

As he walked along the city streets, he thought about Suzanne. He'd been astounded by the discovery of the letter she'd sent to Karen, but it was nothing to what he'd felt when he found that annotated confession. He'd phoned it in immediately; this wasn't something he could withhold, and of course he'd had nothing to do with her case. He'd picked up a bit in passing. A search of her laptop had made a discovery of several files. One document was the confession, and it was thought that she'd transferred it to her sister's laptop on the night she'd killed her. They'd found a copy on a flash drive. Another was a list of assets her sister had. That, together with what they'd already found, gave them enough to charge her. Her finances weren't in great shape. Or so it was said. There were bills to be paid; she owed thousands on her mortgage. It was all there on spreadsheets for the police to see. But none of it made sense to Mark. He'd seen one of her bank statements, for a savings account; the balance of around £76,000 had been impressive. And she had several accounts. She hadn't received anything from her sister's estate, as probate had not yet been proved, so the money hadn't come from that. He'd tried telling Scrimgeour about the money she had but he wasn't interested; as far as he was concerned it was a motive for her killing her sister and that was that. 'Back off,' he'd been told. 'You need to keep well clear of this case. I've had to do all in my power to stop you being investigated as it is. If you're seen to be interfering...' He didn't need to go on. Mark got the message.

As the rain poured down harder, his thoughts became clearer. Suzanne did not seem like a murderer to him. But he had no way of proving she wasn't. Nor could he explain how the files came to be on her computer.

The blare of a taxi horn brought him right back to the present. He had wandered off the pavement in his reverie and the black cab scraped past him with a swerve and a muffled shout of 'dickhead'. Fair enough. Mark came to a stop. That was a missed opportunity; he should have flagged it down. He looked around to see where he was. A main road, some houses set a little back on one side. On the other side some trees, bare of foliage, branches like crooked fingers against the sky. It took him a few seconds to realise he was nowhere near the cheap bed and breakfast. He was several miles away, on Crookston Road, near the secondary school, just a few hundred yards from his own house where Karen and his children were hopefully having a better night than him. He shook his head and kicked at a Tennant's can lying in the gutter. The noise rattled in the stillness of the street. What on earth was his subconscious trying to tell him? For a moment he fantasised about going round to his house, visualising a rapturous greeting from his children, Karen in the background, smiling a welcome. Who was he kidding? A car drove past, too fast for the road, through a puddle, throwing up a sheet of dirty water that drenched him and brought him back to reality. He shook his fist in a cliché of rage at the speeding car, now a blur. With any luck the speed camera just down the road would have caught the bastard. With even better luck the driver would already have nine penalty points and be facing a ban. That'd teach him. Mark smiled ruefully and trudged on up the dark road. In the distance he could hear the swish of cars on Paisley Road West. He'd catch a cab there.

Chapter Thirty-Two

Suzanne

I WAS IN SHOCK. I'd never seen the pieces of paper before. They flashed them in front of me and I read the words in disbelief. 'These comments, they aren't mine,' I said, but they had made up their minds. Something about my sister's death had been 'off' from day one and now they knew what it was. I wasn't too worried though; they'd said they'd search my laptop and I knew there was nothing incriminating on it. My tiny feeling of hope at that was extinguished when I remembered that it was where Mark had found the letter Karen received. Someone had planted it there, but who? Mark? I didn't think so; he had been very clear he hadn't wanted to leave his family and this had precipitated it. Karen? It was possible, except there was no way she could have got into my flat. I thought of the would-be intruder. Was that Karen after all? I wanted to believe it but found I couldn't. To be honest I didn't think she had the brains to do something like this. I was stumped but I sat there in the interview room saying I had no need of a lawyer over and over. I had done nothing wrong.

When they told me they'd found the original of my sister's suicide note as well as a spreadsheet of my financial difficulties from years ago on my laptop, I laughed. Scrimgeour scowled.

'I wouldn't laugh if I were you.'

'Look, I have savings totalling over a hundred thousand pounds. Ask my bank.'

He looked less certain of himself. 'We have requested a warrant to look at your bank accounts.'

'Good,' I said. 'You'll find that I have no money problems at all. And without that, what's my motive? You were never certain that my sister was murdered in any case. And as for these other people I'm supposed to have killed. What's my motive?'

He left the room muttering and I leaned back, certain I would be out of here in no time. What is it they say? Never count your chickens...

His next visit left me devastated. 'We have found further evidence,' he said before even taking a seat.

'Oh yes? What is it this time? A receipt from the supermarket placing me there at the same time as that poor old woman? A non-existent bump on my car from when I ran over a young woman in the street?'

His voice betrayed his triumph. 'Better than that, Ms Yates. We found a knife buried in one of your plant pots. There was blood on it... and you know what? It matches that of the man you killed in Pollok Park.'

Mark

Mark was called in to see Scrimgeour. At first he feared it was something to do with Suzanne, but it was to tell him about a case they'd just been handed. Scrimgeour outlined the details of a stabbing that had taken place after a football match. They'd arrested two men who were still to be questioned.

'I'll fill you in on the details, and then you can join me in the interview room. It'll take you fifteen minutes to get up to speed, then we'll have them.' He started to go over the details of what was an all too common occurrence in Glasgow after an old firm game. This time it was a little different, with both the suspects and the victim being supporters of the same team, Rangers. Mark suspected the stabbing had more to do with drug deals than with football. The victim wasn't talking, but he was a well-known drug addict who'd been done in the past for dealing. He'd probably owed money, and the big boys had chosen to stab him after a football match thinking that a Celtic supporter would automatically get the blame. That was the trouble with drug addicts and dealers; they had little imagination. The few brain cells they'd had were decimated by the consumption of whatever drug was fashionable or easy to get. It wasn't hard for the police to find someone who knew what was going on and who wanted to talk. The two men arrested were small-time dealers who thought they were crime lords. They had no idea what big time crooks were like. Scrimgeour filled in the bare details and handed the file to Mark.

'Right, now have a good look at that, and then we'll go.' He got up and went to open the door, turning as he was about to leave. 'By the way, that woman of yours. She's screwed. We found the knife that was used in one of the murders in her flat. Hidden in a plant pot. Fingerprints and blood all over it.'

Mark said nothing. Christ, it was hard to believe he'd been

taken in so badly. His phone rang and he fished it out of his pocket and looked at the screen. Unknown number. He declined the call and put it away. It immediately started ringing again. He swiped to answer.

'What?'

'Mark, it's me. Please don't put the phone down. I don't know what to do, who to turn to...'

'I can't speak to you, Suzanne.'

'Please.' She started to sob. 'They've charged me with five murders including that of my sister, and I'm innocent. Please can you come to see me?'

'I'm sorry, Suzanne. I can't.'

'There's no one else I can ask, please. Don't make me beg.'

'Don't you have a lawyer?'

'Yes, but she doesn't know me. Mark, this is important... I think Julie is still alive.'

Chapter Thirty-Three

Mark

SUZANNE'S APPEARANCE SHOCKED MARK. Her face was gaunt and she looked years older. Her hair, usually so shiny and healthy looking, was dull and flat against her head. The laughter lines round her eyes had deepened into wrinkles and there were two hard ridged lines on her forehead. She was a mess. He sat down at the table across from her.

'What makes you think your sister is alive?'

'She set me up.' Her hands were restless, fingers drumming on the Formica topped table.

Mark's voice remained impassive, professional. 'Why would she do that?'

Suzanne didn't answer for a moment. She sat up straighter in her chair. 'You didn't know her – she was, she is devious. A game player.'

Mark thought back to the interview with Julie's ex-husband. He had used those exact words, game player. 'That's not a motive, Suzanne. You don't kill people just as a game.'

'And what's my motive meant to be? Money? I have plenty of money, Mark. You know that. Did I ever stint on spending anything on you? And yet, they're trying to say I murdered Julie to get my hands on her money. It doesn't make sense. Surely you can see that?'

Mark shook his head. 'They found the knife that was used to kill Paterson in your flat. It had his blood on it, for God's sake! This isn't just circumstantial evidence. Your fingerprints are on it.'

Suzanne paled. 'Mark, she's very disturbed. And think about it – only four of those killings have been done. She's going to kill again. And it could be a child this time.'

'Look, she's dead. The DNA tests proved it.'

'But what about that woman who lived next door to her, the one who disappeared? Julie could easily have transferred her hair to a hairbrush so the DNA matched.' Suzanne's words were rushed; the visit was coming to an end.

Mark got up out of his seat. 'I'm sorry, Suzanne. I really am, but there's nothing I can do.'

'Get me a copy of the confession. There will be a clue in there. I'm sure of it.'

'I'm sorry, Suzanne, it's not possible. For one thing I no longer have access to it. They won't let me near anything to do with you.'

His heart ached as he drove back to Glasgow. He was sure she hadn't done these murders, but her sister couldn't be alive, could she? There was only one way to prove it. If he could get a DNA sample from the missing woman...

'I know this is difficult for you, sir.' Mark wished he'd never brought up the subject. Mr Fitzwilliam was proving very difficult to persuade. He was going out on a limb here and risked getting sacked, but the more he thought about it the less convinced was he that Suzanne had done anything she'd been charged with.

'You seriously think that Marianne's next door neighbour killed her, dressed her up in her clothes and left her there to be discovered?'

Put like that, it sounded very unlikely, but so was the possibility of Suzanne being guilty. 'It would be helpful to rule it out. If you had anything of your ex-wife's that might have her DNA on it?'

He scratched his eyebrow so that the hairs stood out. 'Um, well she left a toothbrush at mine and a hairbrush. In case, you know, she ever stayed over.' He blushed at this. He must have been on better terms with his ex than he let on.

'That sounds perfect. I'll send someone round to pick them up.'

Mark decided to wait for the results before telling Scrimgeour what he'd done. If it was what he thought it was, he would be vindicated. If it wasn't, then he was in the shit, but there was no point in putting himself there before it was necessary. The results would come through in a couple of days. Until then he had to hold tight.

The stabbings weren't holding his interest. As suspected, they were drug related. One of the men who'd been stabbed had given them a name. It was most likely a set up and Mark had the feeling that they were as far from the big guys as they'd ever been, but it was over to the drug squad now. He made sure his notes were in order and phoned them to say the file was on its way. He leaned back in his seat and thought about his meeting with Suzanne. What had surprised him most was that he had felt little other than pity for her. Yes, he was sure she had not killed anyone, but there had been a desperation in her request for a copy of the confession. In fact, the more he thought about it, it had been fear. She was frightened of her sister. What the hell could have happened to her to make her so afraid of another woman?

Chapter Thirty-Four

Suzanne

I SAT in my room in the prison, looking round in horror at what was now my home. I was on remand. My lawyer had explained to me that finding the knife was the final straw. 'Not only was it found in your home,' she said, 'it had traces of the victim's blood on it and your fingerprints. It was taken from the knife block in your kitchen.'

'That's been missing for months,' I exclaimed. 'I thought I'd thrown it out by accident.'

Her raised eyebrows betrayed her scepticism. She wasn't on my side. I had to find a new lawyer, someone who would fight for me.

I lay on what passed for a bed, looking at the ceiling. There was a cobweb in one corner and a crack round the light fitting. I shuddered. This place had been notorious for suicides at one point; had someone hung themselves using the light cord? I had no way of knowing other than asking and I wouldn't do that. Best to be ignorant of these things. My eyes closed in exhaustion but I was unable to sleep. My mind was on the day that changed my life as well as Julie's.

I was ten years old, almost eleven. It was the year before I was due to start secondary school, the local comprehensive, popular with parents and pupils. Julie was in her third year there but I had no idea whether she liked it or not. She never spoke to me. We'd never been close. There was too much of an age gap, our mother said. I didn't buy that explanation. She was jealous, pure and simple. For whatever reason, she hated me and I didn't like her much either. Most of the time we avoided each other; not hard when we went to different schools. Our parents were always out at work so we were left pretty much to our own devices – for me that was staying in my room and drawing. That helped block out the rows that were a constant background in our house. If Julie wasn't fighting with one or other of them, then they were fighting with each other. I don't know why they had children. They didn't like me, the interloper, but they didn't seem to like Julie either, though she was their own flesh and blood as she liked to tell me.

Drawing took the pain away. I'd known for years I was adopted. I'd heard one of my mother's friends talking to her about it when I was about eight.

'Do you think you were right to adopt Suzanne?'

My mother glanced over to where I was lying in front of the fire, reading. I must have appeared engrossed, for instead of shushing her friend, she said, 'I don't know. I thought it would help Julie to have a sister but it seems to have made things worse.'

I was paralysed by what I'd heard. Somehow I managed to make it look as if I continued to read, but inside I was devastated. As I got older though, I was glad Julie wasn't my real sister. It explained so much about her. I couldn't find out anything about my adoption, so that allowed me to fantasise.

By the time I was ten, my artistic talents were obvious and I would dream for hours of how my real parents were artists, my mother a painter, my father a sculptor. They had been very much in love but parted before I was born. My mother torn between her child and her art. Even at that early age I was aware of how seductive talent is, how if you can do something well you become obsessed. So I didn't blame my mother for giving me up. I imagined her in a studio somewhere, paint spattered, her hair long and wavy, working on a canvas, stopping occasionally to wipe away a tear when she thought of the child she'd given up but knowing she'd done what she had to do. I had inherited my artistic ability from this romantic young couple. The reality of course was a little different; my mother had been in care and had had me at the age of fifteen. Father unknown.

But it was many years before I would discover that, and for years I lived happily in my fantasy world, drawing cute pictures of a woman working on a painting while a baby gurgled in a Moses basket at her feet. Meanwhile Julie was in torment.

It was a hot day in July. We were alone at home. As usual I was in my room, drawing. I was working on perspective. I had taken several books out of the library and I was trying to understand the rules. Vanishing point, horizon: the terms had me befuddled and I wished I had someone I could discuss them with. I couldn't wait to get to secondary school where I would have proper art lessons at last, where someone who knew what they were talking about could explain things to me. Over the past year, I had learned that primary school teachers were expected to know everything but in fact knew very little. I had my ruler out trying to draw a fence going off into the distance when I heard it: a low groaning noise coming from Julie's room. At first I ignored it; she probably had a stomach ache from eating too much. I'd noticed she'd put on weight over the last few months. But the noise grew louder and more alarming. I knocked on her door, tentatively. She could be vicious with her tongue and if it turned out to be nothing I risked a tongue lashing.

'Julie, are you all right?'

'Help me.' It was barely more than a whisper.

I turned the handle and went in.

She was on the floor on all fours, grunting like an animal, naked from the waist down. There was something bulging between her legs. I stood immobile in the doorway, my hand to my mouth.

'Fucking get over here and help me, you stupid bitch.'

I should have turned and run, phoned for an ambulance, but I couldn't move. She shouted at me again and I moved towards her. 'What do you want me to do?' I whispered.

The door to my cell opened and a prison officer walked in. I'd never get used to the lack of privacy here. The constant feeling of being watched. I shook myself out of the depression I was falling into and waited for her to speak.

'Someone to see you,' she said.

It was Mark. I hadn't expected to see him so soon. I sat down at the table opposite him and reached a hand towards him but he recoiled. Embarrassed, I withdrew it, sat on both my hands so they couldn't betray me again.

'I have news for you,' he said. 'I spoke to Mr Fitzwilliam a few days ago – you know, the man whose wife went missing?'

I nodded. I didn't want to speak. It was enough just to watch him.

'He gave me his wife's toothbrush and some hair from a hairbrush she'd left in his house. The DNA from both is the same as that taken from the body. The body that was in your sister's house is not that of your sister. She must have taken Mrs Fitzwilliam's hairbrush as well as her toothbrush and substituted them for her own. Forensics went back through the house. They found some hair under your sister's bed and tested it. The DNA from that was different. We now think your sister may be alive.

'But I thought you looked at her dental records?'

'Apparently not. The original DNA results were thought to be enough.' He sounded embarrassed.

Adrenalin rushed through me. 'Does that mean I'm free?'

'Not yet, I'm afraid. But the evidence is being reviewed right now. It's likely that you will be released soon.'

I took a deep breath, 'Thank you for believing me.'

He handed me an envelope. 'You asked for this. If you find anything, you will let me know?'

I opened it. The confession.

Chapter Thirty-Five

Mark

BACK OUTSIDE IN the fresh air, Mark breathed deeply. Prisons depressed him. He felt sorry for Suzanne but knew it was over. She knew it too. He could tell by the look on her face when he didn't take her hand. He'd give it a few days and then go to get his stuff from her flat. He walked quickly back to the car park and got into the unmarked police car he'd borrowed from the car pool. He sat for some moments before turning the key. Perhaps Karen would be home by now. He had to see her. To apologise for his terrible behaviour. He had been like a man possessed. It was unlikely she would have him back; he wasn't even sure if he wanted to go back, but in either case he had to let her know he was sorry. He drove back to Glasgow along the M8, cursing the road works, trying to look past the blue Ford Transit van in front of him to see how busy the traffic was. He steered the car without conscious thought to Paisley Road West, his windscreen wipers on at maximum, for rain was hurtling out of the sky now. It was dark and the yellow lights of the cars coming the other way dazzled him. One hooted as he swerved towards the middle of the road, his eyelids drooping. He was worn out, exhausted with all the emotion of the past few weeks. He forced himself to concentrate on the drive and not to think about what he would say to Karen.

There were no friendly lights on when he reached the house. He sat in the car opposite their driveway, wondering what to do. She was probably at Debbie's. Mark didn't want to see her there. Debbie would listen in on their conversation, make little sardonic comments, needle him and Karen. There was no possibility of a conversation in her house. Maybe he should phone Karen and arrange to meet somewhere neutral. Christ, he couldn't think, couldn't formulate even the simplest of plans. His fingers tapped the steering wheel. Perhaps it would be best to wait here. Fingers tapping, rain drumming on the car; it was very soporific. He allowed himself to close his fatigue-scratched eyes and, worn out, fell asleep within a couple of minutes.

Someone was trying to break into the house, tapping on the window. Were they trying to break the glass? What could he do about it? Heart pounding, Mark forced his way back into consciousness. Where on earth was he? He wiped a bit of dribble from the side of his mouth and forced his eyes to focus. He could hear a muffled voice and recognised it as Karen's. Still befuddled from sleep, he thought at first that Suzanne had broken into the house and was somehow harming Karen, and then, as reality started to impinge, he remembered where he was. Eyes open, he stared at Karen, who was patiently tapping on the window. He opened the car door and stepped out into the cold night. At least it had stopped raining.

'What are you doing here?'

'I wanted to see if you were all right.' His voice wasn't working properly; it was thick with sleep. Christ, he must have been asleep for ages. He looked at his watch – five past seven, was that all? He felt as though he'd been unconscious for years; his mind was woolly and his limbs felt cramped.

'I'm fine.' Karen turned away as she spoke. 'What do you really want, Mark? You didn't come all this way just to see if I was OK.'

'I'm sorry, Karen. Sorry for everything, I've been a complete dickhead.'

'So?'

Mark felt deflated. Foolishly he'd allowed himself to hope Karen might forgive him, but there was no hint of that in her tightly closed face. He kicked at the kerb with his foot.

'Don't do that. You'll ruin your shoe.'

Mark laughed. 'You sound like my mother. She was always on at me for doing that.'

She smiled then, but sadness showed through. 'Mark, I don't want you here. I don't care if you're sorry. What did you think? That I'd open my arms and welcome you back, the prodigal husband? I've moved on. I'm trying to get a job. I had an interview today. And if I don't get that job, I'll get another. Things have changed, I've changed.' This last was said with a touch of pride, and looking at her, Mark saw a confidence that hadn't been there for some time.

'Oh Christ, I'm so sorry for what I've done. You can't imagine. No, let me speak. I know it's over between us; I wouldn't dare presume otherwise. But I do care for you and I want you to know that I would like to come back.' Mark surprised himself by saying that, but even as the words were forming, he felt the truth of them. 'I know everything has changed. How could it not have? But I needed to know that you and the kids were OK.'

'I'm fine. Now go away.' With that she walked away up the short path to the front door. She opened it and stepped inside, then suddenly came out again. She called to him.

Mark swallowed. What now? 'Yes?' he said as he neared the house.

'Look, Mark. No hard feelings. I know you regret what you've done and I won't stop you seeing the children. In fact, if you want, you can babysit tomorrow evening.'

'I... Yes, of course. What time?'

'If you come round before seven you'll be able to see them before they go to bed.'

Mark returned to the car. It wasn't much but it was a start. It looked as though she was going to allow him more access to the children. He sat for a while, trying to think, his emotions tumbling and churning him up. There was so much to do. First things first. He'd buy some bin liners to put his clothes in and then find a place to stay. Who knows, maybe Scrimgeour would put him up. He couldn't think of anyone else. He turned the key in the ignition and drove off.

Chapter Thirty-Six

Suzanne

BACK IN MY CELL, I took out the sheets of paper that Mark had given me. I was sure there was a clue in there. Julie had ways of doing things, ways of getting others to do things for her. Like on that day in so many years ago.

'Get it out of me,' she screamed again.

'I don't know what to do,' I cried. 'I'll phone an ambulance.'

She turned to look at me. Her face was covered in sweat. The heavy eye make-up she always wore was in streaks across her cheeks. She looked demented. 'Don't you fucking dare,' she panted. 'This is between you and me. Get over here, will you?'

I approached her in the way you might approach a rabid dog; that is to say, I stayed where I was. 'I don't know what to do,' I repeated.

'Get some string,' she panted. 'And a pair of scissors... and a towel.'

'I ran into the bathroom and grabbed the first towel I saw. Then I ran downstairs and into the kitchen where I knew there were some scissors. I looked at the phone. I could just quickly dial 999, but she screamed for me, and terrified, I mounted the stairs two at a time.

'Pull it out,' she said.

I put my hands on the baby's head. Tears were streaming down my face. The head was covered in blood and some sort of white stuff. My hands couldn't get a grasp on it. There was something round the baby's neck and I tried to loosen it, but she slapped my hands away. At last I managed to get a grip and I pulled. It slid out of her body in a gush. I'd seen a video at a friend's house about childbirth a few weeks before. We knew we shouldn't be watching it, but sniggering we'd put it on and watched, fascinated at first then in horror. It had been gruesome to watch, but it meant I knew what to do. I cut the cord and tied it with a piece of string, held the baby upside down and slapped it gently on the back. It was a boy. His cries joined with his mother's. I held him close, unsure what to do. Remembering the video, I gave him my finger and he held on to it tightly. I smiled down at him, before Julie interrupted. 'Bring it here.'

'It's a boy,' I said as I walked towards her.

'Get me a drink, will you?'

I nodded and ran out of the room. My heart was thumping. I was worried about what our parents would say. I stood in the kitchen waiting for the kettle to boil. Perhaps this baby would bring our family together; perhaps he would stop all the fighting. I made toast for her. The damn video again; I remembered the midwife coming to the new mother with a cup of tea and two slices of toast. Pleased with myself for my consideration I walked slowly upstairs, taking care not to spill the tea. Perhaps if I'd been quicker, she wouldn't have done it.

I opened the door to her bedroom and went in. After all the groaning and shouting from Julie and the baby's cries, it was unnaturally peaceful. It took me a few seconds to realise until I saw him, the baby, lying silent and still on the floor.

I tossed the sheets of paper aside impatiently. I'd read through the damn thing more than ten times now and I was still no further forward. I'd looked at the musical clues to see if there was anything there but they were banal: the Spanish hairdresser was *Il Barbiere di Siviglia,* the music for killing the young woman was Schubert's *Death and the Maiden,* the man walking to work was straight out of Verdi's *Rigoletto.* She'd even put in Talking Heads' 'Psycho Killer'. There was nothing there; I was certain. And yet there had to be something. Julie was always fond of riddles and puzzles. She liked to keep everyone guessing. Was all this her trying to get back at me? My mind went back to that awful day.

When I saw the baby lifeless in her arms, I ran towards her. She screamed at me to get away from her.

'He's not moving,' I said. 'Is he all right?'

'He's a monster,' she said. 'An aberration. He had to die.'

I can still remember the shock of those words, the coldness and hatred with which she said them. I opened my mouth to protest but she continued.

'Don't you want to know why?'

I said nothing; I was crying too much.

'You've heard him, haven't you?'

I shook my head, bewildered. 'I don't know what you mean.'

'Night after night, he comes to me. Waiting until he thinks everyone is asleep, but I know you've heard him. You must have – there's only that thin wall between us.'

It was true I had heard strange noises coming from Julie's room. Grunts and sighs, and I had heard her crying. But I had no idea of what was going on. I was barely eleven years old and no one had explained the facts of life to me. Yes, I had a vague idea of what might happen, but in my innocence I thought it only happened when you were married. 'Who comes to you?' I said.

'Why, Daddy of course.' She spat out the words. 'And you'll be next.'

I was rigid with shock and terrified. I had been denying it to myself but I was wary of my father. He pressed himself against me sometimes in a way I thought was odd, and one day he had grabbed my chest and laughed. 'Not much there, yet. But it won't be long.' I knew it was wrong but I had no one to tell.

The hours, days, weeks that followed this were terrible. My mother coming home from work to find us distraught with a dead baby on the floor in Julie's room. My halting explanation of what had happened. Julie saying nothing, just lying on her bed staring at the ceiling. A stream of people coming to speak to us: police, doctors, social workers. They're a blur now. My father being taken away in a police car, neighbours watching, whispering. Julie being taken to hospital, still silent. Then the tiny body being taken away for an autopsy. I wanted to stop them, to hold him again and tell him I was sorry, but I was too scared to ask. And afterwards, when we were alone, the self-hatred of my mother. She railed at herself for hours: how could she not have known, why hadn't she seen the signs? But people weren't aware of child abuse in the way they are today. I tried to comfort her but it was impossible.

We moved away as soon as we could. Put the solid, comfortable house up for sale and moved to a small flat in Knightswood. My adoptive mother and I co-existed in a lukewarm affection. She sometimes went to see Julie in hospital; I never did. As soon as I could, I left home and put it all behind me. After all, they weren't my real family.

I picked up the confession and started to read again. There it was, leaping out at me. The first letter of the first word in each sentence in the first paragraph.

I*t's as simple as this: I'll be dead before sunrise.*

A *number of years ago, I went to a dinner party where we talked about what we'd listen to or read if we had only a few hours left to live.* ***M****ahler or Strauss, Shakespeare or Dickens, what would it be?* ***S****hakespeare yielded to Beckett and Mahler to Nono as the choices became ever more obscure.* ***T****he discussion went on for hours; you should have heard us, trying to outdo each other until it came to what we'd eat.* ***I*** *shut everyone up with my choice of shiokara.* ***L****ook it up.* ***L****ovely.* ***A****nd now my end is near and I quite fancy scrambled eggs – baveuse naturally – but there's no time if I am to tell my story.* ***L****istening to music will have to do.*

It will help me relax. Various people at that dinner party went for the obvious choices: Vier Letzte Lieder, the finale of Tristan und Isolde, but these are too sombre for me. Excruciatingly so.

I wrote them out. *I am still alive.* The message could only be for me.

Chapter Thirty-Seven

Mark

Mark rang the doorbell at precisely seven o'clock. It was a minute or so before Karen opened the door.

'You look lovely,' he said, following her inside.

She went into the cupboard under the stairs for her coat and didn't answer.

'Where are you going?'

'Is that any of your business?'

He lowered his eyes from her gaze. 'Sorry.'

Karen relented. 'I'm off to the pictures with Sheila and Victoria and then we're going for a drink.'

'That's nice.' He tried but didn't quite succeed in hiding his relief. At least it wasn't a date. He wondered what had happened to the man she'd been seeing.

'I'll be back around eleven, maybe a bit later. Is that OK?'

He nodded. 'Where are the kids?'

'Upstairs; they've had their bath but they want you to put them to bed. Oscar's waiting for a bedtime story.'

'I'll go on up then.' He started up the stairs.
'Mark,' Karen said. 'I—'
'Yes?' He turned round.
She shook her head. 'Nothing. I'll see you later.'

Mark sat down in front of the fire with a beer he'd found in the fridge. He'd forgotten how exhausting his children could be. It was one thing taking them out for half a day at the weekend as he had been doing, but quite something else putting them to bed, making sure their teeth were cleaned, telling them stories, playing with them. It had almost broken his heart when Sophie asked him when he was coming back to live with them. He'd been overcome, unable to answer, and when Oscar had joined in, shouting, 'Daddy come home, Daddy come home,' he thought he was going to cry. With some difficulty he extricated himself; they were overexcited at him being there, but eventually they'd gone to sleep, around half past eight.

He flicked through the TV channels wanting something to watch to take his mind off all his problems, but there was nothing worth bothering with except a rerun of a crime drama he'd already seen. Resigned, he fetched another beer and settled down to listen to some music.

He must have fallen asleep. He heard a taxi draw up, the door slam, and knew it was Karen. He looked at his watch: twelve thirty. She'd had a good night then. He blinked the sleep from his eyes and stood up, swaying a little as she came into the room. Her eyes immediately alighted on the four empty beer bottles.

'Bloody hell, Mark. Have you had all that beer?'

He looked down at the bottles. 'Um yeah, I suppose I did.'

'I'll call a taxi.'

Emboldened from the beer he'd drunk, he said, 'Can't I stay here?'

Karen picked up the empty bottles and took them through to the kitchen. 'Oh yeah, right. You think to yourself, Karen's out on the piss. She'll come home feeling happy and we'll kiss and make up. A quick drunken shag and everything will be fine. No, Mark, you can't stay here.'

'I didn't mean that. Karen, I'd never take advantage of you, drunk or otherwise. I meant can I sleep on the couch?'

'Oh.' Karen's voice was flat. She unplugged his phone which he'd been charging and handed it to him. 'Yours, I think.'

He took it from her and put it in his jacket pocket. 'I'll be off, then.' He rose from his seat, his face grey with weariness.

'Oh, all right then. You can stay. I'll fetch a pillow and a sleeping bag. But don't you dare read anything into this.'

'I won't,' he said.

'Good.' Karen went to get a sleeping bag from the cupboard in the hall.

Mark couldn't sleep and wondered if Karen was awake too. It was strange being in the same house, but nice. He couldn't wait to see his children's faces in the morning. They'd be thrilled. He shifted on to his side. Fuck, he'd never get to sleep. Perhaps if he had a whisky... No, that wasn't a good idea. As it was he'd be pretty hung over in the morning. He hadn't realised the beers were Belgian – had sunk them down like lemonade; 9.5% alcohol. He was an idiot. He turned again on the lumpy sofa, counting slowly to ten as he tried to empty his mind of all thoughts.

When he awoke, he was disoriented, couldn't think where he was. Had he heard breaking glass? What was it? His heart was thumping and he lay in the dark, trying to bring his heart-beat down. It was beating so hard it hurt. Take a deep breath, he told himself, breathe in slowly through the nose and out again through the mouth. He was at home; it was fine. The noise must have been Karen in the kitchen. She'd probably broken a plate. There was a faint burning smell as if of toast and he relaxed. Karen was making breakfast.

He swung his legs onto the floor and stood up. Christ, he was stiff. The sofa was too short by a foot to sleep comfortably. His knees cracked as he padded over to the door to the hall and opened it. Immediately the hammer in his heart started up again. That smell wasn't toast; it was too strong. The lamp on the table by the front door was on fire and it had spread to the pile of papers and letters they always kept there. Even as he watched, a paper fell onto the floor and started to burn the carpet. A second later the smoke alarm shrieked, the noise almost too painful to bear.

'Karen!' he shouted as he thundered up the stairs. 'Wake up!' He banged on her bedroom door and she appeared looking bewildered. 'Phone the fire brigade!' he yelled, but she already had the phone in her hand. 'I'll get the kids.' He rushed past her.

Karen had the phone to her ear. 'There's no dialling tone,' she cried. She ran after Mark. He was outside the girls' bedroom, carrying Emma and holding Sophie by the hand. Emma was screaming. Mark pushed Emma into Karen's arms and gave her his mobile.

'Sophie, go with Mummy. Karen, the hallway downstairs is

blocked. Stay in our bedroom, put wet towels over your heads and I'll get Oscar.'

The smoke was thick now and he could hardly see anything. He rushed into Oscar's room and pulled him from his bed. Oscar, disturbed from his sleep, started to cry. 'Ssh, ssh. It's all right, Daddy's here. The smoke was choking him, his lungs were tightening. Mark dropped to the floor where the smoke was less dense. He crawled along the floor with Oscar a dead weight in his arms. Oscar had stopped crying, Mark thought in terror of how vulnerable his son was and with a huge effort he reached the hall; a couple of metres more and they'd be in Karen's bedroom, but it was so hard to move. As he slipped into unconsciousness he heard Karen crying by his side.

Chapter Thirty-Eight

Mark

MARK FELT terrible when he woke up. No hangover had ever felt like this. His chest was sore and tender as though someone had jumped on it. He prodded it gently with his finger; someone definitely had been using him as a trampoline. His senses started to come alive. The smell of the room was not as it should be – too chemical. He opened an eye. Wherever he was it was very bright. White walls, strip lighting, white sheets. Where the hell was he? He looked again. Hospital. Immediately it flooded back. He sat up in bed and called for a nurse. It came out as a gurgle. He looked around him; there should be an alarm somewhere. He found it and pressed it frantically. You could be dying in this place and no one would bother. Where the hell were the staff? He pressed the buzzer lying on his bed and a few minutes later a nurse came to his bed.

'My family. Are they OK?' he managed to croak.

'Your wife's at her friend's with Oscar and Sophie.'

Emma, where was Emma? Mark felt his stomach tighten

into a spasm of fear. How could he ever have thought her a nuisance? He stuttered the words, pushing them out. 'Where's Emma?'

She looked at him with kind eyes. 'Doctor will be along shortly to let you know how she is.'

He grabbed her hand so tightly that she cried out. 'Tell me, is she OK?'

'Ouch! Yes, but the doctor will tell you more.' She pulled her hand from his now relaxed one and hurried out of the room, shaking her hand as she went.

The doctor came along five minutes later. 'Emma's fine,' she said, 'but because she's smaller than the rest of you, her lungs took in more smoke. We just want to keep an eye on her for a couple of days. You should both be home by the weekend.'

Reassured, Mark leaned back into the pillow then bolted upright again as he remembered what else he needed to know. 'How did the fire start?'

The young doctor held up her hands. 'No idea,' she said. 'I think it's the fire service that lets you know. I'm not sure, sorry.' She left him then.

Visiting started at two and went on till five. Mark lay miserable in his bed as time after time the door opened and another unfamiliar face walked in and past him to someone else. It shouldn't be allowed, he thought sourly, as yet another pretty girl walked up to sit beside the young man two beds away. He forced himself to smile when one of them came up to ask whether she could take one of his chairs. 'Take both, why don't you,' he muttered as he watched her struggle up the ward with it. He picked up a newspaper that had been left by his bed and put it straight back down again. There was a lead story of a fire in

Dundee that had killed two small children. His own plight was mentioned in a small box just down from the main story: *Policeman's family have lucky fire escape*. Who wrote these headlines, he wondered? For a brief moment he allowed himself to think of a metal fire escape, covered with four-leaved clover and rabbits' feet. He picked it up again; a crossword would take his mind off things, divert his thoughts from the misery of no visitors. He flicked through the paper and found one.

It was nearly three before Karen arrived. She smiled nervously as she came into the ward. 'Emma's fine,' she announced before he could speak. 'They'll let her home in a couple of days.'

'Is the house OK then?'

'We're alive; that's what matters.'

'That'll be a no, then.' Mark tried to smile but his eyes filled up. 'Oh, Karen, I thought I'd lost you all.'

'I know.' A tear ran down her cheek. 'But you haven't. We're all still here.'

'And the house?' persisted Mark.

'The house has seen better days.'

'Ah.' He paused to think what this meant. 'Do they know how it started?'

'Not yet. The fire officer has still to write the report but they said it was most likely an electrical fault. They think the lamp by the front door was to blame. I don't understand; I'm sure I put it off before I went to bed.'

'It was on fire when I woke up. It wouldn't have to have been on; it may have been the socket that was at fault. Bad wiring.' He said nothing for a moment, then added, 'You saved my life, and Oscar's.'

Karen shook her head, looked away. He saw tears in her eyes. 'It was horrible. When you didn't come back immediately

I opened the door to the hallway. Oh Mark, the smoke... It was... I can't describe it. It punched me in the chest. I saw the two of you lying there. Emma and Sophie were over at the window in our room, with a wet towel over their heads.' Tears ran down her face as she remembered. 'I said to Sophie to stay where she was and look after Emma. Sophie was crying, pleading with me not to go.'

Mark was crying now too. How close they had been to death. It was unbearable. 'I'm sorry,' he said.

'I dropped on to the floor into a crawling position. Thank God, the smoke wasn't as thick there and I grabbed Oscar. I thought my lungs were going to burst. It was only a few feet but it felt like a marathon. I pushed open our bedroom door and dragged Oscar in. The firemen must have got you because I don't remember anything after that.'

They sat in silence. Mark rubbed his eyes, still sore from the smoke. He wanted to tell Karen he was sorry, that he wanted to start again, but he didn't know whether she wanted to hear it.

'Mark,' said Karen. 'What are you thinking?'

'That I love you, that I really regret having hurt you, that I want to come home.'

'That'll be difficult when we have nowhere to live.' Her voice was sharp.

'Would you consider taking me back?'

Karen stood up. 'Mark, I don't know. I've moved on. Yes, I know you've only been away a few weeks but I've got a job, I feel better about myself.'

'I didn't know you'd got a job,' said Mark.

'I told you last night. I start in a week's time. Clerical assistant at a primary school in the West End.'

'That's great,' said Mark. 'I'm so proud of you.'

Karen's smile softened her words but only a little. 'Mark,

you don't get it, do you? I don't really care what you think. This is something I'm doing for me.'

'Karen, I'm sorry. Please, think about what I've said.'

She shrugged. 'I will think about it,' she said, 'but you think about what I've said too.'

Chapter Thirty-Nine

Suzanne

I HAD HOPED it would be Mark who came to tell me the charges were being dropped but it was his boss, DI Scrimgeour. I listened, horrified, as he told me about the fire.

'It's her, Julie. I know it is.'

He shook his head. 'No, it was a faulty lamp.'

'She could have done that.'

His smile was patronising. 'I don't think so.' I gave up at that. He was obviously one of those men who didn't believe women could cope with anything vaguely scientific. And to be honest I wasn't sure she could. Perhaps it was a coincidence.

'Are they sure it was a faulty lamp? No petrol or anything like that?'

'The fire service is not treating it as arson.'

'OK, so what happens now?'

'With the DNA evidence suggesting that the body was that of Mrs Fitzwilliam, and now with this additional evidence of the confession, we are assuming she is still alive. I have to warn you, Ms Yates, that we think you might be at risk from her.'

He might think it but I knew I was at risk. This entire episode had been her revenge on a child who didn't understand that her sister was being abused. I gave DI Scrimgeour a half smile. 'Yes, I think you might be right.'

'Will you be all right going back to your flat?'

'I might go to a hotel for a night or two, until you find her and lock her up.'

"Good idea. It shouldn't be long until we find her. We're assuming she's been using Mrs Fitzwilliam's cards and we can trace her through those.'

I had to go back to the flat first to get some clothes and things. He offered to send a policeman with me but I wanted to be alone. Once inside my flat I breathed more easily. There was a pile of post behind the door, bills mostly. I put them on the kitchen table and put on the kettle for coffee. When the coffee was made I started going through the letters, putting them into two piles: action and recycling. It was amazing how much rubbish you got through the post these days. I had thought with email there would be less need for this sort of crap. I put yet another charity begging letter on the recycling pile and tore open the next letter. I swallowed hard as I started to read.

I won't start with the usual appellation. You were never dear to me. I hated you right from the start. Mother and Father had been all mine, doting parents, giving me everything I wanted. And I wanted everything. Except you. Did you know they thought it might help if I had a sister, that I'd somehow become less demanding? Apparently I was a 'difficult child'. They went to seek help for me and the stupid, geriatric GP they had seen said the best thing they could do would be to have another child. I was 'spoiled', he said. Being people of little imagination they believed him, but it was too late for them to have another of their own so they adopted through a private agency. They actually told me they had a present for me. I thought it was going to be another Barbie doll. I was desperate for another to add to my collection, and then they showed me this smelly mewling thing that was no fun at all. I thought I would kill you and then everything would be fine again, but it was not to be. They caught me in your pram, thought I was trying to kiss you; kiss, kill – only two letters but what a difference they make. Sometimes I wonder what they would have thought if they knew. A bit upset, I should think. They wanted so much for me to be the loving big sister. And then I got over it, just like that. I withdrew a little from my parents and just got on with life. Until my father started to abuse me. The first time he begged forgiveness, down on his knees, crying, sobbing, and like a fool I did nothing. He took my inability to act as a tacit agreement.

I was in my bedroom when I went into labour. I had no idea what was happening to me. You came in, all wide eyed and open mouthed. Clueless. You helped deliver it. The baby was a monstrous sight when it finally arrived. All bloody. You wrapped him in a towel, took him in your arms and cradled him and I saw you, Suzanne. You thought I was asleep but I wasn't. I saw you put your hand over his tiny nose and mouth. You killed him, not me.

I was in that mental hospital for a long time. Silent, saying nothing. Perhaps it was my fault the baby died. Maybe if I'd been kinder to you, less selfish. But I hated you and it came back to bite me. The hospital burned down. Sometimes I wonder if I did that. I might have. I've surprised myself several times with what I've done, what I want to do. I want revenge, Suzanne. But maybe you already know that. I thought of killing you but I decided that was too good for you. I wanted you to suffer. I wanted you to be blamed for something you didn't do, just as I was.

So I planned it all out. I needed to be dead to do what I needed to do. The confession had been written before, on your computer, and I hid it in a file under an innocuous title. But I had no intention of killing myself. I got over my suicidal impulses years ago. I needed a dead body. When my neighbour said she was off for a few months to Malawi, it was too good an opportunity to miss. So, so long Marianne. Sleeping pills and whisky with Rohypnol first. Come on now, you didn't think she'd sit happily by my side as I typed out the confession into the computer? No, the Rohypnol knocked her out until I was ready, and then at six a.m. precisely, some whisky and some sleeping pills poured down her throat. I knew that by the time the body was found there would be no traces of Rohypnol anywhere.

It suited me perfectly. I told everyone I was off on holiday. I knew there were tenants coming in to Marianne's house and that worried me because I wanted the body to be as decomposed as possible. Marianne and I were similar enough in appearance but if the body was discovered too soon my plan would have been ruined. Fortunately the tenants were clueless, or had no sense of smell. Marianne wouldn't be missed for a while and I could live off her credit cards. I had her keys so it was easy for me to take her hairbrush and toothbrush and swop them with mine. I had to be sure she'd be identified as me. The police would be duty bound to investigate my confession, but they'd soon find it was false and then the fun was going to start. I would murder people in the ways I'd outlined in the confession. Apart from the Derek White murder. That was a decoy. I put it in to confuse. It was that murder that made me think of linking my own to music. Did you realise that Derek and his wife were a modern day Don Jose and Carmen? She had even worked in Wills' Tobacco Factory. That part of the confession was true. Anyway the plan was that once they started putting two and two together there would be a few little nudges in your direction.

It was so easy to break into your flat. If I were you, I'd get a new cleaner. She totally bought my story about me being your sister and needing to get in because I was planning your birthday party. Once in, I found your spare keys easily. Fancy you having that antique key holder that was in my parents' house. Anyway, I copied the keys and then I was in and out whenever I wanted. You're a creature of habit, Suzanne. Monday, Wednesday and Friday mornings at the gym from nine thirty to eleven. Every other Saturday morning the farmers' market at Partick. It was easy to do what I wanted.

I hadn't factored in Marianne's husband reporting her missing so soon. That was a blow. I knew it wouldn't be long before you'd spot the clue in my confession and then they'd be on to me. But in any case, I'd spotted your weak spot. Your handsome policeman. Shame you didn't get to hang on to him, but you still care about him, don't you? And when I saw who his partner was? Christ, I almost wet myself! That was too good an opportunity to miss. A chance to get back at the woman who had stolen my husband. I killed John to get back at her and also at her successor, Lynn, who was looking after my child. I already had the murder on Glasgow Green. It fitted in nicely even though I hadn't planned it that way.

The other three murders were just as I had imagined in the confession. They weren't necessary but I thought the more there were the more likely you were to be convicted of at least one of them.

And then of course there's Mark. It was so easy to get into his house and start that fire. Unfortunately, he got away and managed to save his whole family. Shame that, but it gives me another opportunity. I'm going after one of his children this time. It's your fault, Suzanne, and he'll know it and he will never forgive you.

You'll just have to live with it.

Julie

I let the sheets fall from my hand. She was deranged of course, but her words chilled me, especially the sentence about me killing the baby. I hadn't done that, had I? My head was swimming in confusion as I tried to remember. No I didn't want to remember and there was no time. I had to warn Mark.

Chapter Forty

Mark

The sound of his mobile intruded on his reading. He fished it out of the bedside cabinet. 'Suzanne, you have to stop calling me.'

'Mark, I have a letter from her.'

He rolled his eyes; these women and their letters. 'What are you talking about? Has Karen written to you?'

'What? No! This is from Julie. She's trying to get at you through me. The fire, that was her.'

He closed his eyes; the room was suddenly too bright. He was back in his house, trying to get his children, dying... Suzanne was speaking – it sounded important but he was losing the thread.

'Mark, Mark, are you listening to me? This is important. I've phoned your boss to let him know. He's sent two officers round to tell your wife but you have to be aware of what Julie might do. To you as well as to them.'

'I... uh, OK. Thank you, Suzanne.' He pressed the end call

button and sank back on to the pillow trying to take in what she'd said. Those threats against his family... It was unbearable. But Scrimgeour had sent someone round to protect them; he should phone to thank him. Something was niggling him... Emma. He rang for a nurse.

'I have to see my daughter.'

The nurse pursed her lips. 'I don't know, you're meant to have complete bed rest.'

Mark felt panic rise within him. 'Please, I can't rest until I see for myself that she's all right.'

'OK, I'll check with Sister McIntyre.'

Stuff that, thought Mark. Bloody bureaucrats. He waited until she was out of sight then pushed the bedcovers back. He'd see Emma whether they liked it or not.

The children's hospital was in a different building from the main hospital. It took him only a minute or so to run the short distance.

They cottoned on to him as soon as he entered the building. One of the janitors stood in front of him, an imposing shape, threatening.

'Where do you think you're going?'

'To see my daughter.'

The janitor raised his eyebrows so high they disappeared under the thatch of dark hair. 'Wait here and I'll get sister.'

What was it about this place? You couldn't do anything without some bloody sister's say so. Within a few seconds, the janitor was back with a young nurse. She took Mark into the office.

'Are you a patient here?'

'Yes, and my daughter is too. I'd like to see her please.'

'You should be in bed.' The young woman's voice was firm.

'I'm not leaving until I see her.' Mark was just as determined.

A sigh. 'What's your daughter's name?'

'Emma Nicholson; we were in a fire last night.'

She nodded. 'Yes, Emma's just gone to get an x-ray. Nothing to worry about. It's routine for these sort of cases. She should be back any minute now.' She looked at her watch. 'Gosh, is it really four thirty? She should have been done by now. I'll give them a ring.'

Mark looked round the nursing station as she dialled through to the radiology department. His chest hurt like hell and he wondered how long it would be before he felt well again.

The nurse started to speak. 'Yes, is that radiology? I'm looking for a patient of mine, a two-year-old girl called Emma Nicholson. Someone from your department collected her for an x-ray over an hour ago. I was wondering when she'll be back.' A pause. A frown appeared on her brow and she turned away from Mark. 'Are you sure? Can you check for me, please?' Another pause. Mark tried to ask what was happening but she shushed him as someone else spoke to her. 'You're absolutely certain about that? No, I don't know the name of the person who took her.' Another pause; Mark tried to hear what the person on the other end of the phone was saying but he only picked up a mumble. The nurse put the phone down with a sigh.

Before she spoke, Mark butted in. 'She's not there, is she? And never was. They didn't ask to x-ray her and you don't know who's taken her. I'm right, aren't I?' His heart was thumping, his chest tight from fear and smoke damage.

The young woman nodded, her face miserable.

'Jesus Christ. Hospitals are meant to be safe places.'

'I'm sure it's...' Her voice tailed away.

Mark stood up. 'Call the police,' he said. 'I know who's got her.'

Chapter Forty-One

Mark

THE POLICE STATION was buzzing with the news of Emma's abduction. Every police officer they passed gave them a look of sympathy. Scrimgeour was waiting for Karen and Mark in his office.

'Do you have any idea where she might have taken her?'

Scrimgeour grimaced. 'Your guess is as good as mine, Karen. There's a squad of cars out there, waiting for a clue, any hint at all about where to go.'

Mark was sick with nerves, wondering what she would do to his daughter. Emma was in danger. This woman had killed several people one of whom was her baby. He had no doubt that Emma was in danger.

'Suzanne Yates is coming over with the letter her sister sent her. There may be some clue there.'

Karen stiffened at the mention of Suzanne's name. Mark squeezed her hand but she pulled away.

'When will she get here, do you know?'

Scrimgeour shrugged. 'Shouldn't take too long; she's getting a taxi. Her own car's been impounded of course.' He had the grace to look ashamed.

Mark's heart was beating uncomfortably fast. He was still suffering from the smoke inhalation, and that together with the stress of Emma's disappearance was getting to him. Add the upcoming meeting with Suzanne and he might well have a heart attack. 'Sir, can I have a word?'

Karen glowered at him but he ignored her.

'Sure thing, what is it?'

'In private.' Karen's scowl deepened as the two men walked from the room.

'It's probably best if... er Karen and Suzanne don't meet.'

Scrimgeour nodded. 'Here she is now. I'll interview her. You get back to Karen.'

Several minutes later, he came back in. 'We've got a lead. Julie Campbell's car, which was in the driveway of her house in Braeside Road, has gone. A neighbour has just reported it missing. We've put out an alert on ANPR to see if any of the cameras pick it up.' Mark wanted to ask whether Suzanne had anything to say that might be helpful but didn't want to anger Karen by mentioning her name.

'Anything else?'

'Livingstone's with the witness now. We'll let you know. Meanwhile all we can do is sit tight and wait.'

Half an hour passed. Mark paced up and down the room. 'There must be something we can do – put out a plea, something.'

Scrimgeour rubbed at his temple as if he had a headache. His walkie-talkie crackled, making them all jump. He murmured into it, listened to the answer then punched the air. 'There's been a sighting of her car.'

'Are you sure?' Mark couldn't look at Karen, didn't want to see the hope in her eyes.

'Definitely. It was seen speeding in Bearsden, on the Drymen road.'

Mark's stomach lurched as he thought of his daughter bouncing around in a car without a child seat. Or worse, locked in the boot of Julie's car. 'Why Drymen?' he asked. Something was niggling him... Drymen. What was it about Drymen? No, it wasn't there. Scrimgeour left the room.

'What happens now?' Karen asked him.

'I'm not sure. They'll probably... I don't know.'

'Mark, can I borrow you a minute?' Scrimgeour was at the door. Mark got up, his stomach leaden, sure this was bad news. He left the room. Outside in the corridor was Suzanne. He looked round nervously to see if Karen was following.

'Is there anything you can think of, Suzanne? Anything at all.'

'I think she may have gone to the Whangie,' said Suzanne.

'The Whangie?' said Mark.

'You know – it's near Queen's View on the road to Drymen. We used to go walking there when we were children. And it's in the confession. Don't you remember? When she's talking about how she wanted to see the Virgin Mary. She was convinced she'd find her there and used to look in all the crevices for her. And it's on the way to Drymen.'

Of course. *This* was what had been niggling at him. 'But why would she take Emma there?'

Suzanne's face closed up. 'I don't know,' she admitted, 'but you have to admit, it's a possibility.'

'It's all we've got, Mark,' said Scrimgeour. 'We need to follow it up.'

'You're not going anywhere,' said Karen, when Mark told her what was happening. 'You're too ill.'

'I'm fine,' he said.

'Well, I'm coming too.'

The police car sped through the wet Glasgow streets. When they reached the Clyde tunnel, the siren went on and they raced past the queue of traffic through to Anniesland. 'Can't you go any faster?' urged Mark.

Scrimgeour looked at the speedometer. His face paled. 'We're doing eighty in a forty-mile zone. Any faster and we'll take off.'

Mark tried to relax. He knew they were doing their best, but every minute stretched out like an hour. He glanced at the road behind him. Several squad cars were catching up with them. The car slowed down when they reached the country road that would take them to the Whangie.

'No point in killing ourselves,' said Scrimgeour. 'We should be there in about five minutes.'

Mark leaned his head against the headrest trying to gather his thoughts. He had walked up to the Whangie many times but never at night. They had powerful torches to help them see the way. This meant Julie would have plenty of warning of them coming, though she'd have to have a torch too; it was too black a night to do without one. The sky was covered in dark, angry clouds. He closed his eyes and tried to visualise the route. It took about forty minutes to walk up to the crags, but that was in daylight, in good weather. It was an easy walk. She had probably half an hour's start on them, but she was carrying a child – at least he prayed she was carrying a child. God forbid this was some wild goose chase.

'Mark, we're almost there.' Karen's voice interrupted his thoughts. He unfastened his seatbelt, ready to run as soon as the car stopped. Scrimgeour growled at him. 'What are you doing?'

'Getting ready to run,' said Mark. 'I have to catch her before she reaches the top. It's dangerous up there if you don't know what you're doing, and in the dark...'

'We'll go up together. There's at least twenty men in the cars behind. I want some to go round the back way so we've got a pincer attack on her, coming from all sides.'

'Alex, please let him go,' said Karen. 'God knows what that woman is planning; we can't afford to lose a second.'

The car was drawing into the car park at the Queen's View.

'What's the registration number?' he yelled at Scrimgeour. As soon as he had it he jumped out of the car barely waiting for it to stop. There were several cars – this was a popular place for couples having illicit affairs – and he ran round frantically looking at their number plates. He couldn't see it; Christ, what if it wasn't here after all? No, there it was, as near to the path as you could get. He leapt out of the car as soon as it stopped, pausing only to switch on the powerful torch Scrimgeour had given him. The other police cars screeched in behind them. All around the car park, vehicle lights were switched on and furtive couples drove off, wondering what the hell was going on but anxious to get away before they got caught up in something that would need a lot of explaining to their spouses. One of the police officers gave a derisive laugh as the car park emptied.

'All right, Mark. Go on, but keep your head. Know what I mean? We'll be right behind you.' Scrimgeour turned to instruct the rest of the officers.

Mark caught Karen's hand. 'I'll get her back, don't you worry.'

'I'm coming too,' said Karen.

'You'll...'

'What? Hold you up? I don't think so.' Karen was already ahead of him on the path. He ran after her and cursed as he slipped on the wooden sleepers that formed the first part of the path, slightly raised above the sodden ground. His left foot sank into the murky bog. Shit. He pulled it out and walked on, shining his torch on the path to show the way. Karen was a little way ahead, where the path rose steeply for a short distance. He looked past her to see if he could see anything but it was totally dark; no telltale glimmer from a torch to show where his daughter might be. Pulling his jacket close around him he marched on. The rain had turned to sleet.

Karen was almost running up the hill. He quickened his pace and caught up with her. 'Let me go first, in case there's any boggy bits.'

She nodded; boggy ground had always scared her. Mark strode on until they reached the stile. The path split into two here, the high path and the low one. He decided to take the low one as it was slightly easier and he thought this was the one Julie would choose. Scrimgeour would send some men up the other one. He could see light from the torches of his colleagues coming up behind them.

Mark and Karen walked on in silence. They needed all their strength to keep their balance. The wind drove stinging sleet into their faces and the stony path was slippery. Mark shuddered as he imagined Julie slipping and dropping his daughter onto one of the rocks below. They were at the top now where the path dipped into a hollow before going on to the crags themselves. The wind wasn't as ferocious here.

'Did you hear that?' Karen's voice was urgent.

'What?'

'Listen.'

He stopped and listened. A child's wail. It was Emma. He started to run, not heeding Karen's cries behind him.

The sleet was turning to snow, covering the path. Mark pressed on; he was almost there. He turned a corner and there were the crags beside him. He shone his torch all around. Nothing. Snowflakes hurled down; just looking at them made him dizzy. He picked his way along the narrow passage, stopping every few steps to listen.

'Emma!' he shouted. His voice came back at him, a mocking echo. Or was it? He tried again. It might be imagination but he was sure the final echo was not his voice. He couldn't tell where it was coming from. Stumbling, he carried on, straining to make out anything he could. The snow was disorienting. He looked round but Karen was nowhere to be seen.

He yelled as loud as he could, 'The game's up, Julie. You're surrounded.' The wind howled its derisive reply. He closed his eyes in despair.

'Mark.' He opened his eyes when he heard his name and shone his torch up the side of the rock. There she was, a tiny figure near the top. He started to climb.

'Stop. If you come any nearer, I'll throw her down.'

'Julie, Ms Campbell, please give me my daughter. Please.'

Her laugh echoed round the rocks. 'You know, I think she might be dead.' Her tone was conversational as if she was commenting on the colour of paint she'd chosen for her living room.

Mark couldn't speak, couldn't breathe.

'Oh, no. It's OK, she's just sleeping. Quite a deep sleep though. I can't seem to wake her up.'

'Please, Julie, give her to me.' Mark edged his way up the slippery surface. He was terrified. If he put a foot wrong he'd fall, and the rocks were dangerous. If he fell, he might even kill himself.

'I told you not to come up, didn't I? I told you what would happen.' Julie was holding Emma over the edge of the rock face a little to the right of where he was. It was a sheer drop of twenty feet to the ground.

'Julie, I'll do anything.'

'Anything? So, what... You'd kill my sister if I asked you? This is all her fault, after all. Ask her about how she killed my baby, about how she listened while my father raped me time and time again while she did nothing. She'll deny it of course. I want her to suffer as I have suffered. I thought at first getting her done for murder would be enough, and then I thought of killing someone she loved – you. But now I know this is the best way to get to her. If I kill your child, you will never forgive her and she'll have to live with that for the rest of her life. That's good enough for me.'

'I don't know what to say. For Christ's sake, give her to me.'

Julie leaned over the edge holding Emma under the arms, her legs dangling limply. Mark prayed she was still alive. 'Please, Julie. Let me have her.'

Julie smiled, a slow, menacing grimace that chilled him. 'OK. Catch!'

Mark looked in horror as she let Emma go. Below him he heard Karen scream and somebody swear. He pressed his head against the rock face and started to weep.

Chapter Forty-Two

Mark

MARK STROKED EMMA'S HAIR. 'I can't believe she's alive.'

The doctor smiled at him. 'It was a miracle that your wife caught her, but nonetheless very young children often survive falls like that. You must have read about children falling out of windows.'

'Yes, I remember something about it. Their bodies don't tense in the same way ours would – isn't that it?'

'Something like that. She was very lucky though, it has to be said. If she'd hit the rocks...' He shook his head. 'The woman who did it. Have they found her yet?'

Mark's face tightened. 'No. They searched all night for her. There was no trace of her. God knows how she got away.'

'I'm sure they'll get her.' The doctor laid a comforting hand on his arm.

'They'd better,' muttered Mark.

Karen came into the ward with Oscar and Sophie. Sophie

was carrying a teddy bear almost as big as her. 'Mummy buyed it!' she shouted as soon as she spotted Mark. 'It's for Emmie.'

Mark knelt down to speak to her. 'It's lovely. Did you help Mummy choose it?'

Sophie nodded, her face serious. 'Daddy, has the bad lady gone now?'

Mark smiled at her. 'Yes,' he said as firmly as he could, wishing it was true. Sophie wriggled out of his arms and ran to join Oscar, who had gone into the playroom to find some toys.

'Any news?'

Karen shook her head. 'I phoned the station just before I left Debbie's. They haven't been able to trace her.'

'I don't understand it,' said Mark. 'How could she have got away?'

'Maybe she didn't; maybe she's hiding up there somewhere.'

Mark shrugged. 'I don't know. It was pretty cold last night.'

'I hope she's dead,' said Karen. 'I hope she's up there, frozen to the hillside.'

Mark looked down at his feet. It wasn't his fault but he had to take some of the responsibility. His foolishness had brought his family to the brink of disaster. His stomach twisted as he thought about how they could all have died, how near they had been to losing Emma. 'Will you ever forgive me?' he asked.

Karen sighed. 'Mark, I don't know. I don't blame you for what Julie did. She's a very disturbed woman. You couldn't have known when you started that stupid affair that it would turn out like this. But you hurt me badly and I don't know if I can trust you again.' She turned away from him. 'Look, I don't want to have this conversation at the moment. There's too much else to think about. Like where we're going to stay. The insurance company rang. They sent builders out to the house and apparently the damage isn't as bad as they thought. They've started working on it already.'

'That's good. Did they say whether we can stay in a hotel?'

'To begin with, yes. After that it depends on how long the work's going to take. If it's more than a couple of weeks, they'll get a private let for us. They want one of us to meet with the builder today.'

Mark shut his eyes. He was so tired; all he wanted to do was sleep. His chest was still sore from the smoke, but the hospital had given him the all clear that morning and signed him off.

'Do you want me to go?' asked Karen.

'No, it's OK. I'll get over there now and then I'll pop into the station, see if they're any further forward with catching that woman. Have you booked a hotel?'

'The insurance company did it for us. It's in Queen's Drive, near the park. They've given us two rooms. You can share with Oscar and I'll share the other with Sophie and Emma, when she gets out of here.'

Mark nodded. It was a good sign that she had agreed to him being in the same hotel as her and the children. Perhaps they'd be able to sort things out after all. He smiled at her, 'OK, I'll see you later.'

Mark stood in the front garden and surveyed his house. The damage wasn't as bad as he'd feared: a gaping bedroom window of course, sooty streaks on the brickwork, a buckled and blistered front door. He went round to the back. Looking at the house from this angle, you'd never know there'd been a fire. The back door was open and he went in. He could hear a radio in the front room. The workmen must be in there. The place stank of smoke; it would be hard to get rid of that stench. Mark passed through the kitchen, trailing his fingers through the soot on the worktop; the damage in here was minimal. The hall was a different story though: wallpaper hung in ragged strips, the stair carpet was reduced to a wet sludge, the mirror was cracked and hung askew. His heart sank; it would be weeks before this would be fit to live in once more. He pushed open the living room door. Three workmen were pulling up the carpet. They stopped when he came in.

'Mr. Nicholson?' The oldest of them got up and came over to him. 'I'm John Munro. Terrible business this, but we're hoping it will only take ten days or so to get it back into a liveable condition.'

Mark raised his eyebrows. In his experience builders took about five times the amount of time they said. They started work, caused chaos, then found another job somewhere else to work on. Still, maybe if the insurance company was leaning on them...

'Good,' he said.

'We've checked the wiring and the gas supply. They're both fine, so all your amenities are back on again.'

It was feasible then; they might be back home within two weeks. They chatted for a few more minutes about what needed to be done, then Mark said he'd have to go. He got into his car and set off for the station.

'There's been no sign of her since last night,' said Scrimgeour.

'How can that be? She must still be up there somewhere. I won't rest until she's under arrest.'

'Nor will I, believe me. There's a helicopter up there now, searching the area. It has heat-seeking equipment. Trouble is, there's the usual walkers around so it's hard, though we will of course target women who are on their own. You don't get many out on the hills alone.'

'OK. Well, you'll let me know as soon as you hear anything?'

'You'll be the first to know.'

They shook hands and Mark started on his way home. He'd have no peace of mind until she was under lock and key. He prayed they'd be safe in the hotel; there was no way she could find out where they were.

Chapter Forty-Three

Suzanne

It was almost lunchtime when I let myself into the flat. It had been a long night and I was exhausted by everything that had happened, but I had to know how it had turned out, so I'd gone over to the police station where I met with Scrimgeour.

'If it hadn't been for you, she might not be alive today,' he said as he handed me a cup of tea.

'If it hadn't been for me, she wouldn't have been in danger in the first place.'

He nodded and I wondered if he was going to bring up what was in the letter Julie had written to me, but although I was expecting questions, he said nothing about it. He gave me instructions on how to get my car back. 'I'm sorry we arrested you but...'

'The evidence was compelling. I can see that.' We parted on good terms.

I was happy for Mark; he'd got his family back, but I was worried that they hadn't managed to catch Julie. I don't know how she managed to get away. It had been dark – even with torches everyone said it was hard to keep going and there had been over thirty police officers out there looking for her. They'd scaled down the search once Emma was safe, but many of Mark's friends had stayed on for a few hours determined to get the woman who'd threatened one of their own. She was nowhere to be seen. I wondered if she'd perhaps fallen into a bog and drowned or frozen to death but it was unlikely. The Whangie wasn't remote enough or high enough for the sort of bogs that were on Rannoch Moor. The sort that swallowed up sheep and even, it was rumoured, unsuspecting lone walkers.

'Hello, Suzanne.' Her voice was barely audible because of the music playing in the background, Mozart's *Requiem*.

I walked over to my bed where she was lying. 'What are you doing here?'

'I couldn't keep hiding. There was nowhere else to go and I wanted to see you again, one last time.'

'I'm going to phone the police, Julie. It's over.'

Julie held up her hand. 'Save it, Suzanne. I'll be dead before they get here.' Her voice was slurred.

'What do you mean?' I stepped closer. Her face gleamed with sweat. She was very pale. The shadows under her eyes were like bruises.

She pointed to an empty container on the bedside table, aspirin. 'That's all you had in your medicine cabinet. I would have preferred sleeping pills. I've taken most of them, about forty I reckon – should do the trick. That, and the whisky.' I followed her gaze to a half-empty bottle lying on the floor.

Salt water would do the trick. Force her to drink a half pint and she'd vomit up the lot. I turned to leave the room then stopped. 'Why did you do it?'

'What, this?'

'No, the whole thing.'

'I don't know... You... I didn't want you to be happy.' Her eyelids drooped.

I shook her awake. 'Why not?'

'You killed my baby then told a story that everyone believed. All that stuff about making me tea, caring for me. And when I tried to tell the truth you became hysterical and they turned against me.'

My mouth was dry. 'That's a lie and you know it.'

She laughed softly. 'Dirt sticks. I just wanted to do what you had done to me. It's on the record now, what you did. And you'll pay for it.'

I should call for help; do something. I looked down at her, lying on my bed. She looked so peaceful, almost happy. I took out my phone. For a few seconds I studied it, imagining myself dialling 999, the words I'd say. *Emergency services, please, ambulance. I have an attempted suicide here.* They'd tell me what to do. I could save her. I put the phone away.

'Not going to phone for an ambulance then?' Her voice mocked me. 'That makes you as bad as me.' I picked up the whisky bottle and got onto the bed beside Julie. After I had dragged her into a sitting position I shook her until she opened her eyes. 'Get this down you,' I said, putting the bottle to her lips. She shook her head and mumbled, 'You heard it all, didn't you?' then gulped down the drink.

I owed her this. I nodded.

'Maybe if you'd said something, he'd have stopped.'

I didn't reply, thinking of the times he made me uncomfortable. Touching my hair, brushing too close against me. I don't believe he would have stopped. I would have been next. He needed to be removed. Permanently.

She was barely audible. 'Why did you suffocate my little boy? Why?'

My heart was thumping. I thought back to that day all those years ago. I made her tea and toast, which she ate. 'You should try to sleep,' I told her. I sat with the child in my arms and tried to think what to do. My father, Julie's father, would do everything he could to cover up the abuse and some poor sixteen-year-old boy would get the blame. Neither Julie nor I would be safe from him. If the child was dead though, there would be a more thorough investigation.

'It was you, Julie,' I said. 'You were suffering from post-partum psychosis. And no wonder after what that monster did to you.'

She was beyond arguing. I held the bottle for her, giving her little sips until she fell unconscious. Gradually her breathing quietened, and when I was sure she was gone I wiped the bottle then put her hand round it with my hand on top and dropped it onto the floor before picking up the phone to call for an ambulance.

The End

Acknowledgments

Thanks to Rebecca Collins and Adrian Hobart at Hobeck Books for their professionalism and expertise. Thanks also to Sue Davison for her meticulous attention to detail in copy-editing this book and to Jayne Mapp for the brilliant cover design.

I am very grateful to Di Bruce and to Kenny Gray for taking time out of their busy lives to talk to me about police procedures and for the insights they gave me into police work in general. Any mistakes made regarding these are mine alone.

Thanks are due to my friend, Fiona West, who gave me the idea many years ago of using Paul Simon's 'Fifty Ways to Leave Your Lover' in the way it is used in *The Confession*.

I am so fortunate to belong to two writing groups, both of whom have been and continue to be, a fantastic support. To the Glasgow University editorial group: Ailsa Crum, Alison Miller, Ann Mackinnon, Clare Morrison, Griz Gordon and Heather Mackay, I can't believe it's over twenty years since we started out on our writing journey together. Here's to the next twenty. And to the Glad Group: Ailsa Crum (yes, the same one!), Alison Irvine, Bert Thomson, Emily Munro, Emma Lennox Miller and Les Wood, I am so thankful to have found you.

Finally, thank you to my family, Martin, Katherine, Kevin and Peter who have been so supportive since I started writing. You are the most precious things in my life. Apart from the grandweans that is. Tess, James, Hanna, Leo, Archie and Niamh, you're too young to read *The Confession,* but maybe one day...

Maureen Myant

About the Author

Maureen worked for over 25 years as an educational psychologist but has also worked as a teacher and an Open University Associate Lecturer. She is a graduate of the prestigious University of Glasgow MLitt in Creative Writing course where she was taught by Janice Galloway, Liz Lochhead, James Kelman, Alasdair Gray and Tom Leonard among others. She also has a PhD in Creative Writing. Her first novel *The Search* was published by Alma Books and was translated into Spanish, Dutch and Turkish. It was longlisted for the Waverton Good Read Award and was one of the books chosen to be read for the Festival du premier roman de Chambéry.

Maureen has been a voracious reader since the age of six when, fed up with her mum reading Noddy stories to her, she picked up her older brother's copy of Enid Blyton's The Valley of Adventure and devoured it in an evening. She hasn't stopped reading since and loves literary fiction, historical fiction, crime fiction, psychological thrillers and contemporary fiction but not necessarily in that order. Her favourite book is *The Secret History* by Donna Tartt and go-to comfort read is *Anne of Green Gables*.

Maureen lives in Glasgow with her husband. She has three grownup children and six grandchildren who love to beat her at Bananagrams.

Hobeck Books – the home of great stories

We hope you've enjoyed reading this novel by Maureen Meant. To keep up to date on Maureen's fiction writing please do follow her on Twitter.

Hobeck Books offers a number of short stories and novellas, including *You Can't Trust Anyone These Days* by Maureen Myant, free for subscribers in the compilation *Crime Bites*.

- *Echo Rock* by Robert Daws
- *Old Dogs, Old Tricks* by AB Morgan
- *The Silence of the Rabbit* by Wendy Turbin
- *Never Mind the Baubles: An Anthology of Twisted Winter Tales* by the Hobeck Team (including many of the Hobeck authors and Hobeck's two publishers)
- *The Clarice Cliff Vase* by Linda Huber
- *Here She Lies* by Kerena Swan
- *The Macnab Principle* by R.D. Nixon
- *Fatal Beginnings* by Brian Price
- *A Defining Moment* by Lin Le Versha
- *Saviour* by Jennie Ensor
- *You Can't Trust Anyone These Days* by Maureen Myant

Also please visit the Hobeck Books website for details of our other superb authors and their books, and if you would like to get in touch, we would love to hear from you.

Hobeck Books also presents a weekly podcast, the Hobcast, where founders Adrian Hobart and Rebecca Collins discuss all things book related, key issues from each week, including the ups and downs of running a creative business. Each episode includes an interview with one of the people who make Hobeck possible: the editors, the authors, the cover designers. These are the people who help Hobeck bring great stories to life. Without them, Hobeck wouldn't exist. The Hobcast can be listened to from all the usual platforms but it can also be found on the Hobeck website: **www.hobeck.net/hobcast**.

Other Hobeck Books to Explore

Silenced

A teenage girl is murdered on her way home from school, stabbed through the heart. Her North London community is shocked, but no-one has the courage to help the police, not even her mother. DI Callum Waverley, in his first job as senior investigating officer, tries to break through the code of silence that shrouds the case.

This is a world where the notorious Skull Crew rules through fear. Everyone knows you keep your mouth shut or you'll be silenced – permanently.

This is Luke's world. Reeling from the loss of his mother to cancer, his step-father distant at best, violent at worst, he slides into the Skull Crew's grip.

This is Jez's world too. Her alcoholic mother neither knows nor cares that her 16-year-old daughter is being exploited by V, all-powerful leader of the gang.

Luke and Jez form a bond. Can Callum win their trust, or will his own demons sabotage his investigation? And can anyone stop the Skull Crew ensuring all witnesses are silenced?

Her Deadly Friend

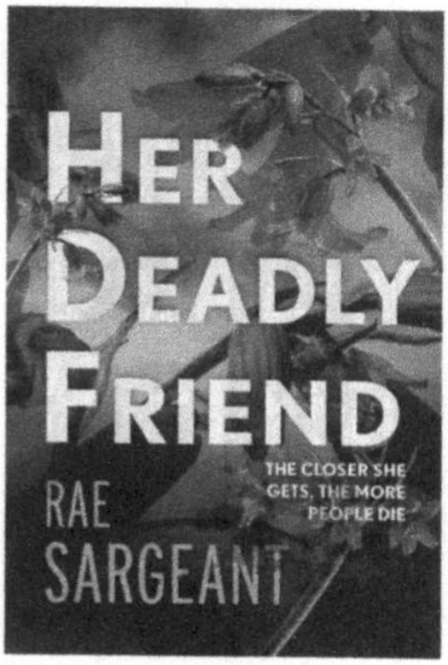

The Suspect
Bullied by Steph Lewis at school, then betrayed by her lover, Amy Ashby still seethes with fury. Despite the decades-old resentment, she's on the hunt for a new man and a fresh start. This time for keeps.

The Stalker
When both women are stalked by a figure from their shared past, danger threatens.

The Detective
Now Detective Inspector, Steph follows a tip-off to her old rival. After quarrels exploded and changed lives forever, she vowed never to see Amy again. But that was then.

The Deaths
Murder rocks the city. The body count reaches five, and all Steph's leads point to Amy. But is Steph obsessed with a schoolgirl vendetta or closing in on a deadly killer?

Pact of Silence

A fresh start for a new life
Newly pregnant, Emma is startled when her husband Luke announces they're swapping homes with his parents, but the rural idyll where Luke grew up is a great place to start their family. Yet Luke's manner suggests something odd is afoot, something that Emma can't quite fathom.

Too many secrets, not enough truths
Emma works hard to settle into her new life in the Yorkshire countryside, but a chance discovery increases her suspicions. She decides to dig a little deeper...

Be careful what you uncover
Will Emma find out why the locals are behaving so oddly? Can she discover the truth behind Luke's disturbing behaviour? Will the pact of silence ever be broken?

Blood Notes

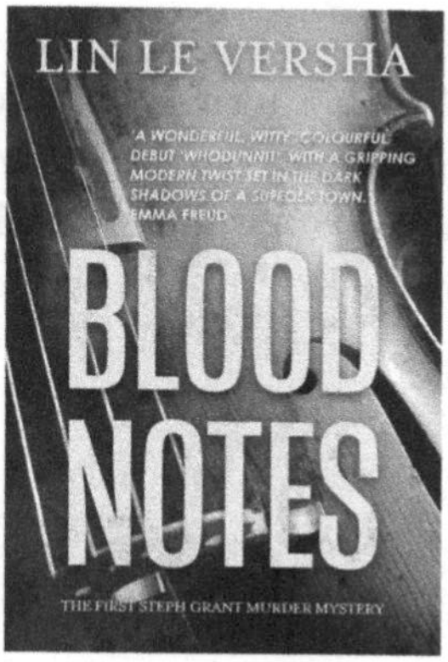

Winner of a 2022 Chill With A Book Premier Reader's Award!

'A wonderful, witty, colourful, debut 'Whodunnit', with a gripping modern twist set in the dark shadows of a Suffolk town.' EMMA FREUD

Edmund Fitzgerald is different.

Sheltered by an over-protective mother, he's a musical prodigy.

Now, against his mother's wishes, he's about to enter formal education for the first time aged sixteen.

Everything is alien to Edmund: teenage style, language and relationships are impossible to understand.

Then there's the searing jealousy his talent inspires, especially when the sixth form college's Head of Music, turns her back on her other students and begins to teach Edmund exclusively.

Observing events is Steph, a former police detective who is rebuilding her life following a bereavement as the college's receptionist. When a student is found dead in the music block, Steph's sleuthing skills help to unravel the dark events engulfing the college community.

Be Sure Your Sins

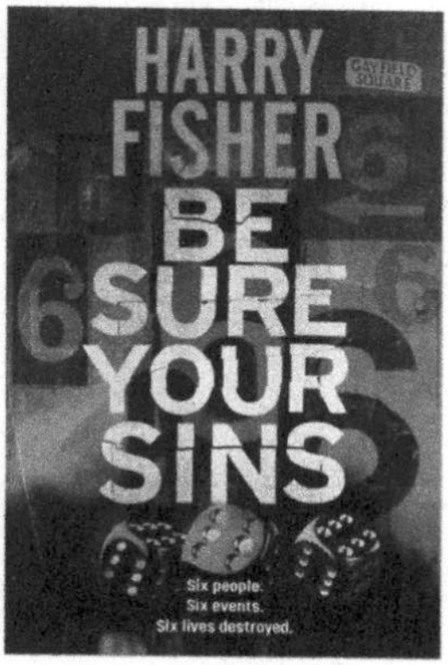

Six people
Six events
Six lives destroyed
What is the connection?

Detective **Melissa (Mel) Cooper** has two major investigations on the go. The first involves six apparently unrelated individuals who all suffer inexplicable life-altering events.

Mel is also pursuing a serial blackmailer but just as she's about to prove the link between this man and the six bizarre events, she's ordered to back off.

So why are her bosses interfering with her investigations? Who are they trying to protect? And how far will they go to stop her?

The answers come from a totally unexpected source.

Also by Maureen Myant

The Search

In Czechoslovakia, 1942, Jan's father has been summarily executed by the Nazis. His mother and his older sister Maria have disappeared, and his younger sister Lena has been removed to a remote farm in the German countryside. With Europe in the throes of war, the ten-year-old boy embarks on a personal journey to reunite the family he has been violently torn from. The experiences he goes through and the horror he faces during this desperate quest will change his life for ever. While examining the devastating effects of war on ordinary families, *The Search* provides an exploration of fear and loss, and of the bond between parents and children. Riveting, moving, at times disturbing, Maureen Myant's debut novel will haunt its readers for a long time after they have put it down.

Lightning Source UK Ltd.
Milton Keynes UK
UKHW041252101122
411975UK00029B/639

9 781913 793890